I come limping out of the hospital leaning on Astin's arm.

EXT. HOSPITAL—DAY

I blink in the pale California sun that shines through a high layer of cloud. People move in and out of the hospital, men and women wrapped in a kind of mental solitude, intent only on the business that brought them here.

Astin eases me into the black SUV. I gasp as pain rockets through my wounded leg. I think about the person who just tried to kill me, and I think about the secret that we both shared.

Once upon a time, I thought that the biggest secret in my life was that I'd killed a friend of mine.

But now I realize that murder is only the second biggest secret. I have a secret that's much, much bigger.

Praise for *This Is Not a Game*

"*This Is Not a Game* is a tale every bit as engaging as one of the intrigues its characters might have dreamed up." —*Bookpage*

"Williams' dialogue is razor-sharp, his plotting breakneck, his eye for trends keen and his empathy with his characters deep." —scifi.com

"The characters are realistic and absorbing, and the story deeply compelling." —*Publishers Weekly* (starred review)

Praise for *Deep State*

"There are powerful ideas stirring beneath the skin of what to a first approximation resembles a taut technothriller, and it's brilliantly executed..." —Charles Stross

"...a slick, intelligent techno-thriller..." —*The Guardian* (UK)

By Walter Jon Williams

This Is Not a Game
Deep State
The Fourth Wall

Ambassador of Progress
Knight Moves
Hardwired
Voice of the Whirlwind
The Crown Jewels
House of Shards
Angel Station
Facets (collection)
Elegy for Angels and Dogs
Days of Atonement
Frankensteins and Foreign Devils (collection)
Aristoi
Metropolitan
Rock of Ages
Ten Points for Style
City on Fire
Destiny's Way
Implied Spaces

DREAD EMPIRE'S FALL
The Praxis
The Sundering
Conventions of War

WRITING AS WALTER J. WILLIAMS
The Rift

WRITING AS JON WILLIAMS
The Privateer
The Yankee
The Raider
The Macedonian
Cat Island

THE FOURTH WALL

WALTER JON WILLIAMS

www.orbitbooks.net

Orbit
Hachette Book Group
237 Park Avenue, New York, NY 10017
www.HachetteBookGroup.com

First Edition: February 2012

Orbit is an imprint of Hachette Book Group, Inc. The Orbit name and logo are trademarks of Little, Brown Book Group Limited.

Library of Congress Cataloging-in-Publication Data
Williams, Walter Jon.
The fourth wall / Walter Jon Williams.
p. cm.
ISBN 978-0-316-13339-5 (pbk.)
1. Child actors—Fiction. 2. Reality television programs—Fiction. I. Title.
PS3573.I456213F68 2012
813'.54—dc22

2011022494

10 9 8 7 6 5 4 3 2 1

RRD-C

Printed in the United States of America

For Kathy Hedges

TEASER

EXT. HOSPITAL—DAY

I come limping out of the hospital leaning on Astin's arm, and I blink in the pale California sun that shines through a high layer of cloud. People move in and out of the hospital, men and women wrapped in a kind of mental solitude, intent only on the business that brought them here.

Astin eases me into the black SUV. I gasp as pain rockets through my wounded leg. I think about the person who just tried to kill me, and I think about the secret that we both shared.

Once upon a time, I thought that the biggest secret in my life was that I'd killed a friend of mine.

But now I realize I have a secret that's much, much bigger.

ACT 1

CHAPTER ONE

HEAVY LUGGAGE BLOG

When you spot someone sitting at the beach wearing a headset for Augmented Reality, or wearing AR specs on the bus, or smiling quietly in the back pew of the church with his video glasses on, what do you think?

I'll tell you what you think. *You think he's watching porn.*

Porn is the killer app for Augmented Reality, just as it has been for practically every other mass-media technology of the last fifty years.

You can do many things with AR. You can get information on the position of stars and planets, you can watch ambitious entertainment videos, you can view the menus of restaurants you happen to be passing. You can play three-dimensional games on a flat surface, you can view historical markers telling you interesting things that happened on the spot where you are standing, you can enhance your museum-going experience.

But you don't need goggles for any of that. All you need is a handheld device.

But for porn, you need the privacy of goggles or AR specs. If you're brandishing a handheld, anyone can look over your shoulder to view your personal kinks. The privacy of video shades permits you to enjoy your sexual fantasies without revealing to everyone around you how sad, lonely, and pathetic you are.

Not that I was thinking of any of these things as I field-tested my first set of AR specs. These were the new ARi designer shades, the handsome result of a collaboration between the Bangalore-based Chandra wireless company and the European designer Aristotle Despopoulos. The specs are the color of champagne, with elegant black ceramic inserts here and there. They retail for about $2,500.

I didn't purchase them—$2,500 is a lot to pay for my entertainment. I found them in a gift bag at a Hollywood party, along with a TAG Heuer ladies' watch, a silk Aristotle Despopoulos scarf blazoned with the AriPop logo, a GPS locator, and a top-of-the-line Chandra handset carrying the signature of Mahesh Singh himself.

I wasn't actually invited to the party in question, but I had a friend who got me in, and whose name I will not reveal. Some of the official guests didn't show up, and I was able to glom one of the gift bags when no one was looking.

This morning I spent a couple hours playing with the ARis. No, I didn't watch porn, instead I took a stroll along Sunset in West Hollywood. Virtual icons have so proliferated there that they almost cover the Strip's famous wall-to-wall advertising. A virtual doorman stands by every door in order to pimp the attractions of every bar, restaurant, or nightclub—or sometimes the bar, restaurant, or club that was located there three or four years ago. A rotating three-dimensional Lana Turner marks the original location of Schwab's drugstore, and if you click her you get a canned history of the drugstore along with a lot of vintage photographs. (It's pretty good actually.) More eerily, a ghostly River Phoenix stands on the sidewalk where he died outside the Viper Room. Actors and musicians are auditioning all over the place, as are sex workers. Political slogans pulse through the air, some of them marking election cycles long past.

Remember when AR was touted as a brilliant, dynamic new electronic tool sure to improve our lives? Advertising and porn, that's what we got.

You really need a traffic cop for all this dreck.

And unfortunately my ARis wouldn't be that cop. I tried to turn the heads-up display off, by sending a command from the Mahesh Singh–autographed handset, but the damned icons just wouldn't disappear.

I looked up the online manual and followed the procedure for turning off the AR function, but nothing happened. After I got home I called customer support, only to be connected to someone whose native language was probably Tamil, and who simply read me the same text from the online instructions that had already failed.

I tried deleting the AR app and reloading it, but it wouldn't delete. Eventually I realized that the ability to switch off the AR function had been disabled. The same people who had given away the ARis *wanted* me to see all that advertising.

The chance to view porn in private sure as hell isn't worth all this.

You might say that I deserve it, having got some video specs I wasn't really entitled to and that now do nothing but laser tons of useless crap onto my retinas. And in my case at least, I might agree with you.

But what about the A-list celebrities who put on their designer ARis for a stroll down Rodeo Drive and discover that they can't rid themselves of all the video hucksters? The same A-list celebrities that Chandra is counting on to tout their specs? How are they going to feel about being unable to turn off all that pimpage?

You might say that Chandra made something of a marketing blunder here.

My ARis are going up for sale on an online auction site, along with the handset and the watch.

Maybe I'll keep the scarf. It goes with some of my jackets.

Comments (0)

INT. ARENA—NIGHT

I come out of the darkness of the tunnel into the brilliant light and the whole arena erupts with a huge, hollow roaring made by thousands of enthusiastic drunken American males. *Whooooooo.* I'm stunned. I haven't heard anything that enthusiastic in ages. Certainly not for me.

I'm so taken aback that I almost stumble, but my cornerman, Master Pak, keeps me going with steady pressure to my shoulder blades. My eyes are dazzled by camera flashes. People are reaching into the aisles to touch me or to offer high fives. I look to my right and see a whole row of bare-chested guys pumping their fists in the air and barking. They're wearing weird alien bald heads, and their beer bellies are painted baby blue. *Oogh-oogh-oogh-oogh.*

Is that supposed to be my *head?* I think. *These are* my *fans?*

In unison they pick up suitcases and hold them over their heads.

Luggage. Oh God.

I blink and they're gone, vanished back into the crowd as I advance.

Whoooooo. The sound seems to pick me up and fling me in the direction of the sky. My heart pounds. My veins are ablaze with adrenaline.

This is what it's like to be a rock star. This is what it's like to *own* an arena full of people.

Ahead the ring is like a silver crown gleaming in a pillar of light. Outlined in the shining argent floods I can see the referee, an enormous 240-pound bodybuilder crammed into a white shirt and bow tie. He wears surgical gloves in the event that I decide to bleed on him. And then an anomaly catches my eye, and I think, *Why is the ref wearing waders?*

When I hop up the stairs to the ring, I find out why.

This is the point where, in my mind's ear, I can hear the television announcer: "This is where the contestant realizes that, without telling him, we've filled the ring with *eight inches of cottage cheese*!"

Oh yeah, I think. *I am so pwned.*

The ring is actually ring-shaped, a circle thirty feet across. It's walled off from the rest of the arena by a six-foot curtain of chain-link. Overhead, against the rows of floods, I can see automated cameras swooping back and forth on guy wires.

My other corner guy, Ricardo, opens a gate on the chain-link wall, and I step gingerly into the cottage cheese. It's very cold, and it squelches up over my bare feet. I stomp around a bit. The cheese is very slippery. It clings to my feet like buckets of concrete.

Pwned, I think. *Totally pwned.*

The ring announcer, who is wearing a rather smart pair of jackboots with his tux, fills the air with hype as I consider my situation. I have these freakishly long legs and arms, which constitute about my only advantage in a martial arts context. For the last four weeks, Master Pak has been drilling me on stick-and-run maneuvers—when my opponent charges me, I'm supposed to stop his attack with a stomping kick to the thigh, or jab him in the face as I shift left or right.

But I'm hardly going to be able to kick at all, not if I have to scoop my feet out of the muck. Even if I get the kick off, I might slip and fall. And I'm going to have a hard time maneuvering in any case.

I look at Master Pak for help. He's just staring down at the cottage cheese with a stony expression. He has a tae kwon do background, and for him it's all really about the kicking, which is something I suddenly can't do.

I don't know what I can do in the upcoming fight except stand there and get run down.

Whooooo. That roaring noise rises again, and I blink off into the darkness and see my opponent and his entourage coming down the aisle from the tunnel.

He's named Jimmy Blogjoy. When he was a kid actor he was Jimmy Morrison, and he starred in a third-rate knockoff of *Family Tree*, but as his career went into decline he renamed himself after his web log. This happened at roughly the time that everyone on the planet stopped reading blogs. They particularly stopped reading Jimmy's, which probably gets even fewer hits than mine. You don't want to do the self-revealing thing when all you've got to reveal is the vacuum between your ears.

Jimmy appears in the gate to the ring and looks down at the cottage cheese, which is as much a surprise to him as it was to me. He's redheaded and stocky and short, and there's a mat of rust-colored fur on his chest.

Jimmy looks over at me and snarls. His fists are clenched. He's really angry. Like it's *my* fault he has to step into the cottage cheese.

I snarl back at him. Fucking asshole.

We are in Episode Four of *Celebrity Pitfighter*, a new reality show. The rules for *Celebrity Pitfighter* are that while everyone in the contest has to have been famous at some point in his life, no one can be an actual pitfighter. We are all brand spanking new to the martial arts. Jimmy and I have trained for exactly three weeks. The world is full of drunks lying under bar stools who could take us with one hand behind their backs.

This is one step up from bum fights.

For my three weeks of training I've had cameras following me around at Master Pak's dojang, and in addition to the training I've been given little challenges, like learning to toss throwing stars at targets, or being made to hold a padded shield while famously large bruisers tried to kick in my rib cage, or trying to look impressed and competent and grateful when martial arts champions taught me their signature moves.

As with most reality shows, everything is scripted. Sometimes I improvise around an outline, sometimes I have to learn lines. The only parts of the show that aren't scripted are the fights—and they are only unscripted *so far as I know.*

None of my special training will be worth a damn when I'm rolling around in the cottage cheese. Because one of the *other* rules of *Celebrity Pitfighter* is that the contestants have to be given a surprise handicap just before the fight. In past episodes fighters have had to fight while wearing handcuffs or had fifty-pound weights attached to their right ankles, or the two opponents had their left arms tied together by a six-foot piece of elastic.

Because having a pair of untrained lames pounding each other in the ring *just isn't enough fun.* You just have to have that extra handicap in order to bring the humiliation to its peak. Because humiliation is what reality television is all about—if the audience can't watch someone utterly destroyed on camera, rejected by his judges and his peers, face not merely lost but annihilated for all time, it won't get its sadistic rocks off.

The witless fucks.

The referee calls Jimmy and me together. As he tells us he wants a clean fight Jimmy looks up at me and snarls. He's wearing a green mouthpiece impressed with silver letters that read KILL YOU. I sneer back.

Bring your worst, you half-assed gump.

We touch gloves and slosh back to our corners. Master Pak touches me and mutters in my ear.

"Look," he says. "You're still bigger than he is. Just beat the shit out of him."

I almost laugh. It's good advice.

I *am* bigger than Jimmy Blogjoy. I'm taller, I have five or six inches of reach on him, and I outweigh him by thirty pounds.

This shouldn't be a fair fight at all. If I knew what I was doing, I'd rip his bowels out.

Master Pak stuffs the mouthpiece in my mouth, leaves the ring, and closes the mesh gate behind him. The audience is baying. It occurs to me that the whole game is set so that Jimmy will win.

"Have Makin train with the TKD guy." I can hear the producer laughing as he says it. "Then put him in goop so he *can't kick.*"

I wonder if the production staff has money riding on Jimmy.

The referee looks at me and asks me if I'm ready. I mumble through the mouthpiece that I am. Jimmy is also ready. The ref punches the air in front of him.

"*Let's rock the world!*" he says.

Whoooooo. My heart is crashing in my chest. I can't see anything outside the ring. Master Pak is shouting at me but I can't hear what he's saying.

The audience noise reaches a crescendo as I slosh forward a couple of steps, then pause to await developments. Jimmy is coming straight on, balled fists on guard, his eyes fixed on my face. I raise my guard. He keeps on. He gets in range and I jab him in the face.

Nothing happens. Jimmy keeps coming. I jab again and he throws a pair of wild punches that miss. I jab and try to maneuver.

The jabs aren't working, even though I can feel them connect and feel the shock all the way to my shoulder. They're supposed to stop Jimmy or rock him back on his heels, but he just absorbs the punch and keeps coming. So I kick Jimmy somewhere in his midsection.

This works, because Jimmy goes down. Except that I go down, too, because my support leg slips in the cottage cheese.

In wild panic I flounder to my feet, cold cheese chilling my torso. Jimmy's already up, charging me, swinging wildly again. He's actually *growling.* I jab, but there's cottage cheese on my glove and the punch slips off him. He wraps his arm around me and the crown of his head butts me under my chin. I see stars and the next thing I know I'm back in the cottage cheese with Jimmy on top of me.

He's sitting on my chest raining punches down. I cover my face and try some of the techniques that Master Pak taught me to reverse someone on top of me but the cheese is everywhere and we keep slipping. At least he isn't hurting me much.

I wriggle and thrash and manage to slide a leg free from beneath his weight. I put my foot against his chest and push and he slides off me.

As I thrash to my feet blackness swims before my eyes. The fight's just a few seconds long and already I've run out of steam.

Before I can quite come on guard Jimmy socks me on the side of the head. It feels like a gong going off inside my skull. I back up, trying to put distance between us, and come up against the chain-link wall. Jimmy clamps onto me again and tries to wrestle me into the cheese. It's like fighting a rabid badger. My chest is heaving with the effort of staying on my feet.

In a rage I pound Jimmy in the body and the back of the head and try to break free, but the punches are too short to be effective, or I'm too out of breath, or both...and then our legs get tangled and I fall into the goop again, twisting away from Jimmy, facedown. A tidal wave of cottage cheese slops across the ring. Suddenly Jimmy's on my back. He snakes a forearm around my throat, but I grab his hand and manage to pull it away and save my windpipe. His feet—his "hooks" as they are called in mixed martial arts—wrap around me and pull my thighs apart. I sprawl face-first into the cottage cheese, and Jimmy begins a flurry of angry punches to the back of my head. None of them is particularly damaging but there are a lot of them.

I can't see. I can't breathe. Cottage cheese fills my mouth, my nostrils, my ears. Jimmy's punches rock my world every half-second. I try to push myself up from the floor of the ring, but I'm pushing up Jimmy's weight as well as my own, and my hands keep slipping out from under me. My lungs are about to explode.

I'm drowning. The thought sends me into a spasm of activity. I wriggle, I slither, I manage to get out from under Jimmy long enough to catch a breath, but he grabs my head and shoves me under again. The bland, salty taste of cottage cheese fills my throat.

Surrender! I've got to surrender! I'm supposed to tap the mat as a signal that I give up, but the floor is covered by cottage cheese, and no one can see the taps that are growing ever more frantic. I begin to flail, clawing at the cottage cheese. My head is full of whirling stars. Pain erupts in my chest, as if my aorta has just exploded.

In the moment before I die, I think of the next day's headline.

HAS-BEEN DROWNS WHILE TRYING TO RESURRECT HIS CAREER. That's what they'll carve on my tombstone.

Then the bodybuilder referee pulls Jimmy off me, reaches his gloved hands under my armpits, and peels me out of the cottage cheese as if I were made of soggy cardboard.

INT. SHOWERS—NIGHT

Later in the darkened locker room I stand under the shower and let warm water sluice the cheese off my body. I pull off my shorts and my supporter and cup and wad them into a ball and hurl them into a corner, where as far as I am concerned they can wait for the end of time.

I try not to think of the expression on Master Pak's face. He was so humiliated by my performance that he couldn't even look at me. The guy was born in the States but is still Asian enough to be turned to stone by the colossal loss of face.

Christ almighty, I've just had my ass handed to me by a brainless loser like Jimmy Blogjoy. Who's the fuckwit now?

First thing tomorrow, I decide, I'm going to fire my agent.

I wash the cottage cheese out of my ears and my pubic hair, then stalk into the locker room. The cheap towel they've given me is about the size of a dishrag, and beads of water are still clinging to my skin as I pull on my clothes. The briny taste of cottage cheese hangs in the back of my throat.

I step to the sink and look into the mirror as I comb my hair carefully over my balding scalp. In the merciless light over the sink I look more freakish even than usual.

Here I am, I think, *twenty-nine years old*. For years I've been working hard to regain some of the love and respect that I possessed when I was at my peak.

My peak, when I was thirteen.

Whoooooo . . .

Dimly, above me somewhere in the arena, I can hear the crowd still cheering. Only they're no longer cheering for me.

I can't get any lower than this, I think. The humiliation is complete, the self-respect has completely drained away. Maybe it's time to give it up. Just walk away, and find something else to do with my life.

I look at myself in the mirror, the huge balding head with the large brown eyes.

What? I think. *And give up show business?*

Then I take my bag and walk off into the night.

CHAPTER TWO

HEAVY LUGGAGE BLOG

I get emails asking what method—or Method—I use when acting.

I don't have any problems with the Method, or whatever other techniques my peers use to jump-start their performances. What I use myself can't be considered a method, because it's too diverse.

I'm a self-taught actor. I was in front of the camera for years of my life, and I found out what worked for me through trial and error.

I've had acting lessons. I've worked with some rather well-known coaches. The lessons were interesting, but they didn't make me a better actor. I think I'd already found my way.

Controlling show-biz parents insist that their children are only playing in front of the cameras, a falsehood that enables the parents to take sole credit for their kids' achievements. Even as a child, I knew this was more than just pretending or playing. I knew there was craft involved, and I knew this was work. Fortunately I had a number of extremely good directors, like Tony McCain and the young Joey da Nova, who worked with me very carefully. They cared enough to teach a child, and they knew *how* to teach me, which a lot of grown-ups didn't.

Sometimes I just know the character right away. Brent Schuyler on *Family Tree* was me, pretty much, only smarter and funnier. Playing a character you know forward and backward is criminally easy.

For characters I don't know instinctively, I try to use imagination to build a character. Even if it's a minor part without a backstory, I'll construct a whole biography for the character. I'll try to work out what the character wants, what is frustrating those desires, what schemes the character might have to achieve his goals. Usually none of that is found in the script, and if it is, it never ends up in the final cut—but knowing it helps me find the character.

I've played a serial killer. I don't know firsthand what it's like to be in a serial killer's head, so imagination was important in building that character. I collaborated with the director, the late Mac MacCartney, on the character's biography, on all the things that made him tick. The character's biography wasn't actually in the film, but I'd like to think that you can see it in my performance.

Of course I'm lucky enough to have an imagination. Some people don't, and they've got to employ some other way to find a character. There are systems for that, and they all work for the people they work for.

I'm also asked for recommendations for acting teachers. Since even the best seem to have made little impression on me, I can't really make any recommendations. Ask around.

Or...what the hell...hire *me*. I'll be your personal acting coach! Just a couple thousand a week, and you're on your way to greatness and fame!

Comments (0)

INT. SEAN'S CONDO—DAY

My first agent, whom I'd had since I was five, fired me when I was seventeen, saying I didn't have a career left. My second agent fired me a couple years later for the same reason. I fired my third agent myself, after she covered her windows with black paint and refused to leave her house.

Cleve Baker is my fourth agent. He's the best agent I could find, which means he's the sort of agent *anyone* can find. He has contacts on the lower rungs of the show business ladder: game shows, voice work, infomercials, reality television. Nude modeling, but not for people who look like me.

People higher on the ladder generally don't return his phone calls. But then they don't return mine, either.

Cleve works alone in a little office on the third floor of a building in West Hollywood. He used to have a secretary but she walked and he never replaced her.

The only advantage to this arrangement is that I can always get him on the phone.

I call him the next morning. I'm lying on the old couch in my sad little condo in Burbank, and my skull is still aching from the pounding it got at Jimmy Blogjoy's hands. My left hand hurts from delivering my useless punches and my back is wrenched in half a dozen places from my attempts to escape Jimmy's clutches. My coffee table is strewn with match stubs and marijuana seeds and a small pool of bong water, because when I got home I got completely chewed in hopes of being able to forget what had just happened to me.

The apartment smells as if a dozen old hippies had died in the middle of the living room, and the back of my throat feels as if a brush fire had raged there for several hours.

I don't mind. It's better than the lingering taste of cottage cheese.

"Baker and Baker," Cleve answers. So far as I know, there's never been another Baker in his firm, but he thinks it sounds better if he has a partner.

"This is Sean," I say.

"How are you feeling?"

"I feel like I've had the crap beaten out of me," I say. "How the hell am I supposed to fucking feel?"

"I heard it didn't go well," Cleve says.

"That's an understatement," I say. "Did you hear about the fucking cottage cheese?"

I've got to work my anger here. I know that I can't fire Cleve unless I'm angry.

Truth is, I don't know if I'll be able to get a better agent. With Cleve I've at least been able to earn a living.

"Yes, they told me about the cottage cheese," Cleve says.

"*Fucking... cottage... cheese,*" I repeat. I've got to keep that anger stoked.

"The show's regularly beating NBC on Tuesdays."

"My cleaning lady dancing the Macarena in a gorilla suit," I say, "could beat NBC on Tuesdays."

Cleve decides to shrug it off. "Well, whatever," he says. "It was a bad call."

Too many bad calls lately, Cleve. That's what I'm about to say, but he gets a word in ahead of me.

"I got a call this morning asking about you. Somebody wants you for a feature."

My anger fades very rapidly.

"Who?" I ask.

"A woman named Dagmar Shaw is producing. I never heard of her—have you?"

I search my memory and find nothing but the drifting clouds of a marijuana hangover. "I don't think so."

"I looked her up," Cleve says, "and she's got some credits—games, mostly."

"And she's going into features?"

"That's what she tells me."

A predator growls somewhere deep in my Cro-Magnon backbrain. I sit up, ignoring the sudden pain in my spine.

What Cleve just told me was that someone who has made money elsewhere is now getting into the motion picture business. That means exactly one thing: Hollywood is going to take her money, and then take some more, and then go on taking until there is nothing left. It happens to every outsider, no matter how savvy, from Joe Kennedy to William Randolph Hearst to Edgar Bronfman, all so dazzled by the bright lights that they never noticed their pockets were being picked. Or didn't care, because they were willing to hand over a fortune to be in the most glamorous business on Earth.

The process of shaking down strangers for all their money is routine and, as far as I'm concerned, inevitable. The main question, therefore, is not whether this Dagmar person is going to lose her money, but how much of this lost fortune is going to go to *me.*

"What kind of part?" I ask.

"The lead."

I jump up from the couch and do a little dance, then wince with sudden pain. In the process of losing all her money, Dagmar Shaw might well do me a *lot* of good.

"I got offered the lead in a feature," I say, "and you didn't call?"

Cleve's tone is cynical. "I never heard of her. The call came out of nowhere, and I get bullshit calls all the time. I was going to do some checking before I got your hopes up."

"Am I going to have to audition?"

"She didn't say. She wants to meet you in person, though."

I grin. "Set it up."

"I'll call her."

"Did she mention the budget?"

"Nope."

"Can I get a copy of the script?"

"I asked. She said she wants to interview first."

"Well," I say, "we'd better interview."

Cleve says he'll call her back, and when the call's over I run to my computer to look up Dagmar Shaw.

She turns out to be a real person, and her wiki shows that she's got a long history in the game industry, producing something called "Alternate Reality Games," or ARGs, for her own company, Great Big Idea.

I've played video games all my life, but I've never played an ARG. One of my friends, Julian Jackson, did some acting for an ARG once, and I make a note to call him.

The wiki features a long list of games produced by Dagmar, along with extensive quotes from their glowing reviews. Most of the games seem to be archived somewhere, which will allow me to check them out.

It's some of the later items in Dagmar's personal history that send my eyebrows crawling toward my hairline. A few years ago, several of her friends were killed in a series of shootings and bombings. The wiki's cautious report of this isn't very forthcoming, but an online search produces a number of other articles, all of which contradict one another. There is a determined minority that insists no one actually died, and that all the murders were part of an online game—but on the other hand I *remember* the bombing of the Hotel Figueroa, and the hysteria about whether Los Angeles had been the scene of a terrorist incident, and I know *that* was real. And there are also links to original news stories from the period—and unless Dagmar managed to hoax a *lot* of major news organizations, those killings were clearly not a game.

A few years later, the wiki informs me, Dagmar was apparently hired by the rock star Ian Attila Gordon to overthrow a foreign government. Dagmar was accused of being a terrorist. I sure as hell remember the fuss over *that*, especially when the coup actually took place, and Attila paraded in triumph past thousands of cheering, recently liberated citizens all waving CDs of his latest album.

There were serious plans to make a film based on these events, with Attila playing himself and doing the film score. I think the movie got stuck in development, because I haven't heard anything about it in a couple years.

I sit in front of my computer and contemplate the job that may be on offer. In the past I've worked for alcoholics, drug addicts, pedophiles, thieves, con men, and megalomaniacs.

I've never worked for a terrorist before. But this is a terrorist with money and the offer of a job.

And I can understand, from personal experience, how your friends can end up dead, and how it can be your fault, but not really, because you didn't mean to do anything bad.

Working for Dagmar seems morally justifiable to me.

INT. SEAN'S CONDO—NIGHT

The only news that I watch is the entertainment news. I turned on a news channel later that day and the news was all about the deteriorating climate and the riots in Seoul and the genocide in Fiji.

I couldn't figure out how there got to be a genocide in Fiji. Isn't it supposed to be an island paradise?

Fortunately I was able to change the channel before the talking heads could get to even more depressing news, and there was the entertainment news, cheerfully floating the rumor of an Andalusian God reunion.

And then Julian showed up with a baggie of weed, and all was well.

"Okay," Julian says. "Imagine a movie—or a novel—that's online."

"Okay," I say.

Julian pushes his glasses back up his nose. "But it's not all at one location. It's hidden all over the place, and you have to *find* it."

I picture this. "How?" I ask.

"You follow clues, or solve puzzles. Or sometimes a fictional person will call your cell phone and tell you to do something, and you need to do it."

I try to process this.

"See," Julian says, "it's *interactive*. You can't just log off and go about your business. The game sort of follows you into real life."

I'm not enlightened. Julian is describing the alternate reality game he worked on, and I'm having a hard time working my mind around it.

Julian looks down at the bong in his hands, which he's packing with the product he's brought with him. "This is dank bud, man," he says. "It's as good as any Amsterdam shit, I swear."

I've known Julian for a long time, and he's part of my circle of former child stars. Julian's fame hit its peak when he was about five, and he did a series of commercials for Nissan in which he played a cute-but-annoying kid pacified by an SUV backseat video screen. Afterward he starred in a sitcom modeled after *Family Tree*, but it lasted only half a season. After that he guested on my show a few times, which is how I know him.

The cute little red-haired kid is now an avocado-shaped adult with a bristly mustache and glasses with heavy black rims. He's still got the mop of red hair. He's earning a decent living as a character actor, and has a steady trade playing accountants, deceived husbands, murder victims, sidekicks, red herrings, and innocent, innocuous bystanders who inexplicably get swept up in the action. He's doing a lot better than I am, but then he looks a lot less freaky than I do.

I decide to give up trying to figure out how ARGs work.

"Did you ever meet Dagmar Shaw?" I ask.

He shakes his head. "I worked for one of her competitors," he said. "They respected her."

I nod. "That's good."

"They said that whatever you do, you shouldn't piss her off." He gives me a quick, mischievous look through his thick glasses. "She'll bomb your car, man."

I give a laugh. "My car? She's welcome to it." Then I see how he's looking at me, and my laughter dies away. "You made that up, right?" I ask.

"No," Julian says. "I didn't."

He's sitting in my easy chair, which is covered with an India-print throw to disguise the fact that it's held together with duct tape. My own butt is dropped into my sagging couch, likewise covered by a throw.

There isn't much to say about my condo. The carpet is beige, the walls are pastel, and the ceiling is that glittery spray-on popcorn that was everywhere in the seventies, ages before I was even born. The framed movie posters on the walls are sort of interesting. I haven't put up posters from my own films, because I don't want to remember most of them.

Julian hands me the bong and reaches for the green plastic lighter on the coffee table. My back gives a twinge as I lean toward him.

"It's showtime," Julian says, and flicks the lighter.

FADE TO:
THE SAME—FIVE HOURS LATER

Julian and I have got into a habit of meeting every few weeks, getting fried, and watching movies. My condo might be a cheap-ass piece of cardboard destined to be condemned after the next earthquake, and my car may have belonged to my mother before she surrendered her material possessions and went into the ashram, but my flat-screen TV gleams with gemlike brilliance, my sound system is powerful enough to raise the Gettysburg dead, and my film collection rivals that of the Smithsonian.

Lately I've become fascinated by the films of the 1970s. Back then, the leads didn't have to be beautiful—ordinary-looking people like Gene Hackman, Walter Matthau, Al Pacino, and Dustin Hoffman could become big stars. All they needed was talent.

I've become a particular fan of Gene Hackman, so tonight we watch him in two pictures, *Night Moves* and *Scarecrow*, the latter of which also costars Pacino. Hackman is brilliant all the way through, in roles that are very different. Pacino is top form. Richard Lynch and the young James Woods and a very young Melanie Griffith are also memorable.

I look at Julian over the half-full bowl of popcorn and the Amstel empties. I am practically swooning with admiration.

"These movies break all the rules," I say. "The heroes aren't supermen. They aren't even beautiful. None of the guys has a six-pack. And the endings are complete downers."

"Which is why they tanked," Julian points out.

"*Scarecrow* didn't tank. It was a major motion picture."

Julian waves a dismissive hand. "It didn't do brilliantly or anything, I bet. If it had done a ton of box office, I would have heard of it before now."

The double feature still has me on a high. "Did you see how long those two-shots lasted?" I ask. "Some of them must have gone a couple, three minutes. Just the two of them talking."

"Boring." The hand-wave again.

"Boring? It's *acting*. It's *great acting*." I reach for my Amstel. "You know," I say, "the women aren't beautiful, either. Jennifer Warren is good-looking, okay, but she's not drop-dead gorgeous."

"But she's *attractive*," Julian says. "And even if Al and Gene don't look like male models, they're still attractive men." Julian, by the way, is a victim of the Hollywood disease where you refer to everyone by their first names, whether you know them or not. He looks at me. "They're better looking than *I* am. All the stars are."

"Bullshit," I say. "A better haircut and some contact lenses, and you could be at *least* as good-looking as Danny Bonaduce."

"Fuck you," he laughs, then grows serious again. "Fact is, we both lost the genetic lottery."

"In the seventies—" I begin.

He looks at me levelly. His glassy pupils seem enormous behind the thick lenses.

"A time machine won't save you," he says. "You are who you are."

"Julian," I say. "I know who I am."

"Sean," Julian says, "you know I've done a hundred things more important than being that kid in the Nissan commercial."

Name three, I want to say.

Fact is, I know far too much about him. He left the business and went to college, but dropped out and went back into the business. He was married just long enough for the wife to take all his money in the divorce. He has a reputation for reliability and he works steadily, but none of his parts are memorable. Over the years he's been a Buddhist and a Catholic and a kabbalist and a pothead. Only the pothead stuck.

He still drives a Nissan. Maybe brand loyalty counts for something.

There is a moment of silence. He plays with the green cigarette lighter while he stares at me, and then he looks down at his hands.

"How's *Mister Baby Head*?" he asks.

"The heirs are still in litigation." My only starring role as an adult, and the producer/director had to go and die without a will. His partners were wrangling in the courts with his ex-wives, his adult children, and a trustee appointed to represent his minor children.

And all the while my performance was sitting in the can, unseen by the world, the whole project worth less and less with every deposition, every motion, every appeal.

"Well," Julian says. "That sucks." He sighs and holds up his baggie. "Want some more moon juice before I go?"

"Yeah."

He packs the bowl, lights up, and I suck in a power hit. My head spins. I hold the smoke in my lungs so long that when I exhale, only a few wisps come out.

Gene Hackman gives me a pitying look from the big flatscreen. I think of Master Pak turning away from me in the locker room, too mortified to speak; and how my agents fired me, and then how I got fired by my family.

I take a swallow of beer to wash away the phantom taste of cottage cheese from my throat. I look at Julian.

"Taking a hit yourself?"

"No. Driving." He puts the baggie in a pocket, then rises from his armchair. "There's this thing called Our Reality Network," he says.

"There's what?" I'm not tracking him at all.

"For ARGs," he says. "I'll send you the URL."

I show him to the door and then step out onto my postage-stamp lawn to take a breath of fresh air. There's a faint frangipani scent to the gentle night.

I think about Hackman's character in *Night Moves*, the baffled, affable detective so completely unsuited to grope his way through the Hollywood labyrinth, through all the players who so completely fucked him over.

I'm not like that, I decide. I grew up here. I know exactly who's going to screw me over, and when.

My chief hope is that, if I just hang on long enough, I can get in a position to screw them all right back.

INT. SEAN'S BEDROOM—MORNING

I flail out of sleep to my cell's ring tone, a feminine shriek I sampled from a horror movie soundtrack. I throw myself out of bed, surfing on a surge of adrenaline, then experience a moment of blinding pain as I stub my toe on a steel dumbbell. Hopping, cursing, I find my phone on the charging stand and answer.

"*Help me! Help me, oh God help me!*" Panic quavers through the woman's voice.

"What?" I'm beyond confusion. Pain shrieks through my toe. "Who is this?"

"He's dead! He's lying here dead! What do I do?"

My mind totters in disarray. It can't help jumbling this terrified woman with the woman who just screamed, even though if I were on top of things I'd remember the screaming woman is just the voice from my ring tone.

"Who is this?" I ask. I make a blind thrust into the shadows of my past. "Is this Melissa?"

"It's Doctor Dexter! Dexter's dead! What do I do?"

I don't know anyone named Dexter. Words stumble across my thick tongue.

"I think you have the wrong number," I say. "I think you should call the police."

"Oh my God, someone killed Dexter! He's lying next to the pool!"

By now my brain is beginning to fumble at reality. There's something about the name Dexter that prods a memory.

The woman wails on in my ear. "*There's a gun! Dexter has a gun in his hand! Should I take it away from him?*"

"Aw, shit," I say aloud.

It's a game. A freaking game. And the woman on the phone is a recording, and nothing I say to her makes any difference.

Julian sent me the URL for Our Reality Network, and yesterday, just to try to make sense of my possible employer, I subscribed to one of the alternate reality games. In it there is a scientist named Lyle Dexter who had gone missing.

My guess is that someone has just found him.

Sometimes a fictional person will call your cell phone... The game sort of follows you into real life. It's not as if Julian hadn't told me what was going to happen.

I bend over and massage my aching toe as the telephone woman continues her hysterics. Now that I know it's an act, I begin to admire the performance.

She's an absolute pro, I have to give her that. It's hard to keep that pitch of hysteria for so long, particularly if you're using just voice.

The phone call ends with the hysterical woman giving an address—which if I were a dedicated player, alert and experienced, I'd know to scribble down. As it is, I just put the phone back on the charger, scratch my armpit, and limp out onto my balcony.

There's no weather at all, which makes it a typical LA day. Midmorning California sun diffuses from a featureless opalescent sky. Palm trees stake out the horizon. My hibachi rusts under the overhang next to a half-empty sack of charcoal. Somewhere I hear the machine-gun sound of a diesel engine-braking. I don't see a single human being, but I see two coyotes sniffing around a plastic garbage can that someone's left at the curb.

If it weren't for the sound of the diesel, you could mistake the scene for one of those movies where everyone dies, and the cities slowly revert to nature.

But no. It's LA, where everyone I know in the business is far more dangerous than those coyotes ever will be.

In a couple hours I'll be having my lunch meeting with Dagmar Shaw. I'll have to tell her that one of her games got me out of bed thinking that someone had been murdered.

Or maybe I won't. Maybe, I thought, she hears that all the time.

I realize that I'm overthinking the meeting. It's too important.

The lead. In a feature. That possibility hasn't existed for me since I was sixteen. Even in *Mister Baby Head*, I was the title character but not the lead.

I step back into the bedroom and consider the dumbbell that

I kicked on my way to the phone. It rolled out of its place, and I nudge it back under the dresser.

I consider doing my workout before the meeting. I used to belong to a health club before money problems forced me to quit, and since then I've learned to enjoy pumping iron at home, first thing in the morning, or running on a secondhand treadmill while watching an old movie on my television. Used exercise equipment, it turns out, is a lot cheaper than a membership in a club.

I work out nearly every day. Actors need to stay in good shape, particularly in these days when taut abdomens and tight glutes are more important than ability.

But today I don't have the time. I shower, dress for the meet—blue polo top, cream-colored slacks—then go downstairs to make coffee. While drinking the coffee and eating half a bagel, I go online and check the entertainment news, and there I find out about Dickie Marks's getting into porn.

Dickie is a few years younger than me. He starred in the hour-long family drama *Hooks & Ladders*, in which he played Benjamin Hooks, the troubled son of a firefighter disabled on 9/11. The series was set in Queens, but of course shot in the parts of Los Angeles deemed by the camera to best resemble New York. For three years in a row he was nominated for an Emmy. I think he won a Golden Globe.

But after *Hooks & Ladders*, nothing. I can't figure out why—Dickie had shown he could act, he was good-looking, he was devoted to his craft, and he remained unattached to any scandals involving sex, drugs, or alcohol. But barring a few guest shots and some theater, he'd stayed unemployed for a decade.

Now he has lent his talent to a porno, using the name Dick Rampant. I can't believe it. Did he really think that no one would recognize him?

What a miserable tool.

I have his private number on speed dial, and in an act of pure sharklike sadism I get my phone and call. It goes straight to voice mail. I'm not surprised that he's hiding out.

"This is Sean," I say. "Dude. What the *fuck*?"

If the public remembers Dickie at all, it remembers him as the thirteen-year-old on *Hooks & Ladders*. And—barring a few genuinely disturbed fans—*nobody wants to see that kid having sex!* Not even after he's grown.

Plus we should consider the puritanical refusal of Middle America, which consumes billions of dollars' worth of porn every year, to forgive porn actors their sins.

Dickie has managed to get into a dead-end job and alienate what remained of his fan base *all at the same time.*

"For chrissake," I say, "you've got to get ahead of the story somehow. Say you were on drugs or something." Inspiration strikes. "Or tell them you were looking for love."

That would be a new one, I think.

"Anyway," I finish, "call me if you want to talk."

I end the call and for the first time I feel better about appearing on *Celebrity Pitfighter*. At least I'm not Dickie Marks's kind of loser. At least I haven't totally lost my mind.

I put the phone in its cradle, then go back online. I avoid browsing anywhere I can find out about the reception of my episode of *Celebrity Pitfighter*, which was broadcast last night.

I accept humiliation as part of the job. But I don't want to wallow in it.

CHAPTER THREE

HEAVY LUGGAGE BLOG

If you saw tonight's episode of *Celebrity Pitfighter*, you'll know that I lost to Jimmy Blogjoy fifty-seven seconds into the first round. I can't say that I'm happy about this.

I'd like to think that it was all the fault of the cottage cheese. If we'd been sloshing around in chicken noodle soup, I'm convinced that I would have done a lot better.

This loss puts me out of the running for Grand Champion, so you won't be seeing me in the ring again.

I'm honored to have been given the chance to participate in this year's tourney, and I wish Jimmy the best of luck. I'd like to thank Master Pak for all his good advice, and all the other teachers who gave of their time and expertise.

I had a great time! Thanks for watching!

Comments (65)

FROM: MaddHaxx

You COMPLETELY sucked! You hit like a little girl!

FROM: HorNyArTie

LMAO when you went dwn for 2nd time. Yoru a pussy, Makin!

FROM: Jaxon31

Blogjoy sez URA fagit!

FROM: Krumble

Kick your ass hahaha

FROM: Verminus

Very interesting. You have an excellent blog. If you're interested in getting a good rate for auto insurance, please contact me at your earliest convenience.

FROM: HvyMtl

Pathetic. Next time bring a howitzer.

INT. SEAN'S BATHROOM—DAY

Before the interview I walk into the bathroom to give myself a pep talk. I stare into the mirror, and the Watcher stares back at me.

The Watcher is a character from Marvel Comics, a member of an alien species dedicated to the acquisition of knowledge. He's lived for millions of years on the Blue Area of the moon, where he observes the Earth, takes lots of notes, practices austerity, and occasionally issues a cryptic warning to the Fantastic Four that a cosmic menace is on the way.

He's very tall, he's got a huge bald head, and he's got weird all-white eyes with no irises.

I look just like the Watcher, except that my eyes are larger and prettier, and he looks better than I do in a toga.

I resemble the Watcher because I have a condition called pedomorphosis. Basically it means that while the rest of my body has aged normally, my head has retained the features of an infant's. Plus my head is really, really huge.

When I was a kid the condition made me cute. I had a big head with huge brown eyes, and my extra-babyish features vastly increased my audience appeal. I always looked younger than my actual age—when I was fifteen I looked twelve or thirteen, all boyish and fuzzy-cheeked, and this hugely increased the number of tween girls who adored me, and massively enhanced my odds of getting sex.

But by sixteen, I was beginning to look a little odd. My dad put it down to an awkward teen growth spurt. By the time I was seventeen, I was two inches over six feet tall and was beginning to look freakish, like a sinister bobblehead doll leering unexpectedly at you from the dashboard of someone's car.

By the time I was eighteen, it was all over. I looked like something stitched together by Victor Frankenstein, I had no work, my fans had turned away or forgotten me, and my parents had run off with my money.

Even my stalkers deserted me, including the middle-aged grade-school teacher who'd been sending me marriage proposals since I was twelve. I thought I'd *never* get rid of that old perv.

For a few years I tried to turn lemons into lemonade by trying to produce a Watcher movie. Marvel had other projects it was more interested in. I tried to get myself attached to those projects, playing the Watcher—or Wolverine, or Kraven the Hunter, or Kitty Pryde, not like I cared. Not like I succeeded, either.

My bathroom is small and smells of mildew. I look at myself in the mirror. "You're a star," I tell myself. "You've got talent. Someday people will notice."

Affirmations. They're one of many cliché approaches that actors bring to their craft. I took acting classes at one point, and though I've forgotten everything else, the affirmations are still with me.

Maybe it works because actors can't get enough of hearing praise about themselves.

"This is going to be a great interview," I say, sincerity glowing like soft candles in my brown eyes.

Actors spend a lot of their lives staring into mirrors. We try on expressions, we try on attitudes, we recite lines, we study how the dialogue looks on our lips.

I look at myself and repeat the encouraging words. My enormous head gazes back at me.

"You're a star," I tell myself. In my dreams.

The bathroom lights gleam off my balding scalp, broad as a piece of armor plate. My eyes are huge and luminous, my nose a stubby afterthought. My ears stand out. The proportions are all wrong for an adult.

At one point I grew a goatee to make myself look more masculine. I shaved it off for *Mister Baby Head* and never grew it back. Another year I shaved off my hair to disguise the fact that I was balding, but it just made my head look bigger, so I let my fringe grow back.

"You're going to nail this interview," I tell myself. "You're going to kill."

The Watcher looks back at me, alight with cosmic power. I turn off the light and stalk back into the world.

The Watcher, leaving the Blue Area for Earth.

EXT. RODEO DRIVE—DAY

Floyd Steneri, who played my older brother on *Family Tree*, is a good guy. He didn't seem to mind that I became the big star, leaving him as a supporting character. If the situations had been reversed, I would have hated him like poison.

After *Family Tree* was canceled, he went to college and got a degree in pharmacy. Because he had his Coogan trust, he was able to actually buy a pharmacy in Wisconsin, after which he got married and had four children. He sends me a photo of the family every Christmas—smiling dairy-fed blond Midwestern kids, wholesome as curds and whey. We talk on the phone every so often, and he tells me about taking them to hockey practice. His business is doing well, and he rarely has a bad word to say about anyone.

Somehow I can't see this as a happy ending. He's out of the business, he's even out of California.

Is this a win? It can't be.

I think about this as I drive to Beverly Hills, where I'm meeting Dagmar Shaw. Even though my mom's pearl-gray Mercedes S-Class is fourteen years old, I've kept it polished and gleaming, because it's the sort of car a successful person would drive, and I want people to think I am that person instead of victim of fraud, catastrophic luck, and multiple felonies, which is what I actually am.

I find a parking place a couple blocks from the restaurant and walk. Bright icons and animated figures jump and wave at me from the corners of my vision. Because I couldn't find my regular eyewear, I'm wearing the stupid Aristotle Despopoulos AR shades that I got in the gift bag at the party, and I can't turn off the icons.

Without the shades I'd see Rodeo Drive in Beverly Hills, with its palms, its rows of tasteful, expensive shops, its perfect glossy appearance marred only by a clump of tourists visiting the site of a crucial scene from *Pretty Woman.* But that's not what I see—instead reality is overlaid by dozens of leaping, cavorting images, doormen touting their shops, ads for adult diapers or sex aids, and the inevitable auditions by actors. The *Pretty Woman* site, for example, is marked by a glowing, rotating Julia Roberts dressed in the spandex shorts and thigh-high streetwalker boots she wore in the film—but here she's only one of a couple dozen sex workers competing for my attention, along with an image of the president garbed as the Antichrist, and various political slogans like STOP WAR! and FIGHT SOCIALISM NOW! Many of these were placed by people who can't exactly spell.

And I see muggers. This is a recent development in AR, created by people who were fed up with the endless proliferation of icons crowding out their cityscape. Muggers are created for the purpose of attacking other icons—to heckle them, to bash them, and sometimes, if they're designed cleverly enough, to actually kill them.

I pass one on the way. He looks like Paulie Walnuts from *The Sopranos*, and he's using a baseball bat to clout an ad for male enhancement. The other ad looks confused and keeps derezzing and appearing somewhere else. It's a clear violation of Tony Sirico's physiognomic rights, but it's hilarious.

"Hey there, Sean," says a voice.

I turn to see my agent, Cleve Baker, loping toward me.

"Hi," I say. "You're not coming to the meeting, are you?"

Cleve is a tall, well-groomed man of about forty. He came out of the music business and has a law degree. His clothes are casual but up-to-the-second, from the handmade Andean alpaca-wool sandals to the blocky Perry Ellis sweater worn over a white crewneck tee. His wrist plays host to a Blancpain Fifty Fathoms chronograph.

I once asked him why anyone would call a watch "White Bread," but he just stared at me.

"No, I won't be at the restaurant," he says. "I'm going to be in the bar in the next room, and after you dazzle this Dagmar Shaw, I'm going to sashay in and nail down the contract."

Agents really shouldn't be in meetings between the producers and the talent—those kinds of meetings are about finding out whether producers and talent are suited to one another, and agents are about what happens if the answer is yes. Agents step in to negotiate contracts if the talent gets hired. Until then, they should stay out of the process, because their presence just confuses things.

"Cleve," I say, "I dunno, that doesn't sound like a hella great idea—"

Then a series of screams sounds from my pocket, and I get out my phone. It's Dickie Marks. I answer.

"Dude," I say to the phone. "I mean, really."

"Yeah. I know." Dickie's voice is subdued, barely audible against the sound of traffic.

"How did you think this was going to end?" I ask. "Did you think at all?"

"I didn't think anyone gave a damn about me one way or another," he says. "My last job was at a *burrito stand*, for Christ's sake. I wore a *bear costume* and a *sombrero*."

"Now you can expect jokes about your burrito for the rest of your life," I say.

I'm taking a certain pleasure in this. The career of another former child star has augured into the pavement, right in front of the whole world, and *he wasn't me*. Thanks to Dickie Marks, the entertainment news didn't even mention Jimmy Blogjoy's drowning me in the cottage cheese.

It isn't enough to succeed, as someone said. Others must fail.

On the other hand, I'm also sorry for Dickie. Because he's yet another wreck in the gigantic freeway pileup of onetime kid stars, like Darlene Gillespie who went in for securities fraud and perjury, or Gary Coleman who declared bankruptcy and was accused of domestic abuse, Melody Chastain who kicked the dog, or Dana Plato or Michael Jackson or Corey Haim or so many others who found ways of killing themselves.

I have no right to feel superior. I too could leap at a chance to bring my career back, and not realize until it was too late how incredibly stupid and destructive it would be, how utterly desperate and insane I would have to be to even *try* such a thing…

What am I saying? I've *been* that guy.

As witness my attempts to get arrested. As witness Timmi's getting killed. Now *that* was crazy.

"Yeah," Dickie says. There is a moment of silence. "The question is what I do now."

"I don't know, man."

Traffic swishes by as I stand on the corner. A chorus of Munchkins from *The Wizard of Oz* march past, singing in silent chorus—I thank God that my AR specs don't have audio.

Dickie's voice mutters in my ear.

"In your voice mail, you said something about telling people I was just looking for love."

"Yeah," I say.

"It makes me sound sort of pathetic."

I say nothing and wait for the sheer pitiful nature of this statement to sink in. Dickie is far beyond pathetic now, so deep in the cottage cheese that he's only seconds away from drowning.

For several seconds I watch an icon of Mickey Mouse brandishing a dildo. He'll be doing that until Disney's lawyers, which tend to be deadlier than Paulie Walnuts at his best, hammer the host with a writ.

"Yeah," Dickie says finally. "Okay. I'm not going to walk away from this without egg on my face."

"Right," I say.

"Maybe," he ventures, "instead of looking for love, I could be in love with... with *one particular person.*"

"Your costar?"

"God, no!" For the first time his voice shows animation. "I have *some* pride left. There's no way I'm going to say I'm in love with Tandee Landes. It was bad enough just having sex with her!"

"If you say so." I've never heard of Tandee Landes, one way or another.

"I mean, she's the most brainless woman I've ever met. And those huge boobs—they don't move. Not even a little bit. They just sit there like flesh-colored concrete and look at you." He gives a growl of exasperation. "The scene wasn't over till four in the morning. It was freezing on the soundstage. It smelled as if someone had died under that couch. And I still had to pretend I wanted to fuck that cow."

I clear my throat. "I don't want to hear about your damn scene, Dickie."

"How about Samantha Hollock?" he says.

It's a name I vaguely remember from about a decade ago. "Is she still in the business?" I ask.

"She's retired from acting, but now she's a producer and director. She produced my movie. I could say I did the movie to get close to her."

"You fell in love with her," I say, "when you were just a kid."

"Yes!" His voice shows enthusiasm. "I did it for love!" He sounds as if he believes it.

"You play that scene, Dickie," I tell him. "You'll absolutely kill."

He'll get nationwide coverage, I think. He'll get another fifteen minutes of fame, plus become the subject of dozens of jokes by late-night talk show hosts. Then maybe he'll do a tour of morning radio shock-jock shows, appearing as the freak-of-the-instant and the butt of yet more fatuous humor.

And then back to the burrito cart. Unless something clicks, and he actually finds work.

But I don't think so. Try to name actors who came back from porn, and you won't find more than a couple. The rest are selling insurance, or working at Burger King. Or dancing in a bear suit in some parking lot.

The traffic light finally changes and I start across the street while putting my phone back in my pocket. Hookers and Mickey and a gaudy ad for Van Cleef and Arpels flash in my AR shades. My phone won't go into my pocket the first time and I pause to open the pocket with my free hand.

Horsepower roars somewhere nearby. My pocket won't cooperate and I keep trying to jam the phone into it. Then Cleve grabs my arm and yanks me out of the way as a battered black Ford Expedition blasts through the intersection. The slipstream tugs at my hair. I stare as the SUV speeds away down Rodeo in a cloud of blue smoke. My heart hammers in surprise and shock. There's a sour oily taste on the air.

"Jesus Christ!" Cleve says. "Get out of the road, Sean, will you?"

I let him pull me out of the intersection. Impudent Smurfs waggle their blue asses at me. I realize the AR shades are a dangerous distraction and take them off.

I look at the traffic light as I step onto the curb. According to the counter on the display, I have another eight seconds left to cross the street safely.

Maybe in other places, New York or someplace, the driver of the Expedition wouldn't be so totally unexpected. But in California pedestrians have such absolute right-of-way over vehicles that it's a little startling that the incident happened at all.

I look at Cleve. "What happened?" I ask.

"Fucking tourist made an illegal left turn across three lanes of traffic," Cleve says.

"Did you get the number?"

Cleve barks a laugh. "I was too busy keeping the car from getting *your* number."

I take a breath and try to calm my thrashing heart. "Well thanks," I say.

"You're welcome." He gestures in the direction of the restaurant. "This way. Your future awaits."

INT. SALO RESTAURANT—DAY

Salo is a kind of neo-Mediterranean fine dining establishment, white plaster walls mounted with bright Moroccan carpets that set off dark iron chairs and tables with deliberately crude, blobby welds. The façade features a couple of massive buttresses that call to mind the pylons of an ancient Egyptian temple. Inside are four dining rooms, each under its own pyramid.

Believers in pyramidology probably think they can eat lunch and get their razor blades sharpened at the same time.

The hostess tells us that our party has already arrived. Cleve calls the hostess by her first name and tells her that he likes her hair. It is generally unsafe to be female when Cleve is around. He keeps up a steady stream of compliments as she walks us to our table.

I'm too keyed up to notice whether the hostess looks good or not. *Lead in a feature.* I'm surprised I'm not drooling.

We pass some well-dressed Ladies Who Lunch, and one of

them looks at me in surprise. "Look!" she says. "It's Luggage Boy!"

Luggage Boy. Something else they're going to carve on my tombstone.

Dagmar Shaw sits at her table, her head haloed from above by a big coach light on a black iron bracket. The first thing I think is *Interesting fashion choice.* Because her hair is a smooth uniform gray, the color of charcoal ash, and you don't see that here, and she's too young for gray hair anyway—she seems to be in her mid-thirties. Because no women in my part of the world have gray hair at all, she looks more striking than all but a few of them.

Her eyebrows are dark, and set above eyes that are looking at me with a kind of half-puzzled expression. It's the look that registers wrongness without quite being able to work out what the wrongness is. I'm used to it, I see it a lot.

Eventually she realizes she's staring too much and her face opens out into a smile, a little strained. I'm used to that, too. She lurches a little coming up out of her chair, and I realize she's pregnant. I'm no expert on pregnancy but hers seems about the middling stage, five or six months.

I jump to her side and steady her, guiding her so that her skull is not impaled by the coach light over her head. While she's murmuring thanks Cleve sweeps in front of me and shakes her hand.

"I'm Cleve," he says.

Dagmar is surprised, but recovers swiftly enough. "I'm Dagmar. This is my husband, Ismet."

I've been so focused on the woman who might offer me work that I haven't even noticed that someone is with her. Ismet is a pale-skinned man, maybe a few years younger than Dagmar, with watchful brown eyes behind dark-rimmed spectacles.

There's something a little foreign about him—the formal way he carries himself, the way he inhabits his clothing—but when he greets me I hear an American accent.

Dagmar looks at Cleve with a degree of suspicion. "Will you be joining us?"

"Well," he says. "I wasn't planning on it, actually—but thanks." He takes a chair and sits. Now *I'm* staring at Cleve.

A waitress is right on the spot, wearing a cute tuxedo with a red sash. She takes our drink orders. I have iced tea.

"Do you think the waitress is hot?" Cleve asks. "I think she's hot."

I look at him. I'm really not happy that he's here. "You like cross-dressers, Cleve?"

"I'm gonna ask her out," he says. His eyes track after her.

Dagmar studies me, her face in a studious cast.

"So," she says. "How are you with children?"

The question takes me aback.

"You mean *your* child?" I ask, waving a vague hand in the direction of her pregnancy. "Or . . . ?"

"Acting with children," she says.

I haven't acted with children since I was a child myself, but I'm smart enough in an interview to accentuate the positive.

"I'm fine," I say. "I like kids."

"Do you have children of your own?"

"No."

"That he *knows of*," Cleve says playfully, and jabs me in the elbow with his knuckles. A jolt of pain shoots up my humerus. I want to hit him over the head with a plate.

"This picture is going to use a lot of green screen," Dagmar says. "Do you have experience with that?"

"Sure," I say. "Green screen is everywhere."

You want to set a scene in Boston or Miami or Singapore without shipping your cast there? Have them act in front of a green backdrop, and then key Boston behind them in editing.

But honestly, the question is a little naive. I turn to Dagmar.

"I'm an *actor*," I say. "I can act on a soundstage or in a fast-moving car or at the bottom of a swimming pool. With green screen all I have to do is *pretend*—pretend that the spaceship's overhead, or that I'm flying, or that I'm talking to a pink, six-armed troll." I mime each of these actions as I speak. I drop the mime and speak directly to Dagmar.

"Pretending is what actors do," I say. "I'm a pro. I've been doing this all my life. Just put me in front of the camera, and I'll give you what you want."

I'm acting as I say this. I'm playing a great actor, and I'm playing it less than three feet from Dagmar's eyes. Most folks aren't used to people being so intense right in their faces. It usually makes an impression.

"Sean is great," Cleve says. "Sean knows what he's doing."

Dagmar considers me. The waitress arrives with the drinks. She puts my iced tea in front of me, and Cleve says, "You have really pretty hands."

Cleve is always complimenting women's hands. Men don't usually do that, so it usually catches women by surprise, and—Cleve assumes—leaves them open to further encroachments.

The waitress is flattered. Cleve asks her name.

"Keisha," she says.

"I've always liked that name," Cleve says.

Keisha hands around the others' drinks. Cleve has white wine and is the only person drinking alcohol.

We order lunch. I have a Provençal fish soup, because the description in the menu sounds interesting. Dagmar asks for a Moroccan chicken dish that's on special, and Ismet orders kofte. Cleve calls for a steak, and hangs on to the wine list so he can decide what red wine he wants with it.

I turn to Dagmar. "You woke me up this morning," I say, and when she looks blank, I say, "With the phone call about Dr. Dexter."

She laughs. "Sorry about that! The sponsor wanted the call going out at eleven New York time. They had a board meeting then, and they wanted the board to hear it live."

"The voice actress was good. Who is she?"

"Terry Griff. And she *is* good."

"Terry? I've met her." Terry is one of those people who've been around forever, talented, continually employed, yet somehow perpetually overlooked for anything but minor roles. You'd recognize her if you saw her, but you wouldn't remember where you'd seen her before.

"You know Terry?" She cocks her head. "Where from?"

"Here and there. Premieres, charity events. We've never worked together."

"She may be in this project. That's why I'm asking."

"It'll be nice to see her again."

Dagmar sips her iced tea, then leans back and considers me. "This is going to be an unusual undertaking," she says.

"Unusual how?"

I see a weary smile on Ismet's face, and I sense he's been through all this before.

"Because it's going to use techniques that have been developed in alternate reality games."

I absorb this. "You're going to have me wake up the audience by phoning them?"

"Maybe," Dagmar says, with perfect seriousness.

I try to remember what Julian told me about ARGs. "So there's going to be—like—interactivity?"

"There will be interactivity going on *around* the film. Games. Puzzles. There will be interactivity *in* the film as well, but that won't really concern you. You'll just act in front of the camera the way you always do."

"Interactivity *in* the film?" A memory floats up. "You mean like the Kinoautomat?"

Dagmar blinks at me. "Kino what?"

"Kinoautomat," I say. "It was a Czech invention back in the sixties. At certain points in the film, the audience would vote on how they wanted the story to go."

She seems both surprised and entranced. "Have you seen any of these movies?"

"I think there was only one. A friend of mine is a collector. Clarence Musselwhite, who owns the Hollywood Museum of Film History. He's got the hardware and everything, for the voting."

The Kinoautomat debuted at a world's fair, and after the fair ended the Czechs didn't want to ship their gear back to Europe, and they sold it for nothing. A collector was on the spot to pick it up, and eventually Clarence got it. But he didn't actually get a copy of the film, *Man in His House*, till years later, after the Soviet Union crashed, and then he had a gathering for some friends in his little theater, and we all sat in the dark and pressed buttons to vote on the way we wanted the film to go.

I explain all this. Dagmar knits her dark brows. "And they made only the one film?"

"The Russians invaded, or something. The technology got suppressed. I think the idea was that people weren't supposed to vote any more, they were just supposed to take their cinema the way the authorities wanted them to."

Dagmar gets out her handheld, calls up an application, and begins scribing letters in the air. Motion sensors in the handheld copy the notes into digital memory.

"There must have been multiple plotlines," she says. "Do you know how they handled that?"

"The last scene was presented first," I say. "The rest of it was flashback. So whatever twists the plot took, they all ended in the same place."

"Interesting..." Her voice becomes a murmur, the words addressed more to herself than to the rest of us. "I wonder if we can do that, start with the end." She's frowning at the screen on her handheld, obviously lost in some kind of internal, writerly calculation.

"So this movie is going to be like that?" I ask. "The audience is going to vote?"

She continues to stare at the screen, and her words come slowly, distractedly.

"Not the audience. The viewer. Each viewer."

"How can that work?" I ask. "There's only one screen in the theater, right? You can't show a separate movie for every customer."

Dagmar holds up a hand. "Just a moment." She scribes another note to herself, then turns to me.

"The picture isn't going to be in theaters," she says. "It's going to be seen through augmented reality."

I feel a wave of disappointment. There have been films presented in AR before, mostly shorts, mostly bad but some all right. But it's still a gimmick.

It's not the *real pictures*. It's not a group of strangers in a large dark room that smells of popcorn, mesmerized by the shimmering images projected on a screen, so caught up in the action that they breathe in unison. AR isn't the cinema. Instead it's something smaller, lesser.

I picture the movie outside on Rodeo Drive, an image of me trying with all the skill I possess to out-dazzle the sex workers, the hucksters, the political slogans, the clumps of tourists.

Ismet speaks for the first time. "I don't think you quite understand," he says. "This is a major picture. It's not an experiment, we really know what we're doing."

Cleve clears his throat. "I don't see the revenue stream here," he says. "If you're not in theaters, you don't have a mechanism for selling tickets."

"The viewers go online and get an account," Ismet says. "The money comes straight to us. It doesn't go through theaters or distributors, so we get a hundred percent."

Cleve seems intrigued by the potential for profit, but he's still skeptical.

"You're going to piss off a lot of important people."

"If we get the viewers," Dagmar says, "that won't matter." She shrugs. "And there probably will be a theatrical release, sooner or later."

"So people are just going to watch this movie in their homes?" Cleve asks.

"No." Dagmar is adamant. "The experience of cinema is special. Movies are something you have to go somewhere to watch. You go to a dedicated place, with friends and loved ones. You don't get that experience with TV or on your computer, and we want to build a community around this experience—so people will have to go to certain places to view it."

"Without theaters," Cleve says, "where will they go?"

"Public places," Dagmar says. "Parks, plazas, community centers. Maybe restaurants or bars, if we can convince the venue they'll make a profit selling food or drink."

I'm maybe a little mollified. Dagmar understands the specialness of cinema, and that wins my sympathy. But that doesn't mean that I think she can re-create the experience in some bar, or in a public square.

I decide not to worry about any of that. I'm the talent. I don't get to pick where the movie is shown.

"I'm still interested in the interactive thing," I say. "How's this going to work?"

"It means," Dagmar says, "more work for *you*. Because you're going to have to film all the various alternate plotlines."

I think about this. "How many alts?" I ask.

"The script isn't final yet—but we think maybe twelve or fifteen actual alternate scenes, all of them fairly short. Each episode will need to have all its big finales in the same place whatever happens, so..."

"*Episodes?*" says Cleve. "So this *is* some kind of TV series?"

"No," Dagmar says. "It's a feature. But we're going to split it into pieces and release it over the course of several weeks."

Cleve just stares at her. "It's a *serial*?"

I sense that he's trying Dagmar's patience.

"We do this all the time," she says, "with alternate reality games."

"Maybe so," Cleve says. "But that's no reason to do it in the movies." He shakes his head. "I'm thinking you've got too many gimmicks all at the same time. Audience voting, augmented reality, releasing the picture as a serial..."

I try to stomp on Cleve's foot, but I miss. I really want to remind him that it's his job to get me paying work, not to crash a meeting uninvited and piss off the producer by criticizing her ideas.

"I'm inventing a new art form," Dagmar says. "And I've got a hundred-sixty-million-dollar promotion budget that says it's going to be a success."

Cleve stares. Dagmar looks at him coldly. "I told you that we're professionals," she says. "Just because you've never seen any of my productions doesn't mean I don't know my way around this town."

"Who's putting up the money?" Cleve asks.

She contemplates Cleve with the same expression she might use to view a booger on the end of her finger.

"None of the usual suspects," she says. "I'll tell you when the time comes."

Cleve's fingers hook around the stem of his wineglass, as if he's thinking about just picking it up and leaving.

He thinks Dagmar is bullshitting him. He's never been connected to a project with that kind of budget in his life, and he's not ready to admit that someone he never heard of can command that kind of muscle.

I must admit that I share his skepticism, to a degree. Three days ago I'd never heard of Dagmar Shaw.

But miracles do happen. And it so happens that I'm badly in need of a miracle.

"What is my part, exactly?" I ask. "Can I see a script?"

She turns back to me. "The script isn't really ready yet," she says.

"It never is, but that doesn't mean I can't read—"

"You play an archetype," Dagmar says.

This intrigues me. I've never been an archetype before, and I consider how it might be challenging.

"Am I the embodiment of evil?" I ask. Because if you look like me, that's something people might see in you.

"The opposite," Dagmar says. "You're sort of an angel." She laughs. "I hope you're not disappointed. I imagine villains are more fun."

I laugh along with her. Angels are not what I expected.

"It could be a challenge," Dagmar says. "Your character is not simply angelic—you're tough, you're fighting for your survival, but you're also in service to—" She pauses for thought. "A higher ideal."

"Interesting," I say. This is more involved than I expected.

When you get right down to it, I would be perfectly happy playing the hero's best friend.

The waitress appears, bringing me a plate of toasted rounds of French bread and a bowl of something that might be aioli. "Want some more tea?" she asks.

"Sure."

The waitress leaves before Cleve can compliment her again, not that he seems in the mood.

"You'll be shooting alternate versions of the story," he is saying. "You can't expect Sean to do that for free."

I'm getting even more pissed off. Cleve is negotiating, and this meeting isn't about negotiation.

"Actors do alternate takes all the time," Dagmar says.

"Not *scripted* ones," Cleve says. "What you're actually making is *several different movies*. You can't expect Sean to get paid for just one."

Dagmar's eyes narrow slightly. "I expect we'll be able to reach an agreement."

"And we'll have to talk scheduling. Because Sean is in demand elsewhere."

Dagmar's narrowed eyes now widen slightly, as if in surprise. I try to control my own expression, because of course my agent is lying his head off. Which is *also* his job.

Dagmar's tone betrays none of the skepticism she must feel. "What am I going to have to work around?" she asks.

"*Celebrity Pitfighter*, for one thing."

This time I can't hold in my amazement. I gape.

"I lost my first fight," I point out. "I'll show up for the reunion show, and that's the end of my commitment."

Cleve turns to me and grins. "Nope." He stabs me in the elbow with a knuckle. "Jimmy failed his blood test. You're back in the rotation."

For a few beats I'm paralyzed by horror, and then I blurt, "They *blood-test*?"

Because, you know, why would they? It isn't like this is a real sport.

Cleve laughs. "They test the winners, yeah!" he says.

I'm staggered. "What was he on?" I ask.

"Ketamine. Which is a horse tranquilizer."

Which would account, no doubt, for the utter indifference Jimmy displayed toward all my attempts to harm him. He was off in Dimension K for the whole fight.

"Jimmy's going to appear on next week's show to show his, uh, *horse remorse*." He jabs my elbow again, and I rub my aching humerus. "He'll tearfully apologize and withdraw from the competition. Then you're going to get the news, and you'll be, like, totally surprised and delighted."

"Oh boy," I say.

"They'll be sending your script in a few days."

So I can rehearse my surprise and delight. Naturally.

"That show got an eight share!" Cleve crows. "The best they've ever done."

Yeah, I think, *that was totally down to me.*

Cleve beams at me as if I've just won an Emmy. I consider grabbing my agent by the ears and head-butting him. Because I'm getting in that ring again when Hell, or maybe the cottage cheese, freezes over.

Cleve is saved from a broken nose by Keisha the waitress, who arrives with our meals. Dagmar's comes in a tajine, one of those conical Moroccan clay pots. Cleve's steak sizzles on a metal plate. Ismet seems pleased with the appearance of his kofte. I get an empty soup bowl. I hope this is not a metaphor for my life.

With a dramatic gesture the waitress pulls away the lid of the tajine, and then she turns to me. "I'll be right back with your soup," she says.

I urge the others to eat and not to wait. "She forgot my malbec," Cleve says.

Keisha returns with a covered tureen. Cleve reminds her about his wine, and she hustles off. I look at the assembly before me, the empty bowl, the tureen, the toasts, and the aioli-like substance. I take the lid off the tureen, and the aroma of garlic and saffron rises up from the orange-colored soup.

Ismet looks at the tureen with surprise. "Is that a Turkish soup?"

"It said on the menu that it's Provençal," I say.

He leans over the tureen and gives a delicate sniff. He seems a little surprised. "We have the same thing in Turkey."

"Good," I say. "Maybe you can tell me how to eat it."

The stuff that I thought was aioli turns out to be garlic pounded with saffron till it's turned creamy. Ismet instructs me to put this on toast, put the toast in the bowl, and then ladle the soup on top. I do this and take a taste. The broth is thick and rich. I taste tomato and fennel and olive oil and the sea.

"Very nice," I say.

"It smells a little smoky," Ismet says. "I'll bet that's Turkish saffron."

Dagmar smiles. "Ismet has a cousin who deals spices."

"He can get you a good deal," Ismet says, quite seriously.

I take another taste. "I wonder how the same soup ended up in Turkey and France both?"

Ismet considers this. "At one point during the Renaissance a Turkish fleet under Barbarossa Hayreddin was based in southern France, because France and Turkey were allied against the German emperor. So my guess is that the Turks provided the bay and the saffron, and the French the fish and the bread."

"Would you like some?" I nudge the tureen in Ismet's direction.

"Yes. Thank you."

He coats his spoon in the thick soup, then takes a tentative taste. A smile of remembrance crosses his face. I try to memorize the look, the eyes half-lidded in pleasure, the close-lipped smile, the reaction to the sound or taste of something familiar from the past, from childhood. I try to burn the look into my memory so that I can use it in front of the camera.

"This is very good," Ismet says. "Much better than the kofte."

"What's wrong with the kofte?" Dagmar asks.

"I... don't know for sure. It's made well. It just isn't right."

Dagmar is amused. She looks at me. "Ismet keeps trying, but he can't get kofte as good as they make at home."

Ismet seems a little embarrassed. "Even ordinary kofte in Turkey is better than- -" He flaps a hand. "Never mind."

"I even got his mother's recipe," Dagmar says. "But it still didn't turn out right."

"The ingredients just aren't the same over here," Ismet says.

So Ismet isn't merely Turkish in ancestry, he was born in Turkey. His American accent misled me.

Ismet makes a tentative gesture with his spoon in the direction of the tureen.

"Help yourself," I say. He takes another spoonful, offers another blissful smile.

"Better watch what you eat," Cleve tells me. "You're going back into training."

"So did you meet Dagmar," I ask, "when you—" *When you were terrorists* is the sentence that comes to mind. "When you worked for Ian Attila Gordon?" I finish.

Dagmar and Ismet give each other an amused look.

"We met just before that," Dagmar says. "I was running a game in Turkey, and Ismet was doing PR for me."

There doesn't seem a graceful way to go from this to bombings and murders and other terrorist activity, so I concentrate on the soup for a while.

After a while, Dagmar puts down her fork and looks at me.

"When can you test?" she says.

I'm about to say that I can test anytime, but Cleve jumps in ahead of me.

"We don't audition," he says. "Sean's body of work speaks for itself."

I find this more than annoying. Here I want to hurl myself to the floor and clutch Dagmar's knees in gratitude, but my agent keeps throwing obstacles in my path.

Dagmar controls her irritation. "I'm not talking audition," she says. "I'm talking *test.* I want to see him in the costumes, I want to see how we can light him. And I want him to meet some of the team and see what they say."

"If the people on the team can say yes or no to Sean's getting the job," Cleve says, "then it's an audition."

"The people on the team can't say yes or no," Dagmar says. She looks at Cleve, and her eyes are hard. "I'm the one who makes those decisions."

"We don't audition," Cleve repeats.

"Call it whatever you want," Dagmar says. "Sean's not my choice for this part anyway, and it's no skin off my nose if he doesn't want to put on a costume and stand in front of a camera."

I can see Cleve mentally flailing around for leverage. The problem is that he has no traction: everyone at this table knows I need the work, and everyone who's seen *Celebrity Pitfighter* knows I have no pride. Cleve's making a bunch of demands and inventing a bunch of conditions demonstrates only his own desperate need to be in control.

I decide to take charge before Cleve gets me canned from the project.

"I'll test," I say. I look at Cleve and shrug. "I don't care. If it makes things easier."

"Right," Dagmar says, very businesslike, and then picks up her fork. "Glad we got that settled."

"My work will speak for itself," I tell Cleve.

I can sense thwarted anger radiating from Cleve like heat from a boiler. There's nothing I can do about that, so I pick up my spoon and help myself to soup.

"I still haven't gotten my malbec," Cleve says. He furiously waves a hand at Keisha and growls in frustration.

Eventually the waitress brings his wine, and he settles down to a sulk for the rest of the meal.

After lunch, Cleve stays behind to try to wangle Keisha's phone number. I hold the door for Dagmar as she steps through. She strides onto the sidewalk, walking in a businesslike way without a hint of the pregnant lady's waddle. I remember a question I'd forgotten to ask.

"You said that I wasn't your choice for this project," I say. "If it wasn't you, who picked me?"

She turns. "The director," she says. "He's worked with you before, and he wanted you."

"Really?" I ask. "Who's that?"

She looks up at me innocently. "Joey da Nova," she says.

She absorbs my utter shock and frowns. "Is there a problem?" she asks.

Other than the fact I killed his wife, I think, *none at all.*

"No problem," I say. "Tell Joey I say hi."

CHAPTER FOUR

HEAVY LUGGAGE BLOG

Every so often someone asks me, "Hey, didn't you have a hit TV series? Didn't it make millions of dollars? How come you don't have any money now?"

It's not like I enjoy telling this story, so I'm only going to go through it this once. If you ask me any questions after this, I'll just refer you back to this post.

What I'm about to give you is a lesson in how to break an unbreakable trust. This is for educational purposes only.

First, a little history. Back in the last century, a boy actor named Jackie Coogan costarred with Charlie Chaplin in *The Kid* and became a star. In fact, he was so successful that he became the youngest self-made millionaire in history.

As happens with a lot of child stars, his popularity didn't survive into adulthood. When he asked his mother and stepfather for the money he'd earned as a child, he found out that they'd spent most of it on high living, and intended to keep the rest. He sued to recover the money, but the judge ruled that all the millions he'd earned as a minor belonged not to him, but to the adults who'd been his legal guardians.

As a result of the scandal surrounding Coogan's suit, the Coogan Law was passed in California, in which fifteen percent of a child actor's earnings are to be placed in a trust until the actor becomes a legal adult.

Personally, I think fifteen percent is a little low. Don't you?

(Coogan, by the way, later went on to originate the role of Uncle Fester in *The Addams Family*, though personally I think his most unforgettable performance is to be found in the equally unforgettable *Mesa of Lost Women* (1953), a movie so completely original that it can rightly claim to be in a genre of its very own.)

I started working in commercials at the age of four, and my loving Mum and Da set up my very own Coogan trust at a local bank. A Coogan trust is "blocked trust," meaning that no withdrawals can be made until the recipient's eighteenth birthday.

Between the ages of four and eighteen I made something like thirty million dollars, between my work on *Family Tree*, commercials and acting gigs, dolls, lunch boxes, and endorsements. The mathematically inclined among you will have noted that when I attained my majority, my Coogan trust should have contained $4,500,000, plus interest

Instead, almost all that money disappeared.

You have to understand the family dynamic at work here. My dad is a thief and a con artist and, now, a fugitive. My mom, on the other hand, is a spiritually evolved individual of a type not uncommon in Southern California, meaning that she's the sort of religious person who would live in Beverly Hills and drive an S-Class Mercedes with a vanity plate reading OMSHIVA.

Remember, first of all, that 85 percent of my income belonged to my parents anyway, minus taxes and dues to the Screen Actors Guild (and boy, did Dad ever complain about the union dues!). The first thing that happened was that Dad became my manager, and skimmed twenty percent off the top. (Agents are legally entitled only to 10 percent, but managers charge whatever the market will bear.)

Maw and Paw saw to it that I became a corporation, Star Child LLC. (I detect my mother's drifty style in the name of the company.) All my disposable income went into my corporation. Mums and Pups were the chief officers, and paid themselves very large salaries out of my earnings. They also bought themselves a large Beverly Hills mansion, a sixty-five-foot motor yacht, and a dazzling array of expensive automobiles. We had servants, my mom had a driver, and we had a cook who specialized in ayurvedic cuisine.

They lived well off my work. But that fifteen percent sitting in a bank in an unbreachable trust—that $4.5 million—clearly nagged at them. From their point of view, they had worked hard to create me and my success. Clearly they were entitled to all the rewards.

I later had to hire a forensic accountant to figure out what happened. Not that it helped, particularly.

First, my dad shopped around for just the right bank in which to stow my earnings. He found a smallish Monterey-based bank with branches in Los Angeles. They'd probably never even heard of Coogan trusts, but that didn't matter. Dad soon enlightened them.

The bank got bought by another bank, which got bought by another. This bank then sold the bank to another bank. Between my fifth and eighteenth birthdays, the bank holding my trust was bought and sold no fewer than seven times.

The result was that the trust officers came in and out as if on a merry-go-round, and soon the only expert on the provisions of the Sean Makin Trust was my dad. The trust officers took his word that certain expenses were necessary—including paying large fees to Mum and Dad for all the hard work they did as trustees.

Withdrawals from trusts are allowed in cases of personal hardship, illness, or the need to provide the principal an education—normally you need a judge's permission for this, but no one at the bank seemed to know this. They were happy to take my dad's word that I was a hardship case who, in addition to a Beverly Hills mansion, needed a Malibu beach house in order to provide a roof over his head. Educational expenses included my dad's trips to Las Vegas, where he dropped a lot of Star Child money on the highly educational roulette tables, and my mother's stays at a health spa in Arizona, where she had her highly educated chakras polished and her aura cleansed, along with her bowels.

I also learned that my father told the bank that I suffered from bone cancer, and had to go to Mexico for secret treatments, because if my illness were known I'd lose my work.

The bank also charged its own fees, which they're not supposed to do. Oops.

The only thing I got from my own trust was my Mini Cooper. I don't know whether that was an educational expense or not.

After *Family Tree* was canceled, my movies flopped, and I began more and more to physically resemble a character from a Tim Burton movie, Ma and Da decided it was time to liquidate. The yacht and most of the cars were sold, along with the Beverly Hills home, which had always been in their name. Mortgages were taken on the beach house.

By that point my mother had become a follower of Babaji Sivadas Kadaitswami, and decided to join him in his ashram and receive instruction at the feet of the master.

The feet of the master, it turns out, are pretty much for sale. Those who choose to leave the world and follow Babaji into the cloister do so on a strict caste system—not caste in the Hindu sense, but caste in the *cash* sense. To live in the same compound as Babaji costs a certain amount. To live in the same house as Babaji costs considerably more. To live in the same house and to become his personal servant costs even more, and nearest to godhead are those who pay for the privilege of sharing at least one meal per day with the swami, assuming of course that he's in town and not off fund-raising in some other district.

My mom bought herself a lifetime of meals for something like $850,000 of my money. Kadaitswami, which means "Master of the Marketplace," turns out to be an appropriate name. He's as larcenous as my father, only more successful at keeping the cash.

When I turned eighteen, Star Child LLC was turned over to me. Mom was already gone to Andhra Pradesh, and I was more traumatized by my parents' separation than my father was. My dad moved to Palm Springs, though he maintained an office in LA, where he pretended to manage my career, and presumably kept his bags packed in case he needed to slip away.

There was a little under two hundred thousand dollars left in my Coogan trust. Star Child was heavily in debt. The Malibu house was mortgaged.

The Mini Cooper, it must be admitted, ran fine.

Now I am aware that there are plenty of eighteen-year-olds who would be happy to start their adult years with a Mini Cooper and a couple hundred grand. I'm not claiming hardship. But I'd also worked hard for fourteen years, and in the end I'd made less than fifteen thousand a year. I could have earned more in a minimum-wage job at McDonald's.

When I asked Dad where my money had gone, he smiled at me. "It just went," he said. When I complained, he laughed. "We had fun, didn't we?"

My friends urged me to take my parents to court. I resisted, but sanity eventually prevailed. I had papers served on my dad's office, but he'd displayed his usual uncanny sense of timing and scarpered ahead of the marshal. There was no way to sue my mother unless she came out of Babaji's compound, and so far as I know she never has.

I had no way of paying the mortgage on the Malibu house, so I was forced to sell, unfortunately at the bottom of the market. I think I ended up making a few thousand bucks.

I sued the bank that had allowed my parents to plunder my estate. The judge ruled that, in view of the fact that the bank had been bought and sold so many times, the legal entity that collaborated in the robbery no longer existed, and the current legal entity was guilty of no wrongdoing. He advised me from the bench to get on with my life.

Another judge—rather grumpily, I thought—refused to hold Star Child LLC responsible for debts contracted before I'd attained my majority. So at least I was no longer in debt, except to the lawyers and the forensic accountant, who took every penny I had left.

I hired some private investigators to track my father, and discovered that some years earlier he'd acquired Belizean citizenship, something that in those days you could get for $25,000 cash. Presumably he's traveling on his Belizean passport, moving from one tax haven to another.

I couldn't afford to keep the investigators on the case. My only consolation is that the way my dad spends money, he won't keep any of it for long.

I even called Babaji to ask him to return the money that my mother had stolen from me. In a sweetly humorous Indian voice, he told me that everything happens for a reason, and that the wise man does not seek enlightenment on the path of materialism.

"In that case," I said, "you'll want to avoid the path of materialism yourself, and send me the money."

Babaji gave a long, merry laugh that went on for some time. And then the Master of the Marketplace hung up on me.

It occurs to me now that Babaji would do very well in the picture business. He has all the right moves.

I survived for a few years on residuals from reruns of *Family Tree*, and scraped enough money together to make a down payment on a third-rate condo apartment in Burbank. I lost the Mini Cooper in a collision with a palm tree. I drive my mother's car now, and probably will till it falls apart, because she still owns it and I can't sell it on my own.

I can't work out entirely what to make of this story. My parents remain a mystery to me.

My impression of Mom and Dad, at least till my eighteenth birthday, was that they were kind, loving parents. My father was controlling, and my mother was a self-absorbed space case, but I have no reason to complain about my upbringing, especially as compared with the chaotic, neurotic, despotic circumstances in which so many of my friends and acquaintances grew up. The work I was doing was hard, but I enjoyed it; I had friends; I was beloved by millions; I had any toy or game that I liked; and my parents threw extravagant parties for me on my birthday and any other day that struck their fancy. I was the center of their world. I never had any doubts that they loved me.

What I have a hard time comprehending is that while I was living my happy life in Beverly Hills, my parents were systematically plundering me. Did they work it out together? I wonder. Did they sit over their coffee in the morning and cold-bloodedly plan exactly how they'd deceive the trust officer and wring another few hundred thousand bucks out of the bank? Was my dad the leader, and my mom his clueless accomplice who never thought to wonder where the money for her yoga vacations was coming from?

I'd like to think so, but the fact that her signature is found on all the incriminating documents argues against this interpretation.

Perhaps they had no more consciousness of their actions than a pair of sharks. Sharks are predators by nature, and not given to self-examination—they consume their prey until they die, and that's that.

My parents saw money and took it. It wasn't doing anything but earning a little interest, it was badly protected, and the possession of it would give them pleasure. Why not?

I wonder if they ever thought of themselves as thieves. The fact that they both planned their exits so carefully suggests that this theory has merit.

The only conclusion I can draw is that I never knew my parents at all. They remain an enigma. I have no more access to their minds than I do to that of the Man in the Moon.

Do they think about the past? Do they wonder where they've been? Do they think about me at all?

Probably not. In Hollywood, you learn it's possible to create a new existence for yourself. You can abandon your old self and become someone new. In Hollywood you can live out your fantasies and the consequences can be nothing more than a few scratched feet of celluloid. People in Hollywood do this every day.

And this is nothing if not a Hollywood story.

Comments (3)

FROM: TooSaint

Whiny rich kid arent you.

FROM: Coldplay

Makin your such a tool.

FROM: Krumble

Cant even beat a junky like Blogjoy hahaha.

FLASHBACK—SEAN'S POV

There are all sorts of things that can kill you: illness, drugs, war, violence. Desperation can kill as well, especially in a place like Hollywood. I'm a case in point.

But the desperation didn't kill me, instead it killed a friend.

Timothea Wilhelm was a staff writer on *Family Tree* during the first season, before she got fired—she really wasn't a sitcom writer at heart. But while she was there, she met the young director Joey da Nova, who early in his career directed twenty or so episodes. Timmi and Joey met on the show and married two months later, and their combination of talents led to enormous success.

Joey provided a brilliant eye for visual composition and a talent for directing kinetic action. His sinuous camera technique made even staid conversations seem like kung fu combat. He worked very well with actors. Timmi had the sense of a film's deep structure, the talent for bright, fresh dialogue, and an ability to create character in just a few brief lines—she wrote all the scripts, whether she got credit or not.

Their combined talent happened to be exactly what was required to produce intelligent blockbusters. *The Third Assassin*, *Hedgehog*, *One Tin Soldier*... the films opened big, stayed in theaters for a long time, and earned the respect of critics.

Timmi was tall and glamorous, with abundant chestnut hair—she seemed a throwback to an earlier kind of style, poised and elegant, that you could see on the cover of a 1940s edition of *Vogue*. Joey was a tough kid from Long Beach, an outspoken Southern California bad boy, often outrageous just for the hell of it. He got headlines with his opinions and public feuds with celebrities, and his delight in sarcasm equaled that of the average eleven-year-old.

Joey and Timmi were forever associated with the words "power couple." They were seen at premieres, Sundance, exclusive parties, Cannes, the Academy Awards ceremony. They jetted from place to place in their Gulfstream. They had a famously rowdy premiere party on a converted minesweeper on the Thames in which Joey was thrown into the drink and had to be rescued by Bill Nighy. Joey and Timmi wore leathers and were photographed on their identical Vincent Black Lightnings, classic motorcycles that in their day had been the most powerful production bikes in the world, and that they snaked down Parmenter Canyon every morning on their way to their offices.

I was on the Hollywood A-list myself in those days, and so I saw them often at parties and premieres. My dad was always trying to get Joey to direct me in a big movie, and though the film never materialized, it meant that I stayed in touch.

Despite their formidable reputations, I found them approachable. Maybe they had a weak spot for children. In any case, I was invited to many of their parties, and often I was the only kid there.

Timmi was sweet to me. Even while playing hostess to fifty important people on the A-list, she would take me aside for a cookie and a talk about my work. She hadn't worked in television in years, but for my sake she still pretended to be interested in the world of *Family Tree*. When I was eleven or twelve, I was madly in love with her.

After my career crashed, Timmi and Joey proved to be the two A-listers who still returned my phone calls. I played minor roles in a couple of their films, and earned enough that I didn't have to get a low-paying job in some service industry.

Then I paid Timmi back for all her kindness by killing her.

This was a result of my brilliant plan to garner publicity by becoming a fake alcoholic. The idea was to attend one of Joey and Timmi's parties, be seen to be drinking heavily, and then on my way down the canyon run my Mini into a guardrail. I'd chug some overproof rum to boost my blood-alcohol levels, then sit back and wait for headlines and fame.

This plan wasn't as insane as it sounds. Because the whole point wasn't whether or not I got labeled as an alcoholic, it was whether or not I got headlines.

Because there would be headlines when I got arrested, and more headlines when I pleaded guilty, and more headlines when I went into rehab, and even more headlines when I left rehab and announced I was clean and sober and ready for work.

There had been a long spell with no work, and I was desperate.

I needed to get my name in front of the public again—jog some memories, hit them with some memorable drama, some soap opera. Call attention to the fact that I still existed, and point out that if only I could get a job, the deadly despair that had caused my drinking would abate, and I'd be the happy little boy from *Family Tree* again, the boy who had warmed their hearts and tickled their funny bones. Hundred-dollar bills and beautiful women would then fall like manna from the sky and attach themselves to me, as they had in the past.

The plan had worked for others. It really had. Why wouldn't it work for me?

The night Timmi died started as a typical party at the Parmenter Canyon home. Jean-Marc and Jaydee and Allison and a lot of Joey's regulars were there. The writer/director Sandy McGinnis was present, having just shed her second husband and acquired arm candy in the form of a pool boy from Sonora. Nataliya Hogan was in the house, sixteen years old, with a brand-new driver's license and a brand-new Boxster Spyder. The party should have been typical, but somehow it wasn't. There was a strange vibe in the air, something I couldn't quite identify. I wasn't the only person there drinking heavily—Timmi got completely skunked, and then had a loud argument with Mac MacCartney, the director who later made *Mister Baby Head*. It was unclear to me what the argument was actually about. It was Timmi who stormed out of her own party in her own house, taking her Black Lightning down the canyon road toward who knew where. Joey, who was hammered himself, was bewildered, and couldn't figure out why his wife had gone. Mac mooched around for half an hour, drank half a bottle of wine, and then left.

At any rate, the party had stopped being fun, and I had plans to make myself famous again. I had one last drink and then got in the Mini.

I didn't need the overproof rum—by the time I left the party I was far too drunk to drive safely even if I'd wanted to. I zoomed down the canyon until I found what to my sozzled mind seemed an ideal place for the crash, a sharp left turn with a guardrail to keep drunken drivers like me from going over the cliff. I could scrape the side of my car against the guardrail and end up perfectly safe.

As for the car, it was insured.

I stopped the car, backed, and aimed the Mini at my target. I put the car in first gear and punched the accelerator, and I had shifted into second and got up to thirty or forty miles per hour when suddenly I was blinded by the single headlight of Timmi's Black Lightning.

I never actually hit her. I sawed the wheel back and forth trying to evade the bike that was rushing at me, and she was likewise trying to avoid me and lost control. She missed the Mini by a hair, missed the guardrail as well, and went right off the cliff.

The whole accident took maybe three seconds. I found myself in my stopped car in the middle of the curve. My heart thrashed in my chest, louder than the fading echo of the Black Lightning's engine. I seemed to be entirely alone.

I didn't know where the bike had come from or where it had gone. I didn't know it was Timmi on board. I only knew that I was in horrible, horrible trouble, and that I had to get away as fast as I could.

Panic had me by the throat. I put the car in gear, and though every nerve was screaming at me to run down the canyon road at top speed, I left the scene at a very sedate pace. Farther down the canyon I chucked the bottle of rum out the window. When I got home I checked the car for damage, anyway as far as I could do in the dark, and then I went to my condo and took a shower and brushed my teeth and went to bed.

By the time I fell asleep I'd convinced myself that nothing had actually happened.

I didn't know it was Timmi till late the next afternoon, when I got a call from Jaydee telling me she'd died after a crash. I put down the phone and stared at the wall for a long time, my heart lurching with terror. It wasn't until later that I heard that Timmi had lived for several hours after the crash, and that if I'd called for an ambulance right then, at the scene of the accident, she might have lived.

I was still panicked, too frightened to feel any guilt. I expected to be arrested at any second. I jotted down the name and phone number of a criminal attorney and put it in my pocket. I kept checking the windows to see if police, or paparazzi, or reporters were lurking. I couldn't bring myself to call Joey, though he called me late one night. He was a wreck, slurring words through pills or booze or both. He alternated weeping with furious threats against whoever was responsible. I don't know what I said—probably the usual pointless things you say to someone whose grief is fresh. Every threat Joey made felt like a knife to my throat.

I don't know how they knew there was another vehicle involved. I don't know how, if they knew there was someone else, they didn't know it was me. I've never tried to clear this up. If I start asking questions, it just might point the finger at me.

I didn't leave my condo till the funeral. I made a point of driving the Mini, just in case anyone wondered whether the car had been damaged in an accident. The memorial was a media circus, with Joey a sobbing wreck who pulled himself together just long enough to punch a cameraman.

After a while the fear faded, and gradually I began to realize that I'd lost a friend. I began to mourn—a little late, maybe, but the mourning was genuine.

Turning myself in was never something I considered. I couldn't imagine whom it would benefit. If it would have brought Timmi back, I'd probably have walked into the police station and confessed; but as things were, I didn't see that my being in jail would do the world any good.

Instead I resolved that I'd try to be worthy of Timmi's memory. I'd work hard and make brilliant films and make a success of myself.

But first, I had to regain the fame I'd had when I was younger.

So, a couple of months later than intended, I smashed up the Mini and got myself arrested.

The headlines appeared, then faded. The world still awaits my brilliant films. Fame has not returned. My resolution to somehow justify Timmi's death went nowhere, along with my career, along with Joey's success. All that's left is a desperation so substantial that I can almost reach out and touch it.

I was there once. I had it. It went away, and I need it again the way a junkie needs his heroin.

And when the success doesn't return, the need only grows. I can understand why Dickie went in for porn, and why Jack Wild stayed drunk for a couple decades, why Rusty Hamer put the .357 to his head, and even why stupid Melody Chastain kicked the stupid dog.

After Timmi's death Joey kept making movies, but without his wife the magic had gone. She understood story and structure, she could chart the arcs of the characters. Without her gift the story fell apart. Joey would come up with some idea for a brilliant visual sequence, and he'd jettison part of the structure to insert it, or he wouldn't realize that it would contradict an earlier part of the movie. Exposition was almost nonexistent, and character moments were dull and clumsy. His visual talent foundered in formlessness. Individually brilliant scenes were thrown almost randomly at the audience, without even a semblance of plot or consistency, like pearls falling from a broken string.

But that's just the average summer blockbuster, I hear you say. No, Joey's pictures were far worse than that. I had minor roles in a couple of them, and I saw the frantic way he worked, making decisions impulsively, tossing out lines that we'd rehearsed to replace them with chaotic improvisation. Even Allison, with all her skill, hadn't been able to edit the mess together into anything coherent.

They were scorned by even the most undiscriminating audiences. Joey's movies lost his backers hundreds of millions of dollars. And he kept up his old habit of making enemies and feuding with anyone who pissed him off—except that before, success had made him immune. No one wanted to kill the king who was bringing in so many millions. But now Joey was vulnerable, and his enemies lined up to do him in. I'd seen his picture on the cover of a tabloid under the single word POISON?

He hasn't worked in over a year. No one will finance his films, and though he's worth a lot of money he isn't yet crazy enough, or desperate enough, to finance them himself.

And now, if I'm lucky, Joey will be directing me in Dagmar Shaw's movie.

I'm elated. Though if I had any sense I'd be hiding under the bed, sucking my thumb and staring out into the darkness, trembling at the knowledge that the monsters were just about to come crawling out of the closet.

TRACKING SHOTS

That evening, Dickie Marks leads the entertainment news. At his press conference, he tearfully confesses his unrequited love for Samantha Hollock.

The confession goes much better than I would have imagined, and it's all down to Dickie's talent. Instead of a pathetic has-been desperate for attention, he succeeds in appearing as a romantic loser. Still pathetic, but a higher class of pathetic.

Samantha Hollock, reached by phone, expresses surprise, and says she's flattered.

The jokes on the late-night talk shows will practically write themselves. It's about all Dickie could hope for.

He calls the next day to thank me. I wish him good luck. He'll need it, now that he's an unperson dancing in a bear suit in the darkest circle of Celebrity Hell.

A few days later, I report to the studio where they film the parts of *Celebrity Pitfighter* that don't involve hitting other people—instead, they run various competitions between the contestants to see who can throw the most kicks in a ten-minute period, or who can hit a target the hardest, or who can chop the most targets with a samurai sword. Winners get money for their charities. I'm not particularly good at any of these, but neither are most of the other contestants, and a couple weeks ago I was surprised to win a sit-up contest.

They put me in an office with a closed-circuit television. A couple of cameramen film me as I watch Jimmy Blogjoy being confronted with the evidence of his ketamine abuse. He breaks down and confesses, then makes his reluctant withdrawal from the competition.

It's all scripted. I've even seen the script, because my lines are in there, too. I get to shake my head and say, "Poor guy" and "I hope he straightens himself out."

What I really want to do is beat him with a crowbar till I hear his bones snap.

After Jimmy's exit, I'm brought into the Thirty-Sixth Chamber, which is where the show's judges sit on thrones and make pompous judgments about the contestants. I think of it as the Humiliation Salon. The set is half Chinese restaurant, half Deco Palace of Ming the Merciless. The judges are a sports announcer who got fired from ESPN2, a supermodel spokeswoman for the show's principal sponsor, a couple actors who have made some undistinguished martial arts films, and a Bagua master from Taiwan given to making opaque remarks about chi in a thick accent.

The judges don't really matter. If you look at the closing credits of the show, you'll find the fine print that says that all judges' decisions are made with the consultation of the network. Everything they say is more or less scripted.

If the network *tells* you it's cheating, is it actually cheating? Apparently not.

Bagua Guy looks at me.

"Your last fight showed that you have a warrior heart," he says. "Your opponent has proved unworthy, and now we offer you the opportunity to advance in the competition."

His accent is so broad that I only understand him because I've read the script in advance.

"I am honored by the judges' confidence," I say. "I desire nothing so much as to get back in the ring and justify Master Pak's faith in me."

The words taste like sawdust in my mouth. I don't want to be here. I don't want to be in any more fights.

Unfortunately, a review of my contract showed me that I have no choice.

The most annoying thing is that after my line, the director calls for another take. He feels I wasn't sincere enough the first time.

It takes two more takes before I manage to counterfeit the correct amount of thickheadedness. Bagua Guy, who wants to go outside and smoke, gets more and more fidgety.

Later, when I'm sitting on my balcony drinking a beer and waiting for the coals to burn down on my hibachi so I can grill a chicken breast for dinner, I get a call from my agent to make sure I actually went through with it.

"Good," Cleve tells me. "You're getting good exposure on this show."

I curl my lip. "It's a piece of shit," I say.

"Don't count on that Dagmar cooze to boost your career," Cleve says. "That hundred-sixty-million promotion budget is bullshit—I know everyone in that league, and she's not dealing with any of them."

"Oh yeah? You called them all up and asked?" Like any of them would talk to him.

"I wouldn't buy anything until her check clears," Cleve says.

"That's true of everyone in this town." *Including you, old sport.* "Don't forget, Joey da Nova's directing. He's major."

"Joey can't get a picture made since *The Permeable* flopped." He snorts. "You knew from the *title* that one was going to go into the toilet. What the hell does *The Permeable* mean, anyway?"

I'm not about to defend *The Permeable*, which reeked like a week-old fish, or perhaps a hundred-fifty-million-dollar action film with no script, an ingenue whose line readings were so bad that she had to be dubbed by a veteran voice actor, and a male lead fresh out of rehab with a post-heroin facial twitch so severe that he needed a face double for all his close-ups.

A *face double.* The mind simply boggles.

"When this project craters," Cleve says, "don't say I didn't warn you."

"You didn't warn me about *Celebrity Pitfighter.*"

His exasperation is plain over the phone. "Millions of people enjoy that show. It puts your face in front of the public. People see you, you'll get work."

I gulp the last of the beer and contemplate the empty bottle in my hand. "A bunch of untrained fighters hacking each other under the influence of ketamine," I say, "someone's going to get killed. And I don't want that person to be me."

Plus, I think, *the damn thing will go on for months.* Normally a reality show is filmed very quickly: you pack all the contestants in one hotel, you shuffle them off to a new contest every day, and you keep them sleep-deprived until they get unstable, overemotional, and borderline homicidal. *That's* good television.

Unfortunately for the producers, the athletic commission for the State of California wouldn't let amateur fighters bash each other nonstop every day for a week or ten days or whatever, and insisted that we have a rest period of a minimum of two weeks between each bout. So—assuming that Dagmar hires me—I'll have to schedule training and fights along with shooting the movie.

"It's a piece of shit," I tell Cleve again.

After the conversation is over, I realize that I've surprised myself. *There's something I won't do to get on television.* I hadn't quite realized that before.

There are some brands of cottage cheese, I think, *that I will not eat.*

Cleve hangs up and I stand up to get another beer. I stretch and lean out over the iron rail. Charcoal scent drifts through the air. A middle-aged couple jog past in white eyeshades and Old Navy shorts. A kid on a skateboard sails past in the other direction, head bobbing to music from his earbuds.

I don't pay any attention to the SUV until it starts, and then the engine rumble sounds familiar. I look in growing surprise at the black Ford Expedition parked across the street from me, at the dark silhouette of the driver behind the shaded window.

Tires give a little shriek as the SUV pulls away, accelerating rapidly. The kid on the skateboard looks over his shoulder at the big Ford coming after him, and smoothly moves his board from the road to the sidewalk. The SUV speeds past, brake lights flash, and then the Ford turns left and vanishes from my sight.

I wonder if that was the guy who tried to run me over on Rodeo Drive the other day.

Except that I don't have any enemies that I know of. Through the beer swilling around in my head, I try to think of people who might hate me.

Jimmy Blogjoy? I have his place on *Celebrity Pitfighter*, and he's been caught doing drugs on national television. Maybe he blames me for all that.

And he *did* wear a mouthpiece that said KILL YOU in big easy-to-read letters.

And then I think, well, Joey da Nova, because I killed his wife. But he doesn't know that, and no one else does, either—and if anyone *does* know about it, why wait all these years to come after me?

It can't be Joey, I think, *because Joey isn't trying to kill me, he is trying to give me the lead in his new movie.*

For a half-second I think about digging my pistol out of the back of my T-shirt drawer. But then I decide against it. Who exactly am I supposed to shoot?

I decide to keep a lookout for black SUVs. And to be careful when crossing the street.

INT. WARDROBE—DAY

"I haven't seen you since Mac's funeral," Jaydee says as she hugs me.

"Has it been that long?"

She releases me and looks at me with motherly blue eyes. Her hair is a shade of blond that does not occur in nature. Her breath is scented with the sweet vermouth she drank with, or possibly for, lunch. Her voice is as loud and brassy as her hair color. I love her to death.

I've known Jaydee Martin most of my life. She was costume supervisor on *Family Tree*, and we've kept in touch since the series was canceled.

"I hear I'm supposed to be an archetype," I say. "How does an archetype dress?"

"Ordinary clothes, mostly. But there's an early scene where you dress sort of like Dr. Zaius from *Planet of the Apes*."

Except for the chimpanzee face, I hope.

She reaches to a shelf by her desk for a loose-leaf notebook and flips through it, then turns the illustration to face me. I see a computer-generated image of a man in a long, fawn-colored knee-length jacket with wide sleeves and heavily embroidered cuffs and lapels. He also wears a collarless shirt, baggy Cossack trousers, and boots.

The features of the man are lightly sketched in and don't resemble mine. The character's name, Roheen, is written above the figure in pencil.

Jaydee touches the figure and moves him across the display paper. With little sweeps of her fingers and thumb she calls for him to walk, run, wave his arms, jump up and down. She rotates the figure so we see him from the front, the side, the rear, and above.

Jaydee removes her finger from the display, and the figure stands still, frozen in mid-step.

We are in the costume department that will be Jaydee's domain for the entirety of the shoot. Near the front door is her office. Nearby are worktables, sewing machines, tailors' dummies, and yards of fabric neatly labeled and stacked on shelves. Ironing boards are folded and hung on the wall. Filling the rest of the large room are portable racks, most of them holding nothing more than empty hangers waiting for completed costumes.

Jaydee looks down at the frozen figure of Roheen. "I wish you were wearing stuff like this all through the picture," she says. "When you're wearing contemporary, everyone has a damn opinion."

I point at the figure on the display paper. "Roheen is some kind of Afghan name or something," I say. "I looked it up. Is that an Afghan costume?"

"No. They told me to give them something otherworldly and serene."

"Otherworldly and serene," I repeat. I think about that for a moment. "Dagmar said I was a kind of an angel."

She shrugs. "Can't help you," she says.

I give her a look.

"Do you know what the picture's about?" I ask.

Her blue eyes twinkle. "They didn't tell you?"

"No."

She cackles. "They didn't tell me, either. Even the script is a damn state secret."

"So far," I say, "the secrecy is working."

Because there are places I can usually find copies of scripts, often well before the movie is released, or even shot. Scripts leak out of everywhere, and I've been hoping to find this one, but I've had no luck. The fact that I don't have a title hasn't helped. But nothing by Dagmar Shaw has got onto the market—though it has occurred to me that Dagmar might not be the actual screenwriter.

"But you're auditioning, right?" Jaydee says. "Didn't they give you a script?"

"They gave me three scenes. They're good scenes, but there's no context."

Which I really hate. Because when I say a line, I want not only to know the line, but to know why my character would say it and what he means to achieve by saying it. And without a context to hang my characterization from, I'm going to have to take a stab in the dark.

Angel. Otherworldly. Serene. That's something, at least.

"Do you have the jacket?" I ask.

"Yeah, but it's just basted together. It needs a final fitting."

"Can I see it?"

Actual leather is very hard to light, so the jacket is made of a material that will look like leather on camera. I try it on, feel the weight of it, try to find the character that lives in it. I make an attempt to move in an otherworldly, serene way. Jaydee watches with amusement.

"I can't tell if you're supposed to be an angel or a drag queen," she says.

"Oh shut up." I look at her. "Can I take this?"

"Sure."

"I mean," I say, "it's supposed to be a test. They're supposed to see how I look in the costumes, so maybe I should actually take the one piece of costume that belongs to my character." I clench my teeth. "Even though it's really an audition, so I could fuck this up with or without the prop."

"I *said* you could take the jacket," she says.

I realize that my anxieties are leading me into behavior and dialogue worthy of ridicule, so I thank her and close my mouth.

I operate, I have realized, on hope. I'm always focused on the future, and right now Dagmar and her project *are* my future. It's not just a part, it's the *only* part I have to look forward to. If this feature doesn't happen, all I'll have in my life is sitting in my apartment smoking bud, watching old movies, staring at the old-time popcorn ceiling, and looking back on my glory days on *Celebrity Pitfighter*.

Jaydee reaches into a pocket for a pack of chewing gum and offers me a stick. I shake my head, and she pops one into her mouth. She's recently given up smoking, and this is her substitute.

"You'll be fine," she says.

I sigh. "This whole setup is so strange."

Jaydee gives a little twist of her lips. "They're not film people, that's how I read it," she says. "They don't have any experience in this, they're making it up as they go along."

"Maybe." I look at some of the costumes on the rack, and I see the tags attached to each piece. Surprise floods into me.

"Nataliya's on this picture?" I ask.

Jaydee pops her gum. " 'Fraid so," she says.

Nataliya Hogan was born Natalie, but now pronounces her name nattle-EE-ya, because it's that much more pretentious. She started out as a teen pop star with a TV sitcom in which she played a teen pop star who had a secret identity as a spy, and now she is an actress whose list of credits, appropriately enough, mainly read "Self."

I've noticed she only dates men who are more famous than she is, so she can benefit from the association. Due to her own growing celebrity, the pool of acceptable candidates is growing smaller and smaller.

In a town full of egomaniacs and narcissists, Nataliya is without peer. Nothing can happen anywhere in the world—in the universe—that doesn't have her at its center.

If you tell her there was just an earthquake in, say, Mexico, she'll explain how she has millions of devoted fans in Mexico and that she had a wonderful weekend in Cabo. If you mention that the president is trying to broker peace in the Middle East, she'll tell you that her TV show was a huge hit in Egypt. If she is told about a grisly bombing in Peshawar perpetrated by jihadi fanatics, she'll mention that she once had a manicurist from Pakistan who told her that her hands were beautiful.

"What's Nataliya doing here?" I say in astonishment.

Jaydee laughs. "What do you think?"

"Joey hates her," I say. "He's told me so. Why'd he cast her?"

"Maybe he wasn't the one who hired her."

"Oh... crap." I'm hoping I don't have any scenes with her.

From Wardrobe I go to Makeup, where I piss off the makeup artist by giving him too much advice.

The fact is that I don't need makeup to play a Klingon. The unusual proportions of my face and head cause certain technical problems, and the solutions aren't always obvious. Though my face looks simply wrong, my eyes are large but otherwise normal. They're the features that look most human and I always want to emphasize them. I've found that dabs of yellow eyeliner smoothed up under my brow help to light up my eyes and keep my big Frankenstein forehead from overshadowing my face. It also helps if my giant forehead is contoured with a darker shade of makeup in order to de-emphasize it, and if my stick-out ears are darkened, they don't look so obvious.

The makeup artist might have worked this out on his own, but I'm nervous about the test and I'm not thinking about his sensitivities when I tell him what I want, so he spends most of the session glowering at close range and otherwise not speaking to me.

Not being spoken to by a makeup artist has never been a huge concern of mine. It lets me concentrate on mentally running my lines and thinking about how I am going to deliver them.

There's a knock on the door toward the end, someone's assistant coming to tell me that they are ready for my test.

INT. SOUNDSTAGE—DAY

The assistant waits for me outside the trailer, and escorts me to the soundstage—not that I need escorting, because the stage is the biggest thing on the lot. I wish the assistant weren't around, because I'm thinking about Roheen and how I'm going to play his scenes. The assistant takes me through a door, and I pause for a moment to let my eyes adjust to the dimness of the vast, barnlike building. The place smells musty.

Only one corner of the soundstage is lit, and that's clearly where the test will take place. Cameras gloom on the edges of the spill of light; people sit on folding chairs or stand around; there's a kind of portable tent where the director, remote as a little god, will sit and watch the action on a video screen.

I recognize someone and increase my pace; she hears me coming, turns, and comes to meet me.

"Tessa," I say.

"Sean."

We take hands and give each other Hollywood air-kisses. It's not that we're insincere, it's that she doesn't want to smear my makeup.

Tessa Brettel is a tall, broad woman in her mid-twenties, probably over two hundred and fifty pounds. Her skin is chocolate, and her cornrows are braided in an elaborate geometric pattern. She wears a simple pale linen shift and gladiator sandals.

Twelve years ago she was part of the cast of the family comedy *Life on Top*, where she was the foil to Kendra Toamasina, who played her irreverent younger sister. Tessa was the serious, dutiful sibling, and was the principal target of Kendra's jokes. Somehow Tessa survived years of slurs on her intelligence, her weight, her looks, her fashion sense, and most of all the size of her booty. Making fun of the fat girl was high sport for all America, and *Life on Top* lasted four seasons, until Kendra Toamasina drowned in a swimming pool following an afternoon of binge drinking. Kendra was mourned by millions, and Tessa forgotten.

"What are you doing here?" I ask Tessa. "Are you testing?"

"I'm the second unit director," she says.

"Wow," I say. "Great!"

I mean it, too. For years her career was as dead as Kendra.

"This project is taking me to Namibia in a couple weeks," Tessa says. "We'll see how much fun that is."

"You shooting the desert?" The fact that there's a desert in Namibia is about all I know about the place, and that's only because I once saw a National Geographic documentary.

"Parts of Namibia are doubling for parts of South Africa."

"Right. Okay."

That's normal. Under most conditions Southern California doubles for everyplace.

Tessa grins at me. "After that I go to Swaziland. Which is doubling for Swaziland."

I don't know where Swaziland is, but it sounds African to me. I say something neutral. "That should be fun."

"You should get into directing," she says. "You'd be good at it."

"Well," I tell Tessa, "let's get the test over with first, and *then* I'll take your job."

I turn from Tessa to the little blond woman who's just appeared at her elbow. She holds out a hand.

"Hello, Mr. Makin. I'm Carter-Ann Dixon."

Her voice has a kind of reedy high-pitched Munchkin quality to it, and she speaks with a strong Southern accent. She comes up to about my elbow, and is dressed in a skirt and heels and a white blouse with a fluffy jabot. She wears a few pieces of tasteful gold jewelry. Her smile is a brilliant white, and there is a little mole on the left side of her chin.

"Hi," I say, and shake her hand. Her palm is dry.

"We are all *so* looking forward to your test," she says sweetly. She speaks with a certain amount of slow deliberation, enunciating every syllable as if she's concerned that I might not completely understand her.

"Um," I say, "thanks."

I look at Tessa, and she's looking at the new arrival with a kind of dry, distant amazement, as if Carter-Ann were an alien who has just materialized in the room.

"Are you part of the crew?" I ask Carter-Ann. Because, though she seems completely out of place here, she might just be a script supervisor or something.

"No, not really." She blinks blue eyes up at me. "I'm a consultant."

This tells me nothing. "What kind of consultant?" I ask.

She waves a hand and makes a pishing noise with her lips. "That's all complicated. Let's get on with your test."

She takes my arm and starts walking with me toward the set. I look over her head at Tessa, who seems about as bemused as I am.

"Dagmar sends her apologies," Carter-Ann says. "She wanted to be here, but she had an important meeting she couldn't miss."

"Is Joey da Nova here?" I ask.

"He couldn't make it, either. Miss Brettel will be directing the test." I look over her head again at Tessa, who smiles at me.

Carter-Ann walks me onto the set, such as it is. A metal grid has been lowered from the high ceiling to about twelve feet from the floor. To the grid are attached a bare minimum of three lights. There's no actual set, just a neutral-colored curtain behind me. The only props are a chair and a small table.

Carter-Ann releases my arm and walks off.

"I'll just watch from over here," she says.

"Okay," I say, for lack of anything better. I stand on the bare set and look around, then turn to Tessa. "I see you've left no impediments to the exercise of my imagination."

Tessa smiles. "Wait a second," she says, "till we get up to speed here." She's bossing a very reduced crew for this shoot, but there are still about a dozen people. The various specialists on the set take their places. Tessa gives quiet instructions. She is suddenly very businesslike, very much the professional.

I check the lights overhead. The key light is to my right, a 1K because the area being lit is small and no more wattage is necessary. The fill light is to my left and is another 1K inside a Chinese ball, a paper lantern to diffuse the intensity of the light. The backlight is a 650W tweenie behind a scrim, to keep the curtain behind me from blazing up and overwhelming the picture. The three-light system is basic in the industry and the gaffers can set it while staggering with drink, blind with hangover, or watching a football game on their cell phones.

I look at the lights again. The Watcher, examining the curiosities of Earth. "Tessa?" I ask.

She finishes talking to the camera operator and turns to me. "Yes?"

"The key or the fill needs to be lower," I tell her. "Otherwise you're going to get nothing but forehead."

Over the years I've got really tired of telling people this. My damned forehead is the cross I carry onto every movie set. Tessa studies me, sees my eyes in deep shadow, the tip of my little nose winking out of the darkness like a silver button sewn to the middle of my face, and she nods.

"Yeah, okay." She turns to someone. "Markie? Can you lower the fill?"

Markie is the grip, apparently. Standing in the bright light I can't see him very well off in the dark, but he has a high-pitched voice with a south Boston accent.

"Where's Arthur at?" he asks.

"I think he went to the toilet," someone says.

"Donna," Markie says, "you got the walkie-talkie?"

He gets the walkie-talkie from Donna and calls Arthur in the toilet.

"Arthur," he says, "can I move your goddamn fill light?"

Arthur's indignant voice crackles from the walkie-talkie. "I'm taking a fucking dump here," he says.

Markie gives the walkie-talkie back to Donna. "Arthur says it's okay," he says.

This conversation is necessary because everyone in the room belongs to a union and it is necessary to maintain a proper division of labor. Markie is a grip, and Arthur is a gaffer, and while a grip can tell a gaffer where to put a light, he can't actually touch it himself.

While great union leaders of the past rotate nobly in their graves, Markie turns off the fill light, gets a ladder, takes the Chinese ball off the overhead rack, and fixes it to a standing pipe with an alligator clip.

The crew goes back to whatever it was doing, ignoring me. When Arthur comes back from the john, he doesn't comment.

I mention this episode only to show why film and television actors have to be really good at what they do. A film set buzzes with distractions. The grips are fussing with the tracks on which the cameras move, or they're trying to get a read on the passive fill so they know how to shape the beam that's coming off the fill light. The electricians move the lights around, or are on ladders setting the barn doors that channel the light. The sound technicians are swinging the booms or trying to get readings on the voices and background noise. The director of photography is moving props and furniture around to add to the artistic composition of every shot. The props master is also running in to add to or subtract from the props visible in the frame, and the script supervisor is trying to keep track of all the changes for the continuity. The script supervisor or the director or the writer-on-set produces new last-second lines for the actor to learn. People are sticking light meters in the actors' faces to get a sense of the light coming off them, or running up with tapes to measure the distance from the camera to the actor. The guy with the clapper runs up before every shot and tries to snip off the actor's nose with his little guillotine blade. And on a big production, everyone's got numerous assistants who perform even more of these little tasks, and more often, and with more noise.

Which is why, when the set is finally quiet and the cameras are running, and the director calls for action, the actors have to be right in the zone. They have to ignore all the chaos that has just been going on around them and become their characters. They have to know where the camera is, and where their marks are, and they have to interact with the other actors and with the camera. They have to remember their lines, and—even if the lines are cliché, which they often are—speak them with sincerity, as if this were the first time those lines have ever been spoken or thought of in the whole history of the world.

Once everybody's in place and Tessa calls for quiet, she eases me into the test by just having me stand and walk and sit in various attitudes, just to see how the camera likes me—or not—and how I move in the Dr. Zaius jacket. I try to project angelic sincerity as I stand and walk about. I think about Michael Clarke Duncan in *The Green Mile*. I think about Morgan Freeman in, well, anything. I think of insipid pictures of Jesus and try to be that character, only with a little more edge.

A voice breaks in. "Mr. Makin?"

I blink and look around. Carter-Ann Dixon has risen from her chair and taken a step toward the light.

"Yes?" I say.

"Can you take a step forward with your left foot? And turn your palms a little toward the camera?"

I look at Tessa, who is the director and in charge of the set, and who by all rights ought to be beheading Carter-Ann at this point. Tessa gives me a deadpan look, then nods.

I do as Carter-Ann suggests. She looks at me critically. "Could you turn your left instep out just a bit, Mr. Makin?" she asks.

I do this.

"That's lovely!" Carter-Ann says. Her voice throughout remains distinct and deliberate, each word enunciated perfectly. "Could you say a line for me, please?"

I'm so surprised that I can't think of any of my actual lines, so I just say, "Tallulah Tallulah Tallulah."

Carter-Ann quirks her mouth in a way that says, *I'm going to condescend to you and pretend to be amused, but you'd better not try that again.*

"A *real* line, Mr. Makin," she says.

All right, I think. *I don't know who the hell you are, but I'm going to knock your eyes right out of your head.*

"Teach not thy lips such scorn," I say, "for they were made for kissing, lady, not for such contempt."

It's *Richard III*, Act I, Scene II, where Richard seduces Lady Anne, whose husband he has just killed on the battlefield. I happen to know a lot of Richard's speeches because last year I was trying to get a production off the ground, with myself in the title role. You might think this an odd ambition, a former sitcom star playing the lead in classic Shakespeare drama...but when I thought about it all through the lens of my perfect desperation, I figured Richard was deformed, and I am strange-looking, so it seemed a perfect fit. In the end no one but me thought I was right for the part.

I give Carter-Ann the speech at close range, as intense as I can make it, my large eyes staring into hers. I stay more or less in the posture that Carter-Ann set me in, though I allow myself to turn my shoulders toward her and make small gestures with my arms.

The odd thing is that it's a speech of seduction—Richard is supposed to get on his knees and offer to let Lady Anne run him through with a sword—but I don't play it that way. I tower over Carter-Ann, so I loom over her and *command* her to love me, kill me, love me. Carter-Ann looks up at me with a half-frown, as if she's trying to puzzle me out.

"Take up the sword again," I finish, "or take up me."

There is a moment's silence. Then Carter-Ann offers a sunny smile.

"Thank you, Mr. Makin," she says. "That was very nice."

Nice. My ferocious Richard of Gloster glare freezes to my face. Carter-Ann turns to go back to her seat.

If she says your behavior is heinous, I think, after Cole Porter, *kick her right in the Coriolanus*.

I restrain my foot and look at Tessa.

"Cut," she says. Then, to me, "Let's move on, shall we?"

"Sure." I break out of the stance that Carter-Ann put me into and move around the little set. My nerve endings are still tingling with the aftereffects of the confrontation.

"Shall we do the first scene?" Tessa asks.

"Fine," I say. "Which is the first scene?"

There is some laughter from out of the darkness.

"The exposition scene," Tessa says. "Roheen and Amir."

"Okay," I say. I think about the scene for a moment. "Can I ask a question?"

"Sure."

"What is this scene actually about? And who is Amir exactly?"

There is more laughter. Tessa comes onto the set so she can speak to me more easily.

"You know as much as I do," she says. "The script is a secret."

"So you have no context for this?" I ask. "You don't know what happened in the previous scene, what leads into this?"

"I don't know anything," Tessa says.

"Why am I saying these lines?" I ask.

There's silence.

"Just act the hell out of the scene," Tessa says finally. "Screw the context."

Carter-Ann's double-reed voice comes out of her corner.

"Roheen's just survived an attack," she says. "Amir is a young boy who's helped him out."

Of *course*, I thought, Carter-Ann is the only person here who knows what's going on. Because otherwise this would not be Hell.

I walk to the edge of the set and look for Carter-Ann.

"And these 'Tellurian Gates' that I'm talking about?"

There is a half-second's hesitation, just enough to convince me that whatever Carter-Ann says next is not going to be true.

"I'm afraid I can't help you," she says.

I reply to her half-second's hesitation with one of my own, just to let her know that she's been busted. "Thanks," I say.

I take a little tour of the set, the plastic chair, the little wooden table. Then I decide that the chair is going to stand in for Amir, so I kneel next to it.

When talking to a child, I figure, you try to get on his level so you can achieve eye contact.

Tessa gets the set quiet and puts two cameras on me, one in a close-up, the other in a cowboy shot, from mid-thigh upward. The guy with the clapperboard runs in, claps, runs out again.

"I need the first line," I say.

"'Are you all right?'" Tessa reads.

"Are you all right?" I say. "You weren't hurt?" I'm in character now, and I've got the lines, and I'm talking to the chair that is Amir.

One of the worst things about auditions is that you don't often get to work with another actor. You're trying to stay in character, but the person feeding you lines is someone's assistant who speaks in a monotone, or who can't pronounce any word with more than six letters, or who can't read at all. You're trying to do a love scene with someone named Monique, and the person reading Monique's lines is an unshaven guy named Bernard who's talking through a mouthful of Fritos.

Thank God Tessa is an actor as well as a director. She feeds me the lines beautifully, using her own skill to shape the character of

Amir. She places herself so that the chair stays between us, and I can look up from the chair/Amir and see her.

Directors tend to be a bit remote these days, staying in a special room or tent where they can see everything on video and control everything remotely. Some of them might as well be in Tibet. But Tessa is right there on the set, her warm voice supporting me.

The scene is mostly Roheen explaining things—it's exposition. Exposition can be deadly, because it's hard to rattle out a lot of information and make it seem natural. Apparently Dagmar, or Carter-Ann or somebody, wants to know if I can make exposition look good.

I figure that Roheen and Amir have just been attacked somehow, shot at or whatever, so it's natural if Roheen is still keyed up. And I *am* keyed up, I'm pissed at having my future at stake in this audition and not knowing enough to be able to do a good job, so I use that anger to drive my performance, give an edge to the words. I'm right there, I'm completely in the zone, and somehow Tessa and Carter-Ann, between the two of them, got me there.

Tessa goes into her little tent to review the recordings, and then comes out and tells me she doesn't need a second take.

There are lots of takes on the second scene. It's an action scene, with attacks by an airplane and an armored car and a bunch of gunmen on foot. I have to imagine all this coming at me, and I have to imagine that I'm with another juvenile named Vitalia, whom I'm trying to keep from being killed.

Dagmar said there would be a lot of green screen in this project. I told her I'd have no problem. Now I have to prove it.

Tessa helps me locate all the various imaginary objects in space, so I can track them with my eyes. And I spend half an hour hiding behind the little table, or low-crawling from one location to another, or carrying the chair—standing in this time for Vitalia—to safety. At least I don't have to wear the Dr. Zaius jacket: apparently Roheen loses it early in the movie and just wears street clothes.

After the second scene we all take a break. I sprawl in a chair with a cup of coffee while Tessa goes into her tent to view the scenes as the camera saw them. I imagine her viewing me crawling around like a four-year-old in a sandbox while I pretend to dodge an armored car, and I laugh.

Tessa comes out of her tent, and asks me if I'm ready for the next scene.

"This is an awfully long audition," I say.

"The scenes are short." At least she doesn't insist that it's a test, not an audition. By now we've all forgotten that we were supposed to believe that.

"And it's comprehensive," I say. Because the scenes call on a number of different skills, so that Dagmar, or whoever, can get a good idea of my range. I deliver exposition, I react to imaginary threats, and in the third scene I have some juicy emotional moments.

The next scene is what you might call a conversion scene, a scene where the character articulates the changes that have occurred in his character during the course of the story.

It's a curious thing that the protagonists of films are expected to change during the course of the drama. It's practically required. *What's your character's journey?* is the question that every half-wit producer knows to ask during a pitch session.

But in my experience, real people don't change that much. My father is a con man. I imagine he was a con man when he was five years old, and when he's on his deathbed he'll be trying to scam the hospital.

Cleve will be second-rate no matter where he ends up. No matter how successful Tessa becomes in her new career, somewhere in her head she'll still be the teenager who lived through four years of the entire country making fun of her weight. My formative experiences all occurred before I was twenty, and since then I haven't altered to any great extent. I'm the same person I was when I was thirteen, just older, less successful, and much more sexually frustrated.

Movies used to reflect that. Bogart didn't develop, he was Bogart all the time. Clark Gable was Clark Gable from beginning to end. So was Joan Crawford.

But that's not what happens to movie protagonists now. They change. They grow. They expand, or sometimes contract. And so does Roheen. At some point in his journey, he realizes he owes a debt of gratitude to those who have helped him on his quest or whatever, and he offers his insights on the matter to yet another juvenile companion, someone named Khabane.

Apparently—in addition to dodging planes and armored cars—Roheen goes around collecting young people of diverse ethnic backgrounds. For what purpose, the three short scenes don't make clear.

I look up at Tessa. "Give me a minute, okay?"

"Whenever you're ready."

I drink my coffee slowly while I review the scene mentally, then I get up and look for Tessa again.

"What is Roheen changing *from*?" I ask.

"Sorry?"

"This scene marks a change in Roheen, but I don't really know who he's been before. Was he confused, or afraid, or a selfish prick... what was he?"

Tessa raises an eyebrow. For a second I recognize the glance she gave Kendra Toamasina in every episode of *Life on Top*, just before she tried—and generally failed—to shut her sister down.

"Sean," she says, "I have no damn idea." Her brown eyes travel in the direction of Carter-Ann, who is talking to one of her assistants, a tall, pale blond man. He carries a tablet computer, and the screen illuminates his face from below, giving it a ghostly, bluish quality.

"You could ask the shrink lady," Tessa says.

I raise my eyebrows. "She's a shrink?"

She nods. "Psychiatrist."

"*Whose?*" I'm completely at a loss. Who the hell assigns a psychiatrist to a movie set? I suppose I could understand if one of the actors were on the edge of a breakdown, and irreplaceable; but

I'm the only actor here, and not only do I not need a minder, but I could be replaced in about ten seconds.

Tessa shrugs. Her voice is pitched low so that Carter-Ann won't overhear. "She's why Joey isn't here. He can't stand her."

If Carter-Ann interferes with Joey the way she interferes with Tessa, the wonder isn't that Joey hates her, it's that she's not in traction.

"Won't hurt to ask her, I guess," I say.

I wait for Carter-Ann's assistant to leave, and then I approach her.

"Dr. Dixon?" I say.

She doesn't blink when I call her *Doctor*, but stands with her hands folded neatly before her abdomen in an attitude of polite expectation. Her weight is distributed evenly over her feet. I realize that her body is very controlled, that she's paying as much attention to kinesics as any actor.

"Can I help you, Mr. Makin?" she asks. We are being very Old World polite today.

"I can see in this scene that Roheen has changed," I say, and then I explain my question. While I'm speaking, she cocks her head to show that she's paying attention, and then when I'm done the head comes level and she looks at me with her blue eyes. She isn't looking right into my eyes, which could either be erotic or a challenge depending on the context, but instead she has a soft focus on my face. Showing that she's interested, but not *interested*.

"That's a very good observation, Mr. Makin," she says. "Let me see if I can help you." Her eyes look away into the dark distance of the soundstage, and then she turns back to me.

"Roheen isn't a bad person," she says. "But he's been preoccupied with his own problems. People are after him, and he has to get somewhere in order to accomplish his..."

"Mission?" I suggest.

She shakes her head. "No. It's not like he's a soldier with an assignment. But he has a task that's vital to him. And he's very much focused on that until he realizes..." She thinks again.

I recall what Dagmar told me at our lunch. "That he's in service to a higher ideal?" I suggest.

Her blue eyes glitter with interest. There's something mantislike about her gaze, something intent and predatory, and I'm instantly uncomfortable.

"That's very astute, Mr. Makin," she says.

I want badly to escape her scrutiny. "Thank you, Doctor. You've helped a lot."

"You're very welcome." As I start to move off, she calls after me. "Remember to turn your palms outward, Mr. Makin."

It takes a few minutes more before I'm ready to do my scene. I have to think about where Roheen is coming from and where he's going. He's not Dagmar's angel yet, I reckon, but this is where he makes the choice to become that person. He's been beset by problems, but this is where he realizes that the problems of other people also matter to him.

Once again I get on one knee, and the chair becomes my interlocutor. Tessa stands off camera, behind the chair where I can see her, and reads Khabane's lines.

What's happening is revelation. It's Roheen discovering who he's been all along without knowing, and at the same time it's me showing Roheen's discovery to the audience. I try to show the process, the way Roheen is finding out his own nature. It's not in the dialogue, it's *behind* the dialogue, in my expression, in my eyes. It's a technical challenge and I wish I could call for an eye light—basically a kind of pencil light they shine into your eyes to get a reflection—because that would show a shimmer in my eyes that might help to suggest Roheen's internal process.

I remember to turn my palms outward. *Screw you, Dr. Dixon.*

The scene isn't very long. Tessa calls for another take, then another. After the third she goes into her tent to view the results. I amble up to Markie, the grip, and ask if he's got an eye light.

"Sure."

So when Tessa comes out for the fourth take, Arthur the electrician is lying on the floor shining the light in my eyes while Markie critically observes the effect. Tessa says nothing, just asks if I'm ready.

After the fourth take, she tells me I can go home.

I make a point of thanking everybody on the set. I want them all to think, *Hey, what a nice guy. How easy he is to work with. If I'm ever in a situation where I can find him work, I definitely want to do that. Because he won't be a pain in the ass like that guy we just fired.*

When I go up to Tessa, she's talking to Carter-Ann.

"You'll get me the dailies?" Carter-Ann says.

"I'll do some cursory editing, then zap them to you."

Carter-Ann gets out her cell phone and walks away. I decide that I've already thanked her enough, and turn to Tessa.

"She gets dailies?" I say.

Tessa nods.

"Why?" I ask. "What's going on?"

She spreads her hands. "I only do what I'm told, man."

I thank her for helping me, suggest that we get together some time before she leaves for Namibia, and then grab the Dr. Zaius jacket and leave. The makeup artist has locked his studio and left, but that's all right, I can take off the makeup at home. I find Jaydee behind her desk amid a scent of alcohol and citrus. She's listening to talk radio and drinking a glass of sweet vermouth over ice, with a slice of orange.

She turns off the radio. "Go well?" she asks.

"I think so," I say. "But I've been wrong before." Jaydee starts to stand up, to put the jacket back on its hanger, but I wave her back to her seat and put the jacket in its place.

"Want a drink?" Jaydee asks, rattling the ice in her glass.

I consider this. After the rigors of the audition, a muscle relaxant is definitely in order.

"You bet," I say.

She makes me a drink and refreshes her own. I find a chair and take a welcome sip. The mix of sweetness and citrus is welcome. I realize I'm very thirsty and I take a big gulp. Spinal kinks that I didn't know I possessed begin to relax. I look at Jaydee.

"Do you know anything about this psychiatrist that's on set?"

"Nope."

"Why would you have a shrink on the set? During an audition?"

Jaydee waves her glass. "They're not movie people, that's all I know."

I start to take another gulp of my drink, then discipline myself to take just a sip. I don't want to get loaded before driving home, not even on vermouth. The problem with my history of DUI is that the law doesn't know I was faking it.

Jaydee, who has no scruples in this regard, takes a swig from her own glass.

"Have you seen Joey?" I ask.

"Yeah. He hired me." She laughs. "It was good to see him."

"How's he doing?"

Her lips give a little quirk. "He's more Joey than ever."

By which she means aggressive, explosive, controlling, temperamental, brilliant, and short.

"Jean-Marc is DP," she continues. "Allison will be editing, and Jane Haskill's doing the music."

I'm impressed. "That's quite a lineup."

"And after all this time," Jaydee laughs, "we're all still friends."

Joey likes to work with the same people over and over. Sometimes that's included me, though always in a minor role. But Joey always cared about even the minor parts, always tried to give me something interesting to do, even though, in the editing, I was often as not cut out altogether.

We sit and gossip for the length of my drink. I'd be happy to hang with Jaydee all afternoon, but I'm paranoid about driving while impaired, so I limit myself to the single drink and then leave.

It's when I'm piloting the Mercedes out of the parking lot that I get a big surprise. Because that's when I see Dagmar along down the rows of cars with Deeptimoy Srivastava.

He's very recognizable, with his shaggy white leonine hair and white horseshoe mustache, his platinum-rimmed spectacles, his glossy handmade shoes, and his ash-gray Nehru jacket.

I know he's something like the sixth-richest man on the planet. I know that he's an IT tycoon, and that he wired half of India and all of southeast Asia. I know he's retired from the businesses that made his money and is now devoting himself to charity work. I don't know this because I read *Fortune* or anything, but because he's in the entertainment news a lot, recruiting celebrities to his various causes.

And now he's here, in this rented studio in the Valley, and he's plainly recruited Dagmar, and my antennae are out, twitching in the wind for the scent of money. Because Hollywood is very good at taking money from people, and the question once again is not whether the newcomer will end up lighter in pocket, but how much of it will go to me.

I drive past them slowly in hopes that Dagmar will see me behind the wheel of the car and introduce me to the billionaire who, in my fast-forming fantasy, will become my patron and bankroll my projects from here to the year 3000; but she's locked in conversation with Srivastava, both of them very intent. I wish I could eavesdrop on their conversation.

I pull out of the studio gates and head for Burbank. The Watcher, returning to the moon to do what the Watcher does best.

Wait.

CHAPTER FIVE

HEAVY LUGGAGE BLOG

"You should get into directing." I heard that recently from an old friend, as I've heard it from others over the years.

That simple sentence, "You should get into directing," has meant different things over the years. Sometimes it means *Your career is over, find something else to do with your life*. Usually it's well-intentioned advice.

But even when the advice is well-intentioned, I'm still not interested. I'm maybe the only person in all of Greater Los Angeles who doesn't want to direct.

There are two kinds of artists: creative, and interpretive. Creative artists include writers, painters, directors, composers, and I suppose architects. Interpretive artists are musicians, actors, singers. Some lucky people are both, so you get singer/songwriters, and composers who are also virtuosos on their instruments. And you get actor/directors.

I'm an actor. I'm not very creative except when it comes to envisioning and inhabiting characters invented by other people. As readers of this blog have no doubt observed, I'm better at saying lines written by others than at writing the lines myself.

Directors are creators, or at least the good ones are. I'm perfectly capable of directing a scene—I can work well with the players, and I know lighting pretty well, and I know which end of the camera to point at the actors. Any technical aspects of the craft that elude me can be handled by the director of photography or the cameraman or any of the other specialists who can be found on the set.

But the end result would be mediocre. It would be a by-the-numbers job. Because I don't have the director's gift.

I have the actor's gift. Given the choice between being a so-so director and a good actor, I'll take the acting job. Even if the acting jobs aren't plentiful, I'll stick at what I'm good at.

I'm an actor, dammit! Give me a role, and I'll burn up the stage for you.

Comments (0)

INT. SUPERMARKET—NIGHT

It's a complete coincidence that I'm in the supermarket the same night as Des Andor. I'm contemplating some wilted bell peppers without enthusiasm, and I glance over and see that he's putting some eggplant in his shopping bag. I go over and say hello.

He's got wavy brown hair, three-day stubble, and the sort of physique that allows him to wear a muscle shirt in public. He shakes my hand with enough gripping power to wrench my arm from its socket. But his smile is genuine enough, and he seems pleased to see me.

"Still got those bruises, hey," he says, pointing at my forearms. A televised workout with a Wing Chun wooden man down at the Thirty-Sixth Chamber gave me some colorful souvenirs. They kept calling for more and more takes. Why anyone would spend hours banging their forearms against a long hardwood peg was more than I could imagine.

"I bruise easily," I tell him. At least several days of ibuprofen have eased the pain.

We move along the vegetable bin to the sound of pop hits from decades before either of us was born. The supermarket is full of the sorts of people who shop at ten o'clock: a middle-aged Hispanic in a Southern California Edison jumpsuit who's just got off shift; a schizophrenic woman mumbling to herself over the honeydews; a couple teenage girls staring at Des and giggling. The de-saturated light of the overhead fluorescents makes them all look like vampires.

"So we're scheduled to fight next week," I say.

"Yep," he says. He gives me an under-eyed look as he loads a head of green-leaf lettuce from the organic bin. "No offense," he says, "but I plan to win." He shrugs. "If I have to participate in this turd of a contest, I'll go for the gold."

"I understand," I say. "If it's all there is, it's all there is."

"I have to wish it *was* all there is," Des says.

There's something in his tone that sets my back-brain humming. I wonder what he's getting at.

"Me too," I say. "I got offered the lead in a feature, but I still have to train for this farkakte contest."

"I got an offer too," he says. "But the movie's being shot in Rome. No way I'm going to be able to commute, or keep in training."

I consider this for a moment. "You want to get a cup of coffee?" I ask.

We pay for our groceries and walk across the parking lot to the all-night restaurant. The place was part of a chain that's been extinct for fifty years, and now it's just called The Palms. Whatever charm it once possessed is long faded, and the air outside the front door is smoky with the scent of the waitstaff sneaking cigarettes.

I order coffee and pie from a brawny waitress in a pink uniform. Des asks for herbal tea and settles for Lipton's. I sip my coffee and contemplate my approach.

I take a sip from my cup, and wince at the taste of coffee left on the heat for far too long. "I can't believe how shabby this show is," I say. "It's making the martial arts look ridiculous."

Des nods. "You're right. I thought there'd be—I don't know—some kind of nobility or something. Some sense that this was real competition—but instead it's nothing but..." He makes a helpless gesture.

"Stunts," I say. "It's just stunts."

"Stunts," he repeats. He shakes his head. "At least it wasn't me taking a bath in the cottage cheese."

"The cottage cheese was a classic, that's for sure. I can still taste it." I watch him dip his tea bag into his cup.

"You know," I say, "you can make that flight to Rome."

He cocks an eyebrow at me. "I've thought of that. All I have to do is lose to you."

"Frankly," I say, "I could use a victory around now. And it's not as if there's any credibility at all to this competition. From where I sit, it's a win-win situation."

He dips the tea bag, jigging the string up and down.

"I don't want to look bad," he says.

"I'll make you look good."

He looks up at me, his eyes hard. "I want to win the first round."

I feel my mouth go dry. If I let him win the first round, and then he decides to go all out and try for victory, I'll be at a serious disadvantage. And if he double-crosses me, who would I complain to?

On the other hand, I'd be off the stupid show, and free to make my movie with Dagmar without the distractions of training and fighting.

"All right," I say. "And I win the match in the second."

We discuss strategy for a bit, and we decide that he's going to chase me around the ring for the first round, and then I'll take him out with a guillotine choke in the second.

"Another thing," he says. "Since we both have real work now..."

"Yes?"

"We don't throw punches to the face."

Relief floats into me like a sigh. If he's worried about showing up in Rome with a bruised face, I know our deal is for real. I smile.

"You got it," I tell him.

I treat Des to his tea, and we shake hands in the parking lot. He goes off to his car and I start the walk toward mine. I hear a rumble of exhaust, and a squeal of tires, but I pay little attention—I'm walking by myself on an empty stretch of asphalt under the lights, and there's plenty of room for any vehicle to go around me.

The engine noise grows louder, and I look to my left just as headlights focus on me. It's a big vehicle, and it's coming fast.

I jog faster to get out of its way, but the tires squeal as the vehicle adjusts its trajectory to intersect mine.

I feel a shock to my entire body as I realize that I've been turned into a target. It's like a land mine going off under my feet. I begin to run. My heart pounds in my ears.

Ahead of me is a steel pipe enclosure for holding shopping carts until they can be returned to the supermarket. A few carts glimmer in the light of the lamps overhead, strewn carelessly within and near the enclosure. I run for it so fast that I can almost feel the wings on my ankles. Wind whistles in my ears.

I throw myself—literally *throw myself*—behind the barrier. Asphalt bites my palms, and I roll.

The vehicle—it's a black SUV, parking lot lights reflecting dully off its dusty finish—swerves away at the last second and clips one of the shopping carts standing near the enclosure. It flies tumbling, bits of it breaking away and scattering over the parking lot like glass from a broken bottle, and comes to a stop fifty feet away.

I roll to my feet. If there's one thing Master Pak has taught me, it's how to fall down and spring back up again.

I watch the receding taillights and taste sour exhaust on the air. My heart lurches in my chest. Adrenaline shrieks along my nerves, but there's no way to fight, and no more reason to run.

The SUV swerves out of the parking lot and accelerates out of sight. It's only now that I remember the black Ford Expedition that almost ran me down on Rodeo Drive the first day I met Dagmar, and I wonder if this is the same driver, same car.

And then the next thing I think about is that Dagmar absolutely, completely, can never know about this.

If she learns that someone's trying to kill me, she could fire my ass.

INT. SEAN'S APARTMENT—DAY

If you're an actor hungry for work, but not so hungry that you don't actually have to wait tables or dance around in bear costumes, you spend a lot of time waiting around. For the next week I wait—I play video games, I watch old movies, I go on the Internet to watch naked ladies engage in extreme varieties of interpersonal behavior. I get together with Julian and smoke weed.

I try to ignore the news about the genocide in Fiji and the Indian task force that's heading for the islands. I have no idea how India got involved.

And now there's a civil war in Ethiopia. When did that happen? At least the riots in Korea seem to have died down.

I call Tessa and leave a message suggesting we have lunch or something before she heads for Namibia, but I don't get a call back. I'm used to not getting called back, and it doesn't much bother me.

Right now she's more successful than I am. She doesn't want to catch the curse of failure from me. I understand this.

Then I get the call from Cleve that Dagmar has called with an offer. And, considering the fact that I'm an unemployed television actor, it's a very nice offer.

As soon as I understand this I jump up from my old couch and start doing my victory dance in the middle of my living room. The Watcher doing the Blue Area Boogaloo, trying not to bark his shins on the coffee table.

"The problem is she wants you for five pictures," he says.

That's a *problem*? My dance grows frenzied. My free hand, flung high at the peak of my leaps, brushes the popcorn ceiling.

"Five?" I ask. "Sign me up!"

"I'll try to make it two," Cleve says. "So that if she wants you for the third, she'll have to fork over more money."

I stop dancing and think about this.

"I think you can ask for more money up front," I say. "I found out who's behind Dagmar's picture. It's Deeptimoy Srivastava."

I probably bungle the pronunciation of the name, but it doesn't matter, because Cleve's never heard of him. "He's, like, one of the world's ten richest men."

I sense Cleve's mind shifting into a predatory mode, just as mine did when I first heard of a game designer's trying to make a movie. We're Hollywood sharks, and we're scenting blood in the water.

"And this Sri guy is getting into pictures?"

"I guess. So when Dagmar was talking about the money backing her, it wasn't bullshit if she's got Srivastava's money in her pocket."

"Is he looking at scripts?" Cleve asks. Because he represents writers who need work even more than I do.

"I don't know. There hasn't been anything in the news about him forming a production company or getting cozy with a studio."

Since I saw him, I've Googled the hell out of him to find out everything I can, and there is nothing there. He's never been involved in show business, except to provide conduits for video on demand to half of Asia.

"I'll get back to you about the details," Cleve says. "I just thought I'd pass on the good news."

It's probably the biggest deal Cleve has ever negotiated. I want to tell him not to fuck it up.

"Great," I say. "Let me know what happens."

They happen quickly. I get more money and a three-picture deal, and I call Dagmar and ask her if she'd care to meet me in the Hollywood Museum of Film History, eating buttered popcorn and watching a Czech movie from the sixties.

INT. THEATER—NIGHT

Clarence Musselwhite is a burly black man a few years past sixty, with long white corkscrew curls hanging over the back of his collar, and a full beard so magnificent that it might well be envied by God. He's the ultimate film geek, happier in front of a flickering screen than a kitten with a ball of string.

He was a trial attorney at one point in his life, and made enough money arguing class-action suits—against Big Tobacco, Big Pharma, Big Oil—to leave the law and engage full-time in his hobby of collecting. He has a vast library of films and an immense number of props and other memorabilia, ranging from early Edison cylinders to the special glove that Harold Lloyd wore on his mutilated hand to the C-3PO costume worn by Anthony Daniels in *Attack of the Clones*. The whole collection is capped by one of the five surviving pairs of ruby slippers worn by Judy Garland in *The Wizard of Oz*.

Eventually Clarence ran out of room for his collection, and so he had to open the Hollywood Museum of Film History in order to have a place to put it. In the daytime, tourists wander the exhibits and gawk at the ruby slippers and Ray Harryhausen maquettes. Some nights, Clarence runs film programs in his theater, and other nights his establishment is available for rent to private parties.

It occurs to me that Clarence may be the only happy man I know. He has no money worries, and he spends every day doing exactly what he wants to do. He's completely achieved his ambitions.

Maybe I should hate him. Due to an accident of genetics I am denied the satisfaction of making full use of my talents and energies, and I could convert my frustration to fury with ease. I would certainly hate anyone else in his position. But somehow Clarence evades my hatred. He is simply too good-natured.

Every so often I try to convince Clarence to invest in one of my film projects, but he knows too much about the business and its hazards and just laughs at me. Reluctantly I respect him for this.

Dagmar wants to see the Kinoautomat and Clarence is always willing to show his collection, so he opens his 150-seat theater for the two of us and fires up his 1911 Paragon popcorn machine.

The chair arms of one row of the theater are now equipped with the buttons we use to vote. Originally there were light strips on the walls of the theater that showed how everyone had voted, but these were too complicated to rig for an audience of two.

We don't start with the movie. You never do in Clarence's theater. First we have a cartoon in which Popeye sinks a Japanese task force, a *March of Time* newsreel featuring Amelia Earhart's solo flight from Mexico City to New York, and a silent trailer for Greta Garbo as *The Temptress.*

Clarence is very big on the total film experience. He likes to pretend that his little theater is a giant picture palace of the 1930s, and produces an entire program. We're lucky we didn't get a Three Stooges short.

Eventually we watch *Man in His House.* It opens with an apartment building on fire, and various cast members zooming down the canvas slide that firefighters have set up to rescue victims of the blaze. We then flash back to the start of the problem, with a woman dressed only in a towel wandering the halls of the apartment looking for shelter.

Does our hero, the very married Novak, let her in or not? We both vote yes.

Originally the system required two synchronized projectors, but Clarence has digitized the film onto one huge disk, and all he has to do is type the number of one track or another.

The film's humor is very dark. Dagmar watches with interest, laughing at the amusing bits, scrolling her handheld in the air to make notes to herself. Then she wants to see the various alternate stories, and Clarence is happy to oblige.

The branching stories are a revelation, because they don't branch. No matter which option we pick, the reel ends up in the same place as if we'd picked the other plotline. There are never more than two possible scenes. The audience has the illusion that it has a lot more choices than in fact it has.

"That's a political comment by the director, Činčera," Clarence says. "It's about the elections under Communism. However you vote, you end up in the same place."

"In a building that's burning down," Dagmar says. Her look is thoughtful.

We thank Clarence, and he gives us paper sacks of popcorn to take home.

"After your movie comes out," he tells Dagmar, "we could have a panel discussion here. Get you and Sean and some other people on stage, to talk about your project."

Dagmar considers this. "With alternate reality games," she says, "we don't talk about how we do what we do. We try to preserve the mystery."

"Movies are different," Clarence says.

"Maybe so," Dagmar says. "I'll think about it." But I see her face close down, like shutters falling across a window, and I know she'll never do it.

We step out onto Hollywood Boulevard. The street is shabby and tragic in the daytime, full of hucksters and tourists and cheap souvenir shops, but at night it retains at least a little bit of magic, of neon and fantasy. Cars pass by on hissing tires. Through the buildings we can see fragments of the Hollywood sign.

"Care to go for a drink or coffee or something?" I ask.

"Hey!" someone says. "Hey!" I look up and see a broad grin, cargo shorts, a baseball cap, and a cup from Starbucks.

"Where's your luggage, man?" the guy asks.

"Heh heh." I wave affably. "Nice."

"*Where's your luggage?*" he shouts, as if I didn't hear it the first time. And then he's off, swigging from his double mocha Frappuccino, or whatever the hell. Congratulating himself on his diamond-edged wit.

Dagmar looks after him with irritation. "Your loyal public?" she says.

"Yep."

No one ever planned for Brent Schuyler, my character on *Family Tree*, to have a catchphrase. "Whatever lifts your luggage" was just one line among many, but when I first said it, the studio audience exploded in mirth. And then they laughed again when I used it again two weeks later. And the week after that. And after that, they laughed because they remembered they'd laughed before.

"Whatever lifts your luggage." I never understood why that sent half of America rolling on the floor with laughter.

Though, as catchphrases go, it's fairly benign. I'd much rather have perfect strangers ask me about my luggage than be Jaleel White watching someone do the Urkel Dance for the ten thousandth time, or Henry Winkler sitting in a restaurant while some subnormal cretin bellows "Ayyyyy" in his ear, or Bill Mumy smiling with resigned politeness when someone yells "Danger, Will Robinson!"

"So," I say. "Coffee?"

"It's late," she says, and then hesitates. "Do you have a place in mind?"

I do.

INT. UNTERSEEBAR—NIGHT

Ten minutes later we're at a submarine-themed brewpub, with portholes and periscopes and heavy brass diving helmets propped on shelves. Though I'd expect some kind of Teutonic march, it's Jimmy Buffett I hear on the bar speakers. I order something called a Sonar Side Scan Ale. Dagmar has tonic without the gin. The waiter brings a bowl of nuts with our drinks.

I sip my drink and make a face. The brewmaster made up for the poor quality of his hops by throwing them in by the fistful, and the result is a bitter nastiness that's a waste of everyone's time.

Dagmar looks at me. "Not so good?"

"Maybe next I'll try the lager." I pop some peanuts to clear my palate. "Why aren't you going to do the talk at Clarence's theater?" I ask.

She gives me a startled look. "How do you know I won't?"

"It was obvious."

She glances away, frowning, then decides to answer.

"Because," she says, "the questions might not all be about the movie."

"Ah." I can see where she'd be reluctant to talk about how so many people around her ended up dead.

"A friend of mine told me that I should be careful around you," I say. "He said you'd blow up my car."

She turns away again. Some internal process tugs on her facial muscles. “Not funny,” she says.

I realize I shouldn’t have said that. Contracts, I remind myself, haven’t been signed yet.

I take a swig of over-hopped ale. “Can you tell me about the movie?” I ask.

She toys with her napkin, which has a periscope’s-eye view of a sinking ship. “You haven’t signed the nondisclosure agreement,” she says.

“I have. It’s with Cleve. I assume he’ll send it to you tomorrow.”

The nondisclosure agreement is a piece of weirdness. I’m not allowed to talk about the film to any outsiders, not without permission, for any reason. Usually producers are all too happy to let people talk about their films, except maybe for plot secrets. But apparently the plots and inner workings of ARGs are all secret, and we are all bound to this tradition imported from another art form.

Dagmar comes to a decision, and shrugs.

“Okay,” she says. “Have you seen *E.T.*?”

“Sure.”

“We’re sort of doing *E.T.* Except that E.T. doesn’t go home at the end. Which is why we get to do sequels.”

I consider this. “And I’m E.T.?”

“Sort of, yeah.”

“I’m an alien.”

It’s not like I’m the most human-looking human on the planet, so this is not unreasonable.

“No, you’re not an actual alien.”

“I’m an angel.”

“Not a *real* angel.” And then, as I’m about to ask another question, she raises a hand. “It’s complicated. You’ll see the script.”

“When?”

“You’ve signed the NDA, so I’ll send the script to you as soon as Cleve faxes the agreement to me.” She hesitates. “Of course the script isn’t a hundred percent finished.”

"It never is."

"And there are alternate plotlines, so it may be a little confusing to read."

"I'll manage."

Her anxiety over the script is a little touching, and probably misplaced. It's not as if my opinion of the writing is going to matter in the least. My job is just to speak the words, even if they stink.

I sip my vile beer. The drink catches her attention, and her gaze follows the glass as I return it to the table. She frowns, and is about to speak when klaxons sound over the bar speakers. There is a blast of air from the ballast tanks and a sound of rushing water. I presume we are now submerged.

"Are you going to structure the story like *Man in His House*?" I ask. "Every branch leads only to one place?"

Dagmar shakes her head. "No, I can't. The original audience for that film would see it once, so it wouldn't be obvious to them that the choices were so limited. *Escape to Earth* is more transparent—the audience will be able to see all the alternate scenes whenever they want, so long as they have a paid account. Too limited a choice will disappoint them, so we'll need more scenes."

"*Escape to Earth*?"

She smiles. "There's your title. Make of it whatever you will."

I consider *Escape to Earth*. "It's a good title," I say, and take another sip of beer. Dagmar looks at my glass again, and frowns.

"I did some research about you," she says.

"Yes?"

Dagmar looks pointedly at my glass, then back at me. "Aren't you supposed to be a recovering alcoholic?"

I laugh. "I'm not an alcoholic," I say. "I just play one at AA meetings."

Her eyes narrow. She isn't sharing my amusement.

"Why are you drinking again?" she says.

"I never stopped." Her look hardens. I sigh and begin the long, embarrassing explanation.

"It was a stupid scheme to reboot my career," I admit.

I explain about my idea to crash my car and gain headlines, sympathy, and work.

"Plus," I add, "you've never seen anything like a Hollywood AA meeting. Trust me—people go there to audition. There are big-name producers and directors and agents at the meetings trying to dry out, so the actors chase them down and pull out all the stops to describe their fall into depravity and their desperate pursuit of sobriety. All pretend alcoholics looking for work."

Dagmar looks faintly aghast. "How did your scheme work?" she asks.

"I sacrificed my Mini Cooper for nothing. I didn't get work until people had forgotten I'm supposed to be a drunk. The insurance money from the Mini went to pay lawyers and the clinic. And now I'm driving my mother's car."

The annoying thing is that the scheme has worked for other people. A well-timed arrest can boost someone's career, if they're properly contrite and stay out of trouble afterward. A second arrest, or a second stay in rehab, tends to make people suspicious.

Dagmar eats a cashew and frowns at me.

"I don't want you drinking while you're working for me."

I'm so taken aback that it takes me a few seconds to respond. "I'm not a real alcoholic," I point out.

"You're a *public* alcoholic," Dagmar says. "You pleaded guilty to drunken driving. It's in the public record. You've been seen at AA meetings."

I feel a flash of anger. "It's all fake!"

"*That doesn't matter.*" Dagmar jabs a finger into the surface of the table. "I'm not having my project derailed by speculation over your sobriety. This is a family-friendly film that I'm going to market all over the world, including places where alcohol is illegal—"

I begin to sputter. "I'm going to be held hostage by the bigotry of a clutch of imams?"

"You're going to be held hostage by *me*," Dagmar says. She

points at my Side Scan Ale. "That's your last drink as long as you're under contract to me."

"There's no way you can enforce that!" I say.

Her mouth presses into a grim line. "I can if it's in the contract. And it *will* be in the contract, along with a few other clauses guaranteeing good behavior."

"Like what?" I say.

"No drugs. No criminal behavior. No sex scandals."

I'm appalled. "What the fuck is a *sex scandal* in this day and age? Now I can't even get *laid*?"

"Not with anyone who's married," Dagmar says. "Or underage. Or a prostitute."

"A prostitute?" I'm sputtering again. "I've never paid for—"

I'm totally indignant. I've been with a *lot* of sex workers. And not once did I have to pay.

Of course, that was back when I was a star. I doubt I'd get any freebies now.

Dagmar raises a hand. "No kicking dogs, like Melody Chastain. No public masturbation—remember Pee-wee Herman." She offers a cynical smile. "I'm sure I'll think of a few more restrictions by tomorrow morning."

I lean back in my chair, fold my arms, and give Dagmar a sullen glare. "I'm an actor," I say. "Not a Mouseketeer. I'm not some kid. I don't need protection from the wicked world."

She shrugs. "I don't give a damn about you. I wish you'd understand that."

"Thanks a lot," I mutter.

Her eyes flash. "What I care about is Roheen. He's a role model and he stays pristine."

I am without words. This kind of paternalism is from generations before my time, when studios tried to control the private lives of their actors. Disney, I guess, was the only studio that actually had any success, at least while Walt was still alive—after which the doors of Sleeping Beauty's castle crashed down to admit a wave of hard-partying, drugging, snatch-flashing ingenues.

None of whom, apparently, I am to be allowed to play with.

"I can't believe I'm hearing this," I say. "This is...medieval."

"Medieval would involve a chastity belt."

"You can't put a morals clause in the contract. It's unenforceable."

"You could take it to court," Dagmar says, "but of course you'd have to take the position that you have an inalienable right to screw underage girls, which might not make that great an impression on the judge—not to mention the public." She nods thoughtfully. "And of course you'd have to pay your attorney with something—your mother's car, maybe?"

She nods. "You know, I'm thinking that it's best not to sign the contract at all."

I don't give a damn about you. She was certainly intent on proving it.

She looks at me, and her gaze softens. "There's still at least twenty million women in this country who aren't married, aren't under eighteen, and don't turn tricks." She waves a hand. "Be my guest."

"Thanks."

"I'm not normally a hard-ass," she says. "But this project is too important for me to allow accidents."

Something in her tone makes me look up.

"What *is* this project exactly?" I ask.

She grows grim again. "It's *my...damn...movie*," she says.

CHAPTER SIX

FROM: Parmita <parmita@babaji.edu.in>
SUBJECT: Your "Blog"

Sean, this is your mother. I am contacting you regarding the unjust attacks you have made on Babaji on your "blog." You say that he is larcenous and that is not true. Babaji doesn't care about money. Any money is used for the purposes of education and to help some of his elderly disciples who have no resources of their own. Babaji is God and God doesn't need money! He would not hang on to money without a good reason!

You also say that Kadaitswami means "Master of the Marketplace," and that is true, but you imply that this has to do with his love of money, and that is false. He was called Kadaitswami because he used to do his preaching in markets and bazaars. He preached to the poor and to the humble! This should not be a cause for mockery!

You are deliberately misunderstanding your phone call with Babaji. It was a great honor that he spoke with you at all. He was only interested in your spiritual well-being, and you chose to mock him. No wonder he hung up. You are very ill-bred. You have completely wasted God's time.

As for the rest of your essay, I can only shake my head in disbelief. Any money that I spent was only to give you a good home. If I also took advantage of the opportunity to advance my own development, that is my responsibility as a spiritual being on this plane of existence. We should all evolve toward God. That is our duty to ourselves.

If I gave Babaji money, it is so that I can go to Heaven! I do not understand why a son should be angry that his mother is going to Heaven.

And I don't see what my car has to do with any of this. I bought a good safe car that would hold the entire family. Now you use this to make fun of me.

But I don't care what you say about me. Babaji says that we must all "suffer the slings and arrows."

I do care, though, that you are using your "blog" to slander Babaji. I expect that you will print a retraction now that you know the truth.

Om Shiva,
Your mother (Parmita Subrahmanya)

FROM: Sean Makin
SUBJECT: Re: Your "Blog"

Your name is Parmita now? I guess it beats Stephanie.

I will continue to say anything I like about Babaji, and to waste as much of his time as I like, so long as he continues to hang on to my stolen money. If God doesn't like it, he can send me a check.

I was really interested to know that it's possible to buy your way into Heaven. If that's true, I guess I'm going there, because the trip was paid for with my money.

You and Dad had $25 million legally to buy your way into whatever afterlife appealed to you. You needed my nest egg too?

Is Heaven like a country club or something? You have to be rich to get in? If there aren't any poor people there, who cuts the rich folks' lawns?

But seriously—this is what it takes to get you to contact me? It's been over ten years since I've heard from you. Not even a birthday card. I was beginning to suspect you don't give a shit.

Babaji can kiss my ass,
Your son (Sean Makin, in case you've forgotten my name)

FROM: Parmita <parmita@babaji.edu.in>
SUBJECT: Re: Re: Your "Blog"

It's not true that I don't care about you. I care about everybody. But I also care about God, and God comes first!

Your continual harping on the money indicates how unevolved your soul has become. You should consider eternal things only. Then you will become more perfect and closer to Babaji. If you don't do this, you could be caught on the Wheel for all eternity.

You continue to slander Babaji! This makes me very angry with you, but it doesn't mean that I'm not concerned for you. "Money is not all that matters." If you come to Andhra Pradesh we can discuss this.

Om Shiva
Your mother

FROM: Sean Makin
SUBJECT: Re: Re: Re: Your "Blog"

Did you know that "Om Shiva" is an anagram of "Mavis Ho"? Do you suppose there is some spiritual significance to this?

I'm a little too busy right now to come to Andhra Pradesh. Why don't you come to California? So many of your old friends would like to see you.

Mavis Ho,
Your son

FROM: Parmita <parmita@babaji.edu.in>
SUBJECT: Re: Re: Re: Re: Your "Blog"

There is spiritual significance to everything, even to this Mavis Ho, who I suppose is a pop star or something. Here in the ashram we are a little "behind the times" as far as entertainment goes.

I would love seeing my old friends and talking to them about Babaji and his message, but you know I can't come to California. My own son loves money so much that he might try to have me arrested!

You should pray to Babaji now that your heart will be healed and your eyes "opened."

Om Shiva
Your mother

FROM: Sean Makin
SUBJECT: Re: Re: Re: Re: Re: Your "Blog"

Your fear of arrest is a sure sign of an unevolved soul. What does prison matter if your thoughts are with Babaji? You should come to California. I'll pick you up in your very own car.

Meanwhile, I think I'll post this correspondence on my "blog," as you call it. Perhaps my faithful audience of lurkers and trolls will help to persuade you to come back to the States.

Mavis Ho,
Your son

Comments (58)

FROM: MaddHaxx

Wow Makin no wonder you're so fucked up!

FROM: Krumble

Mavis Ho LMAO!

FROM: DIEgo

Whining about the money really does go on too long. Just sayin'.

FROM: Coldplay

You both such losers ha ha

FROM: Coopz

Yeah Mom come to California! You'll be right at home with the stupid Liberal Democrats and the other wackos!

FROM: Jacky D-Cup

This is an excellent blog. If you would like to meet girls or see my @@EXCITING PHOTOS@@ please click this link.

FROM: Charlotte

You shouldn't mock your mother like this. It's trashy behavior.

FROM: Krumble

OM SHIVA COME TO CALIFORNIA MOM!!!!!

FROM: Trishula

I'm sure your mother does nothing but pray for you. Your treatment of her is bad enough, but your mockery of Babaji is beyond forgiveness. YOU WILL BE HELD RESPONSIBLE.

FROM: Sean

Oh yeah, Trishula, I'm really tremblin' now. You see, whenever people threaten me on the Internet I just quake in my bunny slippers. I'm sure you're the biggest Babaji badass that ever hid from the world in your mother's basement.

I spit on you, and I shit on your God. Go pray to Mavis Ho or something, lame-ass.

FROM: MaddHaxx

Damn, ppl, Celebretty Pitfighter here is calling a throwdown!

FROM: Trishula

As Our Lord destroyed the Tripura, so shall I destroy you.

FROM: Coopz

Careful Sean, you'll get a rattlesnake in your mailbox!

FROM: Sean

I'm sure Trishula is like a total terrorist—NOT!

INT. ARENA—NIGHT

Whoooo. The animal sound reaches me in the ring and sends a blazing rocket up my spine. I'm back in the ring, and I'm trying to catch my breath because my heart is thundering 140 beats per minute, and the match hasn't even started yet. There's so much bloodlust and testosterone in the air that I can barely think at all.

Des Andor looks at me from across the ring. He's completely expressionless and I can't tell if he means to keep our agreement or not.

Whoooo. The crowd roars its craving for destruction. I feel the urge to punch, to smash, to kick. A barely rational part of my mind hopes that Des isn't responding to this the way I am.

I lose the first round. I'll have to keep reminding myself that.

Our surprise handicaps were delivered in the dressing rooms. Each of us was given a sixteen-ounce boxing glove to lace onto one hand. This makes grappling techniques more difficult, and grappling is at least half our training.

Because Des won a majority of contests in the preceding weeks, he got his glove on his right hand, which will let him hit harder with his power hand. My glove is on my left.

The referee calls us over and tells us to fight fair. I can barely hear him over the crowd's roar. I touch gloves with Des and then retire to my side of the ring.

We're asked if we're ready. I hear nothing, and can only see the referee's mouth moving. I nod.

"*Let's rock the world!*" This time I hear him. The referee punches the air.

I restrain an adrenaline-fueled impulse to charge across the ring, and instead I approach cautiously. Des is taking his time as well. We look at each other across the tops of our gloves. His expression is still blank.

Then his hand lashes out, and I catch it on my glove, and the fight is on.

There are some flurries that go nowhere, and we kick a few times, and then Des wades in with a series of body shots, and I know he's holding to our agreement, because he's not striking for the head at all. I take some hits and dance away. Des's hands are still low and I could jab him in the face easily, but I refrain.

More flurries, more body shots. My floating ribs creak from the power of Des's hits. I get in a few punches myself, and throw some kicks that I know aren't going to do any damage. Des gets in a good shin kick against my thigh. We do some ineffectual grappling. He keeps carrying his guard low, and I could paste him over and over again, but I don't. I can taste my own sweat mingled with the plastic taste of my mouthpiece.

The body blows have me gasping for air by the time the two-minute round ends. I go to my corner and take a rest on the stool while Master Pak tells me to hit him, for God's sake. "His head is wide open!" I nod as if I have every intention of following his advice.

Then the bell rings and I go up to scratch. Des is carrying his guard low again, so I aim some shots for his head, but I fire from outside proper range and the punches go nowhere, or hit him only lightly. He throws a series of wild punches that miss. Then, as I backpedal, he shoots forward right into me, his arms going around me.

I sprawl backward to oppose his weight and to keep him from throwing me down. His head rams into my right armpit. It takes a few seconds before I realize that he's giving me an opening.

I snake my right hand down between his left arm and his neck, and then I draw the forearm across his throat. Des turns his head so I don't accidentally crush his windpipe as I awkwardly grab my right wrist with the heavy glove on my left hand. Then I tighten my grip and lean back slightly to draw the guillotine across the front of his throat.

He stands it for maybe three seconds before tapping me on the shoulder in a sign of submission. I release the hold and throw my hands out, and the referee grabs one hand and holds it over my head.

Awhooooo. The crowd bays its pleasure. A pair of battered old suitcases fly into the ring.

Luggage. Oh boy.

Des gives me a hug, pounds my back, mutters "Thanks" in my ear. I shake the hand of Master Pak, who opens the gate and rushes into the ring to give me a hug. His grin is bigger than mine. Then we all have to quiet down for the ring announcer to make the formal announcement—"Thirty-eight seconds into the second round, by submission"—after which I get another hug from Des and then make the trip back to the locker room past a wild crowd of enthusiasts. The men with the blue beer bellies and the weird alien heads are there, and a crowd of people wave suitcases over their heads.

It's a lot better taking this walk as the winner. And I consider myself a winner, even though the fight was fixed... after all, I was the one who fixed it. I saw the opportunity, and I crafted the victory for myself.

I'm already thinking about the next fight. I know it will be against Lenny Castro.

Des wanted to go to Rome. I wonder what Lenny wants?

INT. SEAN'S CONDO—DAY

Once a motion picture is greenlighted, things happen fast. I sign the contract and the next three and a half weeks are a rush of makeup tests, wardrobe fittings, and more tests to see how I and the wardrobe look to the camera. In my spare time I do a lot of sweating with the free weights and on the treadmill, because I want to get in the best shape I can be—not necessarily for reasons of vanity, but because I'm in nearly every scene and I'm going to need a lot of stamina, and I may not have a chance to do any working out once shooting begins. A series of script revisions are hand-delivered to my condo by one of Dagmar's assistants, a security specialist named Richard.

Richard is about my age, olive-skinned and dark-haired. When he shows up at my door he's dressed in a black tee, black cords, and white Converse sneaks. His only concession to style is a Girard-Perregaux chronograph perched on one wrist. He's dressed like this practically every time I see him, as if it's a uniform, and whenever we speak he retains a courteous, attentive seriousness that reminds me of Spanish hidalgos, or whatever they were called, the guys who conquered Latin America while being too proud to be anything but stoic and courtly.

The first thing Richard does is start to go over my condo for bugs or hidden cameras. He has a little handset with dials and a screen, and he's waving it over my living room walls and furniture. He tells me he'll be doing this every week or so.

"When news of this project gets out, you could find yourself under siege," he says.

I long for the time when the paparazzi will spend their time hanging out by my front door, when autograph-seekers will dog my footsteps. If Richard actually thinks this might happen, maybe my fortunes are looking up.

Though personally I don't see it.

"Isn't this a bit premature?" I say. "It's not like I'm on anyone's radar. I'm not important enough to spy on."

I make a point of not mentioning the man in the SUV who is trying to run me over. If Dagmar decides that I could put the project at risk—say by getting run over halfway through the production—the easiest solution to her problem is to fire me right now. Which she easily can, at this point—no footage has been shot, and there would be no loss.

Richard blows out his cheeks. "Dagmar's fans," he says, "are a little extreme." He digs in a pocket and produces a stick of portable memory marked with a picture of Sailor Moon.

"This is the latest iteration of the script," he says. "If you try to move the file from its current resting place, you'll fail. If you try to print it, you'll fail. And if you lose this little wonder, then I'm going to have to wire a generator to your balls and make you dance."

He says this with a perfect calm face, looking at me with his mild brown eyes. I think of hidalgos with rapiers, terrorists with knives in the dark.

Jesus. I'm worried about the guy in the SUV with someone like Richard in the room?

"How am I supposed to work with the script," I say, "if I can't print it?"

"You'll get pages eventually," he says. "This is just to familiarize you with your part in the story." He looks around my living room. "Do you have a safe somewhere?"

"No."

"I'll have one sent over. You can keep the script in it when you're not around."

I look at Richard and ask him the same question I asked Dagmar.

"What *is* this project, anyway?" He ignores my question.

"In the past," Richard says, "Dagmar's fans have followed the actors around hoping to find a dropped script. They try to find out when we're recording video so they can get onto the set and overhear crucial plot developments. They've hacked our computers, and they've bugged our offices hoping to overhear us discussing important developments in the game."

"But," I point out, "this isn't a game, right? It's a feature film."

Richard's lips quirk. "Our traditional audience may not entirely comprehend the distinction. And in any case, there *is* a game component that will launch along with *Escape to Earth*, so you'll probably get stalked anyway."

"I'll look forward to it." It's been many years since I've had a stalker. Stalkers are how you know you've arrived.

"By the way," Richard says, "congratulations on winning the *Celebrity Pitfighter* fight."

"How'd you know I won?" I ask. "That episode hasn't been broadcast yet."

He looks at me deadpan. "We're paying somebody on the *Pitfighter* team. We don't want you getting hurt during our production."

I absorb this. "If you could find out what the handicap's going to be in my fight with Lenny Castro, that would be very useful."

"I'll see what I can do."

Richard finishes going over my audio components, then looks at my coffee table.

"It might be a good idea to put the bong in a cabinet," he says.

"Weed's legal now," I remind him. "Nearly."

"If you leave it out and someone gets a picture of it through the window or something, he could blackmail you into handing over bits of the script."

"But it's *legal*." I stare at him. "You think they'll *do* that?"

He looks thoughtful. "For sure they'd make the *threat*. Whether or not they carry it out is another matter."

Richard moves into my kitchen and deploys his scanner. I drift after him.

"How long have you worked for Dagmar?" I ask.

"Originally I worked for AvN Soft, which was Great Big Idea's parent company. When Great Big Idea got spun off, I went along." He gives a grin. "Working for Dagmar was a lot more fun."

"Even the, ah, bombings?" I ask. "The coup?"

"The bombings were sort of before my time," Richard says. "I got in right at the end." He is apparently intent on discovering whether someone has bugged the dirty dishes in my sink. "And the coup?" he says. "We were just enablers really. They staged their own coup, we helped them talk to each other."

"Didn't Odis Strange's daughter get killed?"

"Yes. Assassinated." He turns to me. "We all liked her. She took a bullet meant for Dagmar."

"Ah." I feel my mouth go dry. I think about those hidalgos again, a deadly intensity behind the formal politeness.

Richard turns away, frowns at my kitchen door, and makes adjustments to his scanner. He walks to the door, reaches up, and touches a bolt that's been screwed into the wall near the door.

"It's okay," he says. "The laser reflected off it as if it were a lens."

"There's a laser?"

He points to an aperture on his little box. "Built to reflect off camera lenses." He opens my refrigerator door and scans the contents. "You know," he says, "if that six-pack of Amstel disappears between now and my next visit, I won't have to report to Dagmar that you're in breach of contract."

"Oh, please," I say. "This is ridiculous."

He looks at me. "You signed the contract, right?"

I sigh. "I'm not an actual alcoholic, you know." I figure I'm going to get tired of pointing this out.

He shrugs. "Guess you get to prove that."

Richard checks my dining nook and my downstairs bathroom,

then heads upstairs to the bedroom and the master bath. Discouraged, I trudge after him.

"Did you have to take the pledge, too?" I ask. "Or is it just me?"

"All that's between you and Dagmar," he says. He waves his scanner over the door leading to the balcony.

"But she lets you drink."

"I don't drink much." He smiles to himself. "But she puts up with Helmuth, and so far as I can tell he parties every night."

The name tickles something in memory. "Helmuth?" I ask.

"Helmuth von Moltke. He's our head programmer."

Memories float to the surface, then focus. "Blond?" I say. "Dresses well? Goes to all the clubs?"

"That would be Helmuth. You know him?"

"We've met."

I've been in the club scene. I started when I was maybe fifteen, and my girlfriends, who were over twenty-one, got me in the door—and then my celebrity would get *them* into the VIP rooms. Sometimes the clubs would ask me to be their guest DJ, and they drew a good crowd.

I've clubbed intermittently since then, often in hopes of being seen by someone who might give me a job. Sometimes I can't afford the scene at all. And sometimes the guy on the door won't let me in—and once I'm in, I don't get in the VIP rooms. I don't enjoy being in bars where, even if you have money, your money isn't good enough, because *you* aren't good enough.

The gatekeepers on the door have social antennae more acute than even the most experienced tabloid reporter's. They know exactly who is important enough to drink a vodka tonic in the same room as Alex Skarsgård and Taylor Momsen.

Richard looks at me. "Helmuth hasn't mentioned that he knows you."

"He might not remember me," I say. "Or he might remember me, but not know I'm the same actor you people hired."

"I'll ask him." He clears my closet of eavesdroppers.

"Say," I say, "about this alcohol thing. Can I just give you fifty bucks, and you forget anything you saw here?"

He turns to me again, and again I feel the Spanish swordsman behind the polite façade.

"It's my own place," I say. "I don't drink on set, and I won't drink in public."

He narrows his eyes. "You know," he says, "you're utterly failing to convince me you don't have a drinking problem."

"It's Dagmar who has the problem," I say.

He considers this, then speaks. "Dagmar's father was an alcoholic," he says. "She doesn't like drunks much. And she's pregnant, and that makes her nervous and a little paranoid and overprotective of her... project... and of course there's a lot riding on this. So if you make her life easier, you'll make it more pleasant for everybody, yourself included."

I savor the sour taste of capitulation on my tongue. I am getting very tired of having absolutely nothing to bargain with.

"Fine," I say. "I'm all for keeping things... pleasant."

A short while later I watch him from the terrace as he leaves the condo and gets into his red Mitsubishi. Until he drives away, the neat, precise, black-clad figure is the only moving figure on the block, and then it's the urban desert again.

I wonder how long he's been in love with Dagmar. I wonder if Dagmar knows.

I decide it's time I read the script. But first, I go to the fridge for a beer.

THE SAME—ONE HOUR LATER

The script is called *The Life of Chester A. Arthur*, a phony title given the film to deter anyone looking for Dagmar's latest project. It's a three-beer script, because there are so many alternate scenes. Some of them are sketches that might as well be labeled TO BE FILLED IN LATER. But taken as a whole it's impressive.

The writing is good, for one thing. Incisive, clear-cut, unambiguous. Considering the complexity of the whole project, it's remarkably free of confusion.

And—more importantly for me—Roheen is in practically every scene. I'm central, I have some very smart lines to say, and there's no way I'm not going to love this part.

Roheen turns out not to be an alien, or an angel. He's human, more or less. He's just a human from another dimension, or a parallel world. He's a kind of anthropologist, on our world doing research with his team.

Except that it turns out there's another group of visitors to our world, people called the Steene from yet another parallel dimension, and they're hostile to Roheen's crowd. So they kill Roheen's companions and close the Tellurian Gate that he was planning on using to return to his home world.

So then it's off to the next gate, with the Steene hit team in pursuit. And when the Steene close that gate, it's on to the next, and the next.

Fortunately Roheen makes friends with a highly networked juvenile who has online friends in all the various territories Roheen needs to pass through. The kids are webbed in ways that the bad guys can only envy, and they hand off Roheen from one to another using methods both ingenious and courageous.

And as Roheen progresses, he changes. At the beginning he's a little cold, a little clinical—he's a scientist after all—and he's also afraid of being killed at any moment. Later, he develops a deep gratitude to the kids who help him, and then he realizes that he can help them, and help the Earth. He makes major sacrifices in order to do this. The transformation from scientist to otherworldly angel is, for an actor, very interesting.

It's so unlike anything I know from real life.

Turn your palms out. Show me your instep.

My guess is that it's more complicated than that.

I'm thinking about all this when Tessa calls and asks if I want to go to dinner. She's got only a few days before she has to head out for Namibia.

Hey, I think, *this means I'm no longer a loser! My cooties are no longer catching.*

I suggest sushi.

EXT. JOEY'S HOME—DAY

Here we are at Joey's house. Not the one up Parmenter Canyon where he lived with Timmi, but his newer, bigger place in Bel Air Heights, some kind of French chateau built back in the 1930s, made of ochre-colored sandstone with a gray slate mansard roof and multiple chimneys.

It's Old Hollywood. Ronald Coleman once took a shit here, or something. I'm surprised it hasn't been demolished and replaced with a forty-room monstrosity.

Joey da Nova is playing host to everyone on the production with a lavish party two days prior to the first day of filming. Caterers in pale blue uniforms tend to grilled meats on the patio. Bottles of wine stand in rows on crisp white linen tablecloths. A group of people cluster around the Steinway in the drawing room, singing show tunes, and young women in tuxedos distribute drinks and canapés.

There's security at the door—bullet-headed young men in neat navy blazers—collecting phones and anything else that might have a camera in it. Joey—or Dagmar—intends that no unflattering photos from this party will appear in tabloids or on websites.

It's a laughable idea. There are so many ways to sneak cameras into a private gathering like this that you can almost guarantee that if anybody has their screaming celebrity meltdown in public, video will appear on the entertainment news the next day.

Trust me on this. You could ask Melody Chastain, after the video appeared that showed her kicking the dog.

I'm following my contractual agreements and drinking Sprite. I'm not terribly fond of Sprite in truth, but it's clear, and it looks like it could have vodka in it, and I'm drinking it to make Dagmar nervous. But she hasn't arrived yet, so the effect is wasted.

I wander out by the pool, which is full of children. Among them are two of the kid actors who are going to be working with me.

I've been spending as much time as possible with the kids. I'm trying to develop a rapport with all of them, and it's not as easy as I hoped. I don't particularly know how to talk to children. The fact that I had no childhood of my own probably isn't helping.

So I end up spending time watching them interact with each other. Which is fine.

It turns out that while I was doing my training for *Celebrity Pitfighter*, talent searches were going on all over the world. The kids are from everywhere—India, China, South Africa, Chile, and Germany. Despite the diversity of their backgrounds, the kids have certain things in common. They're all between twelve and fifteen, and they're bright, attractive, smart, and charismatic. Because the parts require good English skills, they're all well educated. They're all from the elites in their own countries, and probably because of that they have a kind of glossy international affect—they're fairly at ease with foreigners, and with each other.

I adjust a poolside umbrella to provide me with some shade, and sit in a lawn chair and watch the kids in the pool. They're getting to know each other and having a good time.

They are so screwed, I think. They're young and hopeful and talented. Some of them may become big stars, and they'll all have dreams, and in time their dreams will be blasted apart, and their hearts will be broken and they'll feel like has-beens for the rest of their lives.

It's the process. It's inevitable. And it's not even as if I can tell them that this is going to happen, because they won't believe me.

I'm thinking about all this when a pair of thin legs appear by my chair, and I look up to see Nataliya Hogan, pouting in a bikini.

Nataliya is attractive, for a mutant. Her lips are too plump and her gray eyes are too big and her face is too long and her nose is too bumpy and too pointy. But somehow it all works, it's all strangely alluring. Her face is actually beautiful, if in much the same otherworldly way that an Afghan wolfhound is beautiful.

Her long graceful head, however, is placed on an anorexic Hollywood body. You can count her ribs. Her elbows are knobs on matchstick arms that look as if they belonged on an Auschwitz survivor. The AriPop swimsuit conceals breasts and hips that belong on a thirteen-year-old.

If there's one thing our business teaches young girls, it's how to upchuck your dinner into Tupperware and hide it under your bed. We could rename our town Bulimia City. And Nataliya Hogan is one of Bulimia City's willing victims.

Hollywood selects for certain physical traits in actresses: very tall, and ten to twenty pounds underweight. You meet one woman like that and you don't think much about it, but you see a whole crowd of them gathered in one place, like here at Joey's party, and you could be forgiven for thinking that a spacecraft from the Planet of the Supermodels had landed, and the invasion was under way.

It's not a physical type that particularly attracts me. I like women with breasts and hips. But casting directors never seem to take my preferences into account, and so Nataliya's type remains the standard by which others are judged.

Nataliya sulks as she looks at the pool, probably because she hoped to be the only person in it, so that she could bob around in her bikini and be the center of attraction. Instead there are all these foreign kids in the water.

"Who *are* they?" she asks.

"Your costars," I say. "Your costars' brothers and sisters. And the children of people who will be working on the picture."

She shakes her head. "I wonder if they'll leave."

"Don't worry," I tell her. "People will still admire your swimsuit even if you don't get it wet."

Nataliya accepts this without any consciousness of irony. She looks down at me and blinks.

"I've met you before," she says. "You were at Timmi's funeral."

My nerves give a little jump. Timmi's funeral is something I try not to think about.

"Yes," I say. "I was."

Her brows furrow. "What's your name again?"

I sigh inwardly. "Sean Makin."

Something clicks in her head, and all of a sudden I have her full attention as she realizes that I'm the star of her next picture. With great insight she realizes that I'm useful to her.

"I'm sorry!" she says. "I didn't recognize you!"

Never mind that I'm one of the most recognizable faces in Greater Los Angeles. "That's all right," I say.

"I think we have a couple scenes together," she says. She draws a chair up next to mine and sits. It's the first time she's ever voluntarily spoken to me.

I wouldn't want to give the impression Nataliya is stupid. She isn't, and people who do as well as she in this business generally have considerable intelligence, even if somtimes it's narrowly focused. In her case, her narcissism is so massive that it's swallowed up all her brains, like a black hole, and left only her ambition behind.

Much as I dislike her, I have to admit that her casting in the film has been inspired. She plays Colleen, the ditzy au pair who is supposed to be looking after Emil, the D.C.-based German diplomat's son who helps Roheen navigate the dangers of the American capital. Colleen is always texting her friends, oblivious of anything important in the house, and never notices that Roheen moves into the house she shares with Emil's family. Nataliya's otherworldly affect fits the character like a fine kidskin glove, another tribute to Joey's uncanny skill at casting.

Joey likes to burnish the minor characters in his films, as I found to my gratitude when I played small parts in *Sunlight and Shadow* and *Never the Reaper*, and I suspect he prodded Dagmar into shining up the role of Colleen so that it would suit Nataliya's gifts.

"I've been thinking a lot about my part," Nataliya says.

"It's a perfect gem," I tell her.

She pouts a little. "I think it can be developed more," she says. "I mean, I think there's a crisis going on in Colleen's life."

"Really?"

"Yes. She's always texting, she's trying to get people on the phone, but there's never any response." She widens her gray eyes and gazes at me with a kind of wonder, as if she's awakened to a new, magical, musical, Disney sort of day. "I think she's really *tragic*."

Laughter bubbles up my spine and threatens to burst out my nose. I can imagine the look that would cross Nataliya's face if that happens, and that's even more funny. I feel the mirth building in me like steam in a boiler. I pinch myself on the thigh to keep my mirth at bay, and then I clench my teeth with pain.

"What do you think is happening with her?" I say. Tears sting my eyes and I blink them away as fast as I can.

"Maybe she's been dumped by her boyfriend," Nataliya says. "Maybe she's pregnant. Maybe both." Her eyes get even bigger, and she gives a little gasp of awe at her own insight. "She works for a diplomat, right?" she says. "Maybe she's a *spy*. Maybe she's trying to get important information out to, I don't know, prevent terrorism or something."

She'd spent years playing a singing spy, maybe old plots are still thumping around inside her head.

"I think the spy story's too big for this movie," I say.

"The script could be changed," she says. "There could be rewrites." She leans closer, lifts her face to mine. "You don't think you could talk to the writer?"

"I don't know her that well," I say. I don't plan *ever* to know Dagmar well enough to advise her to rewrite the movie so it's about someone's character other than mine.

The pout again. "I tried talking to Joey. He said the part's already perfect, and that I'll be perfect in it."

I look at her. "I won't disagree."

She pauses a moment to preen. I feel inspiration descending on me like a ray from Heaven.

"Tell you what," I said. "I'm not very good at talking to people about these sorts of things. But I'd be happy to present Dagmar with an actual proposal."

She looks at me and makes what I believe is called a moue.

"What do you mean, a *proposal*." She says the word as if she'd never heard it before.

"A formal proposal, you know," I say. "In writing, with all of your reasoning laid out. Graphics, even. A whole package."

She blinks as she considers this. I've just presented her with a whole new way of viewing her problem.

"Do you think that would work?" she asks.

"Dagmar is a word person," I say. "Words have a good chance of convincing her. Email me the proposal, and I'll print it and make sure Dagmar gets it."

And Joey will get a copy, I think. *And Jaydee. And a whole lot of my other friends.* We'll gather together on cold nights around the fire, and we'll read aloud from Nataliya Hogan's masterwork explaining why the whole film should be rewritten so she can be a secret agent and maybe have a few musical numbers, and then we'll laugh so hard we'll forget to breathe.

One of Nataliya's posse turns up, a blond girl who's dressed in a less revealing version of Nataliya's bikini. Nataliya surrounds herself with people who are convinced that she's as important as she thinks she is, and who dress just like her, only not quite as well. I don't know where she finds them. The new arrival looks down at me and wrinkles her nose.

"Who's *this*?" she asks.

I sip my Sprite. "I'm the star of Nataliya's new picture," I say. "Who are you?"

"I—" She sort of flutters all over as she realizes she's made a gaffe. She takes a step behind Nataliya, as if for protection. "I'm Soren," she says.

"Pleased to meet you, Soren," I say. I'd like to think that my voice is cool and ominous, like that of a Mafia don quietly filing information away on someone who needs to have her wings, and probably the rest of her, clipped.

Soren looks at Nataliya. "Amber wants to talk to you. About the reception at the Huntingdon."

Nataliya looks at me. "I've got to go," she says.

I point a finger at her. "Don't forget to send the proposal," I say.

She nods at me and leaves. I stand up and wander off to the bar to get my Sprite refilled. When I come back I see Dagmar walk out onto the patio with her crew, Richard in his black clothes and white Converse sneaks, Ismet in gray slacks and a pressed long-sleeved sports shirt, and a big blond man in a light blue Lacoste retro polo shirt and soft washed denim. I recognize him as Helmuth, the man I know from my clubbing days. He's put on about twenty pounds since I last saw him.

I wander over, shake hands, smile, rattle my ice cubes. Dagmar, in stretch pants and a worn tee drawn tight over her pregnant belly, looks as if she has been dressed by Walmart. Dagmar looks at my Sprite with suspicion but doesn't comment. Helmuth recognizes me and reminisces about some night at the Got Real? with some girls I don't remember. I have the feeling that he's probably confusing me with someone else.

I tell Dagmar that I feel energized and ready to start on Monday. She tells me that she's glad to hear it.

"I'm glad one of my actors is ready," she says. "I've got to find a replacement for Torey Richardson."

Torey's the actor who's playing Arrick, the commander of the evil Steene. I know him slightly, but I haven't seen him on the set because I'm in only one scene with him, and that's at the end of the picture. When he's shooting, I'm at home, or training with Master Pak.

"What happened?" I ask.

"He went parasailing yesterday, landed wrong, and broke both legs."

"Jesus!"

She gives me a hard-eyed look. "You better not break any bones in that *Celebrity Pitfucker* show."

"From your lips to God's ears." I glance around the party. "Is Deeptimoy Srivastava going to be here?" I ask.

She's surprised, but handles it well.

"He's in the Persian Gulf somewhere," she says. "Supervising one of his foundations." She tilts her head back and looks up at me.

"How do you know I'm working with him?"

"I saw you together the day I auditioned." I lift my gaze to take in the whole scene poolside, the actors and crew, the caterers in their white uniforms, the kids in the pool...

"Is he financing all this?" I ask.

Dagmar grins. "Joey is."

"I mean the whole project."

Dagmar shrugs. "It's pushing the technology. Sri is all about pushing the technology."

She and her crew stroll away without having quite answered my question. I get my Sprite topped up at the bar and stroll over to the buffet to get some lovely grilled prawns with corn salsa. I find some shade beneath an awning and eat the prawns and watch the party. Jaydee Martin walks up to me and gives me a hug. She's wearing an oversized orange tropical shirt and has a glass in one hand and a bottle of Sailor Jerry rum in the other.

"Here," she says. "Have some love." She pours rum into my Sprite, overfilling and splashing onto my wrist. I repress the impulse to give a guilty start and dart glances in all directions.

"Could you look over my shoulder," I say, "and see if Dagmar's watching us?"

Jaydee lofts herself onto her toes to peer onto the patio. "She sure is," she says.

I make a point of ostentatiously pouring my drink into a nearby planter. The ficus seems none the worse. Jaydee is puzzled.

"What was that about?" she asks.

I tell her. Her blue eyes open wide in exasperation. "You can't *drink*?" she says.

"Not only that," I explain, "I can't have sex with underage girls."

She waves her glass and laughs. "What in hell is this world coming to?"

An idea crosses my mind. "Hey," I say, "I want to give you some money."

I put down my plate and dig into my pocket. I give Jaydee a hundred bucks.

"Buy some liquor for me, okay?" I say. "Keep it in Wardrobe for me."

"What do you want?"

I know that Jaydee's taste in wine leans to the kind that comes in cardboard boxes, so I say beer. Jaydee waves the Sailor Jerry under my nose.

"How about some of this?" she says. "Drink enough, you'll want to go out and get yourself a tattoo."

I give a violent start at the scent of rum. It has associations I'd rather forget. Jaydee looks at me oddly.

"The beer will be fine."

I pick up my plate of prawns, and eat a shrimp with the hand that had rum poured over it. I realize that I should wash that hand, otherwise I'm going to carry an alcohol reek for the rest of the day.

I chat with Jaydee for a bit, finish my prawns, and excuse myself. I go inside to one of the bathrooms, wash my hands until they smell of lilac soap instead of overproof rum, then mosey through Joey's chateau. I haven't been here before. Joey's paid a decorator to go with the French theme and to do things with open-beam ceilings, stone fireplaces, white plaster, and pre-rusted metal accents, but I can tell that Joey himself hasn't put much of his own identity into the mix. The place is as free of personality as a hospital room, in complete contrast to the old house on Parmenter Canyon that he shared with Timmi, which was full of books, papers, scripts, DVDs stacked precariously on every horizontal surface, and empty containers of Pringles rolling around on the counters.

I wonder if Joey has his actual life stashed somewhere else, his office maybe, or if this is really all that's left.

I step into one room and find Carter-Ann Dixon, MD, perched on an armchair amid a small circle of people. She wears a white blouse and a neutral beige skirt. It looks as if she's leading a group therapy session. More than that, it looks as if her group has been chosen to illustrate the ideals of the National Diversity Council. Circled along with her is an Asian woman in polyester, a burly black man in a tropical shirt, an East Indian man with gold-rimmed spectacles, and a woman with a face that seems to have come off a monumental Olmec head.

"Oh, sorry," I say, and start to back out of the room. Carter-Ann looks at me with one of her brilliant white smiles.

"That's all right, Mr. Makin," she says in her reedy Munchkin voice. "Let me introduce you to our group of consultants."

I shake the hands of Dr. Li, Professor Mthunzi, Dr. Godbole, and Professor Chaska. "Call me Sean," I say. I turn to Carter-Ann. "What is it that you're consulting about, again?"

She turns to me, her pose perfectly balanced, her hands folded in front of her. I fully expect her to brush me off. "We're planning to make you incredibly popular throughout the world," she says.

I'm so surprised that I can't manage a reply. I imagine hordes of Russians and Bengalis and Sudanese mobbing my appearances at airports, posters of my smiling face stuck up on walls in student dorms in Madagascar, millions in endorsements coursing into my bank account.

Carter-Ann's smile broadens. "I thought you'd approve," she says.

"I wish you every success," I say, and then hesitate. "Can I ask how you're planning to do this?"

"Well," she says, "first of all we're going to fine-tune your performance to appeal to the widest possible group of viewers."

A cold little icicle of suspicion touches my fantasy. I'm all for gaining the widest possible audience, but on the other hand, when I look around the room, I see that I'm the only actor here—it's not like I need a bunch of professors and doctors and headshrinkers telling me how to do my job.

Turn your palms out, Mr. Makin. Thank you so fucking much, Doctor.

"Then," Carter-Ann continues, "we'll preview your performance before selected test audiences throughout the world, just to make certain that they love you the way you deserve."

"And if they don't?"

She tips her head and gives a sweet smile. "We'll work together to fix it."

I'm appalled from my toes to the roots of my fast-fading hair. Not only is Carter-Ann going to be able to "fine-tune"—maybe even *dictate*—my performance, but if her test audiences don't like it, she'll be able to make me *do it over.*

I offer an uncertain grin. "That sounds complicated," I say.

"We'll try to make it simple."

"And the director," I point out, "is normally the person who, ah, fine-tunes the actors' performances." Because he's the *director,* I refrain from pointing out.

Her sweet smile is unaltered.

"Of course Mr. da Nova is in charge of the set," she says. "I don't anticipate any problems. At most I'll just have a few little comments to make."

She's so reasonable that I can almost see this working, right up to the point where she tells Joey that his work has to be scrapped and he's got to do it over. Then I'll dive for cover and hope not to get hit by the shrapnel.

"I'll look forward to working with you," I lie.

"I expect we'll have a lovely time," she says. I hope she's lying, too, because otherwise she's too naive to be real.

I make an exit and go looking for Joey. I find him by the bandstand, where a number of giant Polynesians are setting up their equipment. Joey is talking with Jean-Marc Barineau, the director of photography. Joey likes to work with the same people over and over again and Jean-Marc has been DP on most of his films.

Joey is five feet five inches tall, but with long arms and a pair of shoulders that would do credit to a football player. He has a rugged face, an olive complexion, dark curly hair, and a mat of tangled body hair that practically bursts out of his embroidered Mexican sailor shirt. He wears canvas trousers and sandals on his hairy feet.

Jean-Marc is an obese Frenchman with a five-day beard, dressed in Bermuda shorts and a faded Universal Studios T-shirt streaked with mustard stains. He's got a hot dog in one hand and in the other is a sixteen-ounce tumbler of white wine on the rocks.

He's not a pretty picture, but he makes pretty pictures in the camera—beautiful pictures in fact, balanced, harmonious, with lovely saturated color that soaks into the retina like the Tuscan landscapes of the Renaissance. Sometimes I think he's wasting his talent on Joey's pictures, particularly the later ones—but sometimes, even in a movie about fighting robots or superheroes, he finds moments of surprising beauty that, for a brief moment anyway, can bring the most hackneyed script to life.

"Hey, Joey," I say.

"Kiddo!" Joey wraps me in his long arms and gives me a hug.

Jean-Marc looks at me over the top of Joey's head. "I haven't seen you since Mac's funeral," he says.

"Has it been that long?" I look at Joey. "I thought you'd promised not to throw things at people."

Joey is currently being sued by a reporter who claims that Joey threw a cell phone at him.

"I don't know that Steve Pocket is a *person* exactly," Joey says. "He's a media titan, you know."

Joey steps back and asks me about *Mister Baby Head.*

"Still in litigation," I say.

"What a fucking circus," Joey says.

I've known Joey since I was eight years old, and we fall easily into our old, friendly relationship. We've always liked each other. Even after I killed his wife, we remained friends.

It goes without saying that he doesn't know it was I who killed Timmi. And it's my mission in life to keep him from finding out.

I look at Joey standing on the grass behind his French Provincial chateau, as desperate for work as I am. Employed by Dagmar, who judging by her script has a good grasp of story, maybe even as good a grasp on essentials as Timmi. Whether she can prevent Joey from wrecking it is another matter.

Behind Joey and Jean-Marc, the Polynesians begin tuning. Joey grins.

"South California Hawaiian Orchestra," he says. "I heard them play once, they're great."

"Good slack-string," Jean-Marc says approvingly.

"Are we ready for Monday?" I ask Joey. I've been consumed with learning my lines, but I'm sure Joey has a better idea how the actual production is going.

"Fuck, yes," Joey says. "There's nothing like throwing money at a project to get it on the rails."

"Who's throwing the money?" I ask. "Dagmar?"

A shriek of feedback from the musicians drowns Joey's reply, but I can lip-read the affirmative answer. Joey spins toward the bandstand and yells.

"What the *fuck*! You're gonna give my guests a fucking heart attack!"

"Sorry, bruddah," someone says.

"Jesus, be a little more careful!"

Any one of the Hawaiians could break half Joey's bones simply by falling on him, but they make pacifying gestures while he storms at them and punches the air.

"Maybe we should listen from farther away," Jean-Marc suggests. He is an old hand at dealing with Joey's temper.

"Yeah, fuck," Joey mutters.

We stroll toward the buffet. Joey puts an arm around my waist. He's cheerful now.

"How about you, champ?" he asks. "Are you ready for this?"

"I was born ready." Which falls under the heading *clichéd but true.*

Joey gets himself a piece of papaya. He takes a bite of it, then licks juice from his fingers.

"I just spoke to Dr. Dixon," I said. "She said she looks forward to working with us."

Joey's good mood evaporates instantly. "Head of the Psy-Ops Division?" he snarls. "Crazy bitch."

"She says she'll only have a few suggestions."

His eyes glitter as they look up into mine.

"She opens her fucking mouth," he says, "I'll rip her tits off."

Ah, I think. *This will be such a happy set.*

CHAPTER SEVEN

HEAVY LUGGAGE BLOG

Visitors are usually disappointed when they first find themselves on a movie set. For the most part nothing interesting is going on: people are moving lights or props around, or eating lunch, or waiting while some technical problem is solved. The actors, who are the people the visitors want to see, are either not present or aren't doing anything interesting, because they're in costume and makeup and can't risk getting mussed.

If visitors are present during actual filming, they have to remain still and silent while some strangely dressed people on a brightly lit set mumble dialogue the visitors can't hear, and do this over and over again while the cameras are moved from place to place and the microphones shift around. It's so unglamorous. It's dull. It's...*unlike the movies*! There's no magic, it's just a bunch of people doing their jobs.

Unlike most visitors, I love a movie set. I'm always interested in the way the various technicians go about their jobs, setting lights and capturing sound and giving fragile temporary sets the illusion of age and permanence. Cameras are fascinating, with their many glass eyes: they're now so light and flexible that they can soar overhead on booms or wires, or get a good picture in murky conditions.

Actors who seem just to be standing around are often working hard: they're trying to remember lines, firm up their characters, and decide how they're going to interact with other cast members in the next scene.

If you know what to look for, a film set is a fascinating place. I love being there, even when nothing is going on, because I know where to find the magic.

Comments (0)

INT. SEAN'S APARTMENT—DAY

I figure it's unlikely that I'll run into Lenny Castro at the supermarket, so one day, after we've both failed to complete the obstacle course that *Celebrity Pitfighter* has made us run—Burt Taylor, the bastard, won the event—I ask him over for drinks. I've recently purged my refrigerator, as per Dagmar's demands, so I have to take a trip to the package store on the way.

I pour us each a vodka and tonic, then take the couch and give Lenny the armchair with the Indian throw. He's unusual among *Celebrity Pitfighter* contestants in that he's not really an actor, but a singer: he made the quarterfinals of *American Idol* a decade or so ago, and his career has been marking time ever since. He's got dark Puerto Rican looks that look good on camera, so he's crossed over into commercials, television, and film, but nothing you'd remember. He starred in a TV series that got canceled three episodes into its run. In the meantime he's singing Latin jazz in the top clubs of Riverside and Palmdale.

"Are you working?" I ask. "Besides *Pitfighter*, I mean?"

"I auditioned for a commercial," he says. "And I'm singing here and there."

He's tall, only a couple inches under my height, and in good shape even though he's not in Des Andor's class. He's got a deep blue five o'clock shadow, and the lightest trace of an accent.

I've seen his fights, too, and he's very fast and very clever. He's won his two matches with submission holds that his opponents were too slow to see coming.

"I got lead in a feature," I say. "Not the real movies though—it's AR."

He nods. "Still, that's good. It's a feature, and it's the lead role."

I decide to approach the cheating cautiously. "You know," I say, "with both of us maybe going in front of the camera, we should go easy on each other during our fight."

He seems a little surprised. "How do you mean?"

I brush my cheek with my knuckles by way of illustration. "Not hit too hard to the face. Either of us show up for auditions with a broken nose or black eyes, we could lose work."

He thinks about this for a moment. "That's sensible. Yeah."

"Just do it better than Des did," I say. "He knew he wouldn't get hit in the face, so he didn't bother to guard the face at all."

His head gives a little jerk of astonishment. "Des made the same agreement with you?"

I flap a hand casually. "Oh, sure. The fights are so bogus anyway, it's silly to take risks. Not when they let a junkie like Jimmy Blogjoy into the matches."

I sip my drink and watch him while he absorbs the information. Finally he sighs and leans forward, resting his elbows on his knees.

"It's all crap," he says.

"It's all showbiz," I say. I cock my head and try to look as if I've just had a terrific idea. "You know, I bet we could choreograph a more exciting fight than the one we're actually going to have."

He just nods, thinking. I decide not to pursue that line, and shift to another.

"Have you ever played a villain?"

"I've played bad guys, sure."

"You heard that Torey Richardson broke his legs parasailing?"

He nods and takes a sip of his drink. I take a sip of my own, deliberately synchronizing my timing to his. I want to get our brain waves falling into the same patterns: I'll breathe when he breathes, sigh when he sighs, scratch my ear when he scratches his.

"Torey was in my feature," I say. "He played the villain, the guy I'm fighting for the whole movie. Now they're going to have to recast."

I'm simplifying—Roheen never fights Arrick, he just runs from him—but that's irrelevant, because Lenny looks up, intent interest on his face.

"The bad guy doesn't die at the end," I say. "They're saving him for the sequels they're planning. It could be an ongoing role in a successful franchise."

I blink at him, as if I've just been struck by a brilliant idea.

"I could mention your name to the producer," I say.

INT. SOUNDSTAGE—DAY

"Mr. da Nova, if I can make a suggestion." Carter-Ann's sweet tones chime across the set.

The words send my heart tottering toward despair.

"What's wrong, Dr. Dixon?" Joey asks. His tone is mocking, as is his use of her title.

"I wonder if Amir might reach toward Roheen." I peer past the lights and see Carter-Ann reaching out hesitatingly. "And then he gets a look at him and jumps back." She pulls the hand back.

"Dr. Dixon," Joey says, "we have had a long fucking day."

Which we have, here on the set of *The Life of Chester A. Arthur*. And I have spent much of the day on my belly in a kind of tunnel, with bits of dust and debris being rained on my head by the property master, who is positioned on a grid twelve feet above my head.

It's now Thursday of the first week of production, and Carter-Ann and Joey have been at one another's throats for the whole shoot, plus all the read-throughs and rehearsals. Joey works out what he wants, Carter-Ann makes one of her suggestions, and then they're at it hammer and tongs.

Things would be simpler if Carter-Ann's suggestions were not, on the whole, pretty good. I keep having to remind myself that she is in fact a psychiatrist, and therefore may have some insights into the ways people behave that she is able to translate into concrete proposals.

Joey and Carter-Ann have their argument, Joey cutting and corrosive, Carter-Ann patient and reasonable. The more patient she becomes, the greater his sarcasm. His face becomes stone, and his lips turn white. I half-expect him to have a heart attack on the spot.

While all this goes on, I lie in the dust, and await Carter-Ann's inevitable victory.

We are shooting the first meeting between Roheen and one of his juvenile supporters, a fourteen-year-old boy named Amir. Amir is played by a talented Indian youth named Samendra, who was the winner of a vast talent search that spanned the entire subcontinent and select parts of England and North America. Samendra crouches on the set a few yards from me, and watches the argument impassively, through Amir's gold-rimmed glasses. He's new to movie acting, and maybe he thinks all film sets normally ring with screaming arguments.

Amir's character has been devised to create the maximum possibility for identification with the Indian audience. Amir is a Muslim, which might enlist the sympathy of Indian and Pakistani Muslims and others; but he also lives in cosmopolitan New Delhi, so non-Muslim Indians are encouraged to identify with him. (In the event, Amir is played by a Hindu.) Amir is a dutiful son but with a hidden imagination: he's got a home computer loaded with his artwork, which features superheroes, science fiction, and characters out of Indian legend.

He and a school friend are returning from a school concert when a nearby building collapses. The friend, unable to get connectivity on his phone, runs to get help while Amir dashes into the building to rescue any survivors.

Unknown to these two, the building contained a Tellurian Gate through which Roheen and his team of researchers have just entered our world. The villainous Steene have destroyed the building and wrecked the gate, and only Roheen survives.

Amir encounters the stranger as Roheen is digging himself out of the wreckage. That is how I find myself in the tunnel, supposedly a part of the collapsed building, with the property master raining kibble on my head.

My struggles in the tunnel are not entirely feigned. It's close and hot in there, and I'm in my bulky Dr. Zaius jacket. I've been made up with fake blood on my face, as well as stripes of dirt. The dust makes it hard to breathe. And Joey calls for take after take as he works out the best angle to reveal my desperation and to conceal the fact that the way the rubble often bounces shows it's made of foam blocks that wouldn't harm a hamster.

As the scene was first shot, Amir crawls into the shattered building, calling out to any survivors in Hindi-Urdu. At first he sees only my arm and the top of my head and runs to help, and then Roheen looks up, with his inhumanly broad forehead and strange proportions and glittering eyes, and Amir takes fright and hides while Roheen frees himself.

Carter-Ann wants to give them a little more interaction—she wants Amir to reach out toward Roheen, take fright, then overcome his fear and reach out again, snatching his hand back at the last second. It's a nice little character moment for Samendra, but Joey hates it because it's not his idea, and the argument goes on and on.

"Look," I shout finally. "Either reshoot the fucker or get me the hell out of here!"

That stops Joey's complaints for a moment.

"Why don't we just give it a try?" Carter-Ann says in her cheerful warble.

So we do. Once Joey commits to the new approach, he behaves with complete professionalism. Jean-Marc maneuvers the Steadicam through the rubble with fluid grace. For the most part I'm a bystander, because the new shots are all about Amir.

As we rehearse, Joey reminds me how well he works with children. First he explains to Samendra what he wants his character to do—how to move, how to gesture, what expression Amir should have on his face. Then he explains the *why* behind it, what Amir is seeing, what he's feeling. Samendra is quick to understand. The rehearsals go well.

"Final checks!" calls the first assistant director, a new guy named Clarke I've met only at the first day's shooting. He has a big voice, glasses, and receding hair, and that's all I know about him.

People dash in to check my makeup, and Jean-Marc rearranges the dust and rubble on the set.

"Picture is up!" calls Clarke. "Quiet, please!" The set falls silent. I conjure up my character, let Roheen look out through my eyes.

"Turnover," Clarke calls, to start cameras and sound. Then, "Smack it!" The clapper-loader runs onto the set with his slate, bangs the clapper, and runs out of the frame.

"Set," says the camera operator.

"Action!" Joey calls, and Roheen takes over.

It's another hour before I'm allowed to finally crawl out of my tunnel. Jean-Marc has the camera down low, shooting from Amir's point of view, as I heave myself out of the rubble and unfold my body, rearing up and up like a giant, angry cobra. There's an electrician there with an eye light to beam a menacing red glitter into my eyes. I take a step toward the camera/Amir, hands coming up as if to crush the life out of him...and then I recognize that he's only a frightened child. Roheen hesitates, and for the first time the audience sees his humanity.

At this moment of revelation, I remember to turn my instep out, even though the camera is on my face and the audience won't see it.

The reveal is crucial, so we shoot it over and over until Joey and Jean-Marc and I all agree that I've got it right. Carter-Ann must like it too, because she doesn't say anything.

There are more shots that follow, Amir and Roheen together in the shattered building, building a tentative sense of trust. Roheen digs for his comrades until he finds a woman—an extra all bloodied up for the occasion—and then the camera moves in close as Roheen realizes that she and the rest of his team are dead. I try to let shock and tragedy radiate from my face, my posture. I figure Roheen and the woman had something special between them, though that's not explicit in the script. Joey tells me I'm not doing it big enough, and after the next take he says it's too big. Eventually he tells me it's good, and then we're on to the next bit, where Roheen hears emergency vehicles coming, and runs off with Amir following, and then—because it's nearing the point in the day when all the union crew are going to start billing vast amounts for overtime—Joey calls a wrap for the day. I make a point of telling Samendra that he did a great job—and then I tell the same thing to his mother, a petite Indian lady in a sky-blue suit who has been sitting quietly out of everyone's way the whole day long.

"Who is this Dr. Dixon?" she demands. "She is a terrible person!"

"I don't know myself." I shrug, and head for Makeup to get my face clean.

Dirty and tired as I am, I am deeply thrilled by the fact that this film isn't being shot on location. After *Family Tree* was canceled, I made two movies in foreign countries, one in Puerto Vallarta and the other on the island of Rhodes. They were quick exploitation films, intended to capitalize on the popularity of *Family Tree.* The idea behind each of these films was to take my sitcom character and drop him into a romantic comedy taking place in an exotic location that the sitcom couldn't afford, so that viewers would feel the story open out into the exotic background and think they were getting their money's worth. I played characters who were more or less identical to Brent Schuyler, but with different names.

I hated being on location. I hated the dust and the bugs and the hot sun. I hated all the foreigners around me talking in foreign languages and causing inexplicable foreign delays and complications, and I knew that I could get better Mexican and Greek food in California than I could in Mexico or Greece.

I don't see the point of travel at all, not when I live in Southern California, which already has everything anyone would want. And on top of that, the movies had terrible scripts and mediocre directors, and nobody wanted to pay box-office prices to see Brent

Schuyler when they could get him on television for free. The movies cratered, and took my career with them.

But at least I got to stay in California, the only place to live in the whole world.

I trudge toward my trailer. The dust and blood and grime on my skin are fake, but the fake stuff is no more fun than real dust, blood, and grime, so I'm relieved to get the makeup off. Then I trudge over to Jaydee's domain to return my costume.

Dressers help me off with the costume and would probably help me into my regular clothes, except that I shoo them out of the fitting room. They like me because I don't make them walk back and forth to my trailer to carry the costume away.

The costume department has blossomed with cutters and fitters and assistants and with hundreds of costumes on racks. Even a modest production requires a ridiculous number of costumes, and this production is far from modest.

Once I'm in my civvies again, Jaydee invites me into her office. The walls are pinned with costume designs and with samples of fabric, and one wall is taken up by a huge chart showing which costumes need to be ready by which dates. Below the chart is a fifty-gallon cooler, and Jaydee pops the top and fishes a Double Swan Porter out of the ice. I take a moment to wonder what a Double Swan is, and then I drop into a chair and take a drink.

Jaydee opens a bottle for herself. "How're things?" she asks.

I consider my answer. On the one hand, the atmosphere on the set is poisonous, with the continual vicious arguments between Joey and Carter-Ann. On the other, *I'm working!* I'm working, I'm doing what I was born to do, and I know I'm doing it well.

Even at the end of the day, I'm more exhilarated than not. I'm thinking about my scenes all the time, ways to make them better, ways to reveal Roheen to the viewers.

I'm having the best time I've had in years.

"It's great," I say.

Jaydee lifts a thickly painted eyebrow. "Even with the fighting on the set?"

I wave a hand. "I'm not the one doing the fighting." I decide to shrug. "And we seem to be getting a better movie out of it."

"And Dr. Dixon?"

I sigh. "She comes off as a cross between Kristin Chenoweth, Mister Rogers, and a Nazi grammar-school nun, but she does actually seem to know her job."

"Everyone hates her."

"*I* hate her." I take a swallow of Double Swan. "But what can I do?"

Jaydee gives a wicked grin. "You'd better pray that Joey doesn't knock her block off."

"In the Battle of the Dwarfs," I say, "my money's on Carter-Ann."

"I'm not so sure." Jaydee looks thoughtful for a moment. "Joey's not the same man he was."

I look a question at her. Jaydee gives a little grimace, pulling her lips back from her teeth. "Joey's changed, that's all. Timmi's death, the pictures that flopped... he's a lot angrier than he used to be."

And desperate, I think. I know how that feels.

"This is his way back," I say. "He won't want to screw it up."

"He never had much impulse control." Jaydee sighs and takes a long drink from her bottle, then looks at me. "You know he was seeing Anna Tupolev."

"Yeah. They broke up."

"That's because he hit her. He beat the shit out of her."

I'm stunned. I don't know what to say.

"He was drunk," Jaydee continues, "and he bought her a Bugatti by way of apology, but that was the end of the relationship."

My mouth is dry. "I imagine so," I say, and take a gulp of Double Swan.

Jaydee shakes her head. "Lord knows I love the man, but still..."

Silence hangs in the air for a while. I finish my beer, and stand to get another.

A grin tugs at Jaydee's lips. "Joey showed me Nataliya's proposal."

"A good read, wasn't it?" I get a beer from the cooler and open it.

"Did you really talk her into writing it?"

"I hardly had to talk her into anything."

Nataliya's proposal arrived by messenger a little over twenty-four hours after I'd made the suggestion, in time for the first day of production. It was a professionally produced work, twelve pages long, profusely illustrated, and heavy on the bullet points. She must have had a whole team of her minions working on it.

The contents were hilarious. The first set of bullet points ran as follows:

- Nataliya Hogan is a name recognized across the world.
- She is an accomplished actress.
- Eleven of her songs have charted on the Billboard Hot 100.
- Nataliya is familiar with the world of spycraft.
- Nataliya Hogan is therefore ideal as the protagonist of a film based on espionage and intrigue, preferably with musical interludes.

"I think it was her familiarity with the world of spycraft that got me," Jaydee says. "That's when I started laughing. And after that, I couldn't stop."

"Yeah," I say. "Spies are so very well known for bursting into song at moments of crisis."

I talk with Jaydee for a couple more beers, then say goodbye and amble over to my trailer. I don't have to worry about driving while drunk, because Dagmar has got me a car and driver. I can cruise from Burbank to the studio in peace and quiet, while studying the script, learning my lines, and drinking a very nice latte the driver has bought for me ahead of time.

And, if someone in an SUV tries to crash into me, I'll have a professional driver and a very large car to help protect me.

My day isn't over. I've still got an hour of training with Master Pak before I can go home, have dinner, and learn my lines for tomorrow. *Celebrity Pitfighter* just won't go away. And I'm not the only one working late—as I walk to my trailer, Joey is still working, along with Allison, who's edited all his films since the beginning.

Because it's done electronically instead of the old-fashioned way, by splicing film together, film editing can now be done very quickly and efficiently. I know that Joey doesn't leave for home until every bit of the day's work that can be edited *has* been edited, after which it can be sent to Jane Haskill for scoring.

I'm glad I don't have Joey's job. My hours are bad enough.

I leave the costume department only to run into Dagmar and the line producer, a man named Sawicki. He tries to maintain a kind of dapper John Waters thing, complete with the thin little mustache, but his eyes have blue-black pouches under them and he has a wide lipless frog mouth that droops in an expression of perpetual anxiety.

"Hi there," I say.

Dagmar looks at me and I felt a sudden unease as I realize that I am probably surrounded by a cloud of beer fumes.

"I understand you're responsible for Nataliya's little essay," Dagmar says.

"It was my idea," I say, "but she was the one who wrote it. Or hired the writers. Whatever."

"It was funny as hell," she says. "But don't do it again. I don't want to have to deal with her if she ever realizes she was played."

"Roger-dodger," I warble cheerfully, and then mentally kick myself in the shins. The alcohol has thrown me just enough off-balance that, as Nataliya Hogan might put it,

- I'm acting like a goof, but
- I'm still sober enough to *know* that I'm acting like a goof, therefore
- I'm in danger of overreacting to my own goofiness and acting in a bizarre or inappropriate way, which

- might be taken for drunkenness,
- which would piss off my employer, and what's worse is that
- I probably reek of beer anyway, and therefore
- Oh Christ, I'm fucked.

"We wanted to talk to you about the problems on the set," Sawicki says.

"Okay," I say. I figure I'm probably safe as long as I keep saying "Okay."

"How bad is the situation between Joey and Carter-Ann?" Dagmar asks.

"Bad," I say. "But it's producing results."

Sawicki blinks up at me anxiously. "You aren't feeling threatened or anything?"

I consider explaining that even with my modest martial training I have little to fear from either of the Tiny Titans, but I decide against expressing this complex an idea in my current state, and stick to simple English sentences.

"Nobody's going to hit *me*," I say.

Dagmar looks at me intently. "Has anyone on the set threatened to hit anyone?"

"Not while I've been there."

"I can hear Joey screaming when he's in his office," Sawicki says.

"That's Joey's creative process," I tell him. "It's normal."

"Maybe you should sit in on the set," Dagmar tells Sawicki. "See if you can calm everything down."

Sawicki looks horrified. "I'm the *line producer*," he says. "I can't tell the talent what to do!"

Dagmar rolls her eyes. "Right," she says. "I'll come on the set myself."

Wonderful, I think. Because what we need on this set is *another boss*.

They start walking toward my car, and I find myself falling into step with them. I turn to Dagmar, who is walking along thoughtfully, one hand resting lightly on her pregnant stomach.

"Can I ask a question?"

"Sure," she says.

"How many people were up for the part besides me?"

She frowns at me. "Maybe half a dozen names came up."

"How many did you test?"

"Just you."

I blink. "Why only me?" I ask.

"You were the one Joey wanted," Dagmar says, and then smiles. "Plus," she adds, "you gave a damn good test."

"Oh," I say. "Thanks."

She says nothing, just gives a half-wave as she leaves me at my car. As I get in the Lincoln, I realize that this is the first time Dagmar has ever complimented me on anything.

Maybe, I think, *she's actually beginning to like me. Maybe I'm growing on her.*

I think pleased thoughts about this all the way home. I'm in a sunny mood till next afternoon, which is when I hear that Jaydee has been murdered.

ACT 2

CHAPTER EIGHT

Our Reality Network

Live Feed

LadyDayFan says:

Hey folks. I've just seen a notice in the Movie and TV Production Guide. As follows:

> THE LIFE OF CHESTER A. ARTHUR (Docudrama, Great Big Idea), Los Angeles. Seventh Symphony Casting, 10203 W. Pico Blvd., Bldg. 310, L.A., CA 90064.

Could this be our Dagmar making a film about the 21st president? Or did someone else in L.A. have a Great Big Idea?

Hanseatic says:

Could this be a trailhead for Dagmar's new game?

Corporal Carrot says:

This seems suspicious, if for no other reason that I doubt anyone's actually making a movie about President Arthur. Maybe one of us should show up at the audition.

LadyDayFan says:

It doesn't give a time.

Corporal Carrot says:

Call for an appointment?

Hippolyte says:

I'll just go. That's near where I work.

Corporal Carrot says:

I don't know why they *wouldn't* make a movie about Chester Arthur. I just looked him up, and he's pretty interesting.

INT. SOUND STUDIO—DAY

The morning is taken up with a chase scene on foot through the winding alleys of New Delhi. This is done on a green screen set, the whole structure completely covered in material of a uniform shade of green. When the film is edited, scenes of New Delhi will be keyed in to replace the green material, and we'll appear to be in the middle of the Indian capital.

Some of the New Delhi shots are taken by Delhi cameramen hired for the purpose, but most of the New Delhi neighborhoods were built entirely of zeroes and ones. Dagmar has crowdsourced all the CGI—there are little special effects studios all over the world, many underemployed, many of which are capable of coming up with a New Delhi street, alley, pakora stand, or neighborhood. Dagmar and Helmuth weeded through their offerings and offered payment for the stuff they liked, the actual fee depending on the length, the complexity of the programming, and the willingness of the programmers to accept a percentage of the gross instead of payment up front.

Dagmar is on the set for the morning shoot, though for once everything proceeds in a businesslike manner, and she doesn't have a chance to witness any battles between Carter-Ann and Joey. Maybe her presence calms things down, or maybe it is the fact that Carter-Ann has no suggestions to offer.

After lunch in the trailer, I get my makeup touched up and report to the set just as Clarke is calling out, "Waiting on talent!"

"Talent is here," I say.

Clarke doesn't change expression. "Waiting on gaffers!" he calls.

After the gaffers finish shifting the lights around, we start the exposition scene with Amir, after we've just escaped the Steene. It's the same scene I used in my audition, when I had to pretend the chair was Amir.

Instead of the chair we have Samendra, who has a harder time than the chair getting into his character. The kid's just too mellow for someone who's just escaped a gang of otherworldly assassins. Joey takes him aside and talks to him about how he's got to be more nervous, and I stand and wait and try to keep my own edge.

Carter-Ann walks up. "Mr. Makin," she chirps, "may I make a suggestion?"

"Of course."

"When you're talking to Samendra, could you make this gesture?"

She raises her hand with the forefinger and thumb forming a circle, the rest of the fingers straight.

"Chest-height," she says, demonstrating. "Palm out. Just hold it a second or two."

I try this. Carter-Ann seems to approve.

"Why am I doing this?" I ask.

"It's a Buddhist teaching mudra," Carter-Ann says. "Use it when you're giving Amir important information."

I know about mudras from my mother's spiritual investigations. "You're trying to give me credence with Buddhists," I say.

She looks up at me with a white-toothed smile. "Exactly," she says.

"Okay," I say. It's a little daffy, but I don't mind. The more Buddhist fans I have, the better.

We start the scene. I'm down on one knee, talking with Samendra on his level. He isn't keyed up enough, so Joey rushes in from his blind side and gives a yell to startle him. Samendra jumps and from that point he's okay.

"Cut," Joey says at the end of the shot, and then he looks at me. "One more take, and this time without the jack-off sign."

I'm blank. "The what?"

Joey forms a ring with his finger and thumb. "The jack-off sign."

"Mr. da Nova," Carter-Ann says, "it's a Buddhist teaching mudra."

"It's like he's making a sign for mutual masturbation!" Joey says. "You don't want your hero showing that to a juvenile!" He sneers. "Jesus, we'll all go to jail!"

And they're off. While the argument snarls back and forth, I get to my feet and walk off the set to look for a water bottle I've set on a ledge. I uncap and drink, and then I see Dagmar talking with Ismet and Sawicki the line producer. They have their heads together and look serious, and I figure it's got to be damned important if they're ignoring the fight that's going on a few feet away.

They break, and Sawicki goes hustling past me. I grab his arm.

"What's happening?" I ask.

"I've got to replace the wardrobe mistress," he says, and then pulls away. I grab him again.

"What's happened to Jaydee?" I ask. A whole series of possibilities goes through my mind, most of them having to do with alcohol: a drunken auto accident; drunk and passed out on the job; in the hospital with the d.t.'s.

"She's been killed," Sawicki says.

I'm too surprised to stop him when he pulls away again. I turn to Dagmar, and walk to her.

"Jaydee's been killed?"

"Hit and run," Dagmar says. "A car jumped the curb in front of her house and ran her down."

"Cripes!" I stare at her. "When?"

"Last night, apparently. She didn't turn up in Wardrobe this morning, and Sawicki called and couldn't reach her, so I sent one of her assistants to her house to see if she needed waking up. There was crime scene tape over the lawn and some evidence techs taking pictures of tire prints, and they told her what happened, and she went to the morgue and identified her."

I can see the morgue, cold tiles and refrigerated cabinets, reflected in Dagmar's eyes. Maybe, with her history, she's been in a lot of morgues.

"Did they catch the guy?" I ask.

"I don't know." Dagmar looks up at me. "Do you know her next of kin?"

"She's got an ex-husband somewhere. Also three grown children, but I don't know how to reach them."

Dagmar looks up, and for the first time she seems to become aware of Joey striding about the set growling, while Carter-Ann watches him from her balanced stance, her hands folded in front of her.

"Jesus," Dagmar mutters. "What's this about?"

"The Buddhist mudra of teaching," I say.

She gives me an incredulous look, then steps onto the set.

"What's going on?" she asks.

Both try to explain, but Joey has a louder voice. "It's the freakin' Buddhist wanking sign!" he says.

"How long is the shot?" Dagmar asks.

"Thirty-five seconds," Jean-Marc says from the sidelines.

"Thirty-five *seconds*?" Dagmar asks. "Why are you wasting time? Shoot it both ways, and if we look at the mudra in dailies and it looks weird or suggestive, we just won't use that take."

"Fuck yeah!" Joey says. Apparently he thinks Dagmar's agreeing with him.

Dagmar gives him a cold look.

"If I have to mediate a dispute, I want it to be about something bigger than a thirty-second shot. You're wasting everyone's time."

"That's what I keep *saying*," Joey said. "I just want to get *on* with it, with no interference!"

Apparently Dagmar decides there's no reasoning with Joey when he's secreting testosterone at this rate. "Just take the damn shot," she says, and walks off the set.

I'm only paying partial attention to the dispute, because I'm still trying to process Jaydee's being killed. Some useless bastard in a car, drunk probably or high, jumped his car over the curb and killed her.

I hope she didn't suffer. I hope she didn't linger, like Timmi, for hours, unable to call for help.

I feel Joey's hand on my arm. "Hey, champ. We're getting ready for the shot."

"Jaydee's been killed," I tell him, and while he stares at me I walk past him onto the set and kneel next to Samendra.

I'm thinking about hit-and-run. I'm thinking about Timmi's getting killed, about the black SUV that's tried to run me down.

Jaydee's getting run down on her own lawn doesn't make any sense. She lived in a quiet part of Studio City, in the hilly country backed up against the park: people don't drive madly through those quiet residential streets. It would be impossible, for one thing—the roads are too twisty.

Clarke calls for quiet and the camera moves in close. I try to summon Roheen. Joey calls for action. I hesitate.

"Line," I say.

"'Are you all right?'" reads the script supervisor.

"Are you all right?" I say.

"I'm not hurt," Samendra responds.

I wonder whether the person who tried to kill me is now trying to kill my friends. I wonder if Jaydee got killed because the guy in the SUV missed twice.

I hesitate too long before giving my next line.

"That's okay," says Joey. "Start again."

"Are you all right?" I say.

"I'm not hurt," Samendra says.

Again I hesitate. My mind is blank. "Line," I say.

"Cut!" Joey's call interrupts the script supervisor before she can begin. There's a silence, and then Joey comes onto the set. He puts his hand on my shoulder.

"Do you need a moment?" he asks.

"Yes," I say. "Yes I do."

I stand up and walk off the set and leave the soundstage. Joey probably didn't intend for me to leave the building, but he doesn't stop me. I go to the Wanderlodge that I use as a dressing room and sit in the chair where I have my makeup done in the morning, and I look at myself in the mirror.

My face is covered again with fake blood and dirt, because in the movie it will only have been a few minutes since I escaped from the wrecked warehouse. I look like death. I look as if the killer hit me instead of Jaydee.

It occurs to me that Jaydee was probably my oldest friend. I've known her since I was eight. I met her before I met Joey, before I met Timmi. Anyone I knew before then, I've long since forgotten.

I try to remember that first wardrobe fitting, but it blurs with all the others. I remember Jaydee efficiently adjusting my clothes, a laugh in her voice and the smell of sweet vermouth on her breath.

My mind whirls. I try to work out if I'm the one responsible for Jaydee's death. I don't know.

I can't see how. Even if the guy in the black SUV is crazy, I can't imagine him crazy enough to aim at Jaydee. Of all the people leaving the set at night, why her?

And then the ice-cold finger of paranoia touches my heart. *Jaydee was hiding my beer.* Dagmar saw me leaving Wardrobe on the previous day in a state of intoxication. Dagmar hated alcoholics on account of her father.

What if Dagmar had Jaydee clipped in order to keep me sober?

It's an insane thought, but then terrorists aren't supposed to be exactly the most levelheaded people in the room.

I decide that the safest thing is to quit drinking for real.

INT. ALDRIDGE FUNERAL HOME—DAY

Jaydee was reported dead on the first Friday in June, and the weekend is lost waiting for the next of kin to make arrangements. In the end the funeral is postponed to the following weekend so that everyone from the production can attend.

The funeral home is built along the lines of a Spanish mission church, with white plaster, open beams, and high windows with Romanesque arches. Jaydee's daughter and two sons are there, with their families. There is a minister I doubt Jaydee ever met in life, who discourses on her general goodness and her achievement as a loving parent. He informs us that we are celebrating her life rather than mourning her death.

Speak for yourself, I think. The light that was Jaydee is out. I've been depressed all week.

I'm too young to be as accustomed to funerals as I am.

The minister assures us that there is a Plan at work. That's what I'm afraid of. I'm afraid that whoever killed Jaydee has plans to take out more of my friends.

Eventually the minister opens a prayer book and gets around to the ritual. *Flesh and blood cannot inherit the kingdom of God, neither doth corruption inherit uncorruption. Behold, I show you a mystery.*

Yeah, sounds like a mystery all right. I make the Buddhist sign of wanking and stop listening.

After the service we troop off to another room in the funeral home, a beige barnlike place with stained glass windows set high in the walls. A line of trestle tables holds a buffet. The air is heavy with the scent of coffee. I express my condolences to Jaydee's children, who are all ten to fifteen years older than me, and then take a plate of cookies and a plastic glass of fruit punch off into the gloomiest corner I can find.

Jean-Marc is already there, along with Jane Haskill, who scores all of Joey's films. I never see her around the production, since she works from home, writing and performing the scores on a synthesizer. She's around fifty, with graying hair, prominent teeth, and glasses on a beaded string around her neck. Her dress sense usually runs to ragged cardigans and worn denim, but now she's in a long-sleeved black Ralph Lauren dress that looks good on her.

Normally she really doesn't start her work until the film has been edited into something like its final form, but since the deadlines on this production are so tight, I presume she's been in a writing frenzy all this time.

I ask her about this, and she confirms my premise. "I'm doing a fairly minimalist score, fortunately," she says. "A lot of subdued percussion, and then I've given leitmotifs to the major characters and situations, so I can just throw variations of these onto the soundtrack when I'm out of ideas."

"What motif am I?" I ask.

"*Da-da-da-duaa ta-ta-ta-ta,*" she vocalizes. "But when Amir first gets a look at you we move into a minor key, *da-da da-duaa ta-ta-ta-ta.*"

"Gee," I say, impressed. "I must be scary."

"You sure as hell are." Jane grins. "Haven't you seen the dailies?"

"I don't watch dailies," I say. They make me too self-conscious, too aware of my own limitations and flaws.

Jane picks a vanilla cream cookie off my plate. "I get them as soon as Joey and Allison finish their edits—next morning usually."

"It must help that we're shooting more or less in sequence."

Most films are shot in whatever order is convenient—for example all shots at one location, or on a particular set, are done at the same time, no matter where they are placed in the film; the editor stitches them in the right order afterward. But because *Escape to Earth* is going to be serialized, it's being shot more or less in chronological order. It's easier on everyone, the actors particularly, because we don't have to jump around inside our characters' arcs, and try to remember how our character is different from the character of the previous scene.

Shooting in sequence also allows Joey to rehearse us all thoroughly, which we're all finding very helpful.

Jane looks at me narrowly.

"I last saw you at Mac's funeral, didn't I?"

"I'm afraid so," I say. "We should try to meet on a more cheerful occasion."

"Let's have dinner or something," Jane says, "next weekend."

Jean-Marc seems gloomy even for a funeral. He's dressed in a coat and tie, but he hasn't shaved in several days, and his eyes are beginning to sag with weariness. By the end of production he'll look like something hit by a truck.

"That's three suspicious deaths in a row," he says.

I give him a startled look. It's a reaction fueled by pure guilt: for a half-second, I'm convinced he's accusing me of all three.

But no. He's not being a detective, he's just melancholy.

"Timmi, Mac, and now Jaydee," Jane says.

Jean-Marc gestures with one hand. "Suffering and death is of course the human condition," he says. "That is natural, that is the case of the universe. But my friends don't seem to die of cancer or heart disease—only these strange accidents."

"In Jaydee's case it wasn't an accident," I point out.

Jean-Marc looks at me. "No?" he says.

"Well—" I hesitate, and put my thoughts in order. "Have you been to Jaydee's house?"

They both shake their heads.

"It's a little house on a cul-de-sac in Studio City. It's a hilly residential neighborhood. Those streets south of Ventura follow the curve and slope of the hills. They're twisty and quiet—people don't go drag racing there." I look at Jean-Marc. "What was the hit-and-run driver doing on that little street? He had to have been waiting there."

They look at me with blank fascination. Jean-Marc recovers first.

"What of the motive?" he asks. "Why would someone kill her?"

I raise my hands. "No idea."

"Did she have a lot of money?" Jean-Marc's first thought is to blame the heirs.

"That house was worth quite a lot, I suppose," Jane says, "but not a fortune. Not split three ways."

"People kill each other for two dollars," says Jean-Marc.

Jane takes another cookie from my plate. "If this were a mystery novel," she says, "they'd all be connected."

I happen to know that they're not, because I was responsible for the first death myself, but I'm not going to offer that bit of information.

Jane nibbles my cookie. Jean-Marc shakes his head. "Too many years have gone by," he says. "It's what– five or six years since Timmi's death? And three since Mac went off the cliff."

Not a cliff, actually—the balcony. In the wake of his latest divorce, Mac was renting a house on Cliffside Drive in Malibu, and one rainy winter day he was found washed up on the rocks below the house. There was no sign of foul play, though of course the sea and the rocks had given his body such a battering that there was no way to know if he'd been whacked on the head before being dumped in the ocean. In the absence of any evidence to the contrary, it was assumed he was on a balcony slippery with drizzle, leaned out too far, and tumbled over, aided perhaps by his blood-alcohol content of 0.09. His death began the legal scrapping between his partners and his survivors over *Mister Baby Head*, the film in which he'd directed me.

"If you want to kill someone," Jean-Marc says, "you don't wait so many years. Sooner or later, you're going to stop being angry."

"Besides," Jane says, "what do they all have in common? A writer, a director, a costume designer—colleagues, yes, but they can't all be sharing some great secret that has to be suppressed."

I sip my fruit punch. The ice has melted and the taste is watery.

I try not to think of what it was that Timmi, Mac, and Jaydee had in common.

Me.

CHAPTER NINE

Our Reality Network

Live Feed

Hippolyte says:

I think our question about what Great Big Idea is up to has just been solved. A big billboard has just gone up on Sunset advertising a movie called *Escape to Earth*. "Going Live Worldwide July 28."

There's a sem@code on a corner of the poster that leads to this address, which gives instructions for getting an account and downloading the movie when it becomes available.

I've checked Online Hollywood, which reports Dagmar Shaw and Ismet Kadri as executive producers. The film stars Sean Makin, Nataliya Hogan, and a host of unknowns.

Hanseatic says:

That film has been advertised widely in Europe for weeks.

Corporal Carrot says:

Was it Sean Makin who played Luggage Boy? Or was it the other kid?

Consuelo says:

Have you seen what Sean Makin looks like now? Here's a photo.

Hippolyte says:

Oh my.

Corporal Carrot says:

He's on *Celebrity Pitfighter* now.

Hanseatic says:

Please tell me there isn't a TV show called *Celebrity Pitfighter*.

Consuelo says:

Makin's got a blog. We should look there for trailheads to any new ARG.

INT. ARENA—NIGHT

Whoooooo. The primal sound of the crowd tries to lift me into the air. I keep my feet planted on the canvas, and my mind focused on the script.

Lenny Castro and I have outlined three rounds of slam-bang entertainment. We haven't been able to actually rehearse it, but we pretty well know what we're going to do. And if any of it looks awkward, it's because we're new to the martial arts.

Our handicap consists of a fifty-pound medicine ball we're hauling behind us on a strap. We have to be careful backing up because we could trip over the thing. I consider using the strap as a weapon, a strangling cord maybe, but I decide not to try that kind of improvisation.

We throw punches and kicks, and when we start to get tired, we grapple for a while. I take a few shots here and there, because we're making it look real; but it's nothing I'm going to regret, and nothing that's going to leave a big bruise on my face.

Halfway through the third and last round, I lock up Lenny's arm as we're standing, and then I fall backward to throw him over his head. It's a really spectacular throw, with Lenny doing almost a somersault in the air, and the crowd roars in delighted surprise. Next thing you know I'm on top of Lenny in the half-mount, and I'm tightening up the armlock called the kimura. Lenny surrenders. The crowd goes nuts.

I'm going to the finals. God, it's great to be a winner.

And the best part is that I've got all summer to work out how I'm going to beat Burt Taylor in the final. Recorded episodes of *Celebrity Pitfighter* will stretch into August, and then the final fight will be broadcast live. All I've got to do in the interim is train, and I don't have to worry about getting damaged while *Escape to Earth* is shooting.

It's the best of all possible worlds.

INT. SOUNDSTAGE—DAY

Nataliya looks at me blankly. "Who are you?"

"I'm a friend of Emil."

Her eyes narrow. "Aren't you a little *tall* to be a friend of Emil?"

"I—" I hesitate. "I could try to be shorter."

"Ring ring," says Clarke, from off camera.

"Your phone's ringing," I tell her. They'll dub in the actual ring tone later, in postproduction.

Nataliya half-turns to the cell phone on the kitchen counter, then turns back to me, then turns to the phone again. She holds up a hand.

"Wait there," she says, and reaches for the phone so she can retrieve her text message.

It's a moment of comedy in what has up till now been a mostly serious film. Over the course of June and July, Act I, built around New Delhi and Amir, has progressed to Act IV, built around Washington, D.C., and Emil, another of Roheen's juvenile friends, the son of a German attaché.

In the current scenario, I've been living for several nights in the basement of Emil's Georgetown home without either his parents or the au pair knowing. The parents are always off to meetings, concerts, and receptions. Colleen the au pair is always present, but her head is off in textspace and cyberspace and HerSpace, and she has only the vaguest idea of anything that doesn't come to her via her handheld, let alone what Emil is up to... which is hiding Roheen in the basement, and trying to work out a way to get him to the Tellurian Gate off in the Blue Ridge.

Nataliya's quality of self-absorption makes her perfect for the part, and I have to admit that she's very good at the funny bits. The makeup artist has taken her long-nosed mutant beauty and skewed it slightly, so that it's off-balance and comic. Nataliya can't play to my timing, because she doesn't recognize anyone else as a person worth responding to, but I can play to hers, and it works.

Joey calls for a cut, and then they set up the camera so that I'm getting the close-up instead of Nataliya, and we do it again. And then again, some more. Nataliya goes all unfocused when the camera's on someone else: she saves everything for the close-ups. She's professional that way.

And then the camera moves again, and we shoot another bit of the scene, and then we do all that again, and it's time for lunch. Because Carter-Ann hasn't made any suggestions, Joey's had only a couple of excuses for sarcasm today, once at Clarke, another at Nataliya's entourage of giggling young girls, who got themselves banned from the soundstage after about ten minutes—so far as I could tell, their job was to cluster around Nataliya after every single take and tell her how brilliant she was. Aside from Nataliya and her pack, everyone's happy because we're actually on schedule.

Normally, after a scene is over I tell the other actor how well she did, but I don't this time. It seems redundant when Nataliya pays people for that.

It's six and a half weeks since Jaydee died. All Jaydee's costume designs were completed before her death, and most of the costumes made. All that remains for me is some fittings: her absence has caused scarcely a ripple in the production. One of her assistants was promoted into her place, and everything in the costume department seems to be running smoothly.

I miss Jaydee painfully, but I'm too busy to spend a lot of time mourning. I'm in practically every scene. I remember how, a brief month ago, this seemed a cause for delight.

"Joey?" Nataliya is following him off the set. I trail behind them, because I suspect something amusing is about to happen.

Joey knows Nataliya well enough to be on his guard. He looks at her narrowly. "What is it?" he asks.

"I wrote this monologue."

"Yeah?" He's not terribly interested. "Good for you, sweetheart."

"It's a monologue by Colleen."

He stops on his way to the door and turns to her. "You wrote a monologue for your character."

"Yes. And I think it should be in the movie."

He looks up at her for a moment—she's half a foot taller—and I know his mind is replaying some of the key bullet points from her proposal to make herself the star of the picture. *Espionage. Intrigue. Musical interludes.* He laughs and heads for the door.

"Honey," he says, "we got a script."

She follows, heels clacking on concrete, her perfect Afghan wolfhound hair swaying.

"It's like I understand her," Nataliya says. "I know she's kind of a comic character, but, like, I know how sad she is inside. And I'd like to be able to express that sadness."

She says it very fast, with a kind of weird desperation that causes Joey to slow down. He turns on her.

"What are you talking about?"

"It's—"

"We have a fucking screenwriter," Joey points out. "We have a fucking script. We have a fucking schedule, and we haven't fucking fallen behind." He points at her. "*You* have a part. It's a *great fucking part*, and it was *written just for you*." He slices the air with a hand. "So why are you writing fucking monologues?"

Other people, on their way to lunch, have stopped at the sound of Joey's voice. A circle of shadows stands around Joey and Nataliya, here to witness Nataliya's destruction. Joey can't seem to defeat Carter-Ann; but he can certainly take Nataliya to pieces, and it looks like we're all going to get to watch.

"I—" Words fail Nataliya, and she stomps her heel on the floor, as if to kick-start her brain. "I just think that Colleen—"

"No one cares what you think!" Joey snarls. "Jesus Christ, it's a *small cameo part*." He gets up in her face as far as he can, as short as he is. "I've got a thousand things on my plate with this, and now I'm supposed to worry about your monologue? You're out of your tiny freakin' little mind." He reaches up and taps her forehead. She winces. "Anyone home up there? Anyone up there realize that this project isn't all about you?" He cocks his head and pretends to listen. "No one? No one at all."

"Joey," says Nataliya, "you are not being very nice."

"I'm the director, baby!" Joey sneers. "Where does it say I have to be nice?"

And he stalks away, leaving Nataliya standing by herself. For a moment I feel sorry for her, because the humiliation was so public.

And for another reason as well. There's something in Nataliya I recognize, a feeling that's shared my life for years, intimate as any lover... It's Nataliya's desperation, the hopeless need that made her write a monologue that she knew she'd never have a chance to perform. But why, I wondered, was an A-list celebrity like Nataliya so needy for... for what? To be accepted as a writer? As a serious dramatic actress? A tragedienne?

Good lord, I think, *could her mammoth ego be cracking?* If so, it would be a meltdown on the Melody Chastain scale.

Nataliya looks after Joey for a moment, and then tosses her hair and clacks toward the exit, where her yelping posse waits, the girls she pays to admire her.

Fuck, I think. No use hating her, no use despising her. Nataliya grew up in show business. She's another victim of child exploitation. Just like me, just like Melody Chastain, just like the kids in *Escape to Earth*. Growing up didn't cost her any of her popularity, but that could be tragedy, too. Now she's got millions of fans who expect *something* from her, but who in hell knows what that is?

"What just happened won't make any difference." Carter-Ann speaks at my elbow. I didn't hear her approach, but that's not why I'm surprised. This is the first time she's spoken to me as if I were a normal person.

"Narcissistic personality disorder is the most difficult condition to treat," she says. "Mostly because you can't convince the patient that there's anything wrong."

"I'm an actor," I say. "I can't say anything against narcissism. Narcissism is my best friend."

She gives me a sidelong smile. "Oh," she says. "You thought I was talking about Nataliya?"

A laugh. "I'm not a narcissist," I say. "If I were, I'd want to direct."

"No," she says precisely. "If you wanted to direct, you'd be a megalomaniac." She gives me a wink, and follows Nataliya toward the exit.

If Carter-Ann is confiding in me, I think, *speaking to me as an actual human being instead of a test subject, then she must be confident of winning her war against Joey*.

I decide that I can't disagree.

INT. SEAN'S TRAILER—DAY

I have lunch in my trailer. It isn't a trailer exactly, but a diesel-propelled Wanderlodge RV, a monster as long as a bus. I would be terrified to drive the thing. It has a double bed, a kitchen full of snacks and fruit drinks, and an area where the makeup artist can apply my daily dose of paint. Richard has installed a safe where I can safely hide my script when I'm not studying it.

Today I have pasta salad with little shrimp. Bits of celery crunch between my teeth as I eat. I down a lot of pasta: the carbs keep me chugging through my long days.

I get a menu every day and pick what I want, though presumably I have the juice to dictate a menu if I want to. I've never been one of those people who demand food cooked a certain way, or plates of M&Ms with all the brown ones removed. I'm just delighted to get a catered meal instead of having to sit at the crafts buffet.

I'm drinking apple juice. I haven't had alcohol in the weeks since Jaydee died, and I don't particularly miss it. My life is full.

I'm still experiencing flare-ups of paranoia, particularly when I think about Jaydee. But none of my other friends have been threatened or attacked, and I haven't seen any black SUVs lurking about. I haven't heard from the police about Jaydee or anything else. The case is still open, but I don't know how actively they're investigating.

I turn on the little flat-screen TV, hoping to find entertainment news, but instead I get the regular news. UN troops are now in charge in Fiji, preventing the genocide but protecting the government from the Indians, who are hopping mad. I still don't know what the genocide was about, or why the Indians are involved, but I'm glad it's over.

The war in Ethiopia seems worse, though.

I find the controller and turn to the entertainment news. I hear about the grosses for the previous weekend, and I'm happy.

There's a knock on the door, and I cock my head toward the window to see Sawicki outside. I wave and catch his eye, and he opens the door and comes in.

"Meeting at one o'clock," he says. "Room 201."

This is a room in the Bruce Bennett Building, the shabby office adjacent to the soundstage. It's a big room and we use it for read-throughs.

"Did Nataliya walk out?" I ask.

Sawicki's surprised. "No," he says. "Why would she?"

"What's the meeting about, then?"

He sighs heavily. "Threats and heavy sarcasm, I reckon."

I shrug. "How's that different from anything else happening here in the life of Chester A. Arthur?"

I finish my lunch, take a bottle of mineral water from the fridge, and head for Room 201. Inside the office building the walls, brown and white, have been painted so many times that the plaster is almost smooth, except where there are cracks from one or another of California's earthquakes. The cracks don't bother me: the building's lasted seventy or more years.

I go up the stairs. Dagmar has a corner office here, and the inviting scent from her coffee machine drifts down the corridors. You can tell she's not thinking like a big-shot producer yet: though the electronics in the office are up-to-the-second, the furniture is shabby, and it opens directly onto the corridor instead of making visitors run a gauntlet of secretaries and assistants.

I pause outside her door when I hear a dry male voice inside.

"I was confident in the budget projections," he said, "until you started sending those handhelds to places like Waziristan and Tajikistan. You'll never make back the investment."

"We'll see." Dagmar's tone indicates that budgets aren't really her concern.

"And dubbing the final product into Pashto and six Chinese dialects and half the languages of Africa? You've got two dozen translators standing by full time."

"Consequences of serialization. They're getting the script in pieces. I need them when I need them."

"Well. Don't say I didn't warn you."

"Warned I am." The voices begin to move closer to the door, so I amble forward and glance into the office as I pass by. Dagmar is with a middle-aged blond man who wears an elegant charcoal

Abbey Road suit. Dagmar looks up at me as I pass, nods, returns her attention to her companion.

I continue down to 201 and find I'm the first to arrive. The room is as shabby as everywhere else, with a banged-up wooden oval table and banged-up wooden chairs. Posters of forgotten movies hang on the walls.

I find a seat halfway down the table. Dagmar comes in about thirty seconds later, carrying a cup of coffee, and sits at the head of the table.

"So," I say, "I heard you're going to make me a star in Waziristan?"

"That's the plan." If she is surprised that I was eavesdropping, she doesn't show it.

"Where *is* Waziristan?" The place seems not to be mentioned in the entertainment news, and if there was a documentary about Waziristan on the National Geographic Channel, I must have missed it.

"Pakistan," Dagmar says. "It's a tribal area."

"Spend a lot of time at the cinema, the Waziri?"

Dagmar shakes her head. "I doubt they have much opportunity in their home area."

I consider this. "You figure the—the Waziri?"

"Wazirs."

"You reckon the Wazirs are going to be able to make sense of this picture? Tellurian Gates, parallel worlds, invaders from other planes?"

She offers a tight-lipped smile. "I think the Wazirs know all they need to know about invaders."

"And you're giving away handhelds so that they can appreciate the film for free?"

"Not for free," she says. "They still have to buy a subscription, though it won't cost much out there." She gives a grin and pulls out her handheld. "We're planning a whole series of films," she says, "plus games, online sites, maybe film or television spin-offs featuring our juvenile leads. The giveaway handhelds will be amortized over several productions. They may not produce a profit on *Escape to Earth*, but I'll make money in the long run."

I nod. It sounds smart, though the whole idea of a production company whose financial vision extends past the opening weekend is a little unusual in modern Hollywood.

"Who were you just speaking to, by the way?"

"Morris Galway. He's a producer."

I'm mildly surprised. "Of *this* picture?"

She looks up at me, amused eyes beneath her dark brows. "You don't get to meet them all," she says.

"I guess not."

Then the Psy-Ops Division arrives in the form of Carter-Ann and two of her associates: Dr. Li, whom I met at Joey's party, and a young, pale blond man with a tablet computer. They sit opposite me. Ismet and Helmuth arrive and sit on either side of Dagmar. Then Joey and Clarke enter together, along with their assistants, and lastly Sawicki, carrying the tablet with a red plastic frame, the one he uses for scheduling and budgeting. They sit at the foot of the table opposite Dagmar.

"What's happening?" Joey says. "We've got a full shooting schedule this afternoon."

"We've got a problem," Dagmar says. "Fixing it is going to take a certain amount of logistical dexterity, so I hope you'll all bear with me when I try to deal with the situation."

Joey gives Carter-Ann a baleful look. It's clear he has no doubt where news of this problem originated.

Carter-Ann folds her hands on the table in front of her. She's wearing a dark gray suit and a lace collar and has had her hair done, and she looks like the teacher's pet in catechism class.

"A problem has developed with regard to the banquet scene," she says. "The test audiences aren't giving us the reactions we'd hoped for."

I feel my heart sink. The banquet scene was big and complex and a lot of work.

"*Which* test audiences?" Clarke asks.

"The bad marks are coming from Asia generally, but specifically from China."

My heart, already submerged, plunges through a frigid thermocline into the lightless depths. Asia's our biggest potential audience, and if it's got a problem, we've got a massive one.

"The banquet scene's *great*," Joey says. "It's light, it's funny, it's..."

Dr. Li clears her throat. She's dressed in a sober gray suit, with no jewelry save the gleaming gold fountain pen she has in her hand. "I liked that scene myself," she says. "But then I was raised in the States, and though I've spent years in China, I don't quite have their mind-set."

Joey eyes her. "So it's you who screwed up here?" Li looks down the table. Her gold pen jiggles nervously in her fingers. Joey turns to Dagmar. "Shooting that scene took *four days*. For six and a half minutes of screen time."

Carter-Ann takes the tablet computer from her blond assistant. "Let me show you the data." She taps the touch-sensitive screen with her thumbnail. "I'm sending you the URL where you can watch the scene along with the audience reaction data. You'll need a password—it's 'dimsum,' one word, all lower case."

My handheld chirps. I take it out of the holster, check email, click the URL.

The banquet scene takes place after Roheen arrives in China, in search of a Tellurian Gate somewhere in the wilds of Sichuan. He's had to walk and hitchhike across the Himalayas to get from India, and by the time he arrives he's half-starved. In Chongqing he meets with Lihua, one of Amir's Internet buddies, who helps him hide out and sneaks him some table scraps that don't quite make up for the lack of a real meal. With the help of a pack of mischievous school friends she disguises Roheen as a North American industrialist, someone attractive to her businessman father. Lihua's father invites the visitor to a restaurant, and the famished Roheen falls on the food like a wolf on the fold, and gobbles everything in sight while the locals watch in astonishment.

It's a finely tuned comic scene, and I'm pleased with my performance. I'd hate to have to throw all that in the crapper, though of course I'm used to it. The performances in my last three films all ended up on the cutting-room floor, though at least I was able to console myself with the paychecks.

Carter-Ann explains how she monitored the test audience. It turns out that Psy-Ops wired the hell out of them: one of the displays concerns galvanic skin response, another heart rate, another respiration. The fourth shows data from slide potentiometers the audience members were given—they could slide the potentiometers up or down depending on how they felt about what they were watching.

I watch my performance, and I wince as my ratings plummet. Given the statistics for heart rate and respiration, the audience hates me not only with all their hearts, but with their lungs as well.

"What's happening," Li says, "is that the audience perceived Roheen as grasping and boorish. They're just not approving of this behavior."

"Is Roheen breaking the rules for Chinese table etiquette?" I ask.

"Yes," Li says, "but that's not the problem. The Chinese are perfectly capable of making allowances for foreigners who don't know their customs. It's just that Roheen is greedy, and he's not giving face to the other people at the table. The audience is embarrassed for the host and the other guests, because they're being disrespected. It makes the viewers feel uncomfortable."

Dagmar frowns, taps fingers on the tabletop. "If Sean just tones down his performance . . . ?" she asks.

"I think that would work," Li says. "And we could add some moments where Roheen gives respect to others, like having him offer some of the food to his neighbors."

"How did the stateside audiences like the scene?" Joey asks.

Dr. Lee looks up at him. "Everywhere but Asia liked it. In West Africa they thought it was particularly funny."

"So we have a choice," Joey says, "of pleasing Asia, or pleasing *everywhere else.*"

"Ideally," Dagmar says, "we please everybody."

"It's *funny*," Joey says. "In comedy, funny trumps anything else. Sean's really great in it, and so is everyone else."

I sense a dangerous vibe coming off of Joey, and I decide to step into the scene.

"You'll just be reshooting me, right?" I say to Dagmar. "I'm playing too broad, so I can make it quieter. You don't need to redo the whole scene, just the bits where the camera's on me. The other actors' reaction shots are fine, right? You might not even need to call them back, you can just use stand-ins." I look at Joey. "It's a piece of cake," I say.

"It's possible," Dagmar ventures, "that we could do it entirely in editing, using alternate takes."

"Listen," Joey says. He taps his fingers deliberately on the scarred surface of the table. "I've got Nataliya and a whole crew waiting for me, so let me explain the process as quick as I can."

Everyone watches him.

"It's organic," he says. "What I do is organic." He taps his fingers again. "A vision appears in the mind of the creators, and the cast and crew put in their part, and I facilitate everything." He stirs the air with his hands. "I facilitate. It's magic when it comes together. It's magic when it goes right. And there's one thing I've learned." He thrusts out his forefinger at Dagmar. "*Don't fuck with the magic.* When it's funny, don't fuck with the funny. When it's sad, don't fuck with the sad." He looks up in appeal. "The banquet scene is *great.* You wire up some people in Shanghai or whatever, they don't like what they see, maybe it's because *they're all wired up to machines*. Maybe the machines are getting in the way of the laughter."

"Everyone who liked the scene was also wired—" Li begins.

"Or maybe the Chinese all got fed a box lunch that gave them gas," Joey says. "What the hell do I know? The point is that the scene is magic and as far as I am concerned we shouldn't even be having this discussion." He rises from the table and puts his handheld in its holster.

"I have a crazy superstar to nursemaid through two days of shooting," he says. "So if you'll excuse me, I'll get to where I'm needed."

"Just a minute," says Dagmar. "This meeting isn't over."

Joey looks at her. "You can go on talking if you want. It doesn't have anything to do with me."

Dagmar regards him through narrowed eyes. "Are you doing the reshoots or not?" she asks.

Joey lifts his head. "Of course not. The scene is great as it stands."

I'm watching Joey in growing trepidation. He's cutting his own throat.

She's a terrorist, I tell him mentally. *Don't fuck with this woman.*

"Joey," I say, in hopes of returning sanity to the room. "They're just *reshoots*. You do reshoots all the time." If Joey is going to torpedo himself over a cause, the cause of reshoots is about the lamest one imaginable.

Joey looks back at me. There's this weird saintly glow in his eyes. It's like he's going to his martyrdom.

"You were great, champ," he says to me, and thumps a big hand on my shoulder. "You'll be great in the reshoots, too." He turns to Dagmar. "Look," he says. "I'm just not hip enough for you." He throws his arms wide. "I'm just a filmmaker. I don't have to wire my audiences to machines in fifty countries to know whether I'm any good. I don't have to hire a bunch of shrinks to tell me whether my script is worth shooting. It's—" He clenches his fists. "It's *organic*. That's how I work." He laughs. "You know what the preview comments on *One Tin Soldier* were like? A fucking catastrophe! They hated it! But that was my biggest hit."

He sweeps a hand out to the room, toward Dagmar and Carter-Ann and the others. "You guys had a great script—that's why I signed on in the first place, to work with a great script. And I'm making the script that you wrote. But now with all your data and your focus groups and your—" He makes the Buddhist wanking sign. "You're *screwing it up*. You're so bent on interfering with the process that you're stumbling over each other." He walks past me toward the door. "Look," he tells Dagmar. "You've got a choice between me and all your..." He waves a hand. "Your *apparatus*. And I know what the choice is going to be, so—"

"Oh no, you don't," says Dagmar. Her eyes glitter beneath her dark brows. She clamps her hands on the arms of her chair and heaves herself upright, her pregnant stomach lunging upward as her body bows backward. She straightens with an effort and approaches Joey.

"You don't get to just...walk...out," she says. "You don't get to do that to me." She stands in front of him, her hands on her hips. "You think you can fuck with me just because I'm pregnant? Because I'm a girl?"

Joey makes a noise with his lips and flips a hand as if to brush off an insect.

"Don't call me a sexist," he says. "My wife and I were partners. We were *brilliant*. We—"

"That," Dagmar says flatly, "was long ago." She points a finger at him. "They warned me about you. They said that you were out of control, that you were undisciplined, that you'd lost your timing." She snarls. "And because of all that you were *flat on your fucking ass*. No one wanted to work with you."

Joey makes a little contemptuous twist of his lips. Dagmar cocks her head and looks at him.

"See, I'd seen your movies," she says. "Especially the early ones, the ones that still had soul. I figured that if I shackled you to a good story and made you *film that story*, you'd be brilliant. And I haven't been disappointed." Her eyes flash. "Till now."

She takes a step toward him. "What I realize now is that you've got some kind of damn death wish. You don't want to make good movies, you *want to fuck up*. You're just using your director's ego in the same way a drunk uses alcohol—it's an excuse to keep on screwing up. An excuse not to care. Because if you actually gave a damn, you wouldn't be doing this."

Joey draws himself up and gives her a cold look.

"You've been spending way too much time with your shrink buddy," he says. "Just let me out the damn door."

Dagmar looks at him, then turns and reaches across the table to snatch Helmuth's netbook from between his hands. Helmuth looks up in surprise as Dagmar spins, the netbook at full extension on the end of her arm, the computer swinging right for Joey's head…

I don't know how Ismet does it, but he lunges from his seat and grabs the laptop and falls on it like a football player diving on a fumble. There's a clatter as he sprawls half across the table, the laptop under him.

Joey's eyes widen as he realizes that Dagmar was aiming the computer for his head. Dagmar takes a step toward him.

"I can fuck you up, Joey," she says.

"What are you going to do?" he asks. "Bomb my car?"

She turns white with rage and looks on the table for another weapon, but by that point Helmuth is on his feet. He grabs Joey by the arm and steers him toward the door.

"I will escort Mr. da Nova out of the building," he says.

He and Joey disappear through the door. Dagmar glares after him, jaw clenched in rage. Then she takes a breath and turns to see Ismet rising slowly from the table, the laptop still clenched to his chest. She pats him on the shoulder.

"Good save," she says.

Ismet adjusts his spectacles and offers a slight smile. "It's what I do," he says.

I look across the table at the Psy-Ops Division. Carter-Ann is sitting straight in her chair, watching the event with bright eyes. Whatever expression I see on her face is the one she painted on that morning. Dr. Li looks away, her hand jittering with her gold pen. The male assistant is paler than usual.

Dagmar wrenches free of Ismet's arms, then steps back to her chair. She lowers herself into it carefully.

"Right," she says. "We have Nataliya Hogan for two more days, and we have no director." She looks at Clarke. "You'll have to step in."

Clarke looks uneasy. His *title* is first assistant director, sure, but that doesn't guarantee he knows how to direct, or wants to. In the old days ADs moved up to the director's chair often enough, but now they're mostly trainee producers.

When he speaks, his big voice is unusually subdued. "I don't have a lot of confidence that I'm—ah—right for this."

"We'll manage," I say. The fact that I speak at all catches me by surprise. When I offer the next sentence it feels as if I'm not following my own comment, but answering a stranger.

"The scenes are straightforward," I say. "Jean-Marc will be there. Everyone knows their job." I look at Clarke. "And the whole thing is storyboarded, right?"

In a technique now become standard in the industry, Joey animated the whole film, shot for shot, on his computer, with little stick figures moving around inside a virtual camera frame. The system makes things very easy on the crew, because they always know what setup is coming next.

Clarke nods. "Yeah. It's storyboarded."

"You have a copy of the file?"

"Yeah."

I turn to Dagmar. "There," I say. "We'll be all right."

I find myself wanting to please her. I badly want not to die in a crossfire between Dagmar and whoever she's mad at that day.

Fifteen minutes with the woman, I think, *and I'm coming down with Stockholm syndrome.*

Helmuth returns. His hands brush his tan Hickey Freeman blazer, as if he were scraping Joey off himself. Dagmar's still standing, leaning heavily with one hand on the back of her chair. Ismet stands protectively next to her. She looks up at us, and her voice is weary.

"I want to apologize for that." She lowers herself into the chair. I look at Helmuth's protective expression as he helps guide her to her seat, and I see his expression, and I think, *Holy shit, he's in love with her too*. And then, *I wonder if she knows*.

"That was the sort of behavior I hate," Dagmar goes on. "I was completely out of control. I'm sorry you had to witness it."

I have no idea what to say. *No problem, boss*? Maybe *Joey deserved it*? I decide not to say anything.

Instead, it's Carter-Ann who pipes up. "We can't afford any more scenes, Miss Shaw," she says. "With Joey it seems to be the way he works, but—but really, this is all too important to lose track of ourselves this way."

I look up in surprise. The film is important, yes, because it's my chance at a career again. And it's important to Dagmar, I assume, because it's her company that's making the picture; and it's important to Carter-Ann, because no other film company would ever allow her the sort of power she has.

But I get the impression that's not what Carter-Ann is talking about. It's not the movie that's important, it's something *bigger* than the movie.

What would that be? I wonder. The merchandising? The Roheen action figures and the online games?

What was worth taking a loss in Waziristan for?

Dagmar gives a sigh and looks at me.

"It's a difference in cultures," she says. "I wasn't quite ready for it. I'm used to running a small company with a small group of dedicated people all pulling in the same direction." She shrugs. "The movies are too big. I keep expecting the same sort of spirit of collaboration and I don't always find it."

Yeah, I think. Maybe there actually are industries out there where your colleagues aren't ready to stab you in the back or cut your throat the minute you show weakness. But unfortunately you've entered a business where, if your profile gets too high—if, for example, you crash the party with armloads of new technologies and unlimited funding from an Indian IT billionaire—champagne corks start popping the second you fall on your ass. Because it serves you right for not having to kiss up to get your funding, and for thinking you're smarter than everyone else.

But I'm not going to pop champagne if *Escape to Earth* flops. Because I have no choice but to hope that you'll succeed, and succeed big.

"We're going to need a new director," Dagmar says.

"Tessa Brettel was very good at my audition," I point out.

"We'll want someone more experienced." She turns to Ismet. "But call Tessa and see if she's available. She might be able to bridge between one director and another." Then she looks at me and Clarke.

"Go to the set," she says, "and see if you can save the afternoon."

INT. SOUNDSTAGE—DAY

Save the afternoon is exactly what we do. Jean-Marc and Clarke and I manage the job of directing between the three of us, with help from the camera operator. We tell Nataliya and everyone else that Joey's fallen ill. Nataliya just shrugs off the news without a whisper of emotion one way or another. Joey's ceased to matter to her.

Nataliya is good in all of her scenes. Carter-Ann comes in after an hour or so, but has nothing to contribute. We finish the day's shooting ahead of schedule. I'm so grateful for the peace on the set that when Nataliya brings up her monologue again, I look at Jean-Marc and shrug.

"What the hell," he says.

So we put Nataliya in her bedroom set and sit her on the bed under a poster of Cretan windmills and set up a simple three-light system to light her. We put a camera in front of her. Medium close-up. And then we tell her to start.

During the performance I'm expecting to have to stuff a towel in my mouth to keep from laughing out loud, but you know what? That doesn't happen.

What Nataliya does is magical. She looks at the camera, and she calls up her character's dreams and secret terrors, and she tells us all about them.

She's alone in a strange city. She's afraid she might be pregnant. Her boyfriend won't answer her calls. She's texting everyone she can think of just to have some kind of human contact, but she can't tell them what's really bothering her.

I don't know if Nataliya's actually got her speech memorized, or if she's improvising around an outline, or if she's suddenly possessed by the spirit of an anxious teenager.

She doesn't mention spies. She doesn't burst into song. She gets into the head of a young girl who's completely unlike her, and she's absolutely wonderful.

I don't know how she manages it. My biggest problem on *Family Tree* was that I was supposed to be playing a normal American kid, and I had no idea what a normal American childhood was like. My character, Brent Schuyler, experienced all the typical rites of passage—the big baseball game, the first dance, the transition to high school, the first date, the first kiss; and these were all experiences I had no familiarity with—except for kissing, and I'd actually had sex before I'd ever kissed a girl. In the dance scene I had to ask the other kids to show me what dancing looked like and how to do it.

That's what makes Nataliya's accomplishment so extraordinary. She's put herself into the head of someone she couldn't possibly know. It's even more singular for someone as self-involved as Nataliya. I had no idea she thought anyone else even existed.

When Nataliya finishes, there's a long silence, and then she turns to Jean-Marc and says, "That's it."

I lift my hands and applaud. Everyone else does, too.

Nataliya listens to the applause with her head tilted, as if she isn't quite sure what she's hearing. And then she says, "Do you need another take?"

"I don't think so," I say.

"Hell no," says Jean-Marc. "That was perfect."

"I guess I'm done, then." And then, without any more words—let alone words of thanks—she rises from the bed, smooths her wolfhound hair, and heads for the exit and her pack of admirers.

Jean-Marc and I watch her leave, then turn to each other.

"The old Nataliya's back," he says.

I look after her in amazement. "She's only a human being when she's *acting*."

"I believe," he says, portentous, "that she is not of this Earth."

The door opens, a passage into another, brilliantly lit world. Nataliya's silhouette passes through it, and then the passage closes.

"What are you going to do with the take?" I ask.

"Bump it up to Dagmar. She gets dailies anyway."

"It won't go in the movie, obviously."

"No, but Dagmar's got side projects going. Games and so on. It might end up there, as like a prize or something." Jean-Marc lights one of the 555 brand cigarettes left over from shooting the New Delhi scenes, scratches the stubble on his chin, and looks at me sidelong. He lowers his voice. "What really happened with Joey?"

I look around at the various specialists in the process of packing up for the day. Carter-Ann stands twenty feet away, talking on her cell.

"If you want that story," I say, "you'll have to come to my trailer."

Which he does. We sit in the kitchen, I tell him what happened, and he's not surprised. Joey's been calling him at two in the morning to rant about Carter-Ann's latest outrages. Jean-Marc's attempts to calm him only resulted in greater anger and bitterness.

"Ten years ago he could have gotten away with this," Jean-Marc says. "Now..." He shakes his head. "Now he'll be lucky to be offered a commercial."

Jean-Marc returns to the studio to help Allison deal with editing the day's work. The makeup artist's assistant comes in to remove my makeup, and then my driver takes me home while I relax in the backseat with a fruit juice concoction called a pomegranate surprise. Left at the curb, I punch the code into the wrought-iron street gate and enter the condo complex. I hear splashing from the pool and vintage doo-wop from an open window on the upper floor. There's a strong smell of burning rubber in the air. I'm halfway to my condo when a neighbor—a young Hispanic guy with an Irish name, Murphy—comes running up.

"Hey," he says, "I've been trying to get hold of you for the last couple hours."

I'm surprised. "What's happening?"

"Your car burned up, man." Murphy looks at me out of sad, earnest brown eyes. "There's nothing much left."

I'm too tired to be surprised. This seems the perfect capper to an already shitty day. Goodbye, Mom's Mercedes.

"Well," I say, "thanks for letting me know." I turn for the parking area. Murphy bounces along next to me, doing a kind of skip in order to keep up with my long legs.

"The fire inspector's waiting for you in the clubhouse," says Murphy. "She says it's arson."

"Arson," I repeat, as if trying out the way the word fits in my mouth.

Of course *it's arson*, I think. What else would it be? What else could make my day worse?

I go to have a talk with the fire marshal, a young, nervous-looking Filipina who seems about half my height. I tell her that the car is something like fourteen years old and belongs to my mother, who's been out of the country for some time. I hope she takes this as evidence that I didn't torch it myself for the insurance money.

I tell her that I've been threatened online by a cultist. She does not seem impressed.

She shows me the car. The condo has an automatic gate on a side street that requires a punch code and leads into the parking area. The vehicles are protected by a metal roof but otherwise are open to the elements. There were *two* firebombs, she explains, one thrown through a window, the other thrown under the car. The parking spaces on both sides were vacant, and no other cars were damaged.

It wouldn't have been hard to get into the parking area. The condominium complex is surrounded by an eight-foot-high fence of aluminum pickets with little fleur-de-lis on top, with the one auto gate and two pedestrian gates, each of which requires a code to open. The picket fence wouldn't present much of an obstacle to a reasonably agile person—and in any case, an intruder could just wait for a resident to pass through one of the gates and follow him in.

Police arrive with a tow truck, take a lot of pictures, and haul the car off to their lot, where their evidence techs will inspect it the following day. I'm given a receipt. I mention that I've been threatened by cultists but they say I should come by tomorrow and fill out a report.

They aren't very interested. I guess cultists burn cars every day in LA.

It's nearly nightfall when I finally manage to get to my apartment. I call Joey to see how he's doing, but the call goes straight to voice mail. I go upstairs to shower and change, and then step out onto the balcony to look at the night. The air still smells of burning automobile. I'd love to go out for a meal, but unfortunately someone torched my car.

Looks like I get to microwave dinner again.

I lean on the balcony rail and look out over the neighborhood. The air is still and there isn't another human being in sight.

Then the black Ford Expedition parked across the street rumbles into life, and I feel electric terror shimmering along my nerves.

The SUV roars onto the street and speeds off, trailing a faint wisp of oil fumes.

I feel the cold hand of fear clamp on the back of my neck. I run back into the bedroom and open my T-shirt drawer and claw through it for my pistol.

It's a Glock, one of those blocky weapons used by gangsters on TV, and possibly even in real life. I acquired it from Tito Aragon of *Live Wire*, whose career, like mine, died with his eighteenth birthday. One night a few years ago he showed up at my condo without letting me know he was coming. He was strung out and wanted to sell his pistol to me to get money for drugs. I didn't want to give him money, and I also didn't want him wandering around with a loaded firearm, so I told him I was broke and gave him all the weed in my stash in exchange for the gun. He went off in hopes of trading my stash for heroin, and that's the last I saw him alive. Three weeks later he overdosed on his living room couch. His four-year-old son found him.

I carry the gun around for the next half-hour until I start feeling silly, and then I put it on my bedside table and leave it there till morning. When I leave the apartment the next day in the limousine to the studio, I put it in a shoulder bag and take it with me.

CHAPTER TEN

FROM: Trishula

Perhaps you won't be so quick to dismiss Babaji now that there's a smoking hunk of scorched metal in your parking space.

FROM: Sean

Can I point out just how fucked up my boy Trishula's thinking actually is?

Let me explain this as simply as I can, Trishula—*it wasn't my car that you torched, you moron!* It belonged to my esteemed parent, who lives with Babaji in his own compound and is a far more devoted follower of your deity than you are.

And furthermore, if you had actually read the posts that supposedly inspired your anger in the first place, *you would have known that!* So you've proved yourself both illiterate *and* an imbecile.

Do you think Babaji is going to be pleased that you destroyed valuable property that belonged to one of his closest associates? He's going to make sure your next incarnations are going to be in fifteen different kinds of hells!

FROM: MaddHaxx

Jeezus Trishula URA tool.

FROM: Jaxon31

Trishula more stupid than Makin here ha ha

FROM: Krumble

LMAO!

FROM: Splendour

An excellent post. I recommend your blog to everyone. I would like to recommend Arcane Artie's as a source of magick, Wiccan, and paranormal supplies.

INT. THE STUDIO—DAY

After a visit to the police station and a call to my mom's insurance company, I go to the studio on Thursday even though the call sheet tells me I have the day off. I figure I can maybe make myself useful in much the same way I did yesterday afternoon. Jean-Marc and the others accept my presence without comment.

Nataliya is still on the set, doing scenes with Ferdy, the kid who plays Emil, and his onscreen family. I help out behind the scenes and offer a few suggestions, but mostly I just watch. I'm a little too distracted to be of much use. Too many of my thoughts revolve around the pistol in my shoulder bag.

By now the paranoia that has long simmered in my brain has come to a full boil. I took the news of the arson stoically enough, but by now suspicion and fear have begun to dominate my thoughts.

Some Babaji follower burned my car—with *two* Molotov cocktails, the fire inspector said, one thrown underneath and another through a window. The same person who threw the firebombs, or maybe someone else, had tried to run me down. And Jaydee actually *was* run over by someone lurking on her peaceful street, who might just be the same person who tried to kill me.

It's all too confusing. I can't think of anything that connects these crimes except automobiles—and automobiles connect them to Timmi's death, too, and that connection frightens me.

During the lunch break I go to the Bruce Bennett Building and look for Richard's office.

Turns out he has an engraved plastic nameplate next to his door that actually reads RICHARD THE ASSASSIN. Nothing like a terrorist who puts his job right there on the nameplate.

I knock on the metal door frame and walk in. Richard sits behind three flatscreens and beneath the unblinking eyes of a couple dozen Japanese warriors.

A high shelf rings the office, and it's occupied entirely by action figures. I recognize all of the Seven Samurai standing proudly beneath their homemade banner; I see Toshiro Mifune as Yojimbo and Shintaro Katsu as Zatoichi. If the others are from movies, I don't recognize them. Many seem to be ninjas. Maybe they're from history—except, I guess, for the one that seems to be a white rabbit in samurai drag.

Behind Richard are posters featuring Naruto and the Sega video game character Shinobi.

When I first met Richard I thought of Spanish hidalgos, but I clearly pegged the wrong warrior culture.

Richard looks up. His chair properly belongs to an evil overlord in a film, a tall gray Kevlar-carbon office chair with buttons and studs on the armrests. I see the flatscreens reflected in his eyes.

"Dagmar hasn't sent me your script yet," he says. He or one of his assistants continue to hand-deliver my scripts to me every few days, on their booby-trapped memory sticks.

I close the door behind me and take a seat. "I have a security problem," I tell him.

He takes his hand off the keyboard, drops it in his lap, and focuses his polite attention on me. "Tell me," he says.

I tell him about Trishula and Babaji and my mother and my burned car. I mention the Ford Expedition that's tried to run me down. I offer my suspicion that Jaydee's death was somehow a part of this.

"I'd better call Dagmar," he decides.

Dagmar arrives, an olive-drab tee from something called Magma.com stretched across her pregnant belly. I've never heard of Magma.com, whoever they are. Her hair carries the faint scent of lilacs.

"This better be important," she says. "I'm in the middle of looking for a new director."

Richard offers her his formidable-looking office chair, and as she presses the buttons that adjust it to her figure, Richard sits cross-legged in a corner where he can see both me and Dagmar.

At least he didn't have to remove the swords from his belt before he sat.

I tell my story to Dagmar. She listens intently, writing notes to herself by scrolling her handheld in the air.

"So you've got this Shiva-ist after you," Dagmar says. "The person you provoked on your blog."

"Shaiva," I say. "A Shaiva is a person who practices Shaivism, which is the worship of Shiva." When she looks at me, I shrug. "Sorry, but I've got one in the family."

Richard looks at me. "So this person worships Shiva the Destroyer? Like, a death god?"

"Not exactly," I tell him. "Shaivas believe that Shiva is the supreme god—in Shaivism he's not just the Destroyer, he's everything else, too. Creator, destroyer, sex god, Holy Ghost, and everything in between. The whole package."

"And you've *also* got this SUV after you," Dagmar says, "and that started the day I first met you."

"Right," I say. "He tried to run me down twice, and then he went away. I saw him last night for the first time in weeks."

"And you hadn't pissed off the Shiva-ists—Shaivists—until *after* the SUV started hunting you."

"That's right."

Her eyes narrow. "You haven't mentioned the SUV till now."

"Yes. Well." I try to look abashed. "I thought if you knew that someone was trying to kill me, you wouldn't give me the job."

It wasn't just that, I think. The truth was that I didn't want anything to interrupt my own sudden, surprising happiness. Everything took second place to the fact that I was *working*. And not only was I working, I was the principal character in what might turn out to be a very important motion picture, a movie as important from the point of view of new technology as, say, *The Jazz Singer*—except, I thought, with a better script.

I was living the life I was born to lead, doing the work I was born to do. After a drought of nearly fifteen years, I had the job I hungered for. So what if someone was trying to kill me? All I had to do was be careful when trying to cross the street.

Dagmar's stare turns icy. "You know," she says, "I don't like it when my employees don't tell me the truth."

"I didn't *lie*," I point out. "I just didn't tell you about something that was pretty unbelievable in the first place."

"Right," she says. "You were trying to preserve my sanity out of compassion."

I can only shrug.

"And you also think Jaydee Martin was killed by this SUV person."

"I—" I hesitate. "I'm inclined to think that, yes."

Her stare is still unsettling. The handheld points at me like an inquisitor's sword. "Do you know something about *that* you haven't told me?"

I'm suddenly frightened. "No," I say. "Not at all." Because if the deaths of Timmi and Mac are somehow connected to this, the situation is more weird and complex than I can possibly process, and I don't have any idea who's going to take the next shot at me.

Dagmar swivels her chair toward Richard.

"Find this Trishula," she says.

"That shouldn't be a problem," he says simply.

Dagmar turns to me. "I've been in too many situations," she says, "when people started getting killed. Maybe Jaydee's death is an accident and maybe it isn't, but I'm not about to let it go any further. We're going to put you under protection."

I look at her. "Which means?"

She nods at me. "You get guards. You get armored cars. You get a flak jacket if we think you need one. You get a safe house and people licensed to carry firearms to keep it safe. And we'll go on a hunt for that SUV."

Richard looks up at her. "I'll set it up."

Dagmar rises from her chair. I'm a little too startled by the quickness of her decision to react right away, and she's halfway to the door before I get to my feet.

She stops, looks up at me. "Don't leave the studio before Richard has your protection set up. He'll call you when he's ready."

"Okay." I'm still a bit dazzled. *I'm going to get guards?* I think.

Is that a good thing? I don't know.

At least she'll know for sure I'm not drinking, I think.

Dagmar steps out into the corridor, then swings round and returns. "Sean," she asks, "who inherits when you die?"

"Uh..." I think about it. "I don't have a will, so I suppose it would be my parents."

"And you're estranged from your parents, right?"

I am completely thunderstruck when I realize where this line of inquiry is going—though now I think about it, I guess it's kind of obvious. It's not like I can picture either of my parents as murderers, but then I never saw them as swindlers, either.

"I haven't seen either of my parents in ten years," I say. "But—"

Dagmar lifts her dark brows. "But?" she prompts.

Suddenly I want to defend my folks. It's a reflex I didn't know I still possessed. I figured ten years of desperation and financial struggle caused by their theft of my future had burned any family feeling right out of me.

"My estate wouldn't be worth much," I point out. "All I have is a third-rate condo and a nice sound system."

"No residuals?"

"A trickle, mostly from foreign markets. *Family Tree* isn't being shown on any of the domestic satellite channels."

"Do they know that?"

Again I'm impelled to say something in mitigation, but I can't think of anything. "I don't know what they know," I say.

"Might they know that *Family Tree* is about to be acquired by, say, Nickelodeon?"

I look at her in surprise. "Is it?" I ask.

Dagmar turns to Richard. "Find out where Sean's parents actually are."

"My mom's in an ashram in Andhra Pradesh," I tell him. "Good luck finding out where my father is."

Dagmar looks up at me and pats me on the arm in a gesture meant to be comforting. "It's unlikely that either of your parents wants to kill you," she says. "We're just covering all the bases."

Gee, I think. *Thanks.*

I give Richard as much detail about my parents as I can remember, and then I return to the set for the rest of the afternoon. Nataliya is in some kind of super-intense mode and wraps up all her scenes with phenomenal efficiency and speed—maybe she needs to push off to a pedicure or something. Then there are a few brief scenes with Ferdy and the actors playing his parents, and we wrap for the day.

I go to my trailer, and I call Richard and tell him where I am. Forty minutes later, my new bodyguard contacts me.

His name is Simon. He's in his forties, with a mustache and dark hair both going gray. He wears navy slacks and a tie and a lightweight zippered jacket with lots of pockets. I don't see a gun, but Dagmar told me there would be one, and I don't have any reason to doubt her.

"You have anything you need to bring with you?" he asks.

He speaks with the Okie accent that's common in the Central Valley—or maybe he's a real Okie, who knows?

I heft my shoulder bag and my MP3 player. "Only this." I don't show him the gun.

Simon's car is a dark blue Chevy Impala Super Sport with tinted windows and alloy wheels. He tells me that the body of the car is filled with ceramic and laminated armor stronger, and much lighter, than steel, and that the windows are bullet-resistant.

Simon drives me to North Hollywood, to the NoHo Plaza, a boutique hotel off Magnolia Boulevard. I have a feeling that a lot of the rooms are filled by talent belonging to traveling productions at the Millennium Dance Complex and the NoHo Arts Center, both of which are only a couple streets away. Dominating the hotel lobby is a huge Hockney painting of an avocado-green 1950s California home with a flat overhanging roof that looks like one of Hedda Hopper's hats. There are palm trees in the painting, and a pool and canvas-backed directors' chairs. It's such an ideal California paradise that I want to dive right into the pool. I'm too struck by the painting to even notice the black faux-onyx reception desk with its polite staff in wine-colored blazers. When their existence penetrates my consciousness, they make sure to inform me about the Room Spa Program, and the Arnold Palmer Happy Hour, still going on in the bar for the next half-hour, after which it will be replaced by the evening wine tasting.

I'm put into a two-room second-floor suite that smells of lemon polish and sandalwood. The walls feature silk screens of Marilyn Monroe, and there's a curved wet bar illuminated by a chandelier with an emerald-green cut-glass shade. The Jacuzzi has a refrigerated holder for a bottle of wine or champagne.

I'm more interested in the video game controllers sitting next to the television in the entertainment console. They're likely to be my chief diversion as long as I'm staying here.

"I'll need the keys to your place," Simon tells me. "I'll get you some clothing and supplies for tonight, then tomorrow we'll do a security audit on your home, and teach you a few things you might find useful."

"I have a premiere tomorrow night," I say.

Simon grins. "We'll get you there," he says. "Where is it?"

I sigh. Suddenly this doesn't seem like a very good omen.

"It's in a cemetery," I say.

FROM: Helmuth
SUBJECT: Getting a clue

Sean, I'd like to plant a comment in your blog that will serve as a clue to some of our online gamers. It will be signed "Tempest Royal." I hope that's okay.

Please don't erase the comment when it appears.

FROM: Sean Makin
SUBJECT: Re: Getting a clue

Okay by me.

EXT. HOLLYWOOD FOREVER CEMETERY—EVENING

Los Angeles boasts what is probably the only cemetery with a film program. The Hollywood Forever cemetery, off Santa Monica Boulevard, shows vintage films projected on the wall of a large crypt. They have DJs before and after, and viewers bring picnics and blankets and watch from the lawn next to the single sarcophagus shared by the senior and junior Douglas Fairbanks.

I've gone to the shows myself. There aren't very many places left where you can see old movies as intended, amid an audience of happy enthusiasts, rather than on the small, lonely screen at home.

I've also made a kind of pilgrimage to the child stars interred there: Carl "Alfalfa" Switzer, *Our Gang* star, murdered at the age of thirty-one. Mildred Harris, who starred as Dorothy in a series of Oz films, got knocked up by Charlie Chaplin at the age of sixteen, gave birth to a son who lived three days, and died young. Sharing a crypt with Mildred is another *Our Gang* alum, Darla Hood, who retired at fourteen and died mysteriously at forty-seven. In another crypt is Bebe Daniels, who first toddled onstage at the age of four and never left the business—unlike the other child stars buried here, she had a long, happy, successful career.

Judging by the evidence offered within the cemetery gates, I have only one chance in four of living a natural life span.

Determined to beat the odds, I drive into the cemetery with two bodyguards—Simon brought along a backup, a young man with a goatee, shoulder-length dark hair, and an embroidered vest under his yoked Western jacket. His name is Albert, though I'm sure he'd rather be called Wild Bill.

I've left my pistol in my shoulder bag, which I've left in my closet. Packing a pistol at my premiere might be viewed as a little odd by my peers.

Besides, the place is as secure as a cemetery will ever get. There's security at the gate, and guards in blue blazers and tan trousers wander through the crowds, chatting to one another on their radios. This would clearly be a bad place to murder me.

It's as far removed from a standard Hollywood premiere as possible. It's Hollywood 2.0—or maybe 5.0, or 8.1, or 12.5, since a lot of Hollywoods have gone down the 101 since DeMille made *The Squaw Man* here in 1914.

The scene is set up to remain in keeping with the New Delhi setting for the first episode of the film. There's a bhangra band playing in the Iberian-Moorish Masonic Lodge, the beats of the double-ended drums echoing from the arabesques on the ceiling, the huge wooden thrones, and the ominous inverted pentagram that hangs over the heads of the guests. Outside the crypt shared by Elmo Lincoln and Gregg Toland there's a buffet of Indian cuisine and a bar. Waiters circulate with glasses of champagne.

People in the cast and crew wander among the crypts and tombstones. Since there's no red carpet, reporters and photographers pursue the cast more or less at random. Most of them cluster around Nataliya. I see Deeptimoy Srivastava, in a white Nehru jacket, surrounded by cameras.

I'm wearing a handmade silk shirt, handmade cashmere slacks, and a handmade silk jacket. This isn't because I have a fetish for handmade apparel, but because I'm tall as a lamppost and skinny as a stripper pole, with a neck as wide as my thigh. Regular clothes don't fit me. I get everything tailored at Singh & Son, the Los Angeles branch of a firm founded in Hong Kong.

I manage to give about half a dozen interviews and chatter away as long as they'll have me. I'm relieved that no one asks about arson, murder, or attempts on my life, and from this I conclude that nobody's reading my blog. I am asked about Joey, and I say that he's busy editing further installments of *Escape to Earth*. It's what I've been told to say. So far as I know, there's no director yet.

I hear one of the waiters refer to me as "Luggage Boy." For once I'm not annoyed or depressed.

Simon and Albert hang discreetly in the background, ever alert to jump between me and a bullet. No one opens fire.

Palm trees stand on the horizon like drunken pickets. Drone aircraft circle aimlessly overhead, taking pictures for the paparazzi, hobbyists, and perverts who operate them. They probably aren't seeing anything revealing, except maybe some celebrities' bald spots.

I get a plate of lamb pilaf and a glass of mango lassi and wander among the tombstones. The mint in the pilaf cools my palate. There must be a thousand people here. I find Dagmar standing with Deeptimoy Srivastava near a towering memorial modeled after an Egyptian obelisk. For once she's not wearing a faded tee: in fact she's in a midnight-blue sari of Bangalore silk patterned with silver, with a teal stripe embroidered with vines and red flowers. Srivastava's white suit goes well with his white leonine hair and horseshoe mustache. She's drinking orange juice, and he's sipping something amber from a highball glass.

What are you doing here? I think at him. He's one of the world's richest men, supposedly retired to devote himself to good works, and now he's decided to produce movies. If he wanted profit and glamour, he could have produced Bollywood films and sold them in one of the world's largest markets. Instead he's doing *Escape to Earth*—a very different production designed to be delivered along the IT backbone that Sri's installed all over Asia. Presumably he can make a profit that way, but simply making more money or exploiting the technology doesn't make sense for someone like Sri. Either he's a hardheaded entrepreneur or the second coming of Gandhi, but why would either of those people make movies? It doesn't make a lot of sense to me.

But why should I look a gift horse in the mouth? Sri's expended vast amounts of energy and capital to make me a star. I should forgo second thoughts and settle for being deeply grateful.

"That's incredibly lovely," I tell Dagmar, indicating her sari. It appears that saris make perfectly acceptable maternity garments.

"I got it when I ran a game in India some years ago," she says. "This is maybe the third time I've had a chance to wear it."

"You should wear it more often. It suits you."

"Not enough pockets," she says. "I miss my cargo pants." She looks from me to Srivastava and back.

"Have you met Sri?" she asks.

"I haven't had the pleasure." I'm pleased I can call him Sri instead of trying to pronounce his full name.

I juggle my plate and glass, and then Sri and I shake hands. "We've been discussing you," he says.

I try to conceal my alarm. Tycoons and terrorists, I figure, make bad enemies.

"I hope I haven't caused you too much trouble," I say.

He seems amused. "Building an IT backbone in Bhutan was trouble," he says. "Compared to that, you're nothing."

"I guess not," I say. I'd probably be more offended if I had any idea where or what Bhutan might be. "Did you install the IT just for the movie?"

Sri is even more amused. "In those days," he says, "I was trying to *make* money."

I have no idea what he actually means by this, so I turn to Dagmar. "Is everything going well?"

"So far." She frowns. "Can we talk about your parents?"

I'm not sure I want Sri to know any of this, but then I reflect that I put everything on my blog anyway. "Okay," I say.

"There's no indication that your mother's left India in many years," Dagmar says. "Your father's pretty much dropped off the radar, but no one using either his American or Belizean passport has entered the U.S."

"You won't have much luck finding him," I say. "He's had ten years to establish his new identity."

She sips her orange juice and frowns. "Might I suggest that you write a will giving everything to the Used-Up Actors' Home, or something? And put that information on your blog?"

"You think that'll make me safer?" I'm skeptical.

"It can't hurt."

I think about it, and decide that, in the event that the SUV of Doom gets me, the Motion Picture and Television Fund is as good a place as any for my estate.

A baby drone floats overhead, its rotors whirring. Dagmar raises her voice to speak over the sound. "We're also having trouble finding Trishula," she says. "He's been using a virtual identity wallet and routing his comments through a distributed relay system headquartered in Belarus."

Though I understand not a word of this, I gather it's not encouraging. "So you can't find him?" I ask.

"It'll take longer than expected." She nods reassuringly. "Richard will get him, though, particularly if he keeps posting. I'd suggest that you provoke him with further taunts, but I don't want you to lose any more property"—she offers a thin smile—"so wait till after we've wrapped."

"Ha ha," I say. I turn to Sri.

"I don't suppose you know Babaji, do you?"

Teeth flash beneath the white horseshoe mustache. He adjusts his platinum-rimmed spectacles. "There are a few of India's billion human beings I don't know personally. And I'm not religious, so I don't keep track of those people..." He shrugs. "Sorry."

"I figured it was a long shot." An idea occurs to me, and I turn to Dagmar. "By the way," I say, "how is Lenny Castro working out?"

Even though I'm responsible for Lenny's getting hired, I never see him, since our characters don't meet till the final episode.

"He's working out fine," Dagmar says. She gives a thoughtful look. "He plays Arrick as a kind of dreamy romantic, which you don't expect in an arch-villain. Torey Richardson played the character as a more standard bad guy, so I'm almost happy for those broken legs."

"I'm glad it's working out."

Dagmar narrows her eyes. "Lenny threw the fight, right? In exchange for the recommendation?"

I laugh. "Dagmar, *I* didn't hire him. You did."

She pats me on the shoulder. "Hell, I don't care. Fix all the fights you like. In a fixed fight, you won't get hurt, and that's all I care about." She raises an admonishing finger. "Just don't get caught."

Dagmar's phone plays a few bars of some jazz-type tune I half-remember from somewhere, and she draws it from her bag. The backlit screen glows in her eyes.

"I've got a premiere to get under way," she says. "If you'll excuse me?"

"Sure."

I carry my pilaf and lassi past Johnny Ramone's statue to the lawn near the Fairbanks Memorial, the area where on most summer weekends people go to watch the film program. The Fairbankses, father and son, are in a marble sepulcher surrounded on three sides by a classical portico, with a 120-foot reflecting pool stretching toward me. Behind this is a lawn, so far free of tombstones, stretched out along the blank wall of a long crypt where the pictures are projected during the summer film festival.

Simon and Albert stroll along in the periphery of my vision, their gazes alert, their hands carefully poised and empty of food or drink containers. You'd think that someone would remark on what seem to be a pair of gunfighters guarding my flanks, but no one does.

I pause by Johnny Ramone and bring out my new Chandra tablet. I bought it this afternoon to watch the premiere, but when the time comes I hesitate. I don't watch dailies because it makes me too self-conscious about my work. Normally that doesn't matter at a premiere, when I've completed my work months before, but this is different—I still have a few weeks of shooting to go.

Eventually I decide that I'll watch, but if I start getting that creepy feeling—the feeling that I'm overplaying, or stone-faced and untalented, or so repulsive-looking that even I can't stand to look at myself—if I start getting rattled, I'll turn it off and go get a second mango lassi. I install my plate and glass on Johnny Ramone's plinth.

I fire up the tablet and switch on the Augmented Reality function. As I swing the tablet around I see ghostly icons appear among the tombstones, most having to do with celebrities' graves and the history of the cemetery. Capering right next to me is Johnny Ramone himself, hair flying as he plays a guitar slung low over his crotch. There's a hole in the knee of his jeans.

Towering over Hollywood Forever is a large rotating icon of the globe, clearly intended to indicate the imminence of *Escape to Earth.* Dagmar's installed a gargantuan amount of bandwidth here, and as soon as I click the icon a new screen springs up. I'm surprised by how many items are available besides the film. There are games, making-of videos, biographies of the principals. You can join the project's own social-networking sites. There is a link to a biography of someone referred to as "Mahir Mukerjee, global superstar." I flatter myself that I'm acquainted with the names of most of the world's global superstars, and I therefore suspect Mr. Mukerjee is a trailhead for one of Dagmar's elaborate ARGs.

None of the links work at the moment—functionality has to wait till the magic hour of nine-thirty—but there's a digit counter that informs me I have twelve minutes till the film goes live. I spend the time downloading the free proprietary software necessary to view the picture and finishing off my lamb pilaf.

I stroll along the lawn to the Fairbanks Memorial. It's getting dark, and I can barely make out the big bronze medallion with the bas-relief profile of Fairbanks Sr., or the carved quote from *Hamlet*: "Good night, sweet prince, and flights of angels sing thee to thy rest"—a quote that is also engraved on Tyrone Power's memorial, a short walk away.

I have prepared a private little ceremony. There's a small hole in the back of the huge sarcophagus— allegedly for the cheerful purpose of letting gases escape— and I've got a piece of NoHo notepaper with a little message. My communication is simple and heartfelt.

PLEASE DOUG LET THIS BE A HIT.

When all is said and done, I'd as soon pray to Douglas Fairbanks as anybody. He was one of the first gods to plant his golden feet in his strange kingdom of Hollywoodland, and he still rules here in the cemetery, his bronze face gazing down the length of the reflecting pond.

I approach the sarcophagus, push the paper into the little rectangular hole, and with a kind of breathless unspoken hope let it fall inside.

Behind the sarcophagus, sandwiched between the sepulcher and the classical portico that surrounds it, there's a small marble bench. I sit there, in the silent company of Doug and Doug, and I get out the optional folding screen for my Chandra. I unfold it till it's over two feet across, then dock it to the tablet. I watch the screen light up and await the countdown that will determine my fate.

It's a pleasant summer evening. There are few people around

this corner of the park. My guards have settled into the shadows somewhere and aren't intruding on my privacy.

Birds call from the trees. The lights in the park are going on. A cool breeze is coming down from the hills, bringing the scent of distant mountain flowers. I sit on the marble seat and imagine that I'm thinking of nothing at all.

The magic hour arrives and the links light up. I click the link for the film and am asked what language I'd like to hear it in, and whether or not I want subtitles. I don't know what language the folks in Waziristan speak but I assume it's on the list somewhere. It's already Saturday morning in Asia, and I imagine scores of people gathering to watch the film in parks, or in cafés, or on riverbanks.

Or not. My nightmare is that no one's watching at all, that the technology is all too new or too inaccessible or too strange.

I tamp down my fears, choose English, and put in my earbuds while the buffer fills. There's enough bandwidth to allow everyone in the park to watch the film at the same time. The film begins, and there's Amir and his friend, walking down the street in New Delhi while credits roll. They're having a discussion about the difference between the English words *carrot* and *carat*, and Amir's friend riffs a bit on the idea that diamonds are weighed against carrots at the jeweler's. Then the warehouse collapses, and Amir runs in to help.

I've been awaiting my own appearance with trepidation, but by the time Roheen comes lurching out of the rubble like Frankenstein's monster from a burning mill, I'm not really noticing the sorts of little things that make me crazy when I watch myself. I'm too caught up in the scale of the thing.

I filmed on sets swathed in green screen, and now the green is replaced by shimmering detailed reality. The New Delhi backgrounds are brilliant: they mesh beautifully with the action filmed in California, and the level of detail is astounding. The screen on my tablet seems to have a whole city in it—and it looks like a real city, too, not something obviously created on a computer. I'm fascinated.

Someone *planned* all this, planned how it would look from the beginning. I realize that my own view of the production has been far, far too limited. *Escape to Earth* is far grander than I knew.

Adding special effects is usually part of postproduction, and even though fast computers make it a lot easier now, it still takes weeks if not months. I'm completely taken aback when I realize that all this was done ahead of time—it's *pre-*, not post-, production. Adding the actors in editing was almost the last thing that happened.

There are two moments of possible interaction with the audience, when the action pauses and we get to decide where the movie is going. I tell Samendra not to inform his father of the existence of Roheen, and I also suggest that he stay behind in New Delhi when Roheen begins his run for the Chinese border.

I get more screen time that way.

Since this is Part I of a serial, it runs only a little short of forty minutes. At the end, Roheen is trudging along a forest track in Uttarakhand, heading for China, and the camera pulls back to reveal the mountain valley that holds the forest. The camera keeps pulling back. Mountains rise like great walls to fence Roheen in. Glaciers fill the high valleys, their color a shimmering, sinister, shivering blue. Finally the great peak of Nanda Devi rises up like a vast menacing goddess barring the path. The camera keeps pulling back, tilting to reveal the great ramparts of the Tibetan plateau ahead. Roheen has long since dwindled into nothingness, overwhelmed by the stony, icy fortress that bars his path.

Dramatic music. End of Part I.

I hear distant applause from the direction of the party. Apparently a lot of people began watching the film at the earliest possible moment, like me, and theirs ended just as mine did.

I rise from the marble bench, aware only now of how badly I've cramped. I take a stiff-legged step forward and put both hands on the cool marble sarcophagus.

"Thank you, Doug," I say.

I undock the screen, fold it, and put both it and the tablet in their carrier. I stretch my limbs and step out of the monument onto the lawn. Crickets are sounding in the air.

I find out later that fifteen million people worldwide subscribed to *Escape to Earth* during the first twelve hours that it was available. In the next twelve hours the total went up to sixty-five million. By Sunday morning the numbers stand at a hundred and thirty-five million.

That's a hell of an opening weekend. And the numbers keep climbing.

When I return to the party, I'm a star.

INT. SEAN'S SUITE—DAY

Sunday afternoon I get a call from Joey. I'm half-asleep on my bed at the NoHo, having just had a massage in my suite from one of the hotel's masseuses, in my case a brawny Lebanese lady named Fawziyah. I'm floating, my mind diffused pleasantly into my warm, tingling, completely relaxed body, when my phone begins its series of hysterical shrieks. I grab the handset, intending just to shut it off, but I see it's Joey and answer.

"How are you doing?" I ask thickly. I'm trying to drag my brain back from its post-massage nirvana.

"I've been better," he says. "And by the way, thanks for calling the other day." There is silence. Then, "I really fucked up, didn't I?"

"I'd say there was hella blame to go around. At least you didn't try to hit anyone with a laptop."

"I would have used a shotgun," he says. "Dagmar emailed an apology, by the way."

"She apologized to the rest of us, too."

I swing my legs off the bed and swipe a sheen of sweat off my forehead with a towel. "The premiere went well. The movie looked beautiful. You did a stunning job."

"Have you seen the numbers?"

"I'm checking every ten minutes. I can't believe it."

"Jesus," he says. "The numbers." There's another silence. "Do you think—?"

"Yes?"

He changes tack. "Have I been replaced?"

"Tessa stepped in on Friday, but she's a stopgap. If we have an actual new director, they haven't told me. I'm sure they're calling everyone, but—you know—short notice is a problem."

"Do you think—?" he says again.

"Do I think what?" Because I know what he's trying to say, and I know how hard it's going to be for him.

Escape to Earth is a huge hit. And all the subscription money from those hundred-odd million viewers is going straight into Dagmar's coffers, she doesn't have to split it with theater owners or distributors or anybody. I'll get a chunk of it myself. Once she covers production costs, residuals to certain cast and crew, and the cost of installing infrastructure in places like Waziristan and the Celebes, everything's pure profit.

And the laws of economics will demand a sequel. And, because the infrastructure costs are already paid for, the sequel will be even more profitable.

Joey can't walk out on what has become his first hit in five years. He can't possibly look that ridiculous in public, storming out just ahead of what could be his greatest success. He has to get back in the game.

He sighs. "What are my chances," he asks, "of getting my job back?"

"Joey," I point out, "she tried to hit you over the head with a computer."

"In the heat of the fucking moment. And she apologized."

I towel my face again, a brisk scrub that I hope will bring blood surging to my head. I do my best to calculate the odds. They don't seem to be in Joey's favor.

"It comes down," I say, "to the amount of shit you're willing to eat."

"I'll eat shit," he says. "I know perfectly well I have to eat shit."

"You'll eat shit from Dagmar," I point out. "You'll eat shit from everyone who was at that meeting. And you'll eat every single spoonful of shit that Carter-Ann feeds you for the next month, and you'll do it on your knees. You know that, right?"

"Yeah," he says. He sounds dejected. "Yeah, I know that."

I look down at the floor, still calculating. Now that I'm a star—a star who will inevitably be in the sequel—I maybe have more leverage than I had when I was just a loser in the first round of *Celebrity Pitfighter*.

It might be worth my while to find out just how much leverage I've got.

"I'll call Dagmar, if you want," I say. "But only if you're really serious about crawling your way back into favor."

"God damn!" Joey says. "You're the champ!"

"Not yet," I mutter. I take a needle shower, and I turn the hot water far down, so that I yelp with the sudden cold. My heart lurches into high gear, warm blood and adrenaline flooding my system.

Okay, I'm awake now. Maybe awake enough to deal with Dagmar.

She answers on the first ring. *Maybe*, I think, *I* am *important*.

"A hundred and eighty million," she says. "As of three minutes ago."

"Face it," I say, "we're all geniuses."

"Better than that," Dagmar says, "we're very, very rich."

I don't know what her deal is with Sri, but I'm sure she has more of the gross than I do, and I figure she's sitting pretty.

"I thought I'd report the details of my security audit," I tell her. "For starters, Simon wants to get me out of the trailer."

"I've seen a copy of his report."

Simon started with some fairly sensible recommendations: steel doors and door frames on my condo, barred windows made of one-way glass to prevent anyone from looking inside, cameras and alarms. A panic button worn around the neck that would call security to my aid. An awning on my balcony that would prevent any theoretical snipers from being able to see me. A car with reinforced windows so that no one could toss another Molotov through a window, and with heavy-gauge skid plates attached to vulnerable sections of the underbody to protect it from, say, flaming pools of gasoline—plus of course CCTV focused on my parking place.

After these sensible precautions, Simon's recommendations advance to what might be called Level II Paranoia: evasive driving courses, firearms courses to supplement my martial arts training, and courses in first aid. I would be wearing body armor in public, or at least have it available. The new car would be heavily armored.

Level III involves a whole new home remodeled along the lines of the Führerbunker, with bedrooms for the guards that would move in with me, and a built-in armored panic room where I could hide in the event of an attack, famine, plague, or nuclear strike.

One of Simon's recommendations—I would put this at Level II, myself—involves my moving out of my dressing room/trailer, which is overlooked by several tall buildings in the neighborhood and which isn't bulletproof.

"The Bennett Building has a lot of rooms that were designed as dressing rooms," Dagmar says. "They're offices now, or used for storage, but we can move you into one of them on Monday morning."

"Do you really think someone's going to try taking a shot at me?" I ask. "So far he's only been interested in vehicular homicide."

"I don't want to roll the dice on that," Dagmar says. "If my people need protection, they get it. I've learned the hard way."

Odis Strange's daughter, I think. Took the bullet for Dagmar and died on Cyprus.

I'm not planning on taking a bullet for someone, especially if the someone is me.

"I'll move in," I say. "It's not like I was planning on driving the trailer someplace."

"All right.

"By the way," she says, "we're going to start reshooting the banquet scene tomorrow. Everything else has been pushed back. Do you need a new script?"

"I don't really remember my lines all that well," I tell her. We shot it weeks ago, and since the Chinese section of the serial is going to premiere Friday night, the whole thing has to be wrapped up in the next couple days, so that Allison has time to reedit the scene.

"I'll have a script sent to your room tonight."

"Do we have a director yet?" I ask.

I hear a sigh. "No. But Tessa worked out all right the other day—and all she has to do is a reshoot tomorrow."

"I've got an idea," I say.

"Yes?"

"Why don't we get Joey da Nova? I hear he's available."

Dagmar's tone turns flat. "Not funny, Sean," she says.

"Dagmar," I say, "I got a call. Joey wants to come back."

I hear anger simmering behind Dagmar's voice. "He's burned his bridges, hasn't he?"

"He's willing to forgive you trying to beat him to death," I tell her. "I'd say that's pretty damn generous."

She barks out a laugh. "Tell me why I should bring him back?"

"Well," I say, "first, he gave you the hit you were looking for. Second, he's a terrific director for this project. Third, he's my friend and I work well with him." I take a breath. My heart seems to pause. "And lastly, I want him."

There is a moment of silence on the other end. Both of us, I think, are in the middle of a frantic mental recalibration of the terms of our relationship. Either I have the clout to pull this off, or I don't. Either she's willing to make me happy, or she's not.

Either she has me killed, or she doesn't.

When she speaks, her voice is thoughtful. "You've been a good little trouper, Sean," she says. "And *now* you decide to start waving your dick around?"

"I gave up beer for you," I tell her. "You owe me."

"And I'm protecting you from someone who wants you dead,"

Dagmar says. "I don't think I owe you so much as a stick of chewing gum."

So now the question is, do I push all my chips to the center of the table? *Demand* that Joey be reinstated, on threat of—of what? Walking off the set?

That is ridiculous. I'd never do it. And I have a strong feeling that Dagmar knows I'd never do it.

"I can tell Joey to call you," I say. "You can work it out between the two of you."

"*He* calls *me*," Dagmar says. "He's the beggar here."

"Yes," I say, "yes he is."

"And tell him not to call till tonight. I'm busy till after dinner."

"You got it."

"What I've got," Dagmar says, "is rocks in my head, listening to you like this."

I thank Dagmar and end the call, then call Joey and relay Dagmar's message. He's almost incoherent in his thanks.

"I owe you, champ," he says. "I fuckin' owe you."

Next day he's on the set, directing the reshoot, and I begin to think I've maybe underestimated my clout in this world.

CHAPTER ELEVEN

HEAVY LUGGAGE BLOG

I'd like to thank everyone who watched Episode I of *Escape to Earth*. You've made the project a huge success. If I could kiss three hundred million people, I would!

Comments (178)

FROM: Jaxon31

Kissing those ppl just means URA fagit like Blogjoy sez!

FROM: Coliseum

Its "fagot" moron.

FROM: Jaxon31

URA fagit too haha

FROM: Danishri

That was a terrific episode! Roheen is a great character!

FROM: Vasudev

Was that filmed here in New Delhi? I think I recognized the neighborhood!

FROM: HvyMtl

I gotta admit that ESCAPE TO EARTH was impressive. Of course the fact that Makin is the UGLIEST FREAK IN THE WORLD only helped.

FROM: Tempest Royal

It was terrible what happened to Roheen in New Delhi. I <u>think I might have a solution</u>.

FROM: Corporal Carrot

There's our trailhead!

FROM: Hanseatic

So does that mean that the next episode takes place in England?

FROM: Corporal Carrot

Roheen pretty well looked as if he were going to China.

FROM: Rajkamari

WE LOVE YOU SAMENDRA!!!!

FROM: Jaxon31

Samendra is a fagit hahaha

FROM: LadyDayFan

Tempest Royal might be an agent for the Steyn. Or however that's spelled. But whoever she is, she seems to be London-based.

FROM: HvyMtl

Jaxon, don't you know any other wordz but fagit?

FROM: Jaxon31

HVYMTL YOU ARE A FAGIT TOO HAHAHA

FROM: Trishula

Sean Makin you should enjoy your temporary material success, because soon you will lie in the pit of the lowest hell.

FROM: Jaxon31

HA HA HA WHAT A FAGIT HAHAHA

FROM: Corporal Carrot

Do we think Trishula is a real person or embedded in the ARG somehow?

FROM: HexenHase

Trishula's melodramatic style seems to derive from bad fantasy novels or movie supervillains. I think Great Big Idea employs better prose, don't you?

FROM: Jaxon31

YOU PPL RL FAGITS HAHA!

FROM: Lola17

WE LOVE YOU SEAN!

FROM: MaddHaxx

How about putting out some of that love in MY direction, Lola?

FROM: Corporal Carrot

You know, there are some really unkind people posting on this blog.

FROM: MaddHaxx

Get lost, caporal. We were here first. The loser LUGGAGE BOY belongs to US!

FROM: Jaxon31

hahahahaha hes' ours!

FROM: LadyDayFan

Hmm. When MaddHaxx says that Sean Makin belongs to him, does he mean to David Sivinski, 4801 Crosley Ave, Duluth, Minnesota? Because that's who MaddHaxx seems to be.

FROM: Corporal Carrot

David is the name on the address and the Internet account, but I'm thinking that MaddHaxx is actually David's son Paul, who is thirteen years of age and attends Ordean Middle School.

FROM: LadyDayFan

Good call!

FROM: Hanseatic

Wow! The Sivinskis are in the phone directory! If we called and asked for MaddHaxx, do you think we'd get an answer?

FROM: LadyDayFan

So MaddHaxx— Have we got your number?

FROM: Hanseatic

MaddHaxx? MaddHaxx? Suddenly it's very quiet in here.

FROM: Hippolyte

Amazing how a certain personality type, emboldened by anonimity, is silenced when his true identity is revealed.

FROM: Jaxon31

U ppl R assholes haha

FROM: LadyDayFan

We're not fagits? Whatever those are?

FROM: Hippolyte

I meant "anonymity," of course. Bad fingers!

FROM: Burçak

While you were looking into MaddHaxx, I've been checking out Mr. Jaxon. He seems to be Neal Jackson—clever disguise, there! And his internet account is billed to 1315 South Harbor Boulevard, Anaheim, California.

FROM: LadyDayFan

Uh-oh. It looks like Mr. Jackson has a couple convictions for DUI.

FROM: Hanseatic

Bad credit rating, too.

FROM: Hippolyte

All this in just a few minutes! What else might we discover if we actually put our minds to this?

FROM: Corporal Carrot

Unless I miss my guess, Jaxon has lost his driving license, and he has nothing better to do than drink in front of his keyboard and release his inner troll.

FROM: Jaxon31

I cd do the same 2U, asshats.

FROM: LadyDayFan

Frankly, we doubt you're intelligent (or sober) enough to penetrate our brilliant disguises. But you're welcome to try.

FROM: Hippolyte

I've been looking into Trishula. He seems to be a harder nut to crack.

FROM: Hanseatic

We've only just begun.

FROM: Farzana16

Sean, do you know if Samendra has a girlfriend?

FROM: Corporal Carrot

Yee-haw! Saddle up, boys! There's a new sheriff in town!

INT. SOUNDSTAGE—DAY

Joey's back on the job, but he's not the same Joey. He's subdued. He's cooperative. He accepts Carter-Ann's suggestions without comment and implements them. He watches us all with a dead expression on his face, his eyes walking from one person to the next: me, Jean-Marc, Carter-Ann, the others. His work is professional, but without his usual joy, his usual flair, and without improvisation. He just follows the storyboard he's created for his computer.

Which is fine, as far as it goes. It's a good storyboard. But he no longer seems interested in following up chance opportunities to improve what he's laid out ahead of time. It's like he just wants to get the job over with, then go home.

Whatever he's feeling, Joey isn't letting it show. He's keeping it all under wraps: the resentment of Carter-Ann, the humiliation from the kowtowing he must have done to Dagmar, the fury at the constant interference. I half-expect to see him walk in with an explosives vest and take us all out of the picture.

Joey's disinterestedness isn't as important as it might have been at an earlier stage of the project. By now we've all got momentum. I understand Roheen, and I don't need a director to get me into the character or explain his actions. Everyone else is into their own routines, and the production runs beautifully.

Carter-Ann is quietly triumphant. She doesn't abuse her power in any obvious way, but that's because she doesn't have to. She remains polite and soft-spoken and completely superior. She's got Joey's neck pinned beneath her heel, and that's fine with her.

We reshoot the banquet scene in a single day. I view the old scene before we start, and now I find it bitterly obvious where I failed. Overplaying, turning Roheen into a greedy clown. No wonder the Chinese hated it. I only wonder that people in North America found the scene bearable.

Instead of diving face-first into the food, this time I *yearn* at it. I look at the food, I fondle it with my eyes. I reach out with my chopsticks as if I were about to caress a lover. I look at the meal with something like religious devotion. And when I taste it, I let it rest in my mouth, giving off flavor, barely chewing at all while I screw my features up into an orgasm face.

The cameraman is laughing so hard that the camera keeps shaking and blowing takes.

I'm happy again. I'm working, and I think I'm working well.

Joey doesn't tell me it's good, though. At the end of the day he calls a wrap, and goes off to the editing room with Allison.

INT. SEAN'S SUITE—NIGHT

I know I'm important again when I get a call from Kari Sothern.

"Congratulations," she says. "You seem to be a worldwide phenomenon."

"Yeah," I say. "You should see the fan mail I get from Tanzania."

She laughs. "I'm going to quote that," she says. "Can you give us an interview?"

"Love to," I say, "but—"

"Great! How about right now?"

"But," I repeat, "you'll have to clear it with Great Big Idea. They're controlling all the publicity." I'm already scheduled to make the rounds of local talk shows, and in the wake of the unexpected success of the film—three hundred million subscriptions by the end of the day—I'm being shopped pretty hard to the networks.

It's early evening. Simon has dropped me off at the NoHo, and I've got my feet up on the coffee table, contemplating a hole in one of my socks. A room-service meal of pasta primavera has been wheeled in, and sits half-eaten in my lap. The room smells strongly of garlic.

I'm exhausted, but then I've been exhausted for so long that it's almost normal. I really wish I had a beer.

"Great Big Idea," Kari says, "isn't being very forthcoming."

Probably for good reason. Kari used to be an editor on the *Weekly Tale*, a tabloid newspaper loaded with gossip, innuendo, and scandal, a vast amount of which it either invents or shamelessly creates itself. Now the *Tale* has a daily half-hour show on the Glamour Channel, and Kari produces it. Watching or reading the *Tale* gives you the same odd thrill as, say, professional wrestling, and for the same reason—you know it's fake, but you have to admire the brio with which they put on their act.

"You could just make shit up," I tell her, "like you usually do."

Kari, like most reporters, is immune to insult. "Maybe," she says, "you can give me something off the record."

"Like what?"

"Nataliya Hogan is in this picture, right?"

"Yes."

"Can you give me anything? I won't quote you directly."

My fingers stroke the panic button hanging around my neck—hold it down for three seconds, and guards come bursting in—and I consider telling Kari about the phony proposal, or maybe about the monologue Nataliya wrote. I could go on about the ego, the entourage, the obliviousness to any other person, the complete narcissism... but why?

However much she annoys me, Nataliya is one of *us*. The tabloid reporter is one of *them*. The tabloids prey on people like me, turning us into freaks for the amusement of the sadists and geeks and groupies who read their publications.

Every time I've talked to one of *them*, I've had cause to regret it.

"Nataliya was only on the set for a few days," I tell Kari. "She was perfectly professional. She knew her lines. She was fine."

"What was it like working with her?"

"I only had one scene with her. She was great—very funny."

Her tone turns suspicious. "You're not giving me much."

"I don't *have* much."

"You've been more cooperative in the past, Sean."

I stir my pasta with my fork. "I'm boring," I say. "I'm boring because I'm *working*. I get up in the morning and go to the studio and work all day and then come home and learn my lines for the next day. You want anything exciting from me, you'll have to wait till I have time and leisure. Right now, it's just a fucking job."

It's not true, exactly—I don't mention that I'm being stalked by a homicidal wannabe in an SUV—but what I've told Kari is what I wish were true. I'm an actor, and it's pretty well all I want to be right now. I don't want to be dodging murderous drivers, I don't want to think about Jaydee's death, I don't want to watch snarling people ripping each other to pieces on the set every day. I don't want to try to work out what Dagmar is up to with Deeptimoy Srivastava. All I want to be is in front of the camera and working.

"Listen, Sean," Kari says. "*Escape to Earth* is the hottest thing to hit the planet since New Year. It's the first serial to be presented to audiences since Buster Crabbe's time, *and it's a hit.* Everyone's talking about whether it's the end of conventional cinema."

"Of course it isn't." I feel this hardly needs pointing out.

"*I need something.* What Great Big Idea is handing out is just press releases about the technology. What I need to know about is the *people.*"

I swirl some pasta onto my fork and eat it. Then I take a second bite.

"Or," Kari says, "you could tell me what happens next."

"What happens next," I say, "is that I finish the production and go on vacation. I'll send you a postcard from wherever I end up."

"What happens next *in the story.*"

I laugh. "You want to know how the movie ends?"

"Sure," she says. "You could slip me a script."

I laugh even harder. "Why would I?"

"We'd pay you."

"How much?"

"Last time we paid you ten thousand."

Yes, I thought. For a little thirty-second bit of digital media that wrecked Melody Chastain's career. If I'd known it was going to be that big, I would have asked for more.

"I needed money then," I said. "I don't now."

"Sean," she says, "we've been good to you."

I fork up another bit of pasta. "'*Vodka-raddled has-been*,'" I say. "Am I quoting your paper correctly?"

"Sean—"

"You didn't even get my drink of choice right."

"Sean," she says, "you know we're going to dig."

For a moment I feel a tremor of fear, and then I shrug it off. They're not going to find out about Timmi, not after all these years—and if I'm *very* lucky, they'll find out the identity of my stalkers.

"Dig away," I say.

"We don't have to dig very far," she says. "There's the Melody Chastain video."

She is referring to another desperate episode in my career, when I was broke and provided Kari with candid photos of my fellow celebrities in exchange for money. I took the pics with my handheld, at parties or clubs, and most of them were harmless enough, just the subject looking stupid, unsightly, or silly. They'd end up in the tabloids next to a headline about whether they were too fat, or too thin, or too old, or had benefited from cosmetic surgery, or needed the benefits of cosmetic surgery, or were otherwise inadequate compared to whatever the *Tale* thought they should be on that particular day.

All harmless fun, until I struck gold. There I was at a party at Cindy Ray's, smoking a blunt in privacy on the tennis court, when Melody Chastain had her celebrity meltdown practically in front of me. I was partly concealed by the bushes around the court and no one saw me there.

As a kid actor, Melody had two hit television series, and then went on to star in three big movies. Her career arc was a mirror of mine, soaring up where mine crumbled into the cellar, and she was so talented and so clearly deserving of success that I hardly hated her at all. But her private life was a twelve-car freeway pileup: her engagement to Nathan Marley ended when he dropped her for the tennis player Liz Hughes; Melody then had a widely publicized lesbian relationship that likewise cratered when her partner dumped her; and then there was the wedding in Reno that lasted three days before both parties sobered up and moved to annul.

There I was on the tennis court smoking when it all came down on Melody at once, and she erupted, screaming, throwing drinks, hurling furniture. She is a tiny person, but she showed amazing strength. She kept yelling about a florist and how this florist had screwed with her somehow by delivering flowers to the wrong place. I had my handheld out fast as thought, recording the whole scene. Cindy and Odis Strange and Melody's hapless date were trying to calm her down, and then Cindy's schnauzer—who may have been afraid that Cindy was being threatened or something—ran onto the scene, barking. And Melody, screaming and weeping, kicked that dog, and then kicked it some more while the dog yelped in pain, and then chased the dog around the patio trying to kick it and failing. Then Odis and Cindy grabbed Melody under the arms and carried her off while she collapsed weeping, and that was that.

The video was less than thirty seconds long. Before midnight, I had sold it to Kari and killed Melody's career.

The American public is amazingly tolerant of celebrity behavior on the whole. We can drink rivers of alcohol, snort mountains of cocaine, fornicate till our parts explode. But whatever you do, you can't kick a dog. Kicking a dog is worse than cheating on half a dozen spouses, worse than committing a dozen hit-and-runs. Worse than invading a foreign country.

That video was the end of Melody. Her next films flopped, not because they were bad, but because the public didn't want to see the evil dog-kicker. Her career had collapsed into a sub-basement lower even than mine.

I wouldn't have sold the video if I'd known the sensation it was going to cause. If I thought anything about it at all, I figured the video would cause sympathy for Melody, because she was in such obvious pain.

But she kicked the dog. And that was that. And she became another victim of the public's expectations, Hollywood child exploitation, and most importantly of Sean Makin.

I keep destroying people. I never mean to, I never plan it. But my path is strewn with wreckage, all of it human.

Sometimes I think I might just as well be evil. I could, for instance, become my father, raking in the money and spending it recklessly, not caring how I got it or where it came from or who got hurt. I could become Richard III and strive for power and try to crush those who oppose me. Then there might be a *reason* for all the suffering I seem to spawn. But instead it just *happens*, and I'm left looking at the devastation and wondering how it became connected to me.

"Melody Chastain video?" I hear myself saying. "What Melody Chastain video?"

"You know the one."

It has by now occurred to me that the conversation might be recorded. I am not about to give them any rope to hang me with.

There's no actual record of my sale of the video clip. I handed over a memory stick and got a stack of hundred-dollar bills in return. This happened late in the evening, after banks had closed, and I remember being impressed that the *Tale* had a stack of money that big sitting in the office safe, just in case someone like me wanted to sell it something juicy.

"If you want to talk to me, contact Great Big Idea," I say. "And otherwise, I'll see you around."

"Okay, Sean." Kari sighs. "But whatever you do—*don't kick the dog.*"

Next day I go into Dagmar's office and tell her about Kari's call. "She says she's going to dig," she says.

Dagmar laughs, shakes her head, and thinks for a moment. "I'd better make sure to give her something, then," she says.

I leave and don't think anything about it, not till I see the

Tale that appears midweek. It has a picture of Roheen with the headline ESCAPE TO EARTH—PLOT SECRETS REVEALED! I'm pissed to think that Kari must have got to someone, until I snatch up the rag and read the article, and I discover that someone sold Kari a bill of highly damaged goods. There are no scenes in this film set in Turkey. There's no one in *Escape to Earth* named Kristeen or Fuad or Mehmet.

Someone in Dagmar's organization sold her a fake script—in fact a fake script from one of Dagmar's ARGs with the names changed.

I don't know who handled the trade-off, but I suspect Richard the Assassin. It seems like his style.

I mean to ask him what he did with the money, but I never do.

INT. BRUCE BENNETT BUILDING—DAY

Having a dressing room in the office building instead of the trailer puts me in a completely different scene. Instead of being surrounded by people in the picture business, I'm surrounded by geeks. Richard and Helmuth have staffs. Dagmar has assistants. There are producers I've never met, and this enormously obese man named Mike who slouches around staring at the floor and mumbling—apparently he designs puzzles for the online games, and the mumbling is part of his process. The people from Wardrobe and Makeup who come to tend to me look as if they're ambassadors from a foreign country.

The Bennett Building is full of people rushing off to meetings about hardware and online games and things that have nothing to do with the motion picture. Just walking around, I hear arguments and discussions that are so technical I have no idea what anyone is saying.

I'm reasonably comfortable in my new digs, and my only real problem is that my dressing room doesn't have a shower. There was one once, but it's been converted to storage. But there's a kind of health club downstairs, where the geeks can run on treadmills while arguing over the control to the flat-screen TV, and there's a shower down there. So at the end of the day, when I'm finally out of makeup, I can get a shower and clean up before heading home.

Reshooting the banquet scene changed my schedule, so I've got Friday off, and then will be working all day Saturday. I've also got Thursday afternoon off, because *Escape to Earth*'s popularity has gotten me installed as a guest on a taping of *The Tonight Show*.

Trying out a few witticisms for *Tonight*, I go downstairs on Thursday afternoon, take my shower, and am trudging back up the stairs with my towel over my shoulder when Helmuth overtakes me, turns the corner, and vanishes from sight. All without saying hello.

I feel a warning flutter in my stomach. Maybe there's another emergency. Or another death. I slip up the stairs and turn, and there's the door to Dagmar's office. The scent from her coffeemaker wafts into the corridor.

"Goddamn it!" Dagmar is shouting. "Goddamn it, the tanks are rolling!"

I don't hear Helmuth's reply.

"We weren't in place yet," Dagmar says. "Damn it to hell."

I don't know that I'm supposed to be hearing this, or thinking about what Dagmar has to do with anyone's tanks, but I'm standing right there, and Helmuth passed me on the stairs, and I can hardly pretend I don't exist. So I turn into the office door, and I see Helmuth's back, and Dagmar standing behind her desk. Her face is tight with rage and frustration. Tears glimmer in her eyes.

"What's happened?" I ask.

Helmuth turns to face me.

"War between Thailand and Burma."

"Thailand and Burma?" I don't know why I'm surprised by what foreigners get up to, but I always am. "Why?"

"Stupidity!" Dagmar blurts. "Stupid insecure military men on either side of the border who bluster for the cameras but who won't even *talk* to each other. And now—" She threatens to smash one of her monitors with a white-knuckled fist, but apparently thinks better of it.

"And what..." I approach the subject cautiously. "What do *we* have to do with this?"

"Nothing," Dagmar says. She falls heavily into her chair and gropes blindly for a tissue. "Not a damn thing." She dabs her eyes and sniffles. "Sorry," she says. Her face is partly hidden by her hand and by the tissue. "Pregnant ladies get mood swings."

I don't know why the mood swings should be triggered by a war between strangers on another continent, but then I've never been pregnant, have I?

"We have another problem," Helmuth says. He's speaking very carefully, as aware as I am that we're dealing with a hormone-crazed expecting woman. "We've got server problems."

Dagmar's head snaps up. "Have servers gone down?"

"Eight hundred sixty-six of them," Helmuth is saying. "And they've all crashed."

I relax. We're off the subject of war.

When Dagmar answers, her voice is thoughtful. "Is it any of our old friends with the High Zap?" she asks.

"No. Otherwise we'd have lost whole server farms."

Dagmar blows her nose, and when she speaks her voice is denasal. "Have we been hacked?"

Helmuth shakes his head. "I doubt it. It's only the Top Kick servers made in Korea that have been affected. I think it's an unknown design issue, because the Top Kicks made in the Malaysia factory are doing fine. I've got Hossein and Charlotte on a conference call with the Top Kick people in Seoul, and I've got the Oulu managers listening in."

The scent of coffee is making my mouth water. I turn to the coffee machine, pour coffee into a disposable cardboard cup, and add some white gunk from a packet.

"Where are they?" Dagmar asks.

"Finland, Alaska, and New Zealand."

"And," Dagmar says, "we've got the world premiere of Part II of *Escape to Earth* in something like twenty-nine hours, and now we may not have the bandwidth to put on the show."

Anxiety takes a little nip at my nerves. By the time Part II is broadcast, viewers won't have got into the habit of viewing the episodes regularly—if there's a problem with the downloads, they may just give up.

"Why do you put the servers in places like Finland and Alaska?" I ask. It seems to me that you'd want them somewhere a bit more centrally located.

"Because it's *cold* in Finland and Alaska," Dagmar says. "And also in the mountains of New Zealand. Anywhere there's glaciers, your server farm can save a bundle on cooling." She turns to Helmuth.

"I'll get on the line to Sri and see if any of his companies can let us have some servers," she says. "In the meantime…" She raises her hands and wiggles her fingers, as if summoning something from the ether. "You'll have to go into the cloud. Get us backup routers and servers wherever you can find them."

"It's not in the budget," Helmuth says.

"Take the money from the other budget," Dagmar says.

He nods. His eyes give a little twitch in my direction, trying to gauge whether I understand what just happened, and then he leaves. I sip my coffee.

The other budget. Dagmar's office may look like that of a computer science grad student, but she's clearly wise in the ways of producers. Keeping the real money hidden, where no one—not her backers, not the government, maybe not even Sri—can find it.

This isn't exactly earthshaking news. I am proud to say that Hollywood leads the world in fraudulent bookkeeping. We've been making movies here for over a hundred years, and not a single film has ever made a profit or required the producers to share that profit with anyone else.

When it comes to bookkeeping, the Mafia has nothing on us.

* * *

INT. IMPALA—EVENING

"So who's representing you now?"

It's a question I've been expecting ever since my caller identified himself.

"Cleve Baker, of Baker and Baker."

"Who?" The man is either genuinely baffled or a pretty good actor. His name is Gregg, Gregg with three *g*'s, and he's an agent at Talent Representation International, which is one of the top half-dozen agencies in town.

"Cleve is very exclusive," I say.

"He must be," Gregg mutters. There's a moment's silence. "I was wondering," he says, "if I could buy you lunch and talk to you about what we could do for you at TRI."

I consider making Gregg take me and my entourage—Simon and Wild Bill/Albert—to someplace like Lester's on the Beach, where we could set TRI back a couple grand for a vastly expensive meal, but then I decide I'm too tired and too busy.

"Why don't you pitch me now?" I say. "I figure I've got at least half an hour."

I'm in the backseat of Simon's Impala on Thursday night, stuck on Burbank Boulevard trying to get back to NoHo Plaza, from where I've been taping the great-grandfather of all talk shows. There must be construction or an accident ahead or something. We're boxed in by trucks, buses, and large pickups, and the air conditioning isn't quite efficient enough to keep out the scent of diesel exhaust.

"It might take me more than half an hour," Gregg says. "We're a pretty all-encompassing big agency."

"Just go ahead and pitch," I tell him. "I'm stuck in traffic on the way back from taping *The Tonight Show*."

"*Tonight*? That's great!" he says. "How'd it go?"

"Gregg," I say, "I killed." Which, for the record, I did. Roheen is a fucking icon. Roheen is big enough to get me on *Tonight* on something like three days' notice.

The younger people screamed. The older crowd remembered

Luggage Boy and liked me. I was witty and self-effacing and praised Dagmar to the skies, which can't have hurt me with my bosses.

As with reality television, the audience thinks that talk shows are more spontaneous than they actually are. There's a rehearsal. The host goes over the questions he wants to ask you. You have time to think about amusing ways to answer him, and provided you stay away from the free booze in the greenroom you won't embarrass yourself.

Gregg goes into his pitch. He goes on about how TRI is a creative, forward-thinking entertainment powerhouse with an elite roster of talent and the ability to offer personal attention to each and every client. TRI has worldwide awesome all-encompassing might in the fields of motion pictures, television, music, artist marketing, motion picture financing, book publishing, literary rights, theater, stand-up comedy, commercials, personal appearances, and corporate events.

This last could be a major income producer, I hear. "As big as you are in the online and interactive community right now," he says. "We could book you into gaming and media conventions and get you good money. And—uh—I don't know about martial arts events, but I could look into it."

"Sounds great, Gregg!" I say with great cheer.

"Shall we have lunch?" he asks. "We can go into more detail—"

"One problem, Gregg," I say.

"Yes?"

"Your agency fired me ten years ago. That cocksucker Alan Franz told me I had no career left and that I should find something else to do with my life, like, I don't know, sell vacuum cleaners door-to-door maybe."

"Ah," he says. "Well."

"So has Alan changed his mind?"

I can almost hear his brain gears spinning over the phone. "I haven't, ah, talked to Mr. Franz about you specifically."

"So the aforesaid cocksucker Alan Franz is still at TRI, then?"

Gregg clears his throat. "Mr. Franz is, um..."

"He's executive vice president and chairman of the Management Division—in other words, your boss. Is that right, Gregg?"

"Uh. Yes."

"Well, Gregg," I say, "I'll tell you what we'll do. If Franz comes down to my digs and kisses my ass—and I mean *literally licks my anus*—then I will consider being represented by your company."

"Sean," Gregg says. "Can I call you Sean?"

"You absolutely can," I say.

"Because I want to assure you—"

"Here's what I think, Gregg," I say. "I think that if you leave TRI and get a job with a *genuinely* forward-thinking and creative agency, you should give me a call."

"I—"

"Thanks for thinking of me. I really appreciate it." I hang up.

Simon looks at me in the rearview mirror. "That sounded like fun," he says.

"It whiles away my empty hours," I say.

"Wish I could say that to some of the folks that fired me over the years."

I'm just sorry that I had to have that conversation with some mid-level agent, and not with Alan Franz. What makes the chat all the more sweet is that I know that ten days ago I would have willingly licked Franz's back passage if it had meant getting TRI representation.

Power. It's not just for other people any more. It's for Luggage Boy.

"You know what?" I tell Simon. "I've just finished taping *Tonight.* Why the hell should I go back to the hotel and spend the night playing video games?"

" 'Cuz that's the smart course of action," Simon says, "and you have work tomorrow morning."

"You didn't check the latest call sheets," I say. Because the reshoot of the banquet scene shuffled everything around, and I'm not on call Friday, but will have to come in on Saturday instead, working amid a happy crew delighting in its overtime.

"Take a left and get us to the One-oh-one," I say. "We're getting the fuck out of the Valley and going to the Strip."

"If you say so," Simon says. "But I should maybe call for some backup if you're going out in public."

"Simon," I say. "Nobody's going to be able to follow us in this traffic. And if someone *is* after us, you'll spot them right away."

Wild Bill turns around to look at me. "There could be drones overhead," he says. "Someone could be chasing you that way."

"Can't the two of you deal?" I ask. "There'll be club security as well. And nobody can hit me with an SUV if I'm indoors."

Simon is reluctant, but concedes. I get on the phone and call Helmuth, Dagmar's programming chief, who has these completely false memories of the two of us partying at the Got Real?, and who I gather from Dagmar is quite the party animal. He answers, and I ask if he wants to join me at the clubs tonight.

"I'm already at Panikk."

"Why don't I join you there?"

I also call Julian, but all I get is voice mail. I tell him we're starting at Panikk and I'll let him know if I move anywhere from there.

The doorkeeper at Panikk lets me and my guards in without a blink. He looks like some kind of fashion refugee from 2002, with dental grills and diamond rings on every finger, but his social antennae are very much up-to-the-second.

Panikk has a classic Los Angeles look, with recessed pink lighting, chrome stripes on the bar, and cages for go-go dancers. There isn't much action, and no go-go dancers, but it's early. Helmuth is in a booth behind a couple empty highball glasses, talking with a tall, thin, google-eyed man whose name I can't quite recall, but who I know is a stand-up comic. He recognizes me and calls me Sean, so I respond as if I've known him all my life.

Simon gets a table of his own where he can watch us. I order a burger and a Coke off the bar menu.

Nothing much happens. Helmuth and I leave Panikk after an hour or so and head for Club Kali. The comic stays behind, and I never remember his name. Club Kali features a statue of a big-breasted, multi-armed goddess standing by the entrance, and the interior looks like some kind of Calcutta cult temple, complete with a frieze of gods and goddesses reenacting the *Kama Sutra*. Everyone seems to know Helmuth—and, very encouragingly, everyone knows *me*.

There's more going on at Club Kali, and a DJ with an extremely deep knowledge of Hindi hip-hop, and we stay for a couple hours. By then I've collected an entourage.

You can see it at the clubs. Every successful actor acquires a little crew of less successful actors. It doesn't matter how successful they are—big stars will attract lesser stars, and actors who have just had a walk-on in a sitcom will attract actors who haven't had a walk-on in a long time.

I and my entourage go on to Dove Bar. There's some kind of nuevo-surf band playing and the Dove Bar is jumping. We dance for a while, then chill in one of the VIP rooms.

There is liquor as well as mysterious pills and powders. Aware that I'm with one of Dagmar's employees who would likely rat on me if I did anything against the rules, I indulge in nothing stronger than cranberry juice, but I get high anyway. It's just being in the scene again.

I sink into the club life like a warm bath. I did this for years, when I was younger.

I learned about sex when I was thirteen. I'd finished my scenes for the day and was hanging around my dressing room, waiting for my ride home, and I met a frizzy-haired girl who was actually there for Floyd Steneri, who played my older brother. He'd hooked up with someone else, so the girl took me to my dressing room and showed me some things that up till then I'd only dreamed about.

Within a few weeks I was an experienced player. I was a teen idol, remember, and girls already mobbed the studio gates to catch a glimpse of me driving in or out. I'd get out of the car when I felt like it and sign autographs. If I knew I'd have time to myself at some point in the day, I'd pick the fan I liked and ask if she'd like to take a tour of the studio. (They always said yes.) I'd show her around, then have her wait in my trailer till I had enough free time for a sexual encounter. (They always said yes.)

The delights of amateurs sufficed for a little more than a year, after which I discovered the merit of professionals. Groupies used to be fans or amateurs back in the Stone Age, I gather, but now they're usually placed somewhere in the sex industry—strippers, nude models, actresses who do hardcore, call girls. They had experience, ability, enthusiasm, and giant breasts as artificial and delightful as ice cream sundaes. Since they were over twenty-one, they could get me into the clubs, and my celebrity assured that they were treated well and had access to the VIP rooms.

My parents were busy spending my money, and I'm not sure if they noticed. My father loved peeling hundred-dollar bills off his roll and handing them to me, because it made him look like a tycoon. He never asked what I spent the money on.

My morals might be questioned, but what couldn't be questioned was that I was living the life that every priapic teenage boy in America drooled over. *All the sex I wanted, with practically anyone I wanted.* Everyone else involved got what they wanted, too. No one got hurt.

That wasn't what happened later, when the groupies were gone, and I tried what I assumed were normal relationships. The only women I fell in love with were the ambitious ones who were using me for my industry contacts, and who—once they knew everyone I did—dropped me to climb further up the Hollywood ladder.

I was bewildered. At least it was clear from the start what the ladies from the sex industry wanted.

And so now, here at Dove Bar, I find myself falling into my

former life like a tired field hand into a soft feather bed. It's all familiar. I know the moves.

I don't remember whether I meet Ramona at the Club Kali or at the Dove, but I know that she shares the backseat with me on the drive back to the NoHo, and that the party in my room continues pretty much till dawn.

She's tall and raven-haired and has a winged Eye of Horus tattooed on the small of her back, a butterfly on her upper thigh, and a dragon coiling around an upper arm.

Her breasts have had work, but hey, this is Hollywood.

Simon looks her over carefully before he lets her into my room, but he doesn't give her anything more than an eye-frisk. Apparently even under Level III Paranoia the customer can get laid.

If he'd checked her bag he would have found the cocaine. I decline but she snorts at least half a gram off the polished surface of my bedside table, and then licks up the rest with her active little tongue. When I kiss her I can savor the quinine taste of the drug. The coke probably explains why she's awake at seven and I'm not. She nudges me out of slumber long enough to tell me she's got to go to work, and then she dresses and leaves.

I make sure that she leaves her cell number and collapse back into sleep. Some hours later I rise and shower and call room service for breakfast, only to be told that breakfast is no longer available. I order a pulled pork sandwich. Nothing like red meat to get the day started.

I think about the previous night's call from Gregg with three *g*'s, and realize that it's getting to be time to replace Cleve. Whatever Cleve's virtues might be—and if I think about it real hard I might envision a couple—it has to be admitted that Baker and Baker does not have anything approaching worldwide dominance in, say, artist marketing, motion picture financing, book publishing, literary rights, theater, stand-up comedy, commercials, personal appearances, and corporate events.

Not that I plan to be a stand-up comic any time soon. But still.

So as I eat my sandwich I consider acquiring new representation. I wonder if Joey will set me up with a meeting at Huston-Hauser, the outfit he joined after he fired William Morris years ago when they failed to find him work after his career collapse.

And then my phone gives its horror-movie shriek, and I see that it's Cleve calling.

"I'm not interrupting anything?" he says.

"Nothing but a sandwich."

"Can we talk a minute? I've got some important news."

"Sure."

"I want you to know that I'm going to be closing Baker and Baker."

I'm taken aback, but also delighted. *Problem solved!* I think cheerfully.

In my reply, I affect concern. "You're closing the agency?"

"Yes. I'm moving on to PCTA, and I'm only bringing a few of my clients with me. I hope you'll agree to be one of them."

PanCosmos Talent Associates is one of the top five or six agencies, just like TRI, except that it also has a huge sports division. (Not that I'm planning to join the NBA or anything.) I have to pause for admiration when I consider that Cleve managed to parlay his one asset—me—into a berth at a place like PCTA.

Which, it now occurs to me, means I must be a bigger property than I had assumed.

"I've got a free afternoon," I say. "Why don't you show me around your new digs?"

He hesitates. "I don't actually have an office yet," he says.

"Show me around anyway."

Simon is off, since I kept him busy guarding me till dawn, but a colleague named Astin is on duty, a soft-voiced black man with gold-rimmed shades and a shaved head. He's built like a football player, and probably was one. He drives a black Ford Expedition, which causes me to do a double take and sends paranoia screaming along my veins like the LAPD racing down the Ventura Freeway to a crime scene. For half a second I'm convinced that Astin is my mystery driver, but then I see that his Expedition is new and gleaming, and I remember that the SUV that tried to run me down was older and belched blue smoke.

Astin takes me to PCTA's jade-green octagonal tower in Beverly Hills. It's got weird jagged black objects projecting from the roof, like giant jigsaw pieces, and though they're supposed to have something to do with feng shui, the whole structure is clearly something the Emperor Palpatine built to house an Ultimate Weapon, probably one that sucks in all power for a thousand miles around. Just inside the front door, inset into the marble floor, is another octagon, with each segment marked by an I Ching trigram. More evil magic. Cleve waits in the lobby, wearing a three-piece suit, glossy wingtips, and a chin dark with fashionable two-day stubble.

"Ready to join the Axis of Evil?" he asks me.

He's only half-joking. Even if she is a terrorist, there's a limit to the number of people Dagmar can frighten at a time. PCTA is so huge it can terrify an entire *industry*.

"You're in an awesome new house, man," I say.

"I'd like you to meet Mr. Kravitz."

I figured I could judge my degree of clout by which of the top brass pitched me, but I sure as hell hadn't expected Bruce Kravitz, who is vice president in charge of talent. He was one of the three original founders of the company, and one of the others is dead.

He takes me up to Bruce's office, which is about as big as the set for *Celebrity Pitfighter* and nearly as gaudy, with Chinese vases in every corner, gold Chinese characters set into the walls, and a gold-plated samurai sword mounted under Plexiglas behind Bruce's desk. Bamboo flutes and mirrors, important in feng shui, hang in the corners and on the walls. There are ancient bonsai on little stands. The center of the carpet features a giant mandala, probably one that means *I own the Tao and you can't have it.*

Bruce is lean and balding and has a dry handshake and a dry manner. His eyes are a pale blue. Mild irony seems to surround him like an aura, and I figure John Malkovich should play him in the biopic. I thank him for seeing me on such short notice, and he asks if I'd like anything to drink. I accept a cup of tea, first cuttings from some valley in Oregon that, apparently, has the best microclimate for tea in the world.

Bruce accepts the teapot from his assistant and pours it himself.

I have to admit that it's a pretty darn good cup of tea.

Bruce gives me what I assume is a speech he's given many times before, mostly about the all-consuming mightiness of PCTA. Talented writers will develop or adapt scripts just for me, and PanCosmos will package these with directors and other actors, grab studio heads by their gonads, and demand that they be produced. We will trample Hollywood beneath our collective feet. A future of gold-plated Gulfstream jets and mattresses stuffed with gold double-eagle coins will soon be ours.

While this conversation goes on, Bruce calls in a stream of subagents from various departments: publicity, literary properties—an autobiography is mentioned—and the woman from the speakers' bureau. I have a long talk with her.

"You're hot right now in the tech field," she says. "Game conventions, tech conventions, industry gatherings—you can make a nice packet giving talks."

"And you've got a great story," Bruce says. "Early success, the theft of your heritage, the wilderness years... and now, of course, you've crossed into the promised land."

Great! I think. *I'm Moses!*

I wonder if my mom would be impressed, but then I decide she wouldn't. After all, she knows God personally.

Bruce steeples his manicured fingers. "I'm interested in *Escape to Earth*," he says. "I'm interested in the technologies and the techniques."

Aha, I think. It's not just me he wants, it's also Dagmar and everything she knows and all her skills. But he can't get Dagmar, so he'll settle for stealing as many of her innovations as he can, packaging them with his own people, then selling them himself.

"That's a long conversation," I tell him. "Better save it for another afternoon."

Bruce offers a languid, cynical smile. "Absolutely," he says. He leans toward me. "Sean," he says, "what would you like to do? What's your dream? Because I'd like to make your dream come true."

I feel my mouth going dry as I stare into Bruce's pale eyes. I have absolutely nothing to say. And at this instant, right now, I realize just how pathetic my ambitions have been. All I wanted was to work steadily and not be poor and have women like me— and now I've got that, got it all in the last week, and I can't think of anything more I want.

Cripes, you'd think I could come up with a better fantasy than that, wouldn't you? What the hell can I tell him? *Richard III*? That's ridiculous.

I lean toward Bruce, and put as sincere a look on my face as I can.

"You know," I say, "I've always wanted to play our lord and savior, Jesus Christ."

There's a strange shift that goes on behind the blue eyes as every switch in Bruce's brain resets to zero, and for a moment there's a slackness in the lower jaw as he tries to process the idea of an unnaturally tall, watermelon-headed Klingon playing the Son of God, and how he's now going to have to promise that he'll try to make that happen. But I have to say that he handles it well.

"Just kidding," I say.

Bruce gives a thin smile that tells me he doesn't like being pranked. Cleve breaks into laughter.

"You even had *me* going!" Cleve says. It's the first thing he's said in maybe half an hour.

"Honestly," I say, "it's all happened so fast, I haven't had a chance to reorder my priorities. I have a whole list of ideas, but I'm going to have to look through it and see what really speaks to me now."

Bruce nods. "Fine. Take your time."

He offers to refresh my tea, and I decline.

"Look," I say. "I just need to say this one thing. I got fired by Sam Kripenevitch. I got fired by Alan Franz. Getting fired by Bruce Kravitz would make the trifecta, but—" I try to focus on what I'm attempting to articulate. I have the sense that simply expressing my insecurities would be wrong in this setting.

When in doubt, I think, *try flattery*.

"Okay," I say. "If I go with PanCosmos, it's because I think you're better than those guys. I think maybe that's what I'm trying to say."

Bruce has an expression of professional concern on his face. "Sean," he says. "I won't fire you."

"Fire me if I'm an asshole," I say. "Or if I get drunk and throw up on Michael Jackson's grave or something. But don't fire me just because I have a dry spell."

Bruce nods. "We don't do that here."

He's lying, and I know he's lying, and he knows I know, but it's probably as good a guarantee as I'm ever going to get. I stand up.

"I should stop taking up your time."

Bruce stands. "You can take up my time whenever you need, Sean." He comes around his desk and joins me. "Will we be doing business together, Sean?"

"Yes," I say. "Yes, we will."

We shake hands. Cleve is grinning like someone who's been teetering on the edge of a cliff, and has just been yanked to safety. I turn to him.

"Cleve," I say, "could you possibly check to see if my car is ready?"

"You got it!" he says, and bustles off. I turn to Bruce.

"Beautiful office," I say.

"Thank you."

"It's a big jump for Cleve," I say. "Baker and Baker to here."

Bruce nods. His blue eyes gaze at me palely. "He'll be fine," he says.

"I'm sure he will," I say. "But if he isn't—"

Bruce looks at me in silence.

"It's okay with me if you have to fire him," I say.

There's that little shift behind the eyes again, and I can practically hear the circuits in his brain clicking over.

He nods. A nod from Bruce Kravitz is like a nod from Don Corleone. It's a nod that promises a lot.

Then Cleve comes in, very happy, and he and I hug each other while Bruce Kravitz looks on, smiling, his hand half-raised in a gesture of blessing.

CHAPTER TWELVE

HEAVY LUGGAGE BLOG

I would like to announce to all and sundry that I have made a will. As my family seems to have abandoned me, I decided to leave my entire estate to the Motion Picture and Television Fund, which is a fund that provides assistance to those in our industry who have fallen on hard times.

The MPTF is a noble institution, and I urge those of you with means to contribute.

Comments (1)

FROM: LadyDayFan

I have checked, and the MPTF is a legitimate charity with a long history, and therefore unlikely to be a part of the ARG.

* * *

FROM: Sean Makin
SUBJECT: Your "Car"

Hi Mom.

I don't know if you've been following my adventures here in California, but it appears that one of Babaji's devoted followers has torched your car.

I've filed for the insurance, but you may have to come here to pick up the money.

Yr Son

P.S.: You wouldn't happen to know this "Trishula," would you?

P.S.2: Does Babaji have any comment on this act of violence perpetrated by one of his followers? I mean, is he for or against? And can he make his comment public?

FROM: Parmita <parmita@babaji.edu.in>
SUBJECT: Re: Your "Car"

I don't know why I should respond to you, because you will only put my words on your "blog" and encourage your "friends" to make unkind comments.

Of course Babaji is against violence! He has spoken against violence countless times! But when you speak such slanders against God, it is obvious that God's "true believers" will grow angry! I am angry myself!

There is no reason why you shouldn't send the insurance check to my home here in India.

Parmita

***

FROM: Sean Makin
SUBJECT: Re: Re: Your "Car"

Hi Mom.

Wow, what kind of insurance did you have on that car? I thought the premiums were awfully high, but then I figured, what the hell, it's a Mercedes.

But it turns out that you were paid the *replacement value* instead of the value of the car! I have here a check for $105,249.00, the cost of a brand-new S-Class!

The check is made out to you, and I can't cash it. I also can't send the check to you, because the insurance company won't honor a check deposited in a foreign bank. Apparently there are too many foreigners involved in insurance fraud.

I guess you'll have to come here and pick it up, then open an account with it.

Sean

FROM: Parmita <parmita@babaji.edu.in>
SUBJECT: Re: Re: Re: Your "Car"

My friends here say that you should use it to open a "joint account" in both our names, and then send the money electronically.

FROM: Sean Makin
SUBJECT: Re: Re: Re: Re: Your "Car"

Hi Mom.

I checked with the bank, and they won't open an account in your name without a signature. You'll have to come here for the signature, if nothing else.

I checked to see if I could set up a trust, like you did for me, so that you could pick up the money whenever you wanted, but they say they can't set up a trust in the name of someone who doesn't live in the country.

Apparently there was a lot of fraud connected with trusts and there are new regulations. They've closed a lot of loopholes.

So you'll have to come here after all. Or I could burn the check. Your choice.

Sean

Of course I'm lying. A fourteen year-old Mercedes is worth a little over eight thousand dollars, and that's what the check is actually for. In these emails I'm making up bank regulations wholesale.

I just want to see what will bring my mother to California. Obviously she doesn't care enough about *me* to visit, so I thought I'd tempt her with money. I didn't think eight grand would do the job, so I'm madly inflating the value of the check.

Of course she may be all spiritually advanced and above greed by now, but I'll bet that Babaji would like to get his hands on the cash. We'll see.

INT. NOHO PLAZA LOBBY—DAY

I give Ramona a call from the car on the way home, but instead I get a man with one of those Yat accents they have in Pasadena. He tells me he doesn't know any Ramona.

I must have copied the number into my phone wrong.

We get back to the NoHo, and Astin walks with me into the lobby. On one of the chrome-and-glossy-leather sofas I see Richard the Assassin waiting for me, netbook on his lap, one Converse-clad foot crossed over the other. He gives me a jerk of the chin that means *Come join me*, and Astin and I join him. He rises, glances at his Girard-Perregaux chronograph, then looks at me.

"We have a problem," he says.

Astin is instantly alert, scanning the lobby from behind his gold-rimmed shades.

"Not that kind of trouble," Richard says. He turns to me. "Your room is bugged."

Richard has a key to the room, and also the combination to the safe he's put in a corner of my bedroom, so that he can swap out old scripts for new ones. When he's there he sweeps the room, and he tells me he's found five bugs, two each in the main room and the bedroom, and one in the bathroom.

Hello, Ramona, I think.

"How long have the microphones been in there?" Astin asks.

"The room was last checked Tuesday night."

"Shit, man," Astin says.

"It happened last night," I say. "I mean, early this morning."

They look at me. "I had a lady visitor," I say. "I met her at a club. I guess she brought electronics with her."

And when she was snorting coke off my bedside table she was probably sticking a microphone on the back of my headboard.

I can see how the thing was done. There was no need to do anything so crude as follow me around, although that might have been done with one of the drone aircraft the paparazzi are using these days. But really all you need is a network of informers, folks who hang around places like Dove Bar and Club Kali and other places where celebrities are wont to gather.

Here I came into one of the clubs, and the informant picked up his phone and called his boss, who sent Ramona on her way.

It's news to me that the tabloids are employing prostitutes to gather information, but I suppose I shouldn't be surprised. Still, it's discouraging to know that you can't trust the discretion of a sex worker any longer.

Christ, you might as well fuck a civilian.

I have no idea who Ramona's employers might have been, but I suspect Kari Sothern of the *Tale*. There was something in the way she said "Don't kick the dog" that led me to believe she was planning something for me.

Richard looks at me. "Did this girl film you having sex?"

"She didn't deploy a camera, though I suppose she might have had one in her bag." I try to remember what Ramona's bag looked like. The handbag was small, but I suppose they make cameras small, too.

I *think* she left it in the front room, though. But no, she went back to the bag for a box of condoms and her baggie of blow.

"Well," Richard says, "if a Sean Makin sex tape appears, we'll know one way or another."

"It would also show Ramona snorting a lot of coke," I say. "My guess is she wasn't taking video."

"They're bound to have gotten audio," Richard says. The reference to coke sails right over him. He's so deep into the Ramona problem that he's not even worried what substances I'm consuming.

And I'm not worried about an audio. I recall how much ecstatic moaning and yelling Ramona was doing, and I figure the release of an audio like that would only enhance my reputation with the ladies.

"The range on those bugs isn't huge," Richard continues. "They've got to have a receiver somewhere in the area. In a van, maybe, or maybe in another hotel room."

"I'll ask at the desk," Astin says, "see if anyone checked in late last night." He walks away.

Richard looks up at me. "So is there anything in particular they're looking for?"

I suppress a guilty start. "Other than a sex tape?" I ask.

"I mean, Kari Sothern said she was going to dig, right?"

"Yeah."

"So." He looks at me carefully, and I feel a cold warning finger brush up the back of my neck. "Is there anything in particular she's digging *for*?"

"Well," I say, "I was sort of hoping she might find out who's trying to kill me."

Richard looks bemused. "Interesting idea."

"Set a stalker to catch a stalker," I say glibly.

"But stalkers aren't what she's *looking* for, she's just hoping to find something embarrassing or incriminating. Or— " He holds up a hand. "She's hoping to hear you running your lines or maybe talking with Joey or something about your scenes. She wants the script."

"Ah. Especially if she realized the one you sold her is a fake."

"Well." A trace of a smile crosses his face. "If there's one thing Dagmar's taught me, it's that when someone tries to play you, you play them back."

"So are you playing them back this time?"

"*You* are. A script will be here soon, and all you have to do is practice the lines aloud."

Lead her down another false trail. I laugh. "Yeah, okay."

Astin returns from the front desk. "Bogart Suite," he says. "Right next to yours."

The ghost of a smile returns to Richard's face. "We'll take a look at them in a bit, then. I don't suppose they told you who's paying for that room?"

Astin smiles. "I haven't been provided with bribe money, man."

"We'll fix that," Richard says. "I have to visit an ATM, though."

Astin is helpful. "There's one on the other side of the lobby."

"Excellent." He peers in the direction of the hotel restaurant. "Can we get some food? I haven't eaten since breakfast."

"It's Arnold Palmer Happy Hour," I say. "There should be snacks."

Richard gets some money from the ATM, gives most of it to Astin, and then Richard and I collect taquitos and chipotle-spiced riblets from the buffet, sit, and watch Astin's bribery attempt through the plate-glass window. All we see is that Astin seems to be engaged in a very intense conversation with the young lady behind the desk.

"I wanted to talk to you about Trishula," Richard says as he chews a taquito. "I'm having a very hard time tracking him down through my usual means. His virtual identity wallet is unusually well constructed. So I'm going to have to use a whole other method of working his identity."

"Yes?"

"He doesn't post just on your blog, he's online in other places. Mostly Babaji sites, but he's got a presence elsewhere. So what we do is analyze his social network. From the pattern of his movement online, we can track his relationships. We might find purchases and credit cards. We may be able to find people who know him. And even if we don't, we'll gradually eliminate people till we get to the right guy."

I think about this. "You're saying that while you might not be able to find the right person directly, you can reach him by eliminating *all the other nine billion people on the planet*?"

Richard sips his iced tea. "Yeah. That's what I'm saying."

I eat a riblet as I strive to absorb this. "Isn't that—uh—hard?"

Richard sips again. "Not so much. First off, we can eliminate everyone who wasn't in Southern California in the last week."

"I guess that takes care of most of the nine billion right there."

"The software's been around for a decade or more. It's used by banks, security companies, and intelligence agencies to sift data and find suspicious patterns...and some of Sri's companies use that kind of software, so we have access to it."

"Is that kind of thing legitimate?" I ask.

He gives me a surprised look. "Sean," he says, "you talk as if spying is illegal or something."

"Isn't it?"

"Well," Richard says, "it's not like we're going to look in secure government databases, or anything. We're not looking for nuclear secrets, we're looking for the street address of a crazy person."

"Cool," I say. I give it some thought. "Could we find Ramona?"

"Probably." He gives me a look. "You *want* to find her?"

"To *expose* her. If every bouncer and doorman in LA knows her face, she's going to have a hard time meeting her targets."

At this point Astin returns. "Double Delta Entertainment," he says.

I reach for my handheld and start to call up the Internet. "I bet you that if I check that, it'll be the company that does Kari Sothern's show."

Richard puts a hand over my phone. "Don't use your phone," he says. "Ramona may have cloned it."

I look at the phone in my hand. *Traitor*, I think.

"In fact you'd better turn it off and give it to me. I'll make sure it's not compromised, and I'll give it back to you tonight at the premiere."

As I hand him my phone, I realize that in today's excitement, first with getting new representation and then the excitement over the bugs, it's slipped my mind that tonight is the premiere of Part II of *Escape to Earth.*

Richard looks up Double Delta on his own phone and finds that, indeed, it's the company that produces Kari Sothern's TV show. "Lovely," he says. "Somehow I have a feeling that they're going to suffer a *major* denial-of-service attack."

"Isn't that illegal?" I ask.

Richard blinks up at me. "Didn't say *I* would do it."

At which point one of his lieutenants turns up with the fake script, and so I spend the next couple hours in my suite reading lines like "If we don't stop it somehow, that dirty bomb's going to take out Buenos Aires," and "Those mutant sea creatures are the worst menace your planet has ever faced!"

I have to say I read the lines brilliantly.

The night's premiere is at Griffith Observatory—not in the planetarium, but elsewhere in the building, amid the science exhibits, and in the parking lot and the surrounding area. The place is absolutely iconic, with more than a dozen movies having been made here, and scores of television programs. I take Clarence Musselwhite as my guest, but it takes me a long time to get onto the grounds, because the press presence is massive, and they all want to talk to me. I seem to be a lot more popular than I was last week.

Joey is also mobbed. All I see is the top of his head amid a swarm of reporters and cameras.

Eventually I get past the press area, and Clarence and I and my two guards walk past the pylon with the six statues of strange science-fictional astronomers with blank eyes and long gowns, and then up the long lawn on to the observatory itself and the stairs where Sal Mineo died in *Rebel Without a Cause*. We talk about the movies made here, and Clarence explains what the Foucault pendulum is actually *for*, which I've never known.

We walk out of the building and past the bronze head of James Dean on its plinth. It was Sal Mineo who died in the movie, but it was Dean who got the memorial. Actors with careers that crater, I remind myself, don't get statues built to them.

Still, I touch Dean's shiny nose for luck, and think, *Please, Jimmy, don't let it be a flop.*

There's a band playing classical Chinese instruments on one of the terraces, and the second terrace has a buffet and a bar. I see a lot of women in cheongsams. Dagmar is probably around somewhere but I don't see her. We go out onto the terrace with the food and enjoy the gorgeous view of Los Angeles. As the sun drops into the Pacific we watch the Hollywood sign light up, and then it's time for Part II.

I go by myself onto the lawn and sit cross-legged on the thick grass and fire up my tablet. I unfold the screen and dock it with my tablet and put the tablet on the grass. The uplink goes without a hitch. The download goes fast, and suddenly I'm watching Roheen bouncing around in the back of a truck as he comes down out of the Himalayas into China. I'm still amazed at the level of detail in every single frame. Even on my small screen it seems I could fall into the detail and only find more detail.

And this was crowdsourced, I think. Freaking crowdsourced.

I clench my teeth as the banquet scene comes up. But I hear laughter bubbling up from the dark around me, and I can take heart from the fact that at least a North American audience seems to like it.

Dagmar's done a nifty trick with the ending, one designed to maximize audience participation. Roheen's journey forks at the end of Part II, depending on what the viewer does. By the end he's set up to be shipped in a container to the U.S., but each audience member is given the opportunity to tell him about a scene they've just viewed, in which Arrick, the Steene commander, sends his own men to shut down a Tellurian Gate in Peru. If the player votes to tell Roheen what she knows, then Roheen will jump a freighter to Callao. If not, he'll continue next week to North America.

If the viewer voted for Peru, the vote is recorded in her account, and next week she'll view the Peru episode. But if she elects to keep silent, Roheen goes on to America, to D.C. and his confrontation with the au pair played by Nataliya Hogan.

Whatever choice the viewer makes is locked. Each individual viewer gets only one version of the film. One way to view every possible alternative is to get a whole series of accounts, but the best way is to view the other episode using the account of a friend. The idea is to maximize social networking among the viewers. Dagmar wants the viewers to make friends with each other, to be friends who have *Escape to Earth* in common. She wants people looking to find people who voted the other way, getting involved, arguing over which episode is better.

I listen to the crowd as it watches the episode. I hear little chatter: for the most part they're absorbed. It's like a theater, with everyone sharing the experience with everyone else.

Part II is shorter than the first episode, only a half hour or so. At the end there's rolling applause.

I get up, brush grass off my legs, and wander toward where I left Clarence. I'm surrounded by industry insiders, and they're all smiling at me. Some people cheer.

Four hundred thirty million people watched Part II in the first twenty-four hours of release.

I'm not just a star, I'm a phenomenon.

* * *

INT. THIRTY-SIXTH CHAMBER—DAY

"Sean Makin's going down," Burt Taylor says. "I'm going to cut him off at the knees. By the time I'm done with him, he's going to be nothing but a red smear on the canvas."

Well, that's what I call friendly.

Celebrity Pitfighter's supermodel spokeswoman turns to me. "What do you feel about that?"

"I think that talk is cheap," I tell her.

So is this production. We're filming a one-hour reunion show that will run a week prior to the finale, in hopes of building anticipation for the last fight. We all sit on bleachers on the Thirty-Sixth Chamber set, watch videos of our fights, make scripted comments, and respond to questions from the hostess and the judges.

"I'm going to crush Sean's head," Burt responds.

"Two words for you, Burt," I say. "'International superstar.' Which you will never be."

I have to say that my line is a bit mean-spirited, but then I didn't write it, the uncredited writers did. Besides, I'm Mr. Charm compared to Burt, who has been loudmouthed and annoying for the entire *Pitfighter* series. If this were professional wrestling, he'd be a classic "heel," as I believe the type is known.

Of course if he's the heel, then I'm the good guy, or "babyface." Irony abounds.

The fact is that the audience for reality TV loves a good villain—the annoying, self-centered, obnoxious jerk who shows contempt for his rivals and supreme confidence in his own gifts. The audience loves to see this character rise to the finals, and then get crushed. I'm hoping that the producers have this career arc in mind, and will do their best to make it come about.

Burt is only six feet tall, but he's built like a brick. For this part he's shaved his head, I suppose so that none of us can grab his hair, but he's compensated by growing a villainous little goatee.

He's had a spotty career, mostly playing supporting roles and villains. His two starring roles were in low-budget films that went straight to DVD, and from there to oblivion.

The odd thing is that even though he's in the finals, he doesn't seem to be particularly gifted in his martial arts. I've seen his fights, and he compensates for lack of genuine talent by dogged ferocity. He doesn't give up, every strike means business, and he makes very few mistakes.

We bark at each other some more, and then the hostess reminds the audience that the final *Celebrity Pitfighter* will be broadcast absolutely live in a week, and we fade.

I lurk on the set until I have a chance to talk to Burt, which happens when we're both in the dressing room, standing in front of the mirrors and taking off our makeup.

"Want to get a cup of coffee or something?" I ask.

He gives me a look. "Why? You trying to date me or something?"

"Yeah," I say. "I totally like 'em bald." I wait a few seconds, and then say, "I figured there's no reason why we can't be friends when we're not on camera."

So that's how we end up meeting the next afternoon at a coffee shop on Van Nuys. I collect my chai tea latte from the barista and sit in a beige armchair and read the paper. The headlines are all about the war on the Thai-Burma border, and it's depressing. When Burt arrives, ten minutes late, I'm surprised to see that he isn't alone—he's got two men with him, both young and casually dressed and in very good shape.

Burt sits in the beige armchair near mine, and his two henchmen take some wooden chairs from other tables and pull them up close. I look at him.

"I didn't know I was so scary that you needed bodyguards," I said.

My own guard, Simon, sits discreetly in the corner, out of earshot.

"I wanted witnesses," Burt says.

I look at him in surprise. "To what?"

"To whatever you're going to do."

I look at the two men. "Allow me to demonstrate the proper method for drinking a chai tea latte," I tell them. I take a deliberate sip, and my senses fill with the taste of cardamom. "There," I tell them. "You can leave now."

They look at Burt. He gives me a scowl.

"That wasn't funny," he says.

"Then I won't drink again." I put the coffee cup on the table between us. "There. You're safe from my sense of humor."

Burt folds his arms and looks at me. "So are you here to rumble or what?"

"*Rumble?*" I can't help it, I laugh out loud. "Where did you find that word, some old movie?"

Burt doesn't crack a smile. "If you want to throw down, I'll do it." He nods at his posse. "But these guys make sure it's fair."

I'm experiencing the sensation of having somehow crossed over into an unknown land, where all is mirror and shadow. I've strayed into Burt's head, where nothing is quite as it is in reality.

All I wanted to do was figure out some way to bribe the guy. I didn't want to have to cope with the twists and turns of what turns out to be a supernaturally strange mind.

It takes me a few seconds to recover. "Why in hell would I fight you now?" I ask. "Where's my paycheck? Where's the cameras?"

He gives me a sullen look. "Oh," he says. "So now you're afraid?"

"Fuck yes, I'm afraid!" I tell him. "I'm afraid the producers are going to get one of us killed."

He jabs a finger at me. "Well, I'm *not* afraid, and that's why I'll win."

"The man who's not afraid," I point out, "brought two guards to a meeting in a coffee shop on Van Nuys Boulevard."

That silences him for a moment. I pick up my tea.

"You might as well go," I say. "Or I'll have to drink my tea at you again."

He scowls, his lip curling inside his little goatee, and then he gets to his feet and marches out. His two amigos go with him.

I sip my tea and wonder at the strangeness I've just experienced. *Maybe*, I think, *he's crazy enough to be the driver of the SUV.* Maybe he's been trying to kill *all* the other contestants.

Which leads me to ask myself why I'm still in *Celebrity Pitfighter* at all. Maybe I was out of my mind to fix fights so that I'd win, when it would have made more sense if I'd arranged to lose. I'd be gone from the ring, I wouldn't have to spend hours training, and I'd be able to concentrate on the people who have been trying to kill me instead of the ones who just want to beat me up.

I suppose it was just too easy. I managed to corrupt Des and Lenny without any effort at all. Now I've won two matches, and I've erased most of the humiliation from the cottage cheese incident. I've made it to the finals.

But the problem with that is that I'm going into the ring against a man who's legitimately won three fights. I wonder if I ought to be more frightened than I am.

I wonder how badly I want to be Grand Champion Celebrity Pitfighter, and conclude that I don't, particularly, but since I've got into the finals by hook and crook, I might as well try to win.

I suppose it wouldn't do my career any harm to be known as a martial arts hero. It could even get me parts.

Or, as Gregg with three *g*'s pointed out, I could maybe even make some money giving talks on the martial arts circuit, assuming of course that there is such a thing.

But whatever the case, after my fight with Burt, I'm never going in the ring again, no matter how desperate I get.

INT. SEAN'S SUITE—NIGHT

The screams from my phone echo vastly in the tiled bathroom. I give a start and water moves in a great slide to the other end of the Jacuzzi. I heave my torso out of the tub and grope for my handheld. When I hear the voice on the other end, I realize I've been expecting it.

"Is this Sean? I want to speak to Sean Makin."

I take a moment to deal with the shock, then another moment

to make certain my voice won't tremble when I finally speak. I slide back into the water, which gives another heave.

"Hello, Dad," I say. "I was wondering when you'd call."

"Some of the things you'd written in your blog, I didn't know whether you'd want to hear from me."

"Dad," I say, "I've *always* wanted to hear from you."

I'm soaking at the end of a long day in a tub scented with mountain flowers. I was running my lines in the tub, enjoying the reverb as my voice echoed from the tiles. The guys who had bugged my suite were gone: Astin got the hotel manager to throw them out, after which Richard peeled the listening devices from their hiding places and dropped them into a glass of water.

Richard earlier slipped a tiny camera on the end of a fiber-optic cable under the door of their suite, and also got a microphone in there: he documented their reaction to my declaiming the lines from the fake script, and it sounded as if they'd bought my act.

Richard also returned my phone, scrubbed clean of the malware that Ramona had installed. "Cloned," he said. "They heard every phone conversation you made today, and read every text you sent or received."

I cast my mind over the day's events. So Kari Sothern knew about PanCosmos's trying to sign me up. But I hadn't called everyone on my speed dial saying, "Hey, I just took a meeting with Bruce Kravitz, and he wants to make my dreams come true!" so the story wasn't confirmed.

Not that someone like Kari needs confirmation.

But it's not a bad story, that I'm being courted by a powerhouse agency. I *want* her to report that one.

"That's cool," I said. "I didn't tell them anything that won't be made public in a few days anyway."

"It's lucky they didn't turn the phone into another bug."

I was startled. "They can do that?"

"Well," Richard said, "the phone's on anyway, right? It's got a microphone attached to the handset that's there whether you're talking into it or not. So yes, it's possible to turn your phone into a kind of double agent that reports every word you say to a third party."

"Ouch."

Astin leaned close and put a hand on my shoulder. "You know," he advised, "you can avoid this kind of trouble if you only fuck your friends."

Sound advice, but the sad fact is that I don't have that many women friends, and none of them will have sex with me.

Probably that's my fault. I seem to have trust issues.

And now the principal reason for my trust issues is on the phone. ("Trust issues." Get it? That's a pun.)

"Where are you calling from?" I ask.

"I'm back in the States," he says.

"Are you in town?"

He gives a laugh. I *remember* that laugh. It's the laugh that says, "That question is inconvenient."

Memories are piling up thick around me. It's like fifteen years have melted away and I'm a kid again, waiting for my dad to decide what happens next.

Jesus, I feel like I'm swimming in déjà vu.

"I don't know if I should tell you where I am," he says. There's a smile in his voice. "You might have a warrant out for me or something."

I examine my toes on the far end of the tub. "There aren't any warrants, Dad," I say. "Even if I wanted to prosecute you, the statute of limitations expired years ago."

Which is one of the things that has me grinding my teeth whenever I think about it. The DA had four years to prosecute from the date the crime was discovered. The fact that my father fled added another three years.

But it's now been eleven years. Dad's been away enjoying my money all that time and there's no way he'll ever be brought to the bar of justice.

A civil suit is another matter. But if I file against him, he'll just disappear again, unless I can figure out a way to nail him to the deck somehow. Or find his funds, and then get a court order to seize them.

"So," I ask, "what happened to all the money?"

Nothing like running headfirst at the gate. Dad doesn't seem surprised by the question.

"I had an investment opportunity," he says. "A one-of-a-kind thing. I needed to increase my buy-in." He gives a little delicate clearing of the throat. "That's why I needed your money, Sean. I was trying to make us all supremely rich."

I'm guessing that the buy-in he's talking about was maybe at a poker table.

"It must not have gone well, then," I say. "Because I seem not to be supremely rich."

"There was a change of government," Dad says. "Not our government, theirs. They became a lot more hostile to foreign investment. And then there was a downturn in the economy—not theirs, but ours, except it spread to them, and they blamed us. And..." He sighs. "Things happened."

"Anything left?"

"Oh, I'm doing all right." There's a kind of hearty humor in his voice that's scraping my nerves raw. I want to leap through the telephone and strangle him.

"I'm relieved," I say. "I wouldn't want you to have to move in with me because you're destitute or something."

"No," he says. "That's not going to happen." There is a long pause. Then he says, "You're doing well for yourself."

"Oh, I'm doing all right." In exactly the hearty tone he just used. If he notes the mockery, he fails to acknowledge it.

"Your movie," he says, "I've seen it. You're great."

I feel a little jet of delight pulsing somewhere in my thorax. Some part of me is still longing for Daddy's approval. I slap the feeling down like the reflex zombie emotion that it is.

"Yep," I say. "I'm a sensation."

"You know." There's another pause. "I know you've gone

through some tough times. I know you've been mad at me. But..." Another pause. "I'd like to try to be your friend, Sean. I'd like to make it up to you."

The water in the tub is getting cold. I manipulate the hot water tap with one foot. Water gushes; scented steam rises.

"You could," I venture, "give me my money back. That would be an act of friendship."

"Oh, Sean," he says. He sounds very emotional. "I'd love to. I'd love to be able to do that. But I can't. The money's just...gone."

"Here's the deal," I say. "You say you want to be my friend. But"—I find myself gesturing to the room—"I'm checking through my list of friends, just to see if there's an opening for an embezzler, and there isn't. There just isn't."

There's another pause. Then, "I could make it up to you in another way."

"Yes?"

"What's that rumbling sound, by the way?"

"I'm in the tub. That's the tap running."

"So can you hear me?"

"I hear you fine."

Warmth spreads from my ankles up my calves. "There's a project I'm involved in," he says. "It's a resort complex—a gorgeous thing. You could invest in it. You could make all your money back, and then some."

So there it is. He couldn't even wait till the *second* phone call to make the pitch. He must really be short on funds.

The warm water advances up my thighs. "So where is this resort?" I ask.

"Well." He's hesitant. "I don't know if I should tell you."

Okay, this is too absurd. Too pitiful. I laugh out loud.

"You think I'm going to blindly hand you money for this resort project, without even knowing where it is?"

"Oh no." He seems shocked. "You wouldn't give the money to *me*. I wouldn't have anything to do with your money. You'd give it to the *fund*. The fund is controlled by the corporation, not by me."

I'd have to be out of my senses to believe that. "And where is this fund?" I ask.

"It's in the Antilles. But that's not where the resort's going to be. That's just where the investors keep their money till it's needed."

Warm water floats all the way to my shoulders. I feel sweat prickle on my forehead. "Dad," I say. "Just tell me where the fucking resort is."

"Well," he says. "It's the Mosquito Coast."

I laugh again. "Mosquito Coast? That's where Harrison Ford went nuts in that movie, right? Sounds like a *great* place to put a resort!"

He responds seriously. "There's going to have to be a certain amount of rebranding. But it's a beautiful beach, really. Gorgeous white sand, lovely people who speak English and go to the Moravian church. Columbus visited there."

Before or after the Moravians? I think.

"You have a prospectus?" I ask. "Because I could show it to my business manager, my lawyer. See what they say."

I don't actually have a business manager or a lawyer, but there's no reason my dad should know that.

"Well," doubtfully, "I suppose I could get one."

"You don't have a prospectus? You don't have any numbers or prognostications or data showing rates of return for similar projects amortized over a dozen years?"

For a moment I'm deeply embarrassed by my father. Cripes, I'd thought my dad was a better con man than this.

"I can get one," he says. "But I'm not a salesman, you know? I don't carry sales material around with me."

"When you get one, send it."

"Where to?"

I grin at the opposite wall. "Can't you get my address from the same place you got my unlisted phone number?"

"I don't want it to—"

"Just send it care of PCTA. I'll get it."

The tub is beginning to get uncomfortably hot. I turn off the tap with my toes.

"Yeah," Dad says, "I saw the news item that you went with PanCosmos. Bruce Kravitz is sharp."

"Yes he is."

"But, you know, he's a shark."

"I know that."

"You'll have to watch him."

"I will, Dad."

"You know," he says, "I didn't do so badly for you, when I was your manager."

This is so astounding that for a moment I'm unable to speak.

"Dad," I say, "you *do* know that I had an accountant go over everything, right? And that I know you were stealing from day one."

He sighs. "I wasn't *stealing*, Sean, not really. There were opportunities, and I had to take advantage of them. I always meant to make it right."

Opportunities at the track. Opportunities in Vegas. Opportunities in shabby investment schemes in the Antilles. I find myself clenching my right fist. I look at it in surprise.

"You know, Dad," I say. "You're starting to make me real angry now."

"I didn't mean to do that," he says. "I just wanted to see if we could be friends."

"Yeah, well," I say. "You go on hoping."

I press the End button and then call Richard. I'm expecting voice mail but he picks up.

"I'm sorry to bother you," I say.

"That's okay," he says. "I'm heading for a meeting."

I wonder what kind of meeting he's heading for at nine-thirty on a Monday night.

"I just got a phone call from my father," I tell him. "I've got the number he called from—I wonder if you can figure out where he is. He said he was in the States but there's no reason to believe that."

"No problem," he says.

He reports within the hour. The call came from Vancouver, in Canada, which indicates that Dad's concept of the truth has remained consistent over the years.

"Can you see if he's got property there?" I ask. Maybe I can get a court to seize it.

"I'll check. Would he be using his own name?"

"Who knows? He had his real name on his Belizean passport."

He says he'll check and get back to me. I get back to learning my lines.

Tomorrow we actually go on location. And it's going to suck.

INT. BRUCE BENNETT BUILDING—DAY

I've taken off the makeup and had my shower, and now I'm sitting on a bench in the dressing room next to the exercise room, and I'm smelling pleasantly of floral shampoo. I'm looking at my handheld, because I've just gotten a lengthy text from Richard the Assassin telling me that my father sold his apartment in Cap d'Antibes five years ago, and the house in Belize just last year. Richard and his crew of stealthy cybernauts haven't located any other property, or any substantial sums of money, but he tells me they'll keep trying.

I start to text my thanks, and then the door to the exercise room slams open and a big booming voice laughs. The sound echoes off the tile walls.

"I can't *believe* the amount of data we're getting!" he says. "Hundreds of millions of customers! I don't know how we're going to process it all!"

I can't see the speaker because there's a bank of lockers between me and him, but I gather it's one of the two men who were running on elliptical machines when I came in to take my shower. My guess is that the speaker is the big curly-headed guy, a man almost as tall as I am—he seemed the sort of person who would shout even in a small, echoing room.

"Are you reducing the data here," says another voice, "or remotely?" The second voice is high-pitched, with an accent that comes from the Northeast somewhere.

Locker doors clang open. "I'm doing it remotely," says the first voice. "It's a pain in the ass! I don't even know where the servers are physically that I'm working with."

"Somewhere in the Sri Sphere," the other man says.

I hear this as "Shree Sphere," and for a few seconds I'm trying to figure out what a Shree Sphere is. It sounds like an alien warship in a science fiction film, but I decide it's likely to be a brand name for some kind of router. Then I realize he's talking about Deeptimoy Srivastava.

"Yeah. All this fucking secrecy is—"

The big guy comes around the corner, heading for the toilets, and he sees me and stops dead. I pretend to be absorbed in the text message on my phone, and he pretends he hasn't been talking at all. He walks past me in silence, leaving behind only the bracing odor of sweat.

Later, after I've sent my thanks to Richard, collected my towel, and headed back to my dressing room, I begin to wonder just what becomes of the data I've given Great Big Idea.

When I subscribed to the various installments of *Escape to Earth*, I provided some basic information. Name, address, email, birth date, and credit card. Presumably the system tracked other information, such as usage statistics.

That isn't really a lot. Plenty of online businesses have at least as much information about their customers. But once you have a name, credit card number, and birth date, you can shake a lot more information out of various online trees: profession, credit cards, credit rating, nationality, neighborhood, value of property, relatives, hobbies, business interests, religion, telephone numbers, family members, and all the data about *those* family members once you know who they are.

All that is worth money to a savvy Internet entrepreneur like Sri—and to anyone else who has a product to sell—or anyone interested in fraud or identity theft. The Sri Sphere is a gold mine to anyone who has access to it.

When I get to my dressing room I unholster my handheld, access the login page for *Escape to Earth*, and check the privacy policy. It's short and simple:

Information is for internal use only and will not be sold, given, or otherwise conveyed to any person or entity outside the Great Big Idea network.

Well, that's pretty definite... but even assuming they aren't lying through their teeth, it still leaves them a certain amount of wiggle room. It is not clear what the "Great Big Idea network" is, and there is no guarantee that the network doesn't include all of Sri's vast interests throughout the world.

So that, I think, *answers the question of why Sri became a movie producer*—he intends to exploit the information that he is getting from his hundreds of millions of subscribers. This will provide the windfall that justifies the whole project.

So Sri hasn't turned entirely from Asian tiger to Hollywood pussycat, from entrepreneur to selfless benefactor. Maybe his devotion to good works was a pose, or maybe he just got bored or frustrated with trying to improve the world, and invented a new and ruthless scheme for making money.

Not that I have a real objection. If Sri wants to massage that data, he is welcome to whatever money he can make from it. This isn't anything that other companies haven't done, and aren't doing.

Besides, he is sharing the wealth with me, and making me famous.

I can't see anything wrong with that at all.

EXT. PARMENTER CANYON—DAY

I'm tired. I'm covered in fake dust and real dust, and fake sweat and real sweat, and there's sticky fake blood all over my face, and every time I think we've finally got the take something happens. The hot August sun has turned the landscape into the Anvil of God. Wind blows over one of the reflectors beaming light at me, the sound system goes out, the Steadicam turns spastic and decides to point at the sun, or Roger blows a line. Sometimes he blows a line just to amuse himself—or to tick me off.

Whatever you might think an African name might be, chances are it isn't Roger Cedric Johnston III—that's the name of the kid I'm playing against in the final two installments of *Escape to Earth.* Roger's an upper-middle-class kid from Cape Town, smart and smug as they come. The character he's playing is named Khabane, and the reason he has a name like Khabane is that the audience will know he's African without having to think about it.

Roger is the one kid I haven't managed to get along with, or even like. He thinks I'm a plaything to be tortured for his amusement; and I think he's a stuck-up, annoying, supercilious brat who needs a punch in the nose.

Roger thinks he's a star. He was probably born *knowing* he was a star. It's not something he ever thought he needed to work for, or study for, or practice for. He's just a star, no question, and all others are born to worship him.

It would amuse me to see Roger and Nataliya in the same room, each trying to lord it over the other until someone's spleen exploded in frustration.

We are far up in Parmenter Canyon, a location said to resemble Swaziland, where the action takes place. The climactic scene of the film is supposed to take place near Execution Rock, which is a knob from which the ancient Swazis, or whatever they were called, tossed their criminals. Naturally, because of the cinematic rule that big climaxes have to take place near famous monuments, Roheen's people put one of their Tellurian Gates there, and it's the last one Roheen knows about and the last chance for E.T. to go home.

This is where he makes one last brave effort, and where he's wounded by the Steene and defeated. This is the scene where he realizes that he's trapped on our Earth, and he surrenders the hope of returning to his nation. He'll be an exile forever, hunted by the Steene, supported only by his little cohort of underage sidekicks.

So now I'm dragging my ass around this rough terrain with the fake blood spattered all over me, and during the action I have to lose hope, and then despair, and then ultimately resolve to carry on regardless. My attempts to embody hopelessness and despair are only enhanced by the coincidence that, in order to get to the location, we had to travel past the place where Timmi died.

I've avoided Parmenter Canyon since the accident. At least this time I wasn't driving: I could close my eyes as Simon drove past the corner, and try to ignore the terror and desperation that were clamoring in my head.

I've made it, I thought at Timmi's ghost. *I'm back on top and I'm going to do good work and I'll spend the rest of my life making you proud.*

It occurs to me that, given my interactions with Doug Fairbanks and James Dean earlier, I seem to be spending a lot of time pleading with dead people.

I heard nothing in response, nothing but the song of the tires over the asphalt.

It was the desperation, maybe, that finally got through to Roger. I was staring at him during the take while I thought about taking a knife and flaying his face off, and maybe he sensed what I was thinking, and he decided not to blow his take—and elsewhere on the set nothing fell over, and nobody dropped anything, and the camera and the sound system worked, and Joey finally said, "Cut."

I fucking hate this location. I remember how gorgeous the green screen work was on the early installments of the movie, and during a break I complain to Joey that I don't know why a location is necessary now.

"Because in this scene the background is organic," Joey explains to me. *Organic* seems to be his favorite word these days.

"In the other bits of the movie the scenery was incidental," he says. "Roheen just *happens* to be in D.C. or Peru or wherever. It's like wallpaper. But in this scene you're not just walking past the scenery, you're fighting on it, you're crawling on it, you're bleeding onto it. I don't want to trust that CGI is going to look good a hundred percent of the time in a scene this crucial."

And so he's condemned us to drive past the corner where his wife died for four or five days this week. I wonder if he thought of that when he insisted on a location shoot.

While they set up the next scene I walk off to my chair and settle into it with a bottle of water. I only rinse the dust out of my mouth and spit, because I don't dare drink it. If I have liquids I might have to pee, and that means taking off the costume; and besides my hands are heavily made up, so I can't even take off my own costume or hold my own penis. I'd have to get someone to do that for me. I can just imagine how popular I'd be if I called for volunteers.

Roger Cedric Johnston III, I believe, has someone who will hold his penis for him, or anything else that might need holding. She's a mournful-looking young woman who's supposed to be his auntie, and who has been sent by his family to look after him while he's in California. I can't imagine anyone treating a blood relative as badly as he does, though, ordering her around in Xhosa and yelling at her when she's not quick enough to anticipate his wishes. I think she's probably some hired woman who was passed off as a relative to make it easier to get her into the country.

Or maybe his relatives actually treat him as if he were a little god. I suppose that's possible.

I think about conducting some really vicious practical joke just to let Roger know how everyone feels about him. A bag of dog doo dropped on his head. A slug of laxative slipped into his drink just before the next premiere. Itching powder dumped down his collar just before an interview. Maybe all three.

"Waiting on gaffers!" Clarke calls.

I see Carter-Ann in conference with her assistant and with Professor Mthunzi, her advisor on South African matters, so I heave myself up and walk over to them.

"Dr. Dixon?" I say. She turns to me. "You're a psychiatrist, right?"

"Yes. Of course."

"Can you fix Roger?" I ask. "Because if you don't, I'm going to set him on fire or something."

This gets her attention. She turns to me, eyes fixed on mine, hands clasped in front of her.

"What's the problem?"

"He keeps blowing takes."

She hesitates. "I realize he's not the most experienced actor..."

"It's not a matter of experience," I say. "He knows his lines. He blows takes deliberately because he thinks it's amusing to piss people off. And we can't waste time, because he's a juvenile and under the law he's only allowed to work a certain number of hours per day."

Carter-Ann looks at Mthunzi, then at me. "I'll see what I can do."

"Thank you."

As I start to return to my chair, I see Jean-Marc, Clarke, and Sawicki the line producer in a huddle. Sawicki's on the phone. I know this can't mean anything good, so I join them.

"Fuck no," Sawicki is saying. He's dapper as always in flannel trousers and a sleeveless tartan sweater and a tie. His lipless mouth droops beneath his John Waters mustache. "Fuck fuck fuck."

"What's going on?" I ask. Clarke hisses at me for silence. Jean-Marc watches intently, with a burrito wrapped in aluminum foil in one hand. He absently peels the foil away and takes a bite.

"Fuck," Sawicki says again. "Yeah, okay. Okay. Check. Meeting with Dagmar at nine o'clock. Call me if anything changes."

He lowers his phone slowly and looks at us, a stunned look in his pouchy eyes.

"Nataliya's been killed," he says.

"Hit and run?" I ask. I don't intend to say anything, the words just pop out.

Sawicki nods. "Last night. In the driveway of her beach house on the PCH."

"That's four," Jean-Marc says. "Four deaths." His shoulders are slumped, and he looks like death himself. He's chewing his burrito mechanically. I doubt he's even tasting it.

"The car just hit a glancing blow," says Sawicki. "She got up and started to run, so the driver had to chase her down and finish her off, with—with a club or a crowbar or something..." He gives a hopeless shrug. "Jesus. This is crazy."

"Did anyone get a look at the car?" Clarke asks.

"Yeah. Someone saw it pulling out."

"A black SUV," I say.

"No." Sawicki looks up at me. "A *white* SUV."

I'm surprised, but surprise doesn't stop my mind from racing, and I put my finger on what I suspect is the most important question.

"How did he get her *alone*?" I ask. "She's always surrounded by her claque. What was she doing on the Pacific Coast Highway all by herself?"

They don't have any answers. I look up, past Sawicki, and I see Joey standing there less than five feet away. He's been listening, but he's not engaged with what he's hearing: I see only his profile as he stares off into the arid landscape, his eyes hidden behind wraparound shades.

Whoever got Nataliya alone, I thought, would have to be someone who could *promise* her something. A movie, a recording contract, a free trip to Cannes, something she'd want. "I don't want to be distracted by your posse," he might say. "I just want to look at *you*, sweetheart."

Which meant that the killer was a powerful person in the industry. Someone who could say, "You know, I just looked at the monologue of yours, and I thought it was brilliant. Let's talk about developing a project, just for you."

Which would mean a chance to redefine herself—maybe that would mean she'd be taken seriously as a dramatic actress, or a writer, or whatever her current fantasy might be.

You didn't offer Nataliya worship—she took the worship for granted. If you wanted her attention, you offered her *opportunities*.

That was how you got Nataliya Hogan alone, standing in the driveway of a house to welcome the person who drove right off the highway to run her down.

And as I'm thinking this Joey turns to me, and looks at me from behind the wraparound shades.

"Gaffers are done," he says. "Let's get the shot before we lose the light." He gives me a smile. "Let's go, champ."

A chill runs up my spine as I see myself reflected in his shades, like a target in a gun sight. I go to my chair, take another swig of water, rinse my mouth, and spit. And as I walk back over the dusty ground to stretch out before the cameras covered in fake blood, I think about how I'm going to have to be driven back down Parmenter Canyon tonight to get to my hotel, and how I'm going to see Timmi's ghost standing there, her finger pointed at me as if to say, *You're next.*

CHAPTER THIRTEEN

Our Reality Network

Live Feed

Hanseatic says:

I assume that the Trishula problem is distinct from *The Call of Tempest Royal*, or whatever we're going to call the online game.

LadyDayFan says:

It is never wise to assume these things in Our Reality. But if Trishula is connected to the game, then unmasking him will help us in the ARG. If he is unconnected, then we'll be doing a public service.

Hippolyte says:

As we do, from time to time.

Ballistic Bunny says:

We are one with Clark Kent, we are.

HexenHase says:

Trishula is hiding behind a Tor-type distributed network. These were originally created in order to help citizens avoid the restrictions of totalitarian regimes, but of course they provide anonymity to criminals, terrorists, and crazies as well.

Ballistic Bunny says:

Information wants to be free!

Corporal Carrot says:

And code wants to be wrong.

HexenHase says:

Trishula posts in places other than Sean Makin's blog, mostly Babaji sites and other sites devoted to spiritual topics. We could try seeding one of these with a comment that includes a .pdf or a link to a video or a sound file, and hope he clicks on it. I could manipulate the appropriate plugin to maybe give up an IP address.

Ballistic Bunny says:

Worth trying!

HexenHase says:

If I can get a cookie on his browser, I'm going to totally pwn the guy.

Corporal Carrot says:

I decided to try another approach. A number of Trishula's posts are long and didactic, so I did a search on key words and phrases drawn from Mr. T's posts. Bingo! A number of them are word for word the same as posts by someone named Debashish, which means that Trishula and Debashish are one and the same—or that Trishula loves plagiarizing Debashish and not plagiarizing anyone else.

Debashish is the web monkey of Babaji's ashram in Covina, California, which is apparently a rather distant part of Greater L.A.

Hippolyte says:

I think I'll try to contact him. Not wanting my car to explode at any point, I think I'll use an anonymous remailer for email, and if that doesn't work a prepaid burner phone for the telephone.

Ballistic Bunny says:

Let's ALL try to contact him!

INT. JOLI BLON CLUB—EVENING

I have to say that Dagmar totally steps up. Because the NoHo is too small, she moves anyone crucial to the production to the Lang Towers Hotel, in Burbank, and puts us under guard. We have floors reserved only for *The Life of Chester A. Arthur*, with guards standing at polite attention at the elevators. My room is a tasteful but characterless composition in aquamarine and hunter green. We travel to the studio or to the set in cars or in buses with guards on board. Families move into the hotel along with the crew, so I can never use the hotel pool because it's always full of screaming children. But they'll never drown—they're the safest children ever to play in a swimming pool, because highly trained, heavily armed guards are present at every minute.

Room, food, transportation, all paid for by Dagmar. Everything except alcohol. She really has a bug up her ass about the drink.

From the top floor of the Lang Towers, where I have my new suite, I can walk to the end of the hall and see the Warner Brothers lot and Disney Studios. From my balcony I can look down at the green park of the great cemetery of Forest Lawn, where Nataliya Hogan is going to be buried on Saturday. I don't care much for the view.

This must be what it was like living in a small village in the Middle Ages. We all have our work in common. We all know each other. We're all up in one another's business. And we're all paranoid as hell, because we know the Vikings, or their modern equivalent, could be coming over the hill any second with blood in their eyes and the sun glinting on their steel.

The suspicion that I may have been locked up in the hotel with a killer haunts my mind.

I'm surrounded by guards, but I don't feel safe at all. I figure this must be what it's like to be dictator of some miserable Third World country.

I try watching television to get some relief, but when the news isn't about Nataliya, it's about the Thai-Burmese War. I never thought a foreign war would be less depressing than my life.

I get repeated calls from reporters asking for quotes about Nataliya. I tell them that I didn't know her well but that she was terrific to work with—prompt, professional, and talented. I talk about how she's going to be missed. I say that it's a tragedy she's gone.

I don't mention that I'm afraid I might be next. I don't even mention it to the police, who interview me. I tell them what I can. I also tell them about the black Ford that tried to run me down, and about Trishula who's threatening me on the Internet. I probably come off as a paranoid lunatic, but they're very professional and keep their opinions to themselves.

I'm on location for two more hideous days, driving up and down Parmenter Canyon, working under Joey's flat gaze, and then that's over. I've got one more scene in the studio, and then

I'll probably need to go into the sound studio and loop some dialogue, and then my part will be over.

The fear will continue.

At least Roger turns well-behaved. He's no longer blowing takes deliberately, or acting badly on the set. I don't know if Carter-Ann succeeded in getting through to him, or if the sudden appearance of a host of armed men intimidated him. Maybe he's figured he isn't the top badass on the set after all.

The only entertaining thing that happens is that Kari Sothern reports that future installments of *Escape to Earth* will feature mutant sea creatures and a dirty bomb in Buenos Aires. It's the only amusing thing that's happened to me in ages.

The night before Nataliya's funeral I attend the premiere of Part III of *Escape to Earth* at Universal CityWalk, a kind of high-concept shopping mall run by Universal Studios. The place is so ablaze with light and outrageous architecture and psychedelic artwork that it looks like the whole Sunset Strip of the last fifty years packed into a quarter-mile pedestrian mall. Since the place is very public, with shops, restaurants, and nightclubs, and since our various stalkers and killers could be anywhere amid the customers, serious thought was given to moving the premiere somewhere else. In the end we were encouraged not to wander through the area but to go only to a club called Joli Blon, where the hoi polloi, their SUVs, and their guns can be firmly turned away by our guards.

It's a far more traditional premiere, with plush ropes and a red carpet and fans kept at arm's length. My guards hustle me down the red carpet so fast that I don't think I achieve eye contact with a single one of the fans. It's depressing.

This leads to a morose scene where I'm in a plush leather booth at the Joli Blon with Jane Haskill, the composer, and Allison King, the film editor. I'm drinking ginger ale, and Allison and Jane are sharing a pitcher of frozen margaritas.

Jane wears a black sleeveless Boss satin dress that looks quite fetching on someone more accustomed to jeans and tatty cardigans. Allison is short and plump, with straw-colored hair cut in bangs across her forehead. She's wearing a deeply elegant gown stitched all over with silvery metal scales, and it deserves a better setting than a New Orleans–themed club that looks like a cross between a Bourbon Street dive and the Haunted Mansion from Disneyland.

We've all just watched Part III. In another of Dagmar's nifty ideas, the people who got D.C. last time will get Peru in Part IV, and those who got Peru will get D.C.—but *it won't be the same Peru or D.C.*, there will be large variation built into the stories—and, to make it obvious, and so that the viewers won't get bored, all this was made clear in a few brief previews tacked on to the end of Part III. No matter the alternatives, both Part IV stories will lead to the same place, Roheen on a ship heading for Cape Town. So once again, viewers will be encouraged to look at the videos through one another's handhelds, laptops, or tablets.

The audience in the Joli Blon seem surprised by this, and intensely interested. They're all chattering away.

At the table I share with Jane and Allison, the success of the episode doesn't seem to cheer us up.

Jane looks at her half-empty margarita, then looks at the pitcher, trying to decide whether or not to top up her drink. She decides against it.

"Sean," she says, "when you told me Jaydee's death wasn't an accident, I didn't quite believe you."

"Someone had already tried to run me down twice," I say. "Let's just say I was alert to the possibilities of foul play."

"Everyone who died was at Joey's party six years ago," Allison says. Somehow it's even more depressing when someone else says it. "That's where it all started."

"Everyone died the same way Timmi did," Jane mutters. "Hit by a car."

"Mac wasn't hit by a car," I point out.

"He went off a cliff," Jane says. "So did Timmi."

I feel a chill run up my spine. I hadn't considered that.

Jane looks at Allison. "So is it a serial killer?"

"Well, duh." Allison rolls her eyes. She stirs her margarita with a plastic straw. The straw has this weird little plastic heart on the top that you can compress to actually do most of the sucking for you. The heart fills up like a little reservoir, and then it requires only a small effort to slurp it up from there.

"Timmi was the first victim," she says. "The first victim is always the most important one. That's where the killer is most, like, unguarded. Because he isn't hardened and he can make a lot of mistakes."

I decide to steer the conversation away from Timmi's death. "The police investigated that one," I say. "They didn't find anything."

"They didn't find anything because they can't see the pattern that we see," Allison says.

"And what pattern is that?" It's Jane who asks the question, because I can't bring myself to speak it aloud.

"It's all about the affair that Timmi and Mac were having," Allison says. "That's where things started going wrong."

Relief floods my mind—*hey, suspicion doesn't fall on me!*—but the relief is soon overwhelmed by blank astonishment.

"Mac and Timmi?" I say. "Mac MacCartney and Timmi were—"

Allison raises her margarita and looks at me over the rim of her glass. "You didn't know?" she says.

I just gape at her, feeling so far beyond stupid that I couldn't find stupid with a ten-meter stupid-dowsing stick.

"No one told me," I say, feeling very alone and forlorn.

Allison takes a long drink of her margarita, then reaches for the pitcher. "That's what the fight was about," she says. "Timmi was trying to break up with Mac, but he didn't want that."

"Did Joey know?" I ask.

Allison gives a laugh. "No. He's such an egotist, you know, I'm sure it never occurred to him that a woman would cheat on him. He never guessed till I told him."

Jane gives her a disgusted look and refills her glass. "I can't believe you did that."

Again I'm staring at Allison with my mouth wide open, only this time I'm not bewildered but appalled. "You told him?" I say. "Why in hell?"

"Because I was fed up," Allison says. Her mouth tightens into a grim line. "We were working ourselves to death editing *Golden Fighter*—we were spending eighteen-hour days stuck in the editing room—and each new edit was worse than the last. Joey had no judgment left; he was half in the bag most of the time—he was a complete wreck. He wouldn't listen to me, he just kept moaning that he needed Timmi there to tell him what to do. He kept going on about how perfect she was, how her judgment was so flawless, how she never let him down..." She raises her hands in exasperation. "It went on for *weeks*. If I didn't get Joey to stop adoring a corpse and get on with the work, I'd never have escaped that hell. What the Christ was I supposed to do?"

"You weren't supposed to tell him that," Jane says, flat anger in her voice. "You absolutely weren't justified in that." I can tell they've had this argument before.

"It may not have been justified, but it worked," Allison said. "We got *Golden Fighter* edited and out into the theaters. And bad as it was, that piece of shit could have been a lot worse."

My mind is spinning like a flywheel out of control. It's going to come clanging off its bearings any second. Allison picks up the pitcher and slops more margarita into her glass. I grab the glass out of her hand and pour the drink down my throat, lime juice stinging my tongue, tequila and ice alternately burning and freezing my throat. I gasp for breath and drop the empty glass to the tabletop.

"That's falling off the wagon with a great big thud," Jane observes. She sounds approving.

I look around the room and see Dagmar and Richard the

Assassin on a second-floor balcony, half-hidden by a French Quarter–style wrought-iron balustrade.

"Excuse me," I say, stand up, and lurch for the stair. The bite of the frozen margarita seems to have stabilized my mental process in some brutal way. I feel ideas slotting into place in my head, dropping from the sky into a perfect pattern like geometrical forms in Tetris.

I remember when *Golden Fighter* came out: I'd just finished shooting *Mister Baby Head* and I'd been doing some looping in postproduction and went from there to the premiere. *Golden Fighter*, the first of Joey's big flops. I remember sweating at the party afterward, knowing I'd have to lie, as I waited in line to tell Joey how great the picture was.

Which means that Mac was still alive when Joey was told of Mac's involvement with Timmi.

I climb up to the balcony, where I find Dagmar and Richard sharing a table. Dagmar wears a natty Panama hat over a velvety Empire-waist maternity dress, and she's talking on her phone. Richard, dressed in his customary black, nurses a glass of beer and listens amiably to Dagmar's half of the conversation. I put a hand on Richard's shoulder, and he looks up in surprise.

"Can we talk for a minute?"

He nods, and I pull over an empty chair from the next table and join them.

"Listen," I say. "I just found something out."

"Okay." Richard gives me the full Zen gaze. As always, having his complete attention is a little unnerving.

"Everyone who's got killed," I say, "attended a party at Joey's place six years ago."

I explain about Timmi's affair with Mac, and how she'd been trying to break it off when she got killed. Then Mac's death a few years later, after Allison told Joey about the affair. And how all the deaths after the first seemed to be imitations of Timmi's death in Parmenter Canyon.

While I'm in the middle of all this, Dagmar finishes her conversation and listens.

Richard follows this without comment, then nods.

"So you're saying it's the same killer," he says.

"He's saying it's *Joey*," Dagmar says.

I nod. "Timmi's death was an accident, okay, but now Joey's hunting down and killing anyone he thinks might be responsible." I wave a hand. Tequila sizzles in my skull. "And another thing—Joey *needs* this production to get him back on his feet. He can't afford to disrupt the proceedings because that might mean the end of his career. Have you noticed that the murders here have been of people *after they stopped being useful to the production*? Jaydee's work was basically finished when she died. Nataliya had her three days on the set and was done. Joey didn't need her any longer, and he disposed of her.

"You know," I go on, "I wondered why Joey insisted we go on location in Parmenter Canyon. Because *every day* we had to drive past the place where Timmi was killed—it's as if he needed to psych himself up for something, remind himself why he was there."

"And of course he humiliated himself to get his job back," Dagmar says. "He went that extra mile to get access to you all."

"I've checked Joey's alibi," Richard says. "In fact I've checked everybody's alibi."

"At least," I say, "you didn't have to check mine."

He gives me an amused look. "What makes you think that?"

"Because I'm trapped at the hotel without wheels. I need to call one of your men to go anywhere."

"But you *can* drive," Richard says. "You might have sneaked out of the NoHo and rented a car."

I'm beginning to get angry. "So you're saying I have no alibi for Nataliya's death?"

"Well, you don't." His voice is matter-of-fact. "But you lack motive. For that matter, so does Joey."

Right, I think. *Get back to the alibis.* "So where was Joey that night Nataliya was killed?"

"Joey was working with Allison till after eight. He was on the phone with Dagmar about nine, and that's right when Nataliya got run down. He'd have to be a pretty cool customer to phone someone just as he was about to commit a murder. Or just after, as he was driving away."

"Can you find out where the call originated?"

There's a little shift in his eyes. "I'll do that. Another thing, by the way—Joey doesn't own a white SUV. Or a black one."

"How do you know? Joey owns so many cars he's got half of them in a warehouse."

"There are websites where you can look up car registrations. He doesn't have an SUV registered in California."

"That—" I hesitate. "That probably doesn't matter so much."

Richard waves a hand. "Yeah, he's got resources. He can get a clean car if he wants one. I'll check the phone call, though."

Dagmar leans close to me, the brim of the Panama touching my temple.

"Another thing," she says. "Don't you think it's a little suspicious that your father contacted you only *after* you announced that you were leaving your money to the old actors' home? It's like he realized he wouldn't get any money from your death, so now he's trying to talk it out of you."

Again I feel a certain reflex to defend my father, but I resolutely suppress it.

"Also." Dagmar touches my arm. "The success of *Escape to Earth* has inspired the New Kidz Network to put *Family Tree* in rotation. All seven seasons. So that should mean a nice chunk of change for you."

I look at Dagmar. "Do you think my father knows?"

She shrugs. "I think he called you for a reason."

I consider the bleakness of a world in which family exists only as a parasite, latching on only to drain you of your blood, sanity, and cash. Then I realize that I've lived in that world for a very long time.

"I do have some good news," Richard says. "The gamers have probably tracked down Trishula."

"The *gamers*?" I'm deeply puzzled. "The ones playing your games online?"

Dagmar gives a little smile. "They do these things sometimes," she says. "It's a kind of hobby."

Richard explains that Trishula seems to be a Babaji follower who lives in an ashram in Covina, and whose birth name was Rick Hawkins.

I'm surprised. "Babaji has an ashram in Covina?"

"Why wouldn't Covina have an ashram?" Richard smiles. "'One mile square and all there,'" he says, quoting the slogan of the City of Covina.

I try to get the conversation back on track—which, since tequila is starting to really slosh around in my brain, is harder than you might imagine.

"So you think Trishula is Debashish, who is actually this Rick person?"

"The gamers have tried to contact him, but apparently he's not one of those authorized to talk to outsiders. Their emails go unanswered, and phone calls have been handled by a woman called Praveena. So a number of them actually went to the ashram, but they weren't allowed inside."

Richard sips his beer. "I went myself. Praveena said that Debashish no longer lives there, and that she didn't know where he'd gone. When I pointed out that it said *on their own web page* that he lived there, Praveena said that the web page was out of date, because they didn't have a web person at the moment."

"So do you think he's still there?"

"I'm trying to find out. I'm trying to watch their traffic, to see if Trishula is posting from there. We also know what Rick Hawkins looks like, so we've got our security staking the place out in case he's still there and tries to leave. They're listening in with parabolic mics and such, but all they're hearing is a lot of silent meditation, plus arguments in the kitchen about who's being the stricter vegetarian. Apparently they're very competitive about it." He gives a little flip of one hand. "We'll see what we see."

My flurry of deduction is over, and it's left me more depressed than ever. "Right," I say. "Thanks anyway."

He returns to his beer. I walk out onto the balcony and look down at the club. Jean-Marc is prowling the buffet and stacking his plate high. I see Jane and Allison calling for a second pitcher of margaritas, and I try to remember whether either of them left Joey's party before Timmi. I decide I should warn them to leave town as soon as their usefulness to the production ends.

Then I see Joey. He's dressed immaculately in a three-piece white linen summer suit, and he's giving an interview to a television journalist. His eyes are hidden by shades even indoors, and his expression looks carved from stone.

Spot the hit man in this picture, I think.

I realize my own usefulness to the production is about to end. I've got one more day of shooting and then some looping, and that's it.

Maybe, I think, *I should buy tickets for someplace safe.*

Greenland seems good.

But Greenland seems very far away. I turn, shoulder my way through the crowd around the upstairs bar, and order myself a double scotch.

EXT. UNIVERSAL CITYWALK—NIGHT

I leave the party an hour later. I've had a number of drinks, but I can walk just fine. I've got Simon and Wild Bill with me, hustling me back down the red carpet, and Astin is waiting in the vehicle to speed us off to safety.

CityWalk is all around me in blazing neon pastel color. A life-size King Kong clings to the side of a building. Fans wave and cheer. Some are holding out pens and autograph books. It occurs to me that some of the fans are female and beautiful.

It's just like my glory days. I realize that I don't have to go home with just my bodyguards. And if I pick a fan at random it minimizes the possibility that she is a Ramona, and in any case Simon and his friends can search her for microphones.

So I stop and take an autograph book and smile, and the young green-eyed lady smiles back. Simon tries to move me on, but I resist. I sign a picture and another autograph book and I realize that I don't have to invite just one woman back to my suite. I can have a party, just me and my fans.

Then someone yells "*Gun!*" and I hear screams.

I turn and see a pale-skinned undernourished man in worn jeans and a checked shirt rushing at me. He's already ducked under the velvet ropes and there's a big kitchen knife in his fist and he's seven or eight feet away and coming fast. I know Simon is behind me and I don't know where my other guard is, but I can't see him, so he's out of position.

I react. I give the man a front kick to the midsection. The impact rattles my teeth. My attacker folds like a bedsheet blown away in the wind.

Then I'm staring, transfixed by my own success, as Simon and Wild Bill pile on my attacker and wrench the knife away.

It was being drunk that saved me. If I'd been sober, I would have stood there and been cut down while I tried to think out what to do. The alcohol kept me from thinking, and freed me to simply react.

There are screams and the crowd is surging around, trying to get away. I'm still looking around, because someone *did* yell there was a gun, and I'm blinded by the flashes of cameras, and I realize that the whole thing is going to be on the entertainment news by midnight.

"Did someone see a gun?" I'm asking. I'm standing and blinking in the flashing lights, a perfect target. "Is there a gun?"

If I keep standing here, I think, *I'll get shot.* But if I just run off in some random direction, I could be dashing right at the person with the gun, and I'll *still* get shot. I need someone to tell me what to do.

Simon looks up from the ground, where he's got one of my attacker's arms twisted behind his back.

"I couldn't remember the word 'knife,'" he says. "Not in the heat of the moment."

"Dude," I say, "I'm just glad you didn't say 'pencil.'"

CityWalk security arrives and helps to restore some kind of order. Real police are there within minutes, and my assailant is handcuffed and hauled to his feet. He's wheezing and gasping for breath. My kick completely knocked the wind out of him.

I look at him as he gasps and slobbers and I see the smudge of red on his forehead, the tilaka he must have applied earlier that evening, and I realize that he's Trishula. An angry laugh bursts from my lips.

"Om Shiva, motherfucker," I tell him.

INT. SEAN'S SUITE—NIGHT

It takes a couple hours to finish giving statements at the police station, in part because I'm interrupted by frantic phone calls from Dagmar and Richard and any number of other people who want to make sure I'm all right. After reporters start calling I turn off the phone.

One of the cops comes out to talk to me, and tells me that Trishula started confessing about two seconds after he got in the cruiser. The people at the ashram knew he was Trishula, he said, and they hid him until just yesterday. That's when they were spooked by people showing up asking for him, and kicked him out. He had no place to go but looking for me.

I've just beat up a homeless guy. Not that I'm sorry.

Astin drives me back to the hotel in time for me to watch myself KO Trishula on television.

Damn, the kick is a thing of beauty. Up comes the right knee, "chambering" as they say; and then the foot drives out like a piston, the support foot turning, the hips going straight for the target, all my weight behind the strike as the ball of the foot contacts Trishula's solar plexus. My fists are raised, on guard, ready to finish off the foe if the kick doesn't do its job, but he was coming so fast and so unguarded that he impaled himself on my foot, and that finished him.

After the kick I look completely poised, fists still up, ready for action. The camera can't tell that I'm just standing there because I'm blinded by camera flashes and I can't think of anything else to do. The camera makes me look awesome.

I look like a hero. I look like Kato in action. I look like a Bandit King of Ancient China.

Fuck, I look like *Roheen.*

I don't want to go to sleep. I want to celebrate. I've kicked the stuffing out of at least one of the people who have me holed up in a hotel room under guard, and even if he was some weedy whack-job who's been living on a diet of brown rice for the last ten years, that's reason enough to have some fun.

I'm sobering up and that's not the party I'm looking for, so I walk to the elevator, past the guards there, and go down to the hotel bar. But the few people in the bar are strangers, and I've missed last call. The bartender is emptying the snack bowls and eager to go home.

I decide I can maybe call some folks and invite them to my suite, so I go upstairs again. Once in the room I go to the suite's minibar, get out a miniature of Johnnie Walker, and pour it into a glass. I add a single cube of ice, swirl it a bit, and take a drink. The warm bite of the liquor latches onto my throat, then slowly lets go. I look at my phone to see who's been calling me.

Almost all of them are reporters, including Kari Sothern. Both Cleve and Bruce Kravitz have called, and the thought that my agent cares is enough to warm the cockles of my heart, wherever those might be. I call Bruce back, and after I assure him that I'm unharmed, we agree on a statement that PCTA can release tomorrow in which I modestly claim credit for single-handedly capturing a heavily armed homicidal cultist maniac.

"I don't know if this is what you want," Bruce tells me, "but you're one big step closer to getting big action hero roles."

"I'll take them!" I say.

Then I call Cleve and tell him what Bruce and I decided, and then I look through the list of reporters and call the important ones and give them quotes. I humbly credit Master

Pak with instilling such exemplary martial skill in me. While this chatting is going on I drain a couple more miniatures of Johnnie Walker.

My phone rings just as I've finished talking with the woman from *Hollywood at Night*, and I see it's my father. I answer.

"Hi, Dad."

"Are you all right?" He's talking very fast. "I saw on the news that you were attacked."

"I'm fine," I say. I laugh. "I'm better than fine, I'm *great*."

"That's good. That's good."

"I'm a freakin' whirlwind of martial badness," I babble. "Did you see that front kick? Was that perfect or what?"

"They said the whole production is being threatened. They said you're forted up in a hotel with everyone on the crew."

I laugh. "Yeah, we're all hiding out. Not for long, though . . . we're only shooting for another few days."

"And what happens *then*?"

It's something I haven't quite considered. If I'm no longer needed for the production, will Dagmar withdraw my security? And—if my theory about Joey is correct—isn't that exactly when I would *need* someone to step between me and a speeding SUV?

A front kick, I think, *isn't going to stop a two-and-a-half-ton mass of hurtling Detroit steel.*

"Looks like I'll have to take care of business before the end of production," I say. I go to my closet and grab the shoulder bag with the Glock in it. "Thanks for calling, Dad," I say. "I've got some stuff to do now."

"Say—Sean—did you get the package—?"

I hang up, take the bag to the desk in the front room, and take out Tito Aragon's gun. I contemplate the weapon for a moment, then decide to make sure the gun and I can never be put together in the same frame. I take a hand towel from the bathroom and scrub the gun of prints, and then I realize my prints are probably on the clip and the bullets, so I take the clip out and remove the bullets and scrub each one of them.

While I do this, I drink another miniature from the minibar. The bar's out of scotch, so I start on the Jack Daniel's.

I've played heavies, so I know how to work a gun. I've fired pistols on any number of television shows—my characters always have charming names like "Freak-Face" and "Luke Stiltwalker"—but I've never actually fired live ammunition.

Using the towel, I reload the bullets in the clip, then put the clip back into the gun. I work the slide and put a bullet in the chamber. Then I wipe the whole thing with the towel again, and put it back in the shoulder bag with the towel on top of it.

I keep my hand on the gun, so I can pull it and draw it and fire with my hand still in the towel. I make sure that my finger, wrapped in the towel, can fit through the trigger guard. Once I shoot, I can drop the pistol and walk away and no one will ever connect the weapon to me. If it's registered to anyone, it's registered to Tito Aragon, and he's been dead for eight years.

The plan is perfect! I'm invincible. I'm the Bandit King of Ancient China, and all I need is another Jack Daniel's and I'm on my way.

I have my drink, and then I open the door and look down the corridor. There's no security in sight. The guards sit around a couple corners, by the elevators, because the stairs are alarmed and the elevators are the only way to get to this floor. I leave my own door slightly ajar so I can dash into my room quickly, and then I cruise on silent ninja feet ten yards or so to the big double doors of Joey's suite. The suite has a doorbell, so I press the button. When there's no response, I press it again.

I've got my hand in the shoulder bag and the towel in my fist. In the towel is the pistol. Except that I can't shoot anybody right now because the door is shut.

I ring the bell for a third time, and as I'm retracting my finger the door jerks open and Joey's there, and I give a little surprised jump. Joey's shirt is halfway open, and he's still wearing the trousers belonging to his white summer suit. He's in his stocking feet, and his hair is mussed. He looks up at me.

"What's the problem?" he says.

I could shoot him right now and be back in my room before the guards are even out of their chairs. But somehow the plan is not working. Joey doesn't look like a monster or a multiple murderer. He looks like a tired middle-aged man who's kicked off his shoes after a long, hard day. He looks like an old friend who wants to help me with the problem that's brought me to his door in the middle of the night.

I realize that Joey the director is going to have to help me with this scene.

"You didn't call, Joey," I say. "Everyone else called to make sure I was okay, but you didn't call."

"Everyone said you were all right. They said you beat the shit out of the creep." He narrows his eyes as he looks up at me. "Have you been drinking?" he asks.

"Hell yes," I proclaim.

He swings the door open wide. "Come in before someone sees you and reports you to fucking Dagmar."

I close the door behind me. Joey's room is decorated in shades of cream and gold. A big bouquet wafts floral scent through the room. His vest and suit jacket have been thrown casually over the back of an overstuffed chair. A stack of scripts sits on the table next to the sofa.

"I'm getting scripts again," he says. His tone is dismissive. "It's all crap that other people have turned down, but I can always hope to find something good the others have missed."

"Good luck," I say. "Let me know if there's a part for me."

Joey sits heavily on the cream-colored couch. I sit in one of the overstuffed chairs and stare at him. I'm telling myself just to pull out the pistol and shoot him, but I can't do it.

I need to work myself up to it. I need to get angry.

"What do you have in the bag?" Joey asks me. "A bottle or something?"

"No," I say. "I don't need another drink." I try to glare at him. I try to grow some indignation. "What the fuck's going on, Joey?" I ask.

"It's a freak show, is what it is." Joey's gaze is leaden, his mouth frozen in a snarl. "Dagmar's never made a feature before and doesn't know what she's doing, Carter-Ann is wiring audience members in Timbuktu or some damn place in order to tell us how to do our jobs, and—"

"That's not what I'm talking about, Joey," I say. "I'm talking about all these people getting killed."

He just looks at me.

"Everyone who got killed," I say, "was at your house the night Timmi died. Mac, Jaydee, Nataliya—Jesus, Nataliya couldn't have been more than sixteen at the time."

"She got older," Joey says. "Everybody got older—except for Timmi, who couldn't get older *because some shithead killed her.*"

"They all died the way Timmi died!" I blurt. "A crash, or—Mac went off a cliff!"

Joey's stare challenges me. "Am I supposed to be in mourning? Am I supposed to care?" He snorts. "I got all the mourning and caring done six years ago. I'm not going to do that again, not for a talent-free piece of crap like Mac MacCartney, not for a drunk like Jaydee and not for a spoiled pop star."

"*Jaydee was my friend!*" I'm shouting now.

"She was a lonely old soak," Joey says. "You were the only friend she had, and you only saw her when you were working. You never saw her when she was passed out in front of the TV set at home. The hit-and-run saved her from a painful death by cirrhosis. It's all for the best."

Fury blazes up in me. Let it blaze a little more, and maybe I can do what I came here to do.

"What are you going to say about me, Joey?" I ask.

His tone is suspicious. "What do you mean?"

"Mac was a piece of crap, Nataliya was spoiled, Jaydee was a drunk... if I'm killed, what do you say about me? That I was a *has-been*, a *freak*, a *ham actor*..." I'm shouting again. "*What are you going to say about me once I'm dead?*"

He stares at me frozen-faced. He looks like the bronze statue of some Renaissance duke or something, glaring down from a plinth.

"Did you kill Timmi?" he asks.

I gape at him. Guilt and fear come up out of nowhere and start tugging, yanking at my muscles. It's all I can do not to twitch like a dog.

"What the fuck?" I demand.

"It's a simple question."

I challenge him back. "How did you know Mac didn't kill her?"

"I thought he had." Joey's words are matter-of-fact. "But then six or seven months ago Sandy McGinnis reminded me that Mac was too drunk to drive, so Sandy took him home, and Sandy's pool-boy boyfriend drove Mac's car to her house. And Sandy was sober that night—" He laughs. "And she's a bad liar. I'd know if she wasn't telling the truth."

I stare at him. So Joey had tipped Mac onto the rocks at Malibu, and then discovered only years later that he'd got the wrong man. And now he was making up for lost time.

"What are you going to do to me, Joey?" I ask. "I've got a couple more days of production—and then I'm no use any more. Do I get hit by an SUV then?"

"You didn't answer my question," he says.

"*I loved Timmi!*" I scream. I'm on my feet, one arm waving, the other stuffed deep in the bag. "*I loved you both!*"

"*Answer my question!*" Joey lunges out of the sofa and heads for me, and it's worse than Trishula coming with a knife, because this is a man I've known and respected all my life, and there's pure homicide in his eyes . . . in panic I yank the pistol out of the shoulder bag and point it at him.

He stops dead. He looks at the gun, appearing from the towel like an angry hornet from a bedraggled flower, and then he looks at me.

"You must be mistaking me for someone who gives a damn," he says. "Go ahead and fucking shoot, if that's what you came for."

I snarl and point the Glock right between his eyes. The gun is shaking but there's no way I can miss.

He looks up at me. There's a contemptuous twist to his upper lip.

I try to shoot. I try to will my finger to squeeze the trigger. Nothing happens.

"Fuck!" I shout. "Fuck, fuck!"

My words fail to propel the bullet from the barrel. I stare at Joey over the sights, at the stony eyes that already have me dead and buried.

I flee the room and lock and chain the door to my own suite. My hands are shaking. I finish off the bourbon and start on the vodka. After that things get a little dim.

Later I remember hanging over the toilet and wiping vomit from my lips with a piece of toilet paper while stomach acid burns in my sinus. I remember watching myself on the TV behaving like a hero. I remember seeing Burmese tanks burning in the jungle. I remember looking out my window at Forest Lawn and thinking that the next funeral would be for me.

I'm the Watcher, forting up in the Blue Area, unable to act. I remember making sure the gun was with me wherever I went around the suite.

Some unknowable amount of time later, I wake to find someone standing near the bed and reaching for me. I give a yell and grab the gun and brandish it in his face. I see staring eyes and a gaping, startled mouth.

"Sean, Sean!" he says. "It's me, Simon!"

I blink at my bodyguard and lower the gun. My eyes are gummed and there's some kind of nasty residue on my lips. The room smells of vomit and sweat and gun oil.

"What time is it?" I ask.

"I came to see if you were all right," Simon says. "I knocked, but you didn't answer. I called your phone, but all I got was voice mail." He looks at the gun. "Have you been packing this whole time?"

"Sort of." I wipe crusty stuff off my eyelids. "Why are you here?"

"There's a problem," he says. "I'm sorry to tell you—" He looks away from me for a brief instant. "Joey da Nova's been killed," he says. "We're checking everyone in the hotel to make sure they're okay."

I open my mouth to say something, but nothing comes out. I look at the gun in my fist.

I didn't kill him, I think.

And then, *Did I?*

ACT 3

CHAPTER FOURTEEN

Our Reality Network

Live Feed

LadyDayFan says:

So we've all seen the video of our boy Sean taking Trishula down last night? Nice work from all concerned.

Consuelo says:

Ought we to be congratulating ourselves? If we'd left Trishula alone, maybe he would have remained a harmless crank instead of trying to kill someone.

Hippolyte says:

He was hardly harmless. He burned Sean's car, remember?

Chatsworth Osborne Jr. says:

What concerns me is the mortality rate in this production. Reuters just said that Nataliya Hogan was the second person on this production to be killed.

LadyDayFan says:

Chatsworth! We haven't seen you here in a long time.

Chatsworth Osborne Jr. says:

I moved to New Zealand to be near my daughter. It was a long process.

Consuelo says:

Welcome back. I know you have "resources." Perhaps you can apply them in this instance.

Chatsworth Osborne Jr. says:

I'm retired. I don't have those resources any more.

Consuelo says:

Too bad. Maybe someone here knows where we can get some reports from LAPD?

INT. FUNERAL CHAPEL—DAY

A few hours later, cleaned up, badly hungover and relieved of my firearm, I find myself at the Wee Kirk o' the Heather. "Wee Kirk o' the Heather" might sound like something built on the Munchkinland set, but in fact it's the name of a chapel at the enormous Forest Lawn cemetery, one of several reproductions of moldy old European buildings used by the cemetery as props in weddings and funerals.

Someone has probably made the joke that it really ought to be called the "Twee Kirk o' the Heather," but that wouldn't be me.

The media circus is insane, not only because Nataliya was a

transcendently famous pop star, but also because news of Joey's death has leaked. It's the sensation of a decade already buried to its eyebrows in sensation. Multiple homicide! Cultists attacking movie stars with knives! Martial arts! Celebrities! Simon and Wild Bill practically have to crowbar open my path through the crowd of journalists to the chapel.

The reporters demand details, but I couldn't give them even if I wanted to. All I know is that Joey was found dead in his suite. I don't know when he died, or how, or who killed him. All I can guess is that he was unlikely to have been run over by an SUV.

Once inside the chapel I find the air thick with the scent of sandalwood incense and noisy with the chanting of a group of old, bald, wizened Buddhist nuns. It's news to me that Nataliya thought of herself as a Buddhist, and probably news to the rest of the world as well.

The Wee Kirk is the size of a modest country church, so flatscreens set up outside broadcast the proceedings to the hordes who can't fit inside. Nataliya's gold-plated coffin, fine enough for a pharaoh, sits in front of the altar under soft spotlights. The nuns chant. A man with sleek white hair delivers a homily. He's from the local Buddhist Center and tries to make Buddhism sound as much like the Prosperity Gospel as possible. I had no idea that Buddha so badly wants me to be rich.

Various friends testify to Nataliya's essential goodness. There is weeping. Cameramen run up and down the aisles trying to catch all the action, or at least the tears. Nataliya's horrible show-business mom, from whom she'd been estranged since her eighteenth birthday, waits for a camera to point in her direction and then breaks down weeping. Her father, a record producer, sits as far from the mother as proprieties permit and looks disgusted. It's easy to figure out which half of the family gave her the narcissism.

All this, remember, taking place in the rather confined space of a replica medieval Scottish church, the original of which has long since crumbled to dust.

I'm feeling wretched, not only because the hangover is stabbing needles into my eyes, but also because I'm wearing a Kevlar vest under my shirt. It was Simon's idea, but I was paranoid enough to think it might be a good one. The armor helps prop me up in the pew, when what I really want to do is sag down and take a nap.

At the end of the service we are directed to view another flatscreen that has been set up behind the altar, and there we see the monologue that Nataliya recorded during her last day on the set of *Escape to Earth*.

All the insanity of the funeral fades away, and there's Nataliya as Colleen, facing the audience and revealing one layer after another of loneliness, desperation, and fear.

I look away. Here, with Nataliya's coffin in sight, her character's naked desperation is too difficult to watch.

That's how I happen to find myself viewing the audience, and one woman in particular. She's dark-haired and quite young and is looking up at the flatscreen with tears streaming down her face. I recognize her: she's part of Nataliya's entourage, but I don't know her name.

The thing that interests me is that she's reciting the monologue along with Nataliya. Her lips are moving along with the words. I wonder if she's the person who had to run lines with Nataliya when she learned the monologue. Or—just maybe—she had more to do with it than that.

When the monologue ends the audience breaks into sustained applause. Then the nuns start chanting again, and it's over.

I rise to my feet and wince at another bolt of hangover pain. As the crowd starts filing out, I manage to elbow my way to Posse Girl. She looks up at me in surprise, mascara streaks on her face.

"Hi," I tell her. "I'm Sean."

"I know." She blinks up at me. All around us the crowd is shuffling toward the exit. We're creating a minor traffic jam, and I plant myself in the aisle as people nudge up against me and squeeze past.

"I'm afraid I don't know your name," I say.

She swipes at her eyes with a handkerchief. New mascara streaks appear over the old ones.

"Corrie," she says. "Corrie van Houten."

I loom over her. "How long did you know Nataliya?"

"I—well—I was one of her assistants. I've known her a couple years. A friend of mine introduced us my senior year of high school." She casts an anxious glance at some of the other posse members, who are murmuring among themselves and giving us strange looks.

"That monologue we just saw," I say. "I helped direct it."

Corrie nods. "Did you? That's—that's good."

"Nataliya was brilliant in it."

Tears well up in her eyes. "Yes," she gulps. "She was."

I put a fatherly hand on her back. "You'll land on your feet," I tell her. "You're a very good writer."

Corrie gives me a startled look. "Oh," she says, "I'm not a writer."

I give a look over my shoulder at the flatscreen. "You wrote the monologue, right?"

Her eyes widen. "No. I just helped Nataliya write it."

"But you wrote the actual words?"

"Well." She's a little defensive. "Nataliya told me what to put in it, and so that's what I did."

I don't have time to probe in order to find out exactly what parts were written by which person, and besides, I think I understand what happened. Nataliya snared Corrie right out of high school, dazzled her with the pop-star lifestyle, moved her into the mansion, paid her a pittance, and consumed her life and talent. I doubt she gave Corrie much direction beyond, "Write me a monologue where Colleen feels insecure an' stuff." And then Corrie wrote the piece, and they rehearsed it together after Corrie explained what was actually happening in it, and then Nataliya took credit for everything, and Corrie felt honored to have helped the star notch up another credit on her résumé.

Child exploitation. Where would this town be without it?

I figured this out because even upon my brief acquaintance with Corrie I had a pretty good idea which of the two knew about insecurity and isolation and tragedy, and which didn't.

"Come with me," I say. "I need to introduce you to somebody."

I take her arm rather firmly and guide her out of the Wee Kirk. California sun lances hangover pain into my skull. Corrie's comrades in Nataliya's entourage look at us suspiciously as we step outside. Cameras flash. I take a breath of Los Angeles smog refreshingly free of sandalwood incense.

There's a zone in front of the door that's being kept clear so people can wait for their cars, and I look around the milling crowd and spot Dagmar, standing next to Ismet. I steer Corrie toward her.

"Dagmar," I say. "This is Corrie van Houten."

"Hello," Dagmar says. They clasp hands, and Dagmar takes in the damp cheeks and smudged mascara. "Did you know Nataliya well?"

"Corrie was one of her assistants," I say. "She wrote the monologue we just saw."

Dagmar gives me a surprised look. "She did?"

"No," Corrie protests. "I didn't."

Dagmar continues to gaze at me. "She says she didn't," she points out.

"She only wrote the words," I say. "And put in the emotions and stuff."

Comprehension dawns. "Ahh," Dagmar says, and looks at Corrie with a new awareness.

"She's a good writer," I say. "Since you're becoming such a huge force in this town, you'll need more assistants now, and Corrie should be one of them."

Dagmar absorbs this, and turns to look at Corrie. "Well," says Corrie. "Ah."

I leave them to exchange contact information and then signal Simon to call Astin to bring up the Expedition. I stand there by myself, sufficiently far from the crowd of reporters that I can ignore their shouted questions.

Nataliya's entourage parks itself somewhere to my right rear, I assume because it's the only space left. I try to ignore the suspicious looks they're giving me. I hear Corrie rejoin them.

"What was *that* about?" one of the Posse Girls says.

"Oh, it was that producer—Dagny?—she heard I helped Nataliya with the monologue, and wanted to interview me about some writing job." Her voice turns dreamy. "Nataliya must have told her how I helped. That was so nice of her."

The others chorus their agreement. I smile to myself. Corrie knows her peers, and knows that saying a potential job offer had come as a result of my noticing her talent wouldn't go over well. Instead it has become the result of a good deed by Nataliya, the shared object of worship. They can't be jealous of Corrie's opportunity if Nataliya arranged it.

I predict Corrie will go far in this town.

I see Astin pulling up into the drive. Simon and Wild Bill shoulder a path through the crowd to get me to the vehicle. Reporters din in my ears all the way.

I still don't have answers to give them.

INT. SEAN'S SUITE—DAY

The police are waiting at the hotel. They're not just waiting for me, they're waiting for everybody—with the high profile that this case has developed, my guess is that half the detectives in LA have lost their weekend, and they're just a little bit grouchy about it.

I have a three-hour interview in my suite with a couple of detectives, a plump Asian guy and a high-strung blond woman who keeps popping nicotine gum. I'm nervous even though the interview is as friendly, I suppose, as these things get.

I'm nervous in part because I don't know where my gun is. I know Simon took it and put it somewhere. I don't know whether it's been fired. I could be framed for a killing that I don't remember.

And of course I could be framed for the killing I *do* remember. So either way it's pretty dicey.

At least someone's cleaned the room, so it doesn't look as if the Seventh Fleet's had a drunken riot here along with all the hookers from West Sunset.

They ask if I have any suspects, any theories.

"Jaydee Martin was the first in the series," I say. "Find out who killed Jaydee, and you'll solve the others."

"Some people have suggested that"—the Asian detective looks at the notes he's scrawled on his handheld—"Timothea Wilhelm was the first."

"Maybe that's true," I say, "but that case is old. You're much more likely to generate evidence for one of the more recent killings."

They don't seem interested in my telling them how to do their jobs. The blonde gives me a look. "Do you have access to drugs?"

I look at her blankly. "What kind of drugs?" I ask.

Her look hardens. "You tell me."

I carefully compose my face. "I do not have access to any kind of drugs at all."

She pops her nicotine gum skeptically. "You don't have prescriptions for . . . for anything?"

"No. I'm in good health, I don't need medication."

My brain is spinning. I don't know why they'd mention drugs unless drugs were somehow involved in Joey's death.

They change the subject again, to Trishula. I explain that complicated history all over again, and then they bring up my complaint about the Ford Expedition that's twice tried to kill me.

"Do you have witnesses to these attempts?"

I realize that they suspect I may have invented the SUV, possibly in an attempt to avoid suspicion while running down a number of my colleagues. I mention that Cleve pulled me away from the first attempt, and give them his contact information.

"Do you have any idea who was trying to kill you?"

I mention Jimmy Blogjoy. I can't think of anyone else.

They leave me their cards and tell me to contact them if I have any more information. I agree to do that, and they leave.

This leaves me too depressed to remain alone, so I head downstairs to the hotel's classic bar, dark wood and brass, with a popcorn machine in one corner. Here I find Allison, Jane, and Jean-Marc. Jane and Allison are working on another pitcher of margaritas, and Jean-Marc is drinking single malt. In front of them there's a half-empty bowl of popcorn on the polished wood surface of their table.

I order a club soda. After the last twenty-four hours, I may not touch alcohol ever again.

"Hello, Sean." By this point in the production Jean-Marc is a complete wreck. His eyes sag half-shut. His sagging jowls are unshaven. He smells of sweat and tobacco. He sags over the table with his elbows propped under him.

Jane and Allison look weary, but not nearly as decayed.

The scent of the popcorn stimulates my gastric juices. I eat a few kernels, and the waiter brings my drink.

I turn to the others and ask if they know how Joey died. They have no answers. We were all asked about access to drugs, though, so that provides a substantial clue.

"It cannot be an overdose," Jean-Marc says, "or homicide detectives wouldn't be involved. Someone has to have drugged him."

"If someone poisoned him," I point out, "it has to be someone who knew him well."

"And who lived on the same floor of the hotel," Jane points out. "The same hotel as the rest of us."

I hadn't considered this. With guards on the elevators and alarms on the staircases, that reduces the possible suspects to a manageable number.

"How many of the crew are on our floor?" I ask. "A couple dozen?"

Jean-Marc shrugs. Jane stares at her margarita.

"I'm on the top floor with you," Allison says, "but I'm on the other side of the building, with the elevators in between. If

I'd come over to Joey's side of the tower, the guards would have seen me."

"Bully for you," Jane says. A tear leaks from her eye, and she wipes it with a crumpled bar napkin.

"Honest to God," Allison says. "I thought it was Joey doing the killings."

I look at her. "And you shared this insight with who?"

Her lip curls. "What good would that have done?"

"If people knew to look out for Joey," I point out, "they might not have got killed."

"Except it isn't Joey killing people," Allison says. "All those times I reminded him that I left the party before Timmi went for nothing."

I search my memory. "That's not how I recall it."

Allison flips a hand in dismissal. "It doesn't matter now, does it?"

No, I suppose it doesn't, though I hadn't quite realized the depth of Allison's selfishness till this moment. Telling Joey about Timmi's infidelity in order to make her editing job easier, assuring Joey she'd left the party early while keeping her suspicions about Joey to herself... Allison, I realize, is quite a piece of work.

Jane dabs at another tear. This conversation is depressing me even more than staying alone in my room, so I'm more relieved than not when I see Dagmar and Richard the Assassin appear in the door. They scan the faces in the bar, and when Dagmar sees me she raises a hand and gives a summoning gesture.

"I'm called," I say, and lurch out of the booth.

Dagmar and Richard precede me into the lobby. Dagmar is out of the dress she wore at the funeral and back in cargo pants and a tee stretched tight across her stomach. Richard is still dressed for the funeral, in a gray cashmere suit and tie. For once he's not wearing only black and white. Through the lobby windows I can see a swarm of reporters outside the building, and a pair of guards on the door who are keeping them out.

"Let's go up to your room," Dagmar says.

"Fine with me."

There are more guards watching the lobby elevators. As we step into the elevator with its mirrors and faux woodwork, Dagmar looks at my glass suspiciously.

"What's that?" she asks.

"Club soda." I wave it under her nose. "Have a taste if you want."

"I have a report that you got loaded last night."

"Yeah," I say. "Being attacked by a knife-wielding fanatic while my guards just sort of stood there... something about that experience made me care a lot less about the morals clause in my contract."

"We can get you a different set of guards," Dagmar says.

I make a dismissive sound with my lips. "They're used to all my crotchets by now. Hate to break in a new set."

The elevator doors open and reveal another set of guards, all strangers to me. They know my face, though, and Dagmar's, so they wave us through.

There are more guards patrolling the hallways. It's going to be a lot harder to sneak around into someone's room, assuming that I'd ever want to do such a thing again.

Tessa Brettel passes us going the other way, wearing a bathrobe and carrying a towel over one shoulder. Heading for the pool, or the spa. We say hello as we pass.

So the second unit director has a room on my, and Joey's, side of the elevators. I suppose it's barely possible that she clipped Joey in order to get promoted into his place, but there are so few days of shooting left that it hardly seems worth the attempt.

I take Dagmar and Richard to my room. In the afternoon heat there's a trace on the air of the previous night's excess, and I turn on the air conditioning.

Dagmar walks straight to the hunter green sofa and drops into it. She kicks off her shoes and props her feet on the coffee table. Her ankles are badly swollen.

"You all right?" I ask.

Dagmar shifts herself on the sofa, trying to find a comfortable position. "Five weeks left," she says. "And after that I'll be hauling a squalling shit monster around on my hip for months and months."

I contemplate this wholesome prospect, and can only fall back on my role as host. "Want anything to drink?"

She takes a ginger ale. Richard has cranberry juice. I freshen my club soda with more cranberry juice and pull up an armchair.

"Why did you want to talk to me?" I ask.

"First," Dagmar says, "thanks for introducing me to Corrie van Houten. Because I'm *all about adopting waifs*."

"No need to thank me," I say. "It was my pleasure."

She gives me a thoughtful look. "The other problem I need to talk about," she says, "is what I'm supposed to do with you."

I sip my cran-and-club and find the astringent taste pleasing. "That's easy," I say. "You cast me in the sequel, as per contract."

She nods. "Yes, but why would I?" She points a finger at me. "You're nothing but trouble. People with knives and big cars follow you around trying to kill you. And just a few hours ago you were waving a pistol in a vomit-spattered bedroom and trying to shoot your own bodyguard."

I put on my innocent face. "He startled me."

"Insuring future productions may be impossible, especially if you're in them."

I'm beginning to get angry. I'm hiding in a hotel and three friends are dead and I'm hungover, and now Dagmar is using a completion bond as a weapon to threaten my job.

"Why blame me?" I say. "May I point out that I'm not responsible for *any* of this?"

She replies with a skeptical look. I put a hand up to frame my face.

"Look at this face, Dagmar," I say. "Who else can play Roheen?"

She frowns at me. "Why did you have a firearm, and why didn't you tell anyone about it?"

I try to project a reasonable façade. "Kung fu won't stop an SUV. A pistol might."

A furrow appears between her brows. She gives me a searching look.

"Did you kill Joey? Last night you were insisting he was planning to kill you, and now he's dead."

I'm so taken aback that it takes a while for my brain to process a reply. "Don't trust *my* answer," I say. "What does your guy say?"

Richard speaks for the first time. "Simon said that he didn't think the gun had been fired in a long time. He said it hadn't been cleaned in ages, like it had been in someone's closet for years."

"Simon knows his guns, yeah," I say. "But you know Joey wasn't shot, right?"

Dagmar tries to heave herself into a more upright posture in order to fix me with a steely glare, but the sofa and her pregnancy combine to defeat her. She tries glaring from her semi-recumbent position, but the ploy lacks impact.

"How do you know that?" she asks finally.

"The detectives asked everyone about access to drugs. I think Joey must have been poisoned or something."

Dagmar and Richard exchange looks. Dagmar turns back to me.

"And you didn't poison him?"

I wave a dismissive hand. "With what?"

"Did you kill Timmi Wilhelm?"

Again I have to take a few seconds to manage an answer. "Now I'm supposed to have killed the *whole family*?"

"Can you just answer the question, please?"

I compose myself on the chair, hands on my lap, sitting up straight, as if I were Carter-Ann Dixon offering a suggestion to a hostile director. Making sure that my posture and expression are absolutely proper and absolutely unreadable.

"I haven't killed *anyone*," I say, and then relax. "There. I hope that saves you a bunch more questions."

Dagmar sighs and sips her ginger ale. Her kid must be kicking, because I can see the flesh under her tee giving little twitches.

"Look," she says. "You're a good actor, and I'd like to have you in the sequel. But what am I supposed to do in the meantime? Surround you with a platoon of guards twenty-four/seven?"

"The 'meantime' is just when I'll need them. Because people don't get killed on this production until their jobs are over."

Richard clears his throat. "Joey wasn't finished," he says. "The shooting isn't done."

"There's just Monday, and then maybe pickups here and there," I say. "Joey isn't really necessary any more."

"I can't afford to keep everyone in this hotel indefinitely," Dagmar says. "I've got to make some progress in uncovering what's going on."

"I got Trishula," I say. "And whoever killed Joey has to have been on this floor, on this side of the elevator."

Dagmar and Richard adopt identical pained expressions. "Not quite," Richard says.

I look at him. "What's the bad news?"

"The alarm on the corner stairway failed when it was tested this morning," he says. "So someone could have come up the stairs, disabled the alarm somehow, and gone after Joey."

For a moment I share their disgust.

"Isn't there someone monitoring all the alarms at all times?" I say. "Wouldn't that person have to be an accomplice to whoever did the killing?"

"They say the alarm was tested yesterday afternoon," Richard says, "and must have failed in the meantime."

I'm beyond astonishment. "So now we're up against some hella super-ninja who knows how to bypass alarms?"

"It's more likely," Dagmar says, "that the alarm failed on its own, and that Joey was killed by someone on this floor of the hotel."

"Have you considered Carter-Ann as a suspect?" I say. "Maybe she couldn't take Joey any longer. And she's an MD, she'd have access to drugs."

"Carter-Ann is in Boston for a meeting of the American Psychiatric Association," Richard says. "She's giving a presentation."

Now that I think about it, I don't recall seeing her at Nataliya's funeral. "Are you sure she actually went?"

Richard shrugs. "I can check, I suppose."

I look at the drink in my hand. "Can I move back to the NoHo?" I ask. "I think I was safer there."

Dagmar takes a deliberate drink of her ginger ale. "After Monday, you can move anywhere you like."

"I've been thinking Greenland."

"You could do worse."

"By the way," Richard says, "I got a report that your father entered the U.S. yesterday. He flew from Vancouver to LAX and came in on his American passport."

I think about this. "Tell your guys to keep him away from me," I say.

"We're keeping *everybody* away from you," Richard points out. He glances at the overpriced watch on his wrist. "Things are a little murky where your father is concerned," he says slowly, "so it's difficult to be certain, but it's very possible that your dad is broke."

"How do you know?" I ask. "I tried for several years to track his money and got nowhere."

"We have somewhat better resources than you do," Dagmar says. "Or rather, Sri does."

I nod. "I suppose Sri knows where all the money in the world is."

"More or less."

I give Dagmar a look. *Maybe*, I think, *I should ask a few questions of my own.*

"Sri's set up to make a bundle on this project, isn't he?"

"Four hundred million subscriptions and counting," she says. "I'm sure we're all grateful."

"And of course there's the data you're getting from the subscribers," I say. I watch her carefully as I speak, and I see her face harden just a little, the eyes turn just a little more opaque.

Something hiding in there, I think.

"That information could be worth a lot," I probe.

She shakes her head. "We're not interested in monetizing it. We'll collate it and use it to improve customer service on future projects."

"Sri's down with that?" I ask.

Dagmar shrugs. "Sri doesn't need any more cash."

"Most rich people don't. But somehow they keep trying to make more money."

Dagmar doesn't bother to respond. I sip my drink. Cranberry bubbles tickle my nose.

"You came to Sri with this project, right?" I say. "He didn't approach you?"

She flashes a thin smile. "He didn't know me from Eve."

"But he financed it anyway?"

"Dagmar," Richard says, "is very persuasive."

I don't know how you persuade a self-made billionaire to do you a favor—not unless you can hand him a huge opportunity, such as the personal data of four hundred million people, all collated in your very own Sri Sphere.

"Getting back to your father," Richard says. "I can show you the report I have on him, but it's incomplete. We're pretty sure that your father sold his place on the Riviera and his place in Belize to raise money."

"He wants me to invest in some kind of resort complex on the Mosquito Coast."

"Oh, that." Richard is dismissive. "It's called Costa Magnifico, which is not only ungrammatical but bankrupt. Construction halted four months ago after funds were exhausted. Your father's hoping that if you get the place back on its feet, his own shares will be worth something again."

"Or maybe he's hoping to sell you his shares," Dagmar says. "You could change the name to Roheen's Rendezvous."

"I'll send you the report," Richard says.

Dagmar takes her swollen feet off the coffee table, jams them back into her shoes, and heaves herself to her feet. "You haven't helped me make up my mind," she says.

"About what?"

She gives me a look. "About whether it's worth keeping you alive after the week is over."

"I'll try not to kick the dog," I say.

FROM: Parmita
SUBJECT: Re: Re: Re: Re: Re: Your "Car"

Babaji has an ashram in Los Angeles. You could give the check to one of the disciples there, and he could carry it to India to sign.

FROM: Sean Makin
SUBJECT: Re: Re: Re: Re: Re: Re: Your "Car"

The last disciple from the ashram tried to gut me with a kitchen knife. I'm not letting anyone from that place near me.

P.S.: It turns out that everyone at the ashram knew that Trishula was making threats and planned to carry them out, but they hid this fact from the authorities. The civil suit sounds open-and-shut to me!

I expect I'll end up owning Babaji's whole stateside operation, and then you can visit and stay in whatever ashram here you want.

TRACKING SHOTS

The weekend goes by without any more deaths. I keep my father at bay by letting his phone calls go to voice mail. He keeps asking whether I've got the prospectus he sent on Costa Magnifico.

The police reveal that Joey was poisoned with a Schedule II narcotic, but decline to say which one. I look this up on the Internet, and conclude that it had to be morphine or some lab-engendered version of morphine like Dilaudid or OxyContin.

At least with an opioid, I think, *you feel no pain.*

I spend the weekend trying to work out what's happening to my life, and what's happening to my friends. I'm happy and fulfilled for the first time in years, but everything else is falling apart. One of the threats to my life has been dealt with, but there are at least a couple more.

It's like I'm Typhoid Mary or something. I have a cloud over my head that rains on everyone near me, and it rains tragedy.

I decide that since no one else is solving the mystery, I should do it myself. The only problem with this is that I don't have any information, and I don't know where to start.

I'm not a detective. I'm the Watcher.

It is small consolation to hear that *Escape to Earth* has picked up another eighty million subscribers, all attracted by the sensational publicity over the murders.

I report to Makeup on Monday for the last day of shooting, to have dust and blood painted on me for the last time. Tessa Brettel stands in as director. Roheen's character is as comfortable as an old glove, and I slip it right on and film the last heart-wrenching scene, where Roheen, wounded and in pain, says farewell to his dream of returning home. I nail the big speech in one take, though Tessa insists on a second, just for insurance.

Even Roger behaves, the little prick.

That evening there's a wrap party on the set, with a buffet of Texas barbecue and a DJ and a blooper reel. People walk around with ketchup-red barbecue sauce on their hands, faces, and clothes, and look like ghoulish extras from a brain-eating zombie film.

Dagmar shows up to give a speech about how we've kept on working despite the tragedies that have beset the production, and that she's proud of us.

I give a present to everyone on the crew, a gold stickpin topped by their initial.

It has to be said that I'm consistent. I'm still pathetic in my desire to be liked.

The party falls flat: too many deaths, too much depression, too much fear. Now we're all going to have to go home and hope that no one targets us with an SUV, or maybe a syringe.

People begin trickling out of the Lang Towers as they finish their work. Some are happy to go home. Some would prefer to stay under the guards' protection. A number decide to visit relatives in other states.

Jean-Marc flies home to France. He'll be safer there, at least from American junk food.

After the party, after Simon has checked my suite to make sure no armed assassins are lurking in the closets, he closes the door, pulls my pistol out of his jacket, and offers it to me butt-first. I look at it in surprise, then take it.

"I didn't think I'd see this again," I tell him.

"Joey wasn't shot," Simon tells me. "I don't have to hold it in case it's evidence."

I leer at him. "I could have held the pistol to Joey's head and told him to swallow pills," I say.

He looks shocked. He clearly hasn't considered this. I relax my expression.

"I'll try not to point it at you again," I say.

" 'Preciate it," he says, in his Okie accent.

I put the pistol in my bedside table.

The next few days I'm in a sound studio, looping dialogue. Sometimes when you're making a movie the sound gear doesn't pick up the words properly, or you mumble without meaning to, or there's too much background noise, or the dialogue gets changed. When that happens you have to rerecord the dialogue in the studio so that the crew can have clean sound.

It's tedious work, just a couple of engineers and me with a pair of headphones on, lip-synching to my own image on a small screen.

In my free time I'm planning my future. I have Bruce Kravitz recommend a good civil lawyer, so I can sue Babaji's organization for sheltering Trishula. The fact that his confession to the police admitted this should make the case much easier.

Maybe I'll get my money back, either as a reward or as a settlement.

I also weigh some of Simon's Paranoia Options, and decide to replace my mom's car with a less flammable vehicle. Since the Mercedes brand has worked well for me, I get a Mercedes crossover with all-wheel drive and a big diesel engine that takes fuel much less likely than gasoline to explode. I then turn the vehicle over to a mechanic of Simon's acquaintance who will pimp it out with steel skid plates, bullet-resistant heavy-duty suspension, four-point safety harnesses, secret compartments for weapons, run-flat tires, and bullbars so I can run someone down without denting the chrome. The whole thing will be armored with lightweight ceramics and laminates.

I also start to think about a new place to live. My condo is a dreary place, and I decide it's time to upgrade. My problem is that I'm not yet Hollywood rich—though I have every expectation of living in luxury eventually, state and federal taxes and the Screen Actors' Guild have each taken a slice out of what Dagmar's paid me so far, and I'm not exactly living in Uncle Scrooge territory right now.

Plus, I'm in the process of becoming an industry. I'm getting calls from people who want to put my image on posters, on T-shirts, on mouse pads, and—my favorite—bobblehead dolls. I don't have time to deal with this stuff, so I'm in need of an entourage—a personal assistant, a publicist who isn't a real Sidney Falco, an accountant, a business manager, and a lawyer, people to smooth my way and investigate these offers and take my checks to the bank without any part of them disappearing.

The only reason I'm not interviewing is that I'm afraid a candidate might show up with a knife, a gun, or a syringe.

They can bring listening devices if they want. I'm way past caring about that.

I end up renting a small two-bedroom house off Mulholland in the Hollywood Hills, frame and plaster with a red tile roof. It was built in the fifties and runs about eighteen hundred square feet, built on a hillside with a basement garage. There's no tennis court, no swimming pool, and only one bathroom. If I bought the place outright I'd spend a million and a half at least.

I can drive off the road right into the garage, and not have to worry about anyone trying to run me down as I walk from the car to the front door. The house already has a burglar alarm, and Simon figures he can upgrade the security system without difficulty. I think he's a little disappointed that I'm not excavating for a panic room.

I make plans to move my belongings to the new place, and to rent the condo once it's empty.

By Friday my work on *Escape to Earth* is done, and I join Cleve and Bruce Kravitz for lunch, to discuss my future.

INT. SALO RESTAURANT—DAY

Ironically Bruce wants to dine at Salo, the restaurant where I first met Dagmar. It's only a couple blocks from his office tower. I amuse him with information about the Provençal/Turkish fish soup. Bruce tells me about some scripts that might be adapted for me, in which I play cops or reformed hit men or spies.

Imagine someone who looks like me being a spy or a hit man. He'd be at large for all of twenty minutes before someone recognized him.

Fortunately we live in Hollywood, where we don't have to think about these things.

I've been considering the sort of roles I want to play, and I have an idea.

"The way I look," I say, "I can't be a conventional leading man. I can't just show up on the screen and have the audience thinking I'm the hero. So I think I have to be someone who starts out bad and ends up the good guy."

Bruce nods. "That's a good story," he says. "We can do that story."

"Also," I say, "I don't want to jump into the first project that offers itself. Roheen's made me bankable, okay, but I don't want to make a movie for the sole purpose of capitalizing on Roheen's success. That's what happened with the two pictures I made after *Family Tree* was canceled, and the movies tanked and took me down with them."

Bruce nods again. It's a little unnerving, the way his head moves but his blue eyes remain completely focused on me. It's as if, instead of his eyeballs rotating inside his head, his body rotates around his fixed eyeballs.

"You've obviously learned your way around this town," he says. He takes a sip of his mineral water. "Speaking of exploitation," he says, "I hear the conflict over *Mister Baby Head* has been settled."

I'm pleasantly surprised.

"I ran into Jerry Singleton the other day, and he mentioned it." Jerry was one of Mac's partners in his production company. "Your success in *Escape to Earth* must have broken the logjam." Bruce gives one of his ironic smiles. "So now you'll be known both as Roheen *and* as a murderous chainsaw killer."

"Acetylene torch," I say. "I used an acetylene torch in that one."

Bruce nods. "Soon you'll be torching human flesh in theaters across the country."

The lunch ends on this delightful note, and with Bruce's dry handshake. Cleve hustles off to get the waitress's phone number. I walk Bruce out to the sidewalk, and then I call Simon, who is in a nearby garage with the Impala, to pick me up.

I've got Simon through the weekend. If I want him after Sunday, I'll have to pay him myself. I still haven't made up my mind about that, though my new two-bedroom house is a little small for both me and guards.

Bruce recedes in the direction of his headquarters. Beautifully dressed people walk past, intermixed with casually dressed 909ers looking for the stars. Rodeo Drive stretches left and right, boutiques and jewelry stores and places where you can get four-thousand-dollar shoes hand-crafted by Tibetan yak-herders out of specially prepared water buffalo leather and stitched with sinew from the intestines of rare snow leopards.

Or rather, you can get them if you're prepared to be put on a very long waiting list.

The gaudy, insistent Rodeo that exists in Augmented Reality is invisible at the moment, since I'm not wearing my AriPop shades. Since I have a minute or two while Simon gets the car out of the garage, I slip my handheld out of its holster and turn on the AR app. I pan along the street, trying to spot the spinning globe that marks a place where you can view *Escape to Earth*. I'm pleased to see it, rather distantly, over a nearby café.

I'm panning along when I hear the growl of a vehicle engine, and there—pulling a screaming U-turn right in the middle of Rodeo—is a black Ford Expedition.

On the little screen, the Ford is almost buried in a host of colorful icons, and for a half-second I wonder if it's real. And then recognition kicks in, and with it the adrenaline.

The Ford's engine bellows like an enraged bull. Blue smoke jets from spinning tires. I'm already running like hell. I sprint down the sidewalk and turn only when I've put a silver Toyota Tundra pickup between myself and danger.

There is an enormous crash accompanied by the sound of smashing glass and shrieking rubber. I'm surprised at how far the SUV's weight and momentum make the Tundra jump—the truck lurches up the sidewalk after me, causing me to skip backward in panic, but the Tundra hits the car in front of it and fails to crush me by a few feet.

Another car, a Honda, enters the scene and hits the Ford's right quarter. There's another crash, another shriek of bent metal.

Steam gushes from the Ford's radiator. The Expedition's engine dies—I can see over the hood of the Tundra that the whole engine compartment is caved in. I hear the starter grinding louder than the crash of my own heart, and then there's a crack as the starter breaks.

A reek of burned rubber and smoking exhaust rolls over the scene. I stare through rising steam at the darkened, cracked windshield, and the vague figure behind it, someone who seems to be struggling with an air bag. And then the passenger door opens, and a small, cursing woman staggers out.

I break into helpless laughter. And because I still have my phone in my hand, I punch the button that will start recording video and aim the camera lens at the driver.

"*God damn it!*" screams Melody Chastain, she of the dog. "*God fucking damn it!*"

Her hair is long and stringy and unwashed. Her eyes are not quite focused. She waves a fist at me.

"*This is all your fault!*" she yells at me. I roar with laughter, holding the phone high and hoping my cackling doesn't shake the picture too much.

"Motherfucker!" Melody kicks the Tundra, slips, and falls on her butt.

"*Motherfuck piss bucket!*" she screams. With a certain amount of effort, she manages to get to her feet, and then staggers in a raging circle, shouting curses and waving her fists.

By now a considerable crowd has gathered. Melody is being recognized, and people are taking her picture with their handhelds. People are calling 911. The Honda's driver has gotten out of his car and is standing there, helpless with shock, holding his insurance card in his hand. I'm gasping for breath and spluttering with mirth.

I've been terrified for months, and it turns out I was scared of Melody Chastain, the star whose career I had unintentionally destroyed with my video of her kicking the dog. Someone must have told her that I was responsible for her career death; and back in May, when she saw me crossing Rodeo on my way to meet Dagmar, she was unable to restrain her thirst for vengeance.

I decide I'm going to stop feeling sorry for her.

A police cruiser pulls to a stop, and the officer gets out. As the cop approaches, Melody sees him, shrieks, runs toward him, and hits him in the sternum with her little fist.

Her capacity for kinetic damage is severely reduced by the fact of her not being inside an oversized Ford, and the officer is more surprised than hurt. Still, he reacts with the impersonal professionalism we expect from the police of Beverly Hills. He grabs her, whips her around, tosses her against the Expedition, and unholsters his Taser.

Melody gets hit with three hundred kilovolts of street justice and goes down twitching. At this point the crowd gets between me and Melody, so I stop recording and walk off to find Simon, who's in the Impala stuck in traffic half a block away.

"What happened?" he asks.

"I'll tell you later," I say.

I review the video and it's about as gratifying as I can imagine. I email it to Kari Sothern with the note, YOU OWE ME TEN GRAND.

CHAPTER FIFTEEN

Our Reality Network

Live Feed

LadyDayFan says:

How many people are in jail now for trying to kill Sean Makin?

Hippolyte says:

This *has* to be a game, right? Or a publicity thing?

TRACKING SHOTS

Here's what happens in my fantasy. I call my new lawyer, and this is what I tell him:

"Talk to Melody Chastain's lawyer. Tell her that I won't press charges for attempted vehicular homicide if she checks into a secure facility for some no-nonsense head shrinkage. And I mean someplace serious, someplace they won't let her out until they've installed some heavy-duty impulse control."

I'm feeling benign about the whole thing. Maybe it's because I finally found out who's been trying to clip me. Maybe it's because I'm living the dream. Or maybe some of Roheen's selflessness is rubbing off on me.

But I really don't see how jail would improve Melody. She'd come out more homicidal than ever, and maybe next time she'd use a more practical weapon, like a shotgun.

Except that this isn't what happens, and it's all because of the cell phone cameras that were recording the accident. There I am on all the videos, a foot taller than anyone else in the crowd, and—being a newly certified international film star—completely recognizable. The detectives who interviewed me after Joey's death see me on the video, and next thing you know I'm talking to them, and they're pissed I didn't call them first. I end up confirming that it was Melody who's been trying to run me down for the last four months.

And then, within a matter of hours, Melody's been declared a person of interest in the deaths of Jaydee and Nataliya, and maybe even Joey.

So it looks like Melody's going to be doing time after all, maybe even for some crimes she didn't actually commit.

So now Melody Chastain has become another one of the casualties that seem to accumulate around me, and in her case it's for the second time.

That night, feeling a bit unsettled by all this, I go to the premiere of Part IV of *Escape to Earth*, which is being held on the Caltech campus. Apparently Dagmar went to school there or something. There are thousands of students and fans swarming around, and my guards are extra-alert. But I do manage to talk to some of my fans, and I manage to connect with one tall dark-haired girl who is exceptionally pretty, and she accompanies me to my suite at the Lang Towers, where she submits with considerable amusement to a search for hostile electronics on the part of Simon and Astin. I think they're a little disappointed to discover that she's not carrying any spy gear.

Soon after, I subject her to a longer, much more detailed search. Nothing unexpected is discovered. I'm beyond joy, beyond delight. I'm able to forget Melody. It's like waking up from a long, horrible nightmare.

Saturday morning I bid farewell to my fan-of-the-night, and then dedicate the rest of the weekend to moving all my stuff to my new place. Simon stands by and guards me as movers carry boxes and my old shabby furniture to and fro. I check out of the Lang Towers and move into my new home.

I'm having second thoughts about renting the condo, and now I'm thinking of maybe keeping it as an office. That way I'd still have access to the condo's swimming pool and other facilities.

Now my house is as much like a fortress as Simon's techs can manage—there are cameras, motion detectors, heat detectors, and glass-break detectors. My armored car won't be ready for weeks, but I was impressed by the way the Toyota Tundra stood up to Melody's assault, so I rent one, a version with a big V-8 and an extended cab so I can carry a full set of passengers. It feels like driving a house on wheels. I figure I'm safe from a collision with anything smaller than a locomotive.

I have to make some decisions about my security now. Two people who were trying to damage me are now in jail. I have to decide if that means I'm now as safe as a newly minted—well, *re*minted—Hollywood star is likely to be.

I suppose it's barely possible that Melody killed Nataliya—since they were roughly the same age and in the same profession, she might have viewed her as a rival or something. But I can't imagine that Melody killed Jaydee, or even knew who she was; and there's no way she disabled an alarm at the Lang Towers and dispatched Joey.

Which means that whoever's been killing the crew of *Escape to Earth* is still among us.

On the other hand, there's no proof that the killer has me in his sights at all. What the victims had in common was their attendance at Joey's party the night of Timmi's death, but Joey was the only plausible candidate for a killer, and someone's taken him out of the picture. I can't think of anyone else who would try to avenge Timmi in such a wholesale fashion.

So I reason the killer's motive has nothing to do with Timmi. There's something else going on; and because I don't know what that something is, I figure I'm out of the crosshairs for the time being.

And besides, if I'm targeted by the super-ninja who got through the alarmed door at the Lang Towers and killed Joey in his own suite, I figure there's not much a bodyguard is going to do to stop him.

With a degree of reluctance I decide that I no longer need Simon guarding me all the time, but I keep him and his firm on retainer in the event that I need personal protection for specific events. Which I will, because suddenly I'm very popular.

Invitations are pouring in: premieres, benefits, parties. I'm on everyone's A-list. I accept invites to some of the more private functions, but I don't want to be swarmed by reporters asking me questions best asked of the police, and so I avoid the big public spectacles.

Besides, I'm tired. I've spent the three summer months in front of the camera, friends have been killed, I've been threatened, and I've had to dodge a crazy star in a big Ford. All I really want to do is sleep and occasionally eat, and that's what I do. The paparazzi haven't learned where I'm living yet, and they leave me in peace.

I continue to train with Master Pak. The *Celebrity Pitfighter* finale is just a couple weeks off. I can't get very excited about it.

On Monday I have a meeting with my lawyer, and he sends a registered letter to the headquarters of Babaji's operation in the U.S., which is in Berkeley. We're demanding five million for pain, suffering, and the fact that Babaji has been hanging on to my stolen money for all these years.

Monday night Julian stops by and brings his bong and a monster movie. We get totally glazed and watch *The Valley of Gwangi* (1969), in which cowboys battle a stop-motion allosaurus in Mexico. There's a wonderful nihilistic climax in which a bullring and a Mexican cathedral are destroyed. It's just what I need.

On Tuesday night I'm drowsing on my sagging couch when the phone begins to scream at me. I grope for the phone on the scarred coffee table and knock over a nearly empty take-out container of ginger beef from the local Thai restaurant. I grab the phone, look at the screen, and decide I've finally regained enough energy to handle one of my dad's calls.

The voice is so familiar. Again the years seem to melt away, again I seem to turn into a kid desperate for his controlling father's approval. He asks me how I'm doing, if I'm still involved in shooting. He tells me that he downloaded my *Tonight* appearance onto his computer and watched it, and that I was great.

I don't tell him that I know he's in the States, or that I suspect he's broke. I just want to see how far he's going to take this.

"Have you had a chance to look at the resort prospectus?" he asks.

"Costa Magnifico?" I say. "It's ungrammatical. It should be Costa Magnifica."

"No one who actually stays at this resort," he says firmly, "is going to care about that."

I look at my varnished open-beam ceiling. "My business manager says the place is bankrupt," I say.

The father is shocked. "Bankrupt!" he says. "We're not bankrupt! We just stopped building because Phase I was complete."

I restrain a laugh. "The funds for Phase II are in place?" I ask.

"They're almost secured."

"What does that mean, exactly?"

"It means," doggedly, "that they're almost secured."

I grin. "So you don't really need my help for Phase II, then."

"Now is the time to get in," says my dad. "You'll maximize profit that way."

"My business manager says the stock is worthless," I say.

"The stock will rebound," I'm told, "once Phase II is built."

"Oh look, Dad!" I say. "There's someone at the door! I've gotta go. Bye."

I end the call and put the phone down, and I close my eyes in hopes of drowsing off again—and two seconds later the phone screams again. I figure it's my dad calling back, but I look at the screen and see that it's Dagmar.

"Hi there," I answer, surprised.

"Richard's on his way to you with the new script," Dagmar says. She laughs. "Guess what? We're getting the band back together."

Through my surprise I manage to stammer a few words. "We're *what*?"

"I thought of a new ending," Dagmar says. "It's the ending the picture should have had all along."

I'm appalled. "*We're going back up Parmenter Canyon?*"

"I'm not sure yet," Dagmar says. "We may end up doing the reshoots in the studio. We're still discussing that."

I want to clutch my head and yank out fistfuls of hair. Dagmar is perfectly within her rights to demand reshoots, but I've had enough of *Escape to Earth* and everything that goes with it, especially the terror, paranoia, and funerals.

"So what's so wonderful about this new ending?" I ask.

In the original ending shot in Parmenter Canyon, Roheen, with Khabane's help, manages to get to Swaziland and find the Tellurian Gate. He is on the verge of escaping to his home, but is wounded by the Steene, who then destroy the gate. In the final scene, Roheen is reconciled with the fact of his remaining on Earth, and vows to become Earth's protector against the sinister Steene.

"The problem with that ending," Dagmar says, "is that Roheen loses because he's *unlucky*. His failure isn't the consequence of his decisions or those of his friends."

"Bad luck seems to be Roheen's constant companion," I point out. "That ending doesn't contradict anything that happens before."

"No, it doesn't. But suppose it's not Roheen who's wounded, but Khabane?"

I begin to reply, and then the idea floods my brain with brilliant light.

"Oh, yeah," I say. "That *is* a better ending."

Because then the ending becomes about choice. Does Roheen abandon his wounded comrade and run for his own world; or does he give up his dreams of home and safety and rescue Khabane, just like the Tellurian angel he's become over the last six episodes?

"How are you going to manage this logistically?" I ask. "The last episode premieres a week from Friday."

"I want to see you in makeup at oh-eight-hundred on Thursday," she says.

"Can you get Jean-Marc back from France?" I ask.

"I'm renting a jet to bring him back."

"Who's directing?"

"That'll have to be Tessa Brettel."

I rub my forehead. "Are we moving back into the Lang Towers?"

"Yes. Nobody's caught Joey's killer, you all stay under guard."

"Can I have the NoHo instead?"

"Maybe. Someone will get back to you about the arrangements."

There's a chime from the motion detectors on the front of the house, and then another chime from the doorbell.

"Richard's here," I say.

"I'll talk to you later," Dagmar says, speaking very swiftly, and hangs up.

There's a security console in the living room, and I check the cameras to make sure it actually is Richard before I open the door. There he is, in his usual cat burglar clothes, with a memory stick in his hand.

"Come in," I say. "I need a better idea of what's going on."

For a moment I'm paranoid about whether Richard can smell

the bud I was smoking the night before, but the only thing I can scent on the air is the leftover ginger beef. I offer Richard some fresh orange juice and sit him down on the armchair. The India-print throw I usually have on the chair, to disguise the fact that it's held together with duct tape, vanished in the move, and Richard sits gingerly on the plastic cushion. Because he looks nervous at the way I put the memory stick on the coffee table, I get up and make a point of locking it in the safe.

"Okay," I say, as I sit on the couch near him. "Do we know how Joey died?"

"Overdose," Richard says. "I don't know any details, but apparently the police have every reason to believe that Joey didn't inject himself."

"Carter-Ann has access to drugs," I say. "Did she actually fly to Boston for her convention?"

"Her tickets were used, she checked into the hotel, and since her presentation wasn't canceled, I assume she delivered it."

"And—" I run a hand over my balding scalp. "There was another loose end I meant to ask you about, but I can't remember what it was."

"Joey's phone call to Dagmar? On the night when Nataliya died?"

I blink. "Yeah," I say. "Maybe that was it."

"The call originated from a cell tower in Beverly Hills. So he wasn't down in Malibu killing Nataliya."

Which, I think, *is both good and bad, at least for me.* Bad because the notion that Joey killed three people for reasons of revenge is pretty much dead, and that means that whatever is actually going on is well-nigh incomprehensible.

Good, because if Joey didn't kill people over Timmi, then nobody did, and that means that the deaths aren't about me. Which means I'm not on any hit list that I know about.

It means that whatever's happening—call it the Secret—is about Dagmar, or Sri, or maybe even someone I've never met. And the only problem *now* is that somehow Jaydee, Nataliya, and

Joey found out enough about the Secret to get themselves killed—and so far as I know they weren't even *looking*. Which means they could have stumbled right over it, then got themselves wiped out, without even knowing what it was they'd found, or why they were being killed.

I look at Richard. "Do you have any fucking idea why any of them died?"

He shakes his head. "I was starting to agree with you that it was Joey, but—" He slices the air with a hand. "But it wasn't."

I look around the living room, shabby furniture in a fine, polished home.

"Maybe while you're here," I say, "you might want to do a bug sweep, just to keep in practice."

INT. GETTY VILLA—EVENING

So on Thursday I report for the reshoot, and by Friday I'm already beat to hell. I had so wanted to escape all of this, but here I am covered again in fake mud and dust and blood, except that now it's supposed to be Khabane's blood instead of mine. At least we're shooting in the studio instead of on location—there were high winds predicted for the end of the week, and they would have made Parmenter Canyon a living hell, so Dagmar decided to rely on studio work and green screen.

Tessa is a little nervous and uncertain helming the project, which is unfortunate, because Roger Cedric Johnston III is being a complete asshat. He'd been having a little vacation in California, seeing the sights, taking meetings with his new agent and manager, and waiting for stardom to descend on his head in the shape of a glowing white dove—but now he's got to work for a living, and he's making everyone as miserable as he can.

I try to get Carter-Ann to terrorize him into obedience, and she does her best, but she seems to have lost some of her mojo, and Roger remains, at least intermittently, a brat.

I get showered and changed in time for the premiere of Part V, which is being held at the Getty Villa in Pacific Palisades—which, being a replica of some kind of Roman mansion, is I guess a completely ideal place to premiere the first of two episodes taking place in South Africa and Swaziland. They do have an African highlife band playing in the central courtyard, at the end of the long, gorgeous ornamental pool, and there's dancing amid the shrubbery. I don't think highlife is South African music, but maybe Ladysmith Black Mambazo was busy.

This is why I love California, because the Getty alone shows how unnecessary it is to visit places like Africa or Italy. You can get it all here.

Inside the museum you can wander among ancient statues of Aphrodite and Zeus, eat from a rather uninspired buffet, and watch *Escape to Earth* on whatever digital device you happen to have carried with you. I go to the statue of Zeus, who sits with curly hair and beard on a throne, and I think a prayer at him. *Please, Zeus, let this be a hit.*

From the buffet I get a kebab and some kind of curried meatball. If the buffet is anything to go by, South African cuisine is some kind of Indian-influenced Dutch food, with occasional native elements—though of course the buffet may just be a buffet and not representative at all. I go to an inner courtyard, where there are modern bronze statues pretending to be ancient ones, and I sit down on a bench with my meal and my tablet. The meatball isn't much, but I like the mealie bread that goes with it, and there's an interesting drink apparently made from fermented maize—it's not alcoholic, but it has an interesting flavor, a little like yogurt, and would taste very good on a hot afternoon.

When the countdown comes, I get out my tablet, unfold the screen, open Dagmar's proprietary software, and watch. The episode opens with Roheen on a little tin-bucket freighter heading for Cape Town, with Table Mountain looming over everything, and again I marvel at how gorgeous the CGI is. I know that I, Sean, was never on that freighter, but you simply can't tell the whole thing was rendered on a computer. And my guess is that you wouldn't be able to tell even if you projected it on a screen sixty feet across.

This leads me to think about Roheen's journey, the climax of which I'll continue to shoot over the weekend. By Episode V Roheen is a lot tougher, but he's also a lot more sensitive to what's going on around him. He's engaged, he's compassionate. He cares for the people who helped him out. He's learned a lot more about Earth than he ever would have as an anthropologist, and it's changed him.

Yeah, he's maybe an angel, but he's a rugged angel. Give him a flaming sword, and he'd know what to do with it.

The episode ends with Roheen and Khabane on a bus for Swaziland and the climax at Execution Rock. As the image fades and the credits roll, I hear applause from inside the museum, and I hear voices raised in Xhosa. Roger doesn't just have his auntie with him any more, his whole extended family has flown in for the premiere. There are at least twenty of them, and they all worship him. It's not making him any easier to deal with.

I met his parents when they visited the set. Dad's a high-powered economist for the Ministry for Home Affairs, and Mom works for some kind of NGO that deals in carbon offsets. They're very intelligent and well-dressed and speak excellent English, and they're clearly a part of their nation's elite, a twenty-first-century power couple.

And now, I assume, they've spent the last twenty-odd minutes sitting or standing in various corners of the museum with handsets and tablets, watching Episode V. They all subscribed to Dagmar's feed in order to do this, and paid their fee, and provided basic information to be uploaded into the Sri Sphere, for Sri to mine for its monetary value...

They are, I figure, exactly the sort of demographic that would interest Sri. The parents are in influential positions, and probably a number of the other family members as well. Though the parents are here as Dagmar's guests, the family has enough money to fly the rest of the clan to California on its own nickel.

What will Sri do with their data? I wonder. Use it to target advertising, predict consumer or demographic trends, chart political and economics changes, inform public health issues...? No doubt someone as smart as Sri could find a lot more uses than these.

And then I think of all the deaths that have happened, and I can't imagine why any of this would be worth killing someone over. So Sri has data on a lot of people—so what? *Lots* of people have data sets.

There's a humming overhead, and I look up to see a drone aircraft flying overhead, mining visual data for one tabloid or another, data that can be sold for money.

The drone with its cameras passes out of sight, and I look down at my Chandra tablet, at the screen that is still rolling credits over an arid South African landscape, at the control buttons and the miniature QWERTY keyboard, the omnipresent little camera that gazes blandly from the frame. The kind of omnipresent camera that enabled me to capture pictures of Melody Chastain's humiliation, and that identified me as a witness for the detectives investigating the series of murders.

I look at the tablet, and I think about the application that Ramona could have installed on my handheld, one that turned it into a bug for Kari Sothern and the *Tale*.

I look at the little camera lens, and the camera lens looks back at me, and I realize what kind of data would be worth killing over.

The kind that comes with audio and video.

Escape to Earth is pitched to a certain class of people, people who can afford the hardware and have credit cards to pay for subscriptions—people like Roger's family, local elites with access to the corridors of money and power. The demographic skews young, but that's all right, because once you've got the software on Junior and Missy's phones, *you can listen to the whole family*. Because what Junior and Missy are carrying around isn't just a platform for downloading video, it's a sophisticated espionage system.

Talk about child exploitation. Sri and Dagmar are bugging the children and sending them to listen to Mummy and Daddy.

Of course you can't listen to every conversation among the four hundred million subscribers, but then you don't need to. Your data-mining algorithms can extract from the raw data which of your clients are *worth* bugging, which have information that's crucial to whatever it is you're interested in.

Politics. Economics. Military. Banking. Law enforcement. *Crime*, for heaven's sake. Whatever will provide the information necessary for you to make the right moves, and make a killing in the markets—or in the backstreets.

I remember the way Richard talked about Dagmar's project, giving it a particular emphasis as if it were so much more than just a movie. I recall what Carter-Ann said when she was admonishing Dagmar after the scene with Joey—*this is all too important to lose track of ourselves this way*. I remember thinking at the time that she was talking about something more than just *Escape to Earth*.

What did Richard say? *You talk as if spying is illegal or something.*

How many people would you actually need to pull it off? I wonder. The loudmouthed guy I overheard in the locker room wasn't one of them—he had no idea what was happening to the data he was processing, or for that matter where the data was physically located.

Dagmar has her group of loyal samurai, like Richard and Helmuth and Ismet. They've overthrown a government and dodged bullets and bombs together, and probably constitute the hard battle-tested core of the project. There is Carter-Ann and the Psy-Ops Division, who have to be involved somehow. And of course on top of the project is Sri, master of the Sri Sphere, boss of his own shadowy collection of Sphere denizens.

It is like the world's most enormous private intelligence agency, disguised as a distributed network with server farms in Finland and New Zealand. And what happens when someone threatens to blow the whistle on them?

People die, that's what.

I can—just barely—wrap my brain around this idea. But what I can't seem to comprehend is how Jaydee and Nataliya and Joey were able to constitute any kind of threat to the Secret Sri Sphere. I suppose Joey might have been smart enough, and sufficiently wired into the production to discover something; but what dangerous information could be gleaned by the costume designer and by a pop star/actress who was on the set for all of three days?

I ask myself that question, and I draw a blank.

On the tablet screen, the credits come to an end. I log out, and then I fold up the screen and turn the Chandra off.

My hands are shaking. I try to put the screen in its carrying case, and manage on the third try.

I make an attempt to rejoin the party. I eat apricot sponge cake and have more of the fermented mealie drink, and I try to talk to some people; but I keep seeing Dagmar and Sri nodding and chatting in various corners of the museum, and whenever I see them my nerves begin to shriek. My brainstorm has me so rattled that I'm thumping around like a zombie, and eventually I call Simon and have him bring up the car.

I have a lot of new lines to learn for tomorrow, anyway.

The rest of the cast and crew have been moved back into the Lang Towers, but I'm at the NoHo, back in the Marilyn Suite. I suspect I'm here because Dagmar has realized I'm irreplaceable and she wants me away from any of the cast and crew who might take it into their heads to kill me.

It isn't until after I'm alone in the room that I realize that, if my new theory is true, Dagmar is guarding me from herself.

The guards aren't working for me, they're working for *Dagmar*: she can have them look the other way when she needs a bit of killing done. And that's what probably happened with Joey, the guards just happened to be in another place when Sri's super-ninja slipped in and gave Joey the contents of a syringe...

In a panic I take my spy-tablet and hide it in the closet. I put a jacket on top of it to smother any sound. And then I remember that Richard had my phone for a whole day, after Ramona installed her spyware on it, and that during that time Richard might have installed his own spyware. So now I have *two* poisoned pieces of electronic equipment.

Of course the whole hotel suite might be bugged for all I know.

But then, of course, Dagmar has no reason to suspect me. I decide that I should give her no such reason, and decide to behave normally.

I try to learn my lines. I'm very distracted.

It occurs to me that I'm caught up in a dilemma. I could try informing the authorities of what I suspect, which might solve the murders but also get me killed. And if the authorities think I'm crazy, which is all too likely, I'd get killed for nothing.

Or I could play along with Dagmar, and become a huge star and make a lot of money, and rejoice in my share of profits from the Sri Sphere.

What's a boy to do?

Given the fact that I have no evidence at all, and am unlikely to get any, my course seems clear.

INT. SOUNDSTAGE—DAY

On Saturday it's me blowing my lines, not Roger. He just sits with a smug little smile on his face and watches me sweat underneath all my makeup, dust, and fake gore.

At the end of the eight hours that mark the legal end of his workday as a juvenile actor, Roger skips off and returns to the semi-divine status he enjoys amid his extended family. I deliver dialogue to his stand-in for another couple hours, and then Tessa calls it a day.

Despite my stumblings, the reshoots are nearly over. A few hours on Sunday should finish the project, and then it's over to Allison to edit the new footage into the film she already thought she'd finished days ago.

I thank Tessa for her patience, then drag myself away. When my eyes adjust to the dimmer light away from the set, I see Dagmar and Ismet watching the scene along with Corrie van Houten, Nataliya's ghostwriter and former assistant. Ismet's face is under-lit by the open laptop he carries in one hand, and one hand taps out a message on its keyboard. I limp over to say hello.

"Hi, Corrie," I say. "Did Dagmar give you a job?"

She blinks up at me with bright eyes. "Yes! Thank you for everything!" She takes a step toward me, arms wide as if ready to offer a hug, but then she sees my grimy clothes and bloody makeup and hesitates.

Dagmar looks at Corrie with amusement. "Corrie interviewed, and we connected. Now I'm exploiting her without mercy."

"Merciless exploitation is what assistants are *for*."

Dagmar looks over the set. "I'm here to see dailies. I want to see if all this is going to work."

"I think it's working fine. If I can just remember my lines, we can wrap this up by noon tomorrow."

Dagmar is wearing bib overalls over her pregnant stomach. Pens, notebooks, and her handheld bulge in the overall pockets. Her swollen feet are stuck in flip-flops. It looks like a comfortable ensemble for this stage of her pregnancy.

It has to be admitted that she doesn't look much like a terrorist, or like a cold-blooded mastermind who would have ordered Jocy's assassination. She doesn't even look like a producer.

"When do we start on the sequel?" I ask.

Her mouth quirks. "Well," she says, "I have to write it first. And somewhere in there, I have to have a kid."

"Next time," I say, "you should probably give yourself more relaxed deadlines."

"Yeah, I know." She nods wearily. "I just wanted to get the episodes out before someone stole a script and made everything public. I'm used to tight deadlines with the games, and..." She waves a hand. "I'll get better at this."

"Kubrick was supposedly editing *2001* in the projection room just before the premiere," I say. "At least things haven't slipped that far."

She looks skeptical. "We'll see."

"I'm just wondering," I say, "if I'm going to have time for another project between now and then."

She cocks an eyebrow at me. "Do you actually have a project waiting?"

"One may come along. My agent gets lots of offers these days."

She nods, not very interested in whatever offers Cleve might be fielding. Then she winces and presses a hand to her side. "The kid's really active today. Seems to be pissed off for some reason."

"I'm glad *I* can't get pregnant."

"All men are. Or so I'm told." She gives a grunt and presses her hand to another part of her abdomen. I continue making conversation.

"Another one of my earlier films, *Mister Baby Head*, will probably be released soon."

A smile tweaks the corners of her mouth. "Why do you think that?"

"It's been held up in legal limbo since Mac MacCartney died. Apparently all that's been resolved."

"That's right," she says. "I was the one who resolved it. I bought the picture from the heirs."

I look at her in deep surprise.

"They all hated each other so much," Dagmar explains, "that they wouldn't sell out to each other, but they'd sell out to *me*."

"So you'll be releasing it?"

"No." A little shake of the head. "I won't."

I gape at her for a few seconds, and then I feel anger begin to burn in my veins.

"What the fuck?" I say.

She sighs. I see that there's a shine of sweat across the bridge of her nose. "I'm not releasing *Baby Head* until we're done with Roheen. I can't have people going into a theater expecting to see Roheen and instead seeing a sadistic maniac who burns women's faces off with a blowtorch."

"Just market it as horror!" I tell her. "Everyone will know what they're getting."

Dagmar looks up at me. "Who do you want to be, Sean? Roheen, who has an audience of over four hundred million fans, or the blowtorch guy?"

The answer to that one seems obvious enough. "Both," I say. "I was great in *Baby Head*. People should see it."

She waves a dismissive hand. "People will. Eventually." And then her eyes narrow as she looks at me from under her dark brows.

"So," she says, "is there any particular reason why Melody Chastain was trying to wipe you out?"

I assume an expression of baffled ignorance. "The police haven't told me."

"I mean, did you even know her?" Dagmar says. "Did you date her, or steal her boyfriend, or…" She frowns to herself, and there's an odd tic at the corner of her lip.

"I know her to say hello to," I say. "We've never been what you'd call friends."

Dagmar's frown deepens. She puts a hand on her stomach. "I think…" she begins, and then she bends over and gives a sudden howl of pain.

For a moment I'm paralyzed, and then I jump forward and grab one arm. Ismet puts his laptop down and takes the other. Corrie takes a step toward Dagmar, her arms outstretched, and then pauses, unsure what to do.

"Get Dagmar a chair," I tell her.

"What's wrong?" Ismet says. "What's happening?"

Dagmar utters a long, wrenching moan, like an animal caught in a steel trap. Corrie dashes to the set, finds a folding chair, brings it. Ismet and I steer Dagmar into the seat. She remains bent over, hands over her stomach.

"It hurts," Dagmar says in a whisper. "Something's gone wrong." I can see pinpoints of sweat dotting her forehead.

I pat my pockets like an idiot, but of course I'm in costume and my phone is in my dressing room. I hold out a hand to Corrie and snap my fingers.

"Phone," I say.

Numbly she hands me her phone. I punch in Simon's number.

"I need you to bring the car to the soundstage, northeast corner," I say. "Dagmar needs to go to the hospital fast."

We're collecting quite a crowd: Tessa, Jean-Marc, a dozen or more technicians. One of the grips overhears me and runs to the big garage doors in the middle of the north wall of the soundstage, and rolls them open. So when Simon arrives with the Super Sport, he's able to drive right into the soundstage, park next to Dagmar, and jump out to open the rear door.

The pain hasn't let go of Dagmar. She's bent over, panting for breath, barely able to talk. Her face is drained of color. Pens clatter out of her pockets as Ismet and I help her stand. We move her to the car and ease her into the backseat. Ismet runs around to the other side and gets in next to her.

Simon is bent over Dagmar, trying to strap her into her lap belt. "Sherman Oaks is the nearest hospital, right?" I ask him. "Straight down the One-oh-one?"

"Valley Presbyterian!" Dagmar gasps. "Big maternity center!"

"The lady knows best," I say.

Simon buckles Dagmar in place and closes the door. "I'll wait for you in my dressing room," I say to him as he jumps into the driver's seat, and he nods.

Then the Super Sport guns its engine, and the car is away, leaving the scent of exhaust. I hand the phone back to a stunned Corrie.

"Call Valley Prez," I say. "Tell them Dagmar is coming, and describe what's happening to her."

"I don't *know* what's happening to her!" Corrie says.

"You know as much as anyone. And when you've made the call, tell Richard and Helmuth, then follow her to the hospital."

She nods, and makes the call.

I join the crowd for a lot of nervous chattering and speculation. "Where's Carter-Ann?" I ask. "She's an MD, someone should have called her."

Nobody knows where she's gone to. I suggest that someone call, and I believe someone does.

The crowd slowly breaks up. I realize how tired I am. I'm on the verge of returning to my dressing room when I see Ismet's laptop still sitting there, on the concrete floor. It's gone to the screensaver, in which brightly colored blobby things bump up against other brightly colored blobby things.

I pick up the laptop, close the lid, and take it with me when I leave.

CHAPTER SIXTEEN

FROM: Parmita <parmita@babaji.edu.in>
SUBJECT: Your Lawyer

I am so angry at you! You have filed a "lawsuit" against Babaji and now everyone here is very upset!

You don't know how difficult a "position" this places me in! People are looking at me as if this is all my fault!

I demand that you drop this "lawsuit" at once! Maybe God will forgive you but I may not!

FROM: Sean Makin
SUBJECT: Re: Your Lawyer

If it's any consolation, we haven't filed a lawsuit yet. We've just told Babaji's lawyer how much he'll have to pay me in order to *prevent* me from filing a lawsuit.

Considering that the local ashram engaged in a criminal conspiracy to murder me, I'm surprised the whole lot of them aren't in jail.

And of course Babaji has been holding on to nearly a million dollars in my money for over a decade now.

You should tell your fellow inmates that this money means nothing, and that I am merely saving Babaji from a life of materialism.

Oh, and by the way, thanks for all the compassion and concern over the fact that someone *nearly succeeded in murdering me*! I'm *so* glad to hear that this is *all about you*!

INT. SEAN'S SUITE—NIGHT

I'm arguing with myself about the laptop all the way to NoHo. Part of me wants to toss it in the nearest trash can, because possession of the laptop could get me killed. Part of me argues that I owe it to Jaydee and the other victims to find out why they died.

Maybe I take the laptop just to shut up the voices that have been screaming in my head for the last twenty-four hours, and I just have to find out if I'm right. Or maybe it's Roheen who dictates my final decision, who tells me that I simply need to discover the truth, and then figure out what to do once I know it.

So once I get home I take the laptop out, put it on the desk in the front room of my suite, and stare at it for a while. If I'm right and anything with the *Escape to Earth* software can be bugged, I should be careful not to reveal that I've been snooping.

I get a tonic water from the minibar while I'm thinking, and some mini pretzels because I'm hungry. Salt and quinine taste surprisingly good together: maybe someone should make a packaged food with that flavor.

I examine Ismet's laptop carefully and see that there's a switch on the outside of the case that will allow me to manually turn off the wireless network adapter. I turn the switch to the off position. And in the unlikely event that the computer simply records everything for later broadcast, I open the lid carefully a crack, then stick a Band-Aid over the camera lens at the top.

I open the lid all the way and see the screen flash into life. Ismet presumably had anything important password-protected, but I've never turned off the machine or closed any files, so whatever passwords he gave it are still operative.

On top of the display is some email Ismet was reading, all of which has to do with the marketing of the *Escape to Earth* finale in Latin America. I minimize the email and scan the icons on the desktop. They're mostly for running software that I've never heard of. I click the option that calls up recently viewed documents, and the name of one jumps right off the screen at me.

Sean/Father02.

I click it, and a program that runs video and audio jumps onto the screen. From the laptop's speakers I hear my father's voice.

"Have you had a chance to look at the resort prospectus?" he asks.

"Costa Magnifico?" my own voice replies. "It's ungrammatical. It should be Costa Magnifica."

"No one who actually stays at this resort is going to care about that."

I listen as my conversation with my father is replayed, right to the point where I pretended there was someone at the door and I hung up. The audio quality is good, which tells me that the audio isn't taken from a bug in the room, but from the phone signal itself.

I was right. Richard has cloned my phone, and he and Ismet and for all I know half the Sri Sphere are listening to my calls.

Then panic jolts me as I realize that my phone is sitting nearby, on the side table in the front room where I laid it down when I came into the room, and that someone might have heard me playing the sound file. In sudden terror I grab the phone, turn it off, and then put it in the closet, under the jacket, next to my tablet, where I hope it won't pick up any more conversations.

I return cautiously to the laptop, which has not exploded or otherwise behaved in an alarming way, and then I do a search to find out where *Sean/Father02* is actually located on the drive.

There's a Sean Makin folder, and *Sean/Father02* is only one file among a couple dozen. I click randomly on some of the others, and discover that most of the files seem to feature me practicing my lines for the next day's shooting. I've been leading a pretty dull life in the last few weeks. The one exception is the night with my fan from Caltech, and mercifully the Sean Makin sex tape seems not to be here. Perhaps some unusually tactful person erased it. I hope so.

I check the other files, most of which have names that I don't recognize, but which generally seem foreign. Some have country names: India-Pakistan, Thailand-Burma, Korea, Mozambique. I click a few audio files at random, and it's all men talking in languages that I don't know. The audio quality isn't very good, though it shows signs of having been cleaned up, probably by an automated program designed to remove background clutter. Then I click another one, and I hear a voice speaking English, though with a foreign accent.

"The current-account deficit for July was higher than what we actually announced. Four point three billion rand."

Well, I think, *I may not know what a rand is, or a current-account deficit, but I know there's no way a savvy entrepreneur like Sri isn't going to be able to make a packet off that piece of information alone, by betting against whoever it is who's covering up his deficit problems*. Maybe Sri will make enough to pay for this whole venture.

I decide that I've learned what I intended to learn, and I close all the files I've opened. Then I panic again, because I realize the computer's history will show what files I've been meddling with. I stop and think about this for a moment, and then I erase the existing history. I bring up the office suite and click a number of files at random—graphics from Ismet's ad campaigns, spreadsheets of who knows what, text files proposing this or that. I fill up the history, and I call Ismet's email back up.

The display now looks exactly as it did when I first opened it. I doubt that Ismet has memorized his own computer's history, and what the history now shows is at least plausible. I stop and think about what to do next.

The laptop contains proof that Dagmar and Sri are conducting widespread, and presumably illegal, surveillance throughout the world. And it's probably why three people were killed, though I still can't figure out how Joey or Jaydee found out enough that they needed to be silenced.

Okay, Roheen, I think. *I've gotten all noble and found out what's going on. What the hell do I do now?*

Roheen seems not to have an answer to this one. So Sean has to take over: I decide very sensibly that I need insurance. I rummage through the carrying case for my laptop until I find some portable memory, and then I plug it into one of Ismet's USB ports, and I try to move a bunch of the files into portable storage.

Except that the computer then asks me for a password. I remember the scripts that Richard's been delivering on portable memory, and that Richard arranged it so I couldn't copy the files to any other drive. Ismet has the same feature here.

I cancel the transfer. I'm completely out of ideas, so I turn the computer off, wipe most of my fingerprints off the keyboard with a handkerchief—they know I handled it *some*, but I don't want it to seem as if I've been groping the thing—take the Band-Aid off the camera lens, and close the lid.

I have a persistent notion that I've just made an idiot of myself, though I can't quite work out how.

Greenland, in any case, is looking better and better.

I decide to have something like a normal evening, by way of covering myself if nothing else, so I get my phone from where I've hidden it, and I let the Sri Sphere hear me call the hotel restaurant and order chicken marsala for dinner.

While I'm waiting I decide it would be polite to inquire how Dagmar is doing, and so I call Ismet. The call goes straight to voice mail, so I call Richard instead.

"Dagmar's still in surgery," he says. "The placenta tried to tear away."

"Good Lord," I say.

"Dagmar almost bled to death in the car. They wheeled her into the hospital and stuck the biggest IV I've ever seen right in her arm and started pouring blood into her. Then she had an emergency C-section."

"Wow."

I'm sort of useless when confronted by gory details. "Good Lord" and "Wow" are about as much as I can manage.

"Her little girl is all right, though."

"That's good," I say.

"Ismet is with her."

"Tell them I called." There is a pause. "When you see Ismet," I say, "tell him that I've got his laptop."

Even through the phone I feel Richard's attention suddenly focused entirely on me.

"You have Ismet's computer." He says this as if the fact is one of many he has to place in the right order.

"He left it on the floor of the soundstage," I tell him. "I didn't know what else to do, so I picked it up."

Twenty minutes later there's a knock on the door. I check the peephole and I see Carter-Ann's pale, blond assistant. I open the door and hand him Ismet's laptop, and we have a brief conversation consisting of a very few syllables.

"Hi."

"Here you go."

"Thanks."

"Bye."

A few minutes after that my dinner arrives, and after that I set my phone near my seat and entertain the Sri Sphere with the recitation of my lines for the next day.

INT. SEAN'S BEDROOM—PREDAWN

"Didn't you know, Sean?" Timmi says. "UFOs are really made of bread. You can put butter on them and eat them." She laughs and puts a finger to her lips. "It was the lilacs who told me. Don't tell anyone that the lilacs can talk."

I wake with my heart pounding in a room that smells of lemon wax, and I fight through tangled sheets to the bedside light.

The light reveals a silk-screen portrait on the wall opposite, Marilyn Monroe laughing and looking at me over her shoulder. Timmi's elegant personality seems to attach itself for a moment to the portrait, and for a moment the sadness is so profound that I feel it like a dull knife twisting its way to my heart.

The dream fades. I remember Timmi and Joey in it, lots of shouting, lots of anger. I don't remember what any of it was about except that it didn't seem to be about vehicular homicide. The fighting was like at that party six years ago, when Timmi and Mac were fighting and I didn't know why.

I rise from the bed and walk naked to the front room and turn on my computer. *There are websites where you can look up car registrations*, Richard said.

It takes me half a minute to find one. In order to search the database you can enter name, address, registration number, or license plate number. I give it my credit card number and a name. A few minutes later I find that Timothea Wilhelm owns a car, a white Dodge Grand Caravan. Which is technically a van, not an SUV, but a motorist at night on the PCH might not be able to distinguish one from the other.

Joey never changed the registration after Timmi died, he just kept paying the registration and the insurance. Just as I'd done with my mother's Mercedes.

I look at the time: it's just after five-thirty. I have a seven o'clock makeup call, so there's no point in going back to bed. As I shower and put on my clothes I try to figure out what it is I've just learned.

It *was* Joey who killed Jaydee and Nataliya: he killed them with his wife's van, which he probably considered poetic justice.

After I told Dagmar and Richard about my theory at the Joli Blon, they realized that Joey was a threat to the production. He couldn't be allowed to continue, but they had no evidence against him. And so Sri's super-ninja assassins were dispatched, and so was Joey.

I restrain myself from telling anyone about any of this until I'm in Astin's Expedition, heading for the studio, and then I call the two detectives who interviewed me after Joey's death. The Asian guy's phone goes to voice mail, and I leave a message telling him to call me. I call the woman who chews nicotine gum, and she answers right away.

"What is it?" she asks.

"This is Sean Makin," I tell her. "I'm calling about—"

"Who are you again?" she asks.

So much for my international stardom. I explain who I am and my connection to one of her cases. Then I explain about the white Grand Caravan that Joey never transferred to his own name.

"If you find that car," I say, "you'll find the vehicle that killed Jaydee Martin and Nataliya Hogan. Joey owned a lot of cars, and he might not have kept this one at his house. But if you find the warehouse—"

"We're looking at someone else for those murders," she says.

"Melody Chastain had no motive for those killings."

She barks a laugh. "So far as we can tell, she has no motive for trying to kill *you*."

Touché, I think. "Does Melody Chastain have a white Grand Caravan?" I ask.

There's a moment of silence. "We'll check into it."

"Sorry to spoil your Sunday morning," I say.

"It was spoiled hours ago," she says sourly, and pops her gum in my ear.

I hang up and call Richard. For all I know, he might have just been listening to my phone call, but I've got one question I need him to answer.

"This is Richard," he answers. For the first time since I've known him, he sounds tired.

"How's Dagmar?" I ask.

"Fine. She's out of danger, and so is her little girl. They're both sleeping."

"I just found out something." I tell him about Timmi's Grand Caravan. "So it looks as if Joey really did those hit-and-runs," I tell him. "But there's one question unresolved."

"Joey's phone call," Richard says. He sounds a lot less sleepy now. "The one he made from Bel Air at the time that Nataliya was being killed at her beach house."

"Can you chain cell phone signals together?" I ask. "Can you call from the Pacific Coast Highway to Joey's house in Bel Air, and then have a device in Bel Air relay the call to its destination? Like Trishula was doing with his distributed network, but for telephone instead of Internet?"

"Yes," Richard says. "It would be relatively easy, I suppose. But what you're really asking is whether it was done in this instance."

"Yes," I say. "That's what I'm asking."

"I'll try to find out."

"Thanks."

Though if Richard was part of the conspiracy to kill Joey on behalf of Dagmar and Sri, there's not a lot I've told him that he doesn't already know. But maybe it will salve his conscience to know that Joey actually did kill two people before he and Dagmar took him down.

Assuming of course that he has a conscience, always a crucial question in our particular line of work.

Astin looks at me in the rearview mirror. "That was unusual. Are you turning detective or something?"

"Someone's got to," I tell him. "And I'm the one people keep trying to kill."

Astin nods his shaven head. "Good point. If I can help in any way . . . ?"

"Just keep me alive."

Astin nods again. "That's what I'm here for."

I call a florist and order a large bouquet for Dagmar's room at Valley Presbyterian, which I hope may soften her in the matter of having me whacked, and then I go in for makeup. When I'm done, and I go onto the soundstage, I see Carter-Ann talking to Tessa Brettel.

I walk toward them. When Carter-Ann turns toward me, I ask her about the psychiatric conference.

"It went very well. Thank you." Carter-Ann is bright and chirpy this morning, and wears a jacket with a plush gathered collar over one of her usual frilly blouses. She looks like a fashionable sorceress in an online fantasy game.

"Have you seen Dagmar?"

"Just briefly, when she got out of surgery. She wasn't functioning very well, as you can imagine."

"Indeed."

"She'll be much better today. I'll call her when shooting is over."

"Give her my regards," I say.

"Waiting on gaffers," Clarke calls.

"I'm going to get Roger's ass over here," Tessa tells me. "And then we'll talk about this scene."

The scene goes extremely well. It's the last scene in the movie, in which Roheen has got the wounded Khabane to a clinic and had him patched up. It's very close to the scene as originally shot, except that this time it's Khabane in the bed and not Roheen. It's a melancholy scene, with Roheen's mission having failed, his friend having been wounded, and his home world a swiftly receding dream.

The trick, as an actor, is to get just the right amount of hope into the scene. Though Roheen's failed, he's changed for the better, he's traveled rough and learned a lot, he's found internal resources he didn't know he had... he's also made new friends who have become important to him, and found a new calling. The audience has to see that.

I can't overplay it, because then it will just be this chirping-birds-and-singing-flowers Disney ending, and that's not what we're after. Roheen's become very real to me after all this time, and I want to send him out on just the right note.

Roger is behaving for once, I think because he realizes this is the last day and he wants to get it over with and get back to his vacation. Tessa keeps having to slow him down and remind him why he's here. Still, this is a minor annoyance compared to his behavior in the past, and I'm so focused on my own part that I barely notice it.

The experience is so intense that I lose track of time. It's slightly after noon when Tessa calls for the last cut, and I stand up out of my trance and look around. The crew is applauding, and for a moment I'm not sure whom they're cheering for, and then I realize it's me.

I stand there stunned, and then Tessa walks onto the set and gives me a hug. I hug her back, and I wave and smile at the applauding people.

I didn't get applause the first time we shot the ending.

I want this feeling to go on as long as possible, so I delay leaving the soundstage until it's clear that everyone else just wants to pack up and go home to enjoy their Sunday. There won't be a wrap party, because we already had one. For a moment I consider inviting everyone to join me at Dove Bar at ten o'clock, but then I realize I'm nearly staggering with weariness, and that what I really need is about ten hours' sleep. I say goodbye to everyone who's still around, and then I leave the soundstage and find Astin waiting for me outside. Normally my guards let me walk around the lot unescorted, but now he's sticking to my elbow.

"You said to keep you alive, man," he says.

"I appreciate it," I say.

There will be more looping, I assume, in the next couple days, and then my part of *Escape to Earth* will be over, everything except various appearances and promotions to help sell the film, and myself, to the public.

I go to my dressing room in the Bennett Building, and the makeup artist's assistant removes Roheen from my skin. I stick my head out the dressing room door to tell Astin to bring the car around.

Then I change out of my costume, which I hang up in my dressing room for the costumers who will collect it, and put my own clothes on. I'm tying my Nikes when there's a knock on the dressing room door.

"Who is it?"

"It's me, Mr. Makin." I recognize the voice of Carter-Ann's blond assistant.

I open the door, and he takes a step inside and swings a pipe for my head.

CHAPTER SEVENTEEN

FROM: Farzana16

Did you see that Samendra's making a personal appearance at the Electronic Superstore in Model Town on Saturday?

FROM: Danishri

I am absolutely going!

FROM: Farzana16

We should go early. There will be a long line.

FROM: Danishri

WE LOVE YOU SAMENDRA!!!

INT. SEAN'S DRESSING ROOM—DAY

Hell, I don't even know the man's name, and here he is trying to kill me.

I don't think he's quite prepared for how tall I am. He's aiming for my temple, but he has to reach up so far that the tip of the pipe hits the top of the metal door frame with a clang. This only delays the strike by a fraction of a second, but it's just enough—I give a startled blind leap away from him and bat the pipe away as it bounds off the door frame. He scrambles after me, swinging, the pipe hissing as it comes within a millimeter of my face.

I poke him in the face with my left fist, but that barely slows him down—it's Jimmy Blogjoy all over again. I duck another wild swing. There's a smashing sound as the pipe connects with my makeup mirror.

The thought of Blogjoy sets me in a fury, rage mixed with terror, and I punch all-out with my right. The punch connects with his cheek and knocks him back. The pipe comes up again and whangs my left forearm, and the shock of pain keeps me from following up my successful strike.

I take a couple steps and put my makeup chair between us. It's a heavy padded swivel chair, like a barber's chair, and I think about picking it up and trying to use it as a weapon, but it's very heavy and I don't know if I'm strong enough.

We stare at each other over the chair and we both reassess. My heart is throbbing so fast and hard that it seems like it's bounding free inside my rib cage, rattling my bones with every beat. The eyes in the blond man's pale face are dead, like the eyes of a shark. His lips are drawn back from his teeth in a silent snarl.

It's a small room, maybe twelve feet by fifteen. The dressing room behind me is smaller, but it doesn't have a door, only a curtain, so I can't keep him out.

I've had my panic button for weeks, the one that will summon aid, but I wasn't wearing it when I was in costume, and I haven't put it on yet. It sits on the makeup table, next to my phone. Apparently the only way I'm going to get help is to shout for it.

"Help!" I call. "Help me!"

Except it's Sunday afternoon, and I'm in an office building where everyone's gone home. If I were on the set, or if this were happening in my old trailer, someone would probably hear me, but here it's unlikely.

When I yell the blond man lunges around the chair to my right, to keep between me and the door to the outside. My martial reflexes are coming back and I kick him, just like I kicked Trishula outside the Joli Blon, but the kick glances off his hip. It doesn't knock him down, but it's enough to unbalance him and stop his forward momentum, and his strike with the pipe cuts the air between us but doesn't hit anything.

We stare at each other and pant for breath. I call for help again. And then a woman screams.

It's the ring tone from my cell phone that sits on my makeup table, but the blond man doesn't know that, and he gives a start and looks wildly for the source of the scream. So that's when I go for him, while he's distracted.

I throw a wild block to his forearm as I charge, intending to intercept the swing that I know he's going to throw. The pain and shock of bone on bone makes me glad I hit the forearm instead of the pipe. Then I smash into him with all my weight and bear him backward. I drive him into the door frame behind him, and I see a start of surprise on his face. Surprise and, perhaps, a dawning fear.

I'm inside the range of his weapon now. There's not a lot of harm he can do with it without room to swing.

I'm screaming with rage. Adrenaline is playing like a blowtorch on my nerves. Three months of paranoia, fear, and suspicion are resolving themselves into shrieking fury now that I finally have something in front of me to attack. My left forearm has his right shoulder pinned against the door so that he can't swing the pipe, and my right fist is pumping a series of short, vicious punches into his floating ribs. I head-butt him hard enough so that I see stars. I take a step back, then drive a rising knee into his midsection.

Gasping for air, he hurls himself forward against me, his arms wrapping me, holding me close. I can smell the herbal scent of his shampoo. I totter under our combined weight and try to throw the knee again, but taking one foot off the ground is a mistake because it unbalances me. We lurch around our common center of gravity like drunken tango dancers, and then I trip and fall. I carom off the makeup chair, the impact knocking the wind out of me, and then we're both lying on the ground on our sides, facing each other, my arms still around him.

I throw a few punches into his back, and he flaps at me with the hand that's holding the pipe, but there's no way to get proper distance and leverage, and neither of us is doing any damage. He tries to lever himself up in order to get enough room to swing, but I stick to him like a piece of cling wrap. He twists within my embrace in order to get both hands on the ground to push himself up; and then even in the midst of my fury and terror I feel a species of relief floating through my mind, because I know that he's just made a serious mistake.

In mixed martial arts it's called "giving your back." It's what happened with me and Jimmy Blogjoy, when I fell and he pounced on my back and began pounding me and driving me into the cottage cheese.

Now the blond man's turned partially away from me, and I wrench myself off the floor and pounce on his back with all my weight. He levers himself up on hands and knees, but I'm clinging like a limpet and he doesn't have anyplace to go. My forearm is trying to snake around his throat. My legs are wrapping his legs. I can hear him gasping for breath as he fights against our combined weight. I'm still screaming, shouting aloud with every exhalation.

He tries to reach over his left shoulder with his right arm and stab me with the pipe. I duck, my head digging into the gap between his right shoulder and head. My right hand reaches around his body to grab his right forearm and pin it in place. My left hand grabs the pipe and tries to wrench it free. He begins to totter.

The only way he can keep his balance is to let go of his weapon and plant his right hand back on the floor, but he won't surrender the pipe, so we both fall to the right and land heavily on the dressing room floor. My legs wrap around his thighs and render both his legs useless. I grab my right wrist with my left hand and begin to squeeze.

It's called an arm triangle choke. I'm squeezing his right arm, right shoulder, and neck all together, with my right forearm cutting into the side of the neck. If I squeeze hard enough, the soft parts—like the throat, and the carotid artery—will collapsc. The blond feels the choke start to bite and he begins to fight it, shooting his right arm up in an effort to buy himself a little extra room within the circle of my arms; but that's the wrong thing to do, because that just lets me cinch him tighter. Now his right hand is trapped high over his head and he can't use the pipe at all.

He begins to flail, and his desperation seems to vastly increase his strength. His legs are thrashing and his left hand is pounding my thigh, which is the only part of me he can reach. Jolts of pain shoot up my leg and hip. His legs escape me and I have to keep hooking them with my feet. All this thrashing makes my choke slip, and gives the blond a chance to gasp for air; but I never let go, and I always clamp down again.

He kicks. He arches his back to try to get me off him. He hits me on the thigh so many times that I'm afraid he's smashed the bone to fragments. I hang on to the choke, working every chance I get to tighten the circle of my arms. The pipe flails over my head, thumps the floor and whangs off the base of the chair, but it's no threat to me now.

Then he goes limp, and it's so sudden that I figure he's shamming. I use his sudden passivity to improve my position and squeeze even harder. I can smell the sour sweat on his neck. I'm still shouting for help.

After a while I stop shouting because my own vision is turning black. I can't seem to get enough air even though I'm not the one being strangled. My back hurts, my head hurts. My thigh hurts where he's pounded it.

There's a limp man partly on top of me, and all I can think to do is hang on.

Eventually it occurs to me that the blond really isn't faking it, and I cautiously relax my hold. The man doesn't spring back to life. I slowly relax the triangle choke and reach up above my head to take the pipe. Now I have his weapon.

I work myself out from beneath the limp body. I kneel near him, the pipe poised to hit him if he starts to move. But he doesn't move, he just lies palely on the carpet, his blond hair untidy as a heap of straw. His eyes, staring vaguely at the door, are blood-red. I give a shudder. I didn't know that could happen.

I grab the arm of the chair and heave myself upright. A bolt of pain shoots through my left thigh where the blond man pounded on it. For a moment I almost topple, and then I swivel the chair around and sit and try to catch my breath. My heart is still crashing in my chest like an engine with the throttle jammed wide open.

I begin to laugh as a mad rush of euphoria hits my veins. *I'm alive! I'm the champion! I took down Dagmar's assassin!*

Bring 'em on, I think. *Bring 'em on, and I'll keep knocking 'em down. Beware the Watcher's mad kung fu skillz!*

My cackle runs dry and I begin to cough. My throat aches. My head is whirling. I close my eyes until things stabilize a bit.

When I open my eyes, I look at the blond man again. Despite the red eyes, he doesn't look much like an assassin to me. I can't help but think that professional assassins probably have access to more effective weapons than a metal pipe. I mean, even *Trishula* had a kitchen knife, and Trishula was pathetic.

If I'd had my pistol where I could have reached it, neither of them would have stood a chance.

I look at the pipe in my hands. It's wrapped in cloth tape, like medical tape, and the tape is dented in several places where the pipe hit a hard surface like the metal door frame. When I see there's blood on the tape I panic and begin patting myself on the head to see if I've been wounded, but then I realize the blood isn't fresh, and that it's Joey's.

OMG! I think. *I brought down Joey's killer!* Maybe now I can find out what the fuck that was all about.

I laugh as I ride another burst of euphoria. Then I look down at the blond man again. He's showing no sign of coming back to consciousness. I spend a while trying to decide if I care about that.

My thought processes do not seem to be functioning with quite their normal vigor.

Eventually I decide I'd better figure out what's actually happening with Assassin Man. I try to stand again, gasp at the pain in my thigh, and then sort of slide out of the chair onto the floor. I have to catch my breath again, and knead my thigh until the pain ebbs. Then I kneel by the blond man's head and brandish the pipe overhead as I use my left hand to feel for a pulse in his throat.

I can't find a pulse, but I don't know if that's because there isn't a pulse to be found, or because I'm simply useless at taking someone else's pulse. I poke at the man's throat for a while, shifting my fingers to a new place every few seconds. There's not only no sign of a pulse, but no reaction at all.

I stare at the man as I realize that I seem to have killed him. A nervous laugh bursts out of me. I wonder if I am in serious trouble.

I decide I should try to summon assistance. My phone is on the makeup table, so I crawl to the table and grope around on top in search of it. A piece of broken glass stabs my finger, and I wince and snatch the hand back and suck blood from my fingertip. While I'm doing this I notice something that's rolled under the table.

It's a syringe. I pick it up and look at it in surprise. I wonder if I was fighting some kind of junkie. Did the man have to get high before he could bring himself to attack me?

I decide I'd better call for Astin and follow his advice about what to do next. I spin the chair around, then heave myself up and into my seat. The pain in my thigh brings tears to my eyes. From the chair I can see my phone, and I can also see that it's been smashed. I sift through the broken mirror glass and look at the telephone parts and decide it can be put back together. I jam the battery and SIM card back into the handset and hold the apparatus together with my hand while I wait for the phone to come alive.

Somewhat to my surprise the screen lights up, and the phone

plays the little tune that tells me it's connected to the network. I try to call up the speed dial directory so that I can call Astin, but my fingers are suddenly too clumsy to manipulate the phone. I try several times and keep pressing the wrong part of the screen. Suddenly I'm all thumbs. Then some vital part of the phone slips out of its proper place and the screen goes dark.

I laugh and put the phone down on the table. Despite my clumsiness, I'm otherwise feeling pretty good.

And then I start thinking about the syringe, and I remember that Jocy was supposed to have been poisoned. I realize that the contents of the syringe might not have been for the blond guy, but for me. In sudden panic I start patting myself to see if I can find a needle poke.

I remember the man hitting my thigh over and over again. I wonder if he had the syringe in his hand, if he unloaded a bunch of poison into my leg. I look at the fabric of my trousers but I can't find a needle mark. Not that it's likely there would be one.

I decide it's time to talk to Astin. He should be just downstairs, waiting in the car. I clamp my hands on the arms of the chair and heave myself upright. I cry aloud at the agony in my leg. Whatever may have been in that syringe, it hasn't suppressed the pain at all.

I lurch to the door and rest a while, leaning on the door frame. Then I set out down the corridor.

All I have to do is walk to the end of the hall, turn right, walk down another corridor, pass Dagmar's office, then go down the stairs. Under normal circumstances the walk would take maybe thirty seconds.

I go reeling down the hallway, one hand trailing on the wall to keep my balance. I keep giggling and talking to myself. I realize when I'm halfway down the corridor that I've forgotten about my panic button, which would summon aid immediately. I haven't seen it, so it must have got knocked off the table. Then, as I approach the corner, I get my bad leg twisted under me and I fall over.

I laugh for a while over that, and then I make an effort to get on hands and knees. There seems to be something seriously wrong with my coordination.

It must also be admitted that the floor is surprisingly comfortable. It feels like the softest, warmest mattress in the world. I wonder if I should lie here for a while and catch my breath.

A faint, receding sense of urgency gets me to my hands and knees. I crawl to the corner, turn right, crawl some more.

I am so very tired. I've been working very hard for months and I really deserve a rest. It's only fair that I take a little break from all the aggravation in my life and catch up on my sleep.

I pitch forward onto my face, and I think this is pretty funny.

I remember thinking that all I need is a nap, and then I'll be all right.

CHAPTER EIGHTEEN

TALE EXCLUSIVE: Kari Sothern reports that a drunk, stoned Sean Makin was seen being carried out of his dressing room by crew from a private ambulance.

INT. EMERGENCY ROOM—DAY

"Can you walk? Dagmar wants to see you."

It's Richard. He's padded into the emergency room on his white Converse sneaks, and now he stands in front of me, looking at me with his usual polite gaze. I sit on the edge of my examination table and look back at him.

Well, I think, *Dagmar probably won't kill me in the hospital.* "I'm supposed to sign some papers," I say. "Give me a minute to do that."

Astin, it turns out, saved my life. He figured I was taking a shower, but after too many minutes passed and I didn't turn up, he went in search of me. First to the shower rooms, and then upstairs; and when he found me collapsed in a heap, not breathing, he applied artificial respiration until the ambulance got there.

The parameds figured that my respiratory system was depressed by an opioid and fired an inhaler of naloxone up my nose, and within about forty-five seconds I was sitting up, chatting with everyone, and feeling just about normal.

Of course they don't let you just walk away from something

like that, so I got bundled into the ambulance and taken to Valley Presbyterian, where Dagmar had been carried the day before, and I underwent a whole series of tests that showed that, barring a few scrapes and the bone bruise on my thigh, I was in fine shape.

I didn't remember about the corpse in my dressing room until I was already in the ambulance, but even with the delay it didn't take long for the police to turn up. These weren't the detectives I'd met before, but a new bunch. They were deeply suspicious and I had to give them a lot of redundant background information, and they spent a lot of time on the phone talking to police who knew more about the case than they did. They encouraged the medics to check me for puncture wounds, of which they found only one, on my left thigh. This evidence that I wasn't a junkie improved the cops' view of me somewhat.

I gave a preliminary interview in the E-room, and agreed to come down to the station and make a more formal statement on Monday morning. I guess they figured that, as I was about the most recognizable face on the planet, I wasn't much of a flight risk.

Which left me there in the emergency room, amid the scent of clean laundry, plastic, and disinfectant.

I sign the forms indicating that I am on my own and no longer the hospital's responsibility, and then I limp out of the emergency ward and find Richard and Astin both waiting for me in the lobby.

"You keep getting into trouble, man," Astin says. "I'm just not going to let you out of my sight ever again."

"You do that," I say. "By the way, is it your birthday? Because I feel like buying you a present."

Richard looks at his fancy watch. "This way," he says.

My leg hurts like a bastard. Astin offers to let me lean on him, but I decide I'm all macho and lurch on my own two legs all the way to the maternity ward.

There I find Dagmar in a private room. She wears a white cotton nightie, and there's a tiny pink infant in her arms. Ismet stands guard, pale and silent in a corner. Bouquets of flowers fill the room with a gentle floral scent. One of them, I assume, is the one I sent this morning.

Dagmar looks up at me as I hobble in, her eyes narrowed.

"You've had adventures," she says, a bit accusingly.

"So have you," I point out.

"Have a seat."

I gratefully drop into one of the chairs and stretch my aching leg in front of me. Richard quietly closes the door behind me. Despite his promise to keep an eye on me, Astin stays out in the corridor. Maybe he thinks I'm safe, maybe he's just doing what he's told.

Surely she won't kill me in the hospital, I think.

Dagmar looks surprisingly healthy. Her cheeks are flushed, I guess with the blood they've poured into her, her skin tone seems good, and her gray hair has been combed and braided.

"You look like you've bounced back," I say.

"I almost bled to death," she says. She still has that accusing tone, like it was somehow my fault. "I spent ten minutes in non-stop labor in the car before I passed out, I had a C-section, and I almost died from shock. The baby almost died from blood loss, from hypoxia, and from an attack of tachycardia so bad that her heart almost exploded." She closes her eyes. "At least they're giving me the good drugs."

"I almost got murdered by one of Carter-Ann's Psy-Ops guys," I say, because I feel this fact ought not to be totally ignored. "He's the man who killed Joey, if you hadn't figured that out. And what's the baby's name, by the way?"

A smile touches her lips. "Anna Fadime," she says. "After my mother, and Ismet's."

"And they let you hold her? She's not stuck in an incubator?"

Dagmar looks at me like I'm an imbecile. "She's not premature. I was in my ninth month. This is a perfectly normal newborn."

"Uh," I say, "good."

That pretty well exhausts my conversation on the subject of Dagmar's baby. I was never a proper child myself, just a working stiff from the age of four, and it has to be admitted I don't know much about children who aren't holding down a steady job.

"So," I say, "did Carter-Ann send what's-his-name to kill me?"

"No," Dagmar says. She's still looking at her baby. "He was doing that on his own."

"And why is that?"

She looks up. Her eyes flash. "Charles didn't exactly send me a memo about what he was going to do and why."

Charles, is it? I think. "Give me your best guess," I say.

"Nietzsche," says Ismet, "said something to the effect that every cause inspires someone who, through his fanatic profession of the cause, drives other people away. Charles was like that."

I look at him. "If that was meant to make anything more understandable, it completely failed."

Ismet raises his hands, then lets them fall. "He believed in the project. Believed totally. He was trying to protect it."

"Like Trishula," Dagmar says. "Trishula believed in Babaji, and when you attacked Babaji, Trishula attacked you. He didn't think of himself as the aggressor, he thought he was defending something he believed in." She presses her lips together into a white line, and then speaks. "Charles thought you were a danger to the project. You and Joey both. After you told us that you thought Joey had killed Jaydee and Nataliya, we had an emergency meeting. Carter-Ann was out of town, so Charles stood in for her." Her eyes turn stony. "Apparently Charles decided to take action on his own."

Richard clears his throat. "My surmise is that he hid in Carter-Ann's suite at the Lang Towers. He had access to her rooms, he was in and out all the time. He went to see Joey, banged him on the head, then gave him a fatal overdose."

"If you're going to hit him with a pipe anyway," I say, "why not just beat his head in?"

Dagmar looks aghast. I think that maybe she's seen a little too much of that kind of violence in her time.

"Hitting him like that would be messy," Ismet offers. "You'd get blood on yourself. Drugs are quieter and, I suppose, more merciful."

"And Carter-Ann supplied the drugs," I say. They all look shocked.

"No," Dagmar says. "She's not—" She strives for words. "She's difficult, I'll admit that."

"She's a freak," I say. "And I say this as a freak who knows a freak when he sees one."

Dagmar is annoyed at my interruption. "She's someone Sri picked," she says, "someone who worked with him on some of his education projects. But she's not a killer."

I must look skeptical. Richard responds.

"Carter-Ann told me that Charles used to work as a counselor in the county hospital rehab center. My guess is that if he kept in touch with some of his former patients, he could get any amount of drugs he wanted. All he'd have to do is take any street drug and cook it down to increase the potency."

I decide to let that go. No doubt the police will determine whether the drugs were from the street or the pharmacy.

"Joey was killing other people on the movie," I say. "I can see how . . . Charles . . . would disapprove. But how did *I* get to be such a threat?"

Ismet gives me an unreadable gaze. "You looked at my laptop. You tried to download my files."

Richard clears his throat. "You tried to cover that up," he says. "But we're better than that."

I shrug. I'm trying to seem casual. "So I found out that Sri is mining data from the Great Big Idea customers in order to make money. So what? Data mining happens all the time."

There is silence. I look at Dagmar and her two samurai, one standing on either side of the bed, and they are all looking at me without sympathy. I'm beginning to feel as if I may be facing a firing squad.

"You listened to the sound files," Ismet says.

I was very much hoping that they wouldn't have noticed that.

I shrug again. "You've got a bunch of files of foreigners talking to each other. Big deal."

Again I face the silence. Dagmar narrows her eyes.

"If you don't mind my saying so," she says, "you're being a little disingenuous."

I doubt I'd be any happier if I actually knew what *disingenuous* means. I flap my hands.

"I don't *care* what Sri does to make money," I say.

"You must know," Richard says, "that making these recordings is illegal."

I glare at him. "You were the one who said it wasn't illegal to spy!"

Anna Fadime stretches, yawns, arches her back, and goes back to sleep. The three of them watch this with tenderness mixed with a rather ferocious protectiveness.

Christ, I think, *Anna Fadime is going to grow up with this crowd protecting her—like the Three Hundred Spartans, only with better tech. I pity any kid who bullies her on the playground.*

"It's not about money," Dagmar says. "It's about the baby."

"I don't care," I insist. "I was just trying to find out why people were dying, and now I know. So I don't care about the rest of it."

"That won't wash, I'm afraid." Dagmar looks at me and gives a little nod of her chin, as if confirming something to herself. "Sooner or later," she says, "you're going to wonder what is so special about our project that a qualified psychologist like Charles would kill people to protect it. Do you really think he'd do that over Sri's profits?"

"He might if he had a piece of them," I say. "Maybe you all do."

"I think it's safer," Dagmar says, "if you actually become a part of our criminal conspiracy."

I'm truly getting exasperated. All I want is to convince them of my harmlessness, and they won't let me do that. Now I'm supposed to sign a blood oath or whatever it is that Mafia soldiers do.

"I'm really not interested," I say.

Ismet glowers at me from behind his glasses. "We don't really care whether you're interested or not."

I give up. "Yeah, fine. Whatever."

Dagmar looks down at the baby again, and strokes the wisp of fine dark hair on its forehead. "I've been through a certain amount of chaos in my life," she says. "Friends of mine were murdered. I've been caught in…in civil disorder." Her eyes are haunted. "Riots. Revolutions. Nasty stuff." She looks up at me. "I was trying to get pregnant, and I realized I wanted to lower the odds of anything like that happening to my child. So I approached Sri with a proposition, and…" She waves a hand. "Miracles happened."

I could imagine that. When billionaires want things to happen quickly and don't care how much money they spend, things happen quickly indeed.

"We're doing things on several levels," Dagmar says. "We're attracting a worldwide audience, mostly young people, and we're integrating them into our social network. People from different cultures are encouraged to encounter one another, and to profit from Roheen's example of courage, compassion, and cooperation." She shrugs. "Eventually they'll lose interest in Roheen, but we'll find something else to catch their attention."

"Very nice," I say. It sounds a little pie-in-the-sky, but I can't say it seems particularly sinister.

"On another level," Dagmar says, "we're spying on them." I look at her in surprise, not that she's doing the spying, but that she admits it so plainly.

She nods. "We're attracting elites and the children of elites. We're sifting through any information we gather in order to find anything that we can use to avert conflict."

Everywhere in the world, she explains, there are flash points, like the border zone that's the scene of the fighting between Burma and Thailand. India and China could collide over competing claims in Kashmir, or over water running off from fast-melting Tibetan glaciers. The Middle East is a perpetual storm front.

Southeast Asia is a brew of competing religions and ethnicities. Conflicts over dwindling oil and mineral resources are inevitable.

In any crisis situation, it's vital to know what the various sides are thinking. Bugging the children of important people—or the important people themselves—might help clear away the fog and enable any competing factions to better judge the other sides.

"We're not using the information to generate income," Dagmar says. "We're giving it away—giving it to the people who need it. If people know what the opposition is actually thinking, they're less likely to make the mistakes that lead to war or civil conflict."

She pauses, and again strokes her baby's forehead. "We're making a more open world," she says. "More transparent. I only wish we'd have been able to gather some information before the Thailand-Burma thing happened."

"It sounds great, though!" I say, as cheerfully as I can. "I hope it works."

Dagmar gives me an angry glance. "Don't condescend. Don't you *dare* condescend."

I raise my hands. "Fine."

"We've already seen some results," Ismet says. "A few days ago, the Pakistani air force had jets on the runway with atom bombs under their wings, ready to head for Delhi."

I look at him in surprise. "I don't believe I caught that on the news."

It's not like I'm a news junkie, but atomic warfare is one of those things even I would have heard about.

"You wouldn't," Richard says. "It's one of those things that people don't talk to reporters about." He offers a slight smile. "You called me right in the middle of it. It was just after your father contacted you for the first time. Remember?"

I nod.

"The Pakistanis were conducting maneuvers near Kashmir," Ismet says. "The Indians saw that and thought that Pakistan was trying to take advantage of the fact that a bunch of India's resources were halfway across the ocean, heading for Fiji in the wake of the genocide there. India went to DEFCON Two. The Pakistanis saw that and went ballistic." He waves a hand. "We—Sri, rather—was able to assure each government that the other had no intention of going to war."

"Sri can open a lot of doors," Dagmar says. "And no one asks him where he gets his information."

"But people must know," I point out.

"Some people do. Some others may suspect. We cooperate with certain agencies, in this country and elsewhere. It's the penalty for doing business."

I shake my head. "All that's necessary is for someone to take a good look at your code, and the secret's out."

"The code is compiled in such an elaborate way as to make that unlikely," Ismet says. "We used—well—an old acquaintance to do that."

"If we're discovered," Richard says, "we're shocked to learn that someone's hacked our program, and we send out a patch. And then another patch, and things are back to normal again."

I try to process all of this. The first thing I'm convinced of is that all three of them believe what they're telling me. They're certain that Sri has turned from Asian tiger to pussycat, that he's using their technology for benign purposes. They believe in this Utopian scheme to open up all the world's secrets, or at least those belonging to people who enjoy Internet-delivered entertainment—who is, I guess, pretty much everyone these days.

No wonder *Escape to Earth* had such insane deadlines. They were anxious to get their program into people's phones as quickly as possible.

But this is also a scheme that Charles believed in, and that he was willing to kill me over. That rather takes the shine off it for me.

It's insanely ambitious. Megalomaniacal. It may not work at all.

But then I think of Dagmar operating in the blue glow of some Secret Headquarters, with Sri on the secure phone from some Southeast Asian trouble spot, and somehow it all seems plausible.

Dagmar as a secret overlord, ruling the world through her monopoly of information...

But still. I don't think I believe in this scheme, but then it doesn't much matter what I believe.

Anna Fadime squirms suddenly in Dagmar's arms. Dagmar looks at her with amusement.

"Okay," I say, "so that's it?" I massage my bad leg. "I don't need to know any more details."

Dagmar and Ismet look at one another. "I suppose not," Ismet says.

"A few more points of information on another topic," Richard says. "The police found Timmi's white van in Joey's garage. The front end had clearly been damaged. The CSI people are processing the van now."

I feel a moment of relief. "So Melody's off the hook," I say.

"For everything except trying to kill *you*," Dagmar says.

"And hitting a cop," Richard adds.

Dagmar gives me a frankly curious look. "What *was* that about?" she asks. "Why is Melody Chastain mad at you? You can tell me."

I try to look baffled. "I can't," I say.

I don't think I convince her.

"One more thing," Richard says. "There was a cell phone call from Pacific Palisades to Joey's house at around the time that Nataliya was killed. And a few seconds later *another* call got routed from Bel Air Heights to Dagmar's phone. So it looks like Joey set up a relay, just like you suggested, to give himself an alibi."

"Great." My friend was not just a crazed hit-and-run killer, he was a conniving, intelligent hit-and-run killer. The thought is deeply depressing. I look at Dagmar.

"Well," I say, "that's that. Are we done?"

Dagmar's look pins me to my chair. "You need to know one more thing," she says. "Which is that I own you."

I feel a warning prickle on the back of my neck. "How so?" I ask.

Dagmar speaks clearly and reasonably. "I own you because *Escape to Earth* is a huge hit, and there will be sequels. You want to be a star again, and you've already shown you'll do anything and swallow any humiliation in order to be a star. *Celebrity Pitfighter* proves that."

I just stare at her.

"But more significantly," Dagmar continues, "I own you because I know that it was you who killed Joey's wife."

My heart gives a lurch. I hold out a hand in protest as I gabble.

"That's not true!" I say. "You can't know that!"

"You told me that you planned to cause an auto crash in order to generate headlines," Dagmar says. "I think your dress rehearsal went sour, and Timmi Wilhelm was killed."

"No!"

She nods at me, and gives a slow smile. "If you breathe a word of what we've just told you to anyone in authority," she says, "that's the story that we're going to tell them. I'll say that you confessed to me while drunk. No one in this town is going to disbelieve that."

"So on the one hand," Ismet says, "there's money, fame, and stardom. On the other, obscurity, poverty, jail, and—if you're lucky—more *Celebrity Pitfighter*."

I look at them all for a moment, and then lift my hands.

"Who would I tell?" I say.

"Who indeed?" Dagmar grins. Her daughter gives a jerk of her arm, and for a second it looks as though she's giving me the finger.

"Are we done here?" I ask.

"I think so," says Dagmar.

I heave myself to my feet and wince at the pain from my bruised thigh. I hobble toward the door and reach for the doorknob.

"One more thing," Dagmar says.

I pause and turn to her.

She grins again. "No more alcohol," she says.

CHAPTER NINETEEN

FROM: Parmita <parmita@babaji.edu.in>
SUBJECT: Re: Re: Your Lawyer

Your vicious "lawsuit" has had terrible consequences. Babaji told me today that I would have to leave the ashram until the legal issues are settled.

I am an old woman now and I don't want to have to leave the place I love, but you have done this evil thing and now I am the one who must pay the consequences.

I will be flying to Los Angeles soon. I hope you will have my check waiting for me, because it is my only source of "income."

INT. ARENA—NIGHT

Whoooo. The crowd goes insane as I make my entrance from out of a billowing artificial fog. Thousands of people are waving luggage over their heads. Dazzling spotlights cut back and forth through the space above the ring. My theme music—which, without consulting me, the producers have decided is AC/DC's "Thunderstruck"—booms out at pane-rattling volume.

For once the sound and frenzy don't lift me off my feet. My pulse isn't thundering in my ears.

It must be admitted that I don't much care that any of this is happening. Less than a week ago, a pipe-swinging lunatic tried to kill me in my own dressing room, and Dagmar revealed her plot to become some kind of secret master of the world, and after all that, *Celebrity Pitfighter* is beyond trivial.

The ring is swathed in some kind of black plastic tent, and there are extra-giant flatscreens set up above the ring, so I figure the producers have come up with something truly special for the finale. I step through the black plastic door, and then climb into the ring.

At least it isn't cottage cheese this time.

Burt Taylor stands across the ring from me, shifting his weight from one foot to the other, staring at me with no expression. I briefly wonder what's going through his strange mind, then I decide it doesn't matter.

The announcer tells us that the final fight will take place in total darkness. Officials will wear infrared goggles, and infrared cameras will relay the action to the fans outside.

Two of us in here swinging blind? I think. The producers really *are* trying to kill one of us.

I shrug. I figure I can deal.

The ref calls us together for our final instructions. Burt clenches and unclenches his jaw muscles. I view him with indifference.

We touch gloves, and I move back to my starting place. I nod when I'm asked if I'm ready, and then the lights go out, and I'm left alone in the dark with only the sound of my heart in my ears.

It's strange, but even though I can't see him, I know all along where Burt is. I can feel his body heat on my skin. I don't know if I'm unusually sensitive that way, or if this is something that anyone can do.

I take a few steps to my left to make sure that he can't mow me down if he charges straight ahead, and then I start creeping toward him. He's taking a few steps forward.

I come up on his right and get close enough to hear him breathing. His body heat is like a lamp burning on my skin. I lash out with a shin kick to the back of his leg. The kick blasts right through the leg, throwing it up into the air, and Burt goes down. I dive on top of him.

From there it's by the numbers. Wrestling is a series of if/then statements, like computer programming—if I do this, Burt counters in a certain way, and then I counter the counter. It's over very quickly, because Burt isn't thinking fast enough to exercise all his options, and then I lock up his arm and he surrenders. The lights go on, and the crowd goes insane.

I suspect Burt may not have been trying very hard to win.

It has occurred to me that since Burt last saw me, I've been twice attacked by people trying to kill me, and I've taken them both down, and I've killed one of them. That might have made an impression on him. It might have convinced him to pay more attention to not getting hurt than to winning the fight.

If I'd been up against someone with my reputation, I would have surrendered as fast as I decently could.

In any event, the strategy of near-indifference seems to have worked for me.

Afterward there is the presentation of the championship belt that I have no intention of defending, ever, and interviews, congratulations from the other contestants, and a triumphant march back to the dressing room, where I meet with Simon and Wild Bill and am driven home. Paparazzi drones swarm the sky above us and follow me all the way home, in obvious hope that they'll be able to watch when someone new tries to kill me.

Reporters wait outside my house, and even a few fans. I smile and wave at the latter as we disembark and go into the house.

I check my messages and find that a detective has called me. This is a brand-new detective, one I've never spoken to before.

The police seem to have a theory that the various people who tried to kill me are all connected somehow, that they were employed by a shadowy third party who is trying to assassinate me. Since they can't find this person, they keep hounding me to tell them who he is. I've told them that the only person I can think of is Babaji; but he's in India, and they can't interrogate him, and they'd prefer someone local.

I decide to call the detective back in the morning. It's not like I have anything to tell him.

Simon and Wild Bill finish checking my house for intruders, and then leave. I check the outside cameras—the reporters and photographers are still there—and I set the alarms.

I'm under siege in my own house. Fans are swarming my blog and have got ahold of my email and are sending me hundreds of letters every day. I can barely move without being recognized. Camera drones are in perpetual orbit over my house, keeping track of everything I do.

My God, it's wonderful. It's everything I've ever dreamed.

CHAPTER TWENTY

FROM: Parmita <parmita@babaji.edu.in>
SUBJECT: In Los Angeles

Your father and I are staying at the Costa Brava Hotel in Manhattan Beach. We would both like to meet you and hope that you can "spare the time."

Your mother

FROM: Sean Makin
SUBJECT: Re: In Los Angeles

You're staying in the same hotel? Have you really been in touch all this time?

FROM: Parmita <parmita@babaji.edu.in>
SUBJECT: Re: Re: In Los Angeles

Of course your father and I have "stayed in touch." We have always had things in common—especially our son!

Your mother

FROM: Sean Makin
SUBJECT: Re: Re: Re: In Los Angeles

Sure, I'll come see you. And please point out to Dad that "Costa Brava" is, in fact, grammatical.

INT. SEAN'S CAR—DAY

"Hi, Mom and Dad. It's been a long time, hasn't it?

"Oh, Mom— here's your check, by the way. I lied about it—it's only for eight grand. Sorry. I knew you wouldn't fly out for a teeny little sum like that, and I really wanted to see you.

"I know that you've both got questions for me, so let me answer them. Mom, I'm not going to drop the lawsuit against Babaji. I'm sorry it made you *persona non grata* over in Andhra Pradesh, but if Babaji wants to settle, he knows what to do.

"And Dad, I'm not going to invest in your resort. Everyone advises against it. You'll have to find some other victim for that.

"But here's what I will do. I understand that you're both strapped for cash, so I thought I'd buy you a nice house in, say, Belize, where Dad's already got citizenship. It doesn't *have* to be Belize, not if Dad's got too many creditors there, but I think it should be somewhere out of the U.S., and tropical. Because the tropics are nice.

"Because that's how I *want* it, okay? I've got used to your being abroad, and though I'll be glad to have these reunions every now and again, I kind of like to keep my family at a distance. Because that way you won't be asking me for money all the time.

"So I'll buy you the house, and then you can live there. Or, if you don't want to do that, you can rent it and live somewhere else on the money.

"But what you can't do is sell the house, because I'll own it, and it will be in my name.

"And then we can go on from there. Dad can try to sell the neighbors on his various money-making schemes, and Mom can hang pictures of Babaji on all the walls. Won't that be fun?

"All you have to do is learn to live on a budget, and you should be just fine.

"So there. I don't want it said that I let my parents starve. Not when I'm this big star making potfuls of money. Or is it potsful?

"Full pots, anyway, that I intend to keep. Because I'm a grown-up now, and I get to keep what I earn, or spend it on any damn thing I want."

That's the speech I rehearse as I drive to Manhattan Beach, near the airport, to meet my parents for the first time in over ten years.

I don't know if I can stick as firmly to my speech, and my plan, as I'd like. My father can be awfully persuasive. Maybe if he keeps after me he'll actually talk me into putting some money into Costa Magnifico.

That's why I want him in Belize, not here. A safe distance from my susceptible heart.

Because that's where I'm weak. I want to be loved. I'll always have at the back of my mind the thought that maybe my parents will love me if I give them money.

But I think I'm probably over that.

I believe I wrote earlier in this memoir of my belief that while people change and grow in the movies, they don't do it so much in real life. I'm much the same person I was when I was thirteen—a star.

Have I became a better person? Has playing Roheen improved me somehow?

To be honest, I don't think so. I think what's made me better is success and money.

Lack of success made me desperate and crazy. All the bad things I've done in my life came out of that desperation. Killing Timmi, crashing Melody's career... all that happened because I was in the middle of a ten-year-long panic attack caused by the collapse of my career. I wasn't thinking. I *couldn't* think. I needed to have the love back.

Now I'm a star again, and the desperation is gone, and with it any inclination to behave in any way that will get people hurt. I'm benign now, and I don't hate anybody, and it's all because I got to play Roheen.

But will I be so benign as to accede to my Dad's scheme to re-brand the Mosquito Coast?

I don't think so. My father can't own me any more, because I've become Dagmar's property. I started as a tool of other people's ambitions, and that's how I've ended up.

I do what she tells me. But she doesn't tell me to do much that I don't already want to do—she tells me to work at a job I love, and to cash my checks, and to be a huge international star adored by millions. She tells me to fulfill my dreams.

If you're going to be owned by someone, this is the way to be. What does it matter if I'm not quite my own man?

And it's not as if Dagmar is a demanding master. She's off most of the time being the secret master of everything, or training her daughter to be ruler of the world, or whatever she's actually doing.

But whatever it is she's working at, I hope she's writing the sequel.

ACKNOWLEDGMENTS

With thanks to my first readers for their inimitable intelligence and advice:

Ian Tregillis, Daniel Abraham, Melinda Snodgrass, Victor Milán, John Miller, Emily Mah, Steve Stirling, Jan Stirling, Terry England.

extras

meet the author

Walter Jon Williams

WALTER JON WILLIAMS has been nominated repeatedly for every major SF award, including Hugo and Nebula Award nominations for his novel *City on Fire*. His most recent books are *The Sundering*, *The Praxis*, *Destiny's Way*, *This Is Not a Game,* and *Deep State*. He lives near Albuquerque, New Mexico, with his wife. Find out more about the author at www.walterjonwilliams.net.

introducing

If you enjoyed
THE FOURTH WALL,
look out for

EQUATIONS OF LIFE

by Simon Morden

Samuil Petrovitch is a survivor.

He survived the nuclear fallout in St. Petersburg and hid in the London Metrozone—the last city in England. He's lived this long because he's a man of rules and logic.

For example, getting involved = a bad idea.

But when he stumbles into a kidnapping in progress, he acts without even thinking. Before he can stop himself, he's saved the daughter of the most dangerous man in London.

And clearly saving the girl = getting involved.

Now, the equation of Petrovitch's life is looking increasingly complex.

Russian mobsters + Yakuza + something called the New Machine Jihad = one dead Petrovitch.

But Petrovitch has a plan—he always has a plan—he's just not sure it's a good one.

1

Petrovitch woke up. The room was in the filtered yellow half-light of rain-washed window and thin curtain. He lay perfectly still, listening to the sounds of the city.

For a moment, all he could hear was the all-pervading hum of machines: those that made power, those that used it, pushing, pulling, winding, spinning, sucking, blowing, filtering, pumping, heating and cooling.

In the next moment, he did the city-dweller's trick of blanking that whole frequency out. In the gap it left, he could discern individual sources of noise: traffic on the street fluxing in phase with the cycle of red-amber-green, the rhythmic metallic grinding of a worn windmill bearing on the roof, helicopter blades cutting the gray dawn air. A door slamming, voices rising—a man's low bellow and a woman's shriek, going at it hard. Leaking in through the steel walls, the babel chatter of a hundred different channels all turned up too high.

Another morning in the London Metrozone, and Petrovitch had survived to see it: *God, I love this place.*

Closer, in the same room as him, was another sound, one that carried meaning and promise. He blinked his pale eyes, flicking his unfocused gaze to search his world, searching...

There. His hand snaked out, his fingers closed around thin

wire, and he turned his head slightly to allow the approaching glasses to fit over his ears. There was a thumbprint dead center on his right lens. He looked around it as he sat up.

It was two steps from his bed to the chair where he'd thrown his clothes the night before. It was May, and it wasn't cold, so he sat down naked, moving his belt buckle from under one ass cheek. He looked at the screen glued to the wall.

His reflection stared back, high-cheeked, white-skinned, pale-haired. Like an angel, or maybe a ghost: he could count the faint shadows cast by his ribs.

Back on the screen, an icon was flashing. Two telephone numbers had appeared in a self-opening box: one was his, albeit temporarily, to be discarded after a single use. In front of him on the desk were two fine black gloves and a small red switch. He slipped the gloves on, and pressed the switch.

"Yeah?" he said into the air.

A woman's voice, breathless from effort. "I'm looking for Petrovitch."

His index finger was poised to cut the connection. "You are who?"

"Triple A couriers. I've got a package for an S. Petrovitch." She was panting less now, and her cut-glass accent started to reassert itself. "I'm at the drop-off: the café on the corner of South Side and Rookery Road. The proprietor says he doesn't know you."

"Yeah, and Wong's a *pizdobol,*" he said. His finger drifted from the cut-off switch and dragged through the air, pulling a window open to display all his current transactions. "Give me the order number."

"Fine," sighed the courier woman. He could hear traffic noise over her headset, and the sound of clattering plates in the background. He would never have described Wong's as a café, and resolved to tell him later. They'd both laugh. She read off a number, and it matched one of his purchases. It was here at last.

"I'll be with you in five," he said, and cut off her protests about another job to go to with a slap of the red switch.

He peeled off the gloves. He pulled on yesterday's clothes and scraped his fingers through his hair, scratching his scalp vigorously. He stepped into his boots and grabbed his own battered courier bag.

Urban camouflage. Just another immigrant, not worth shaking down. He pushed his glasses back up his nose and palmed the door open. When it closed behind him, it locked repeatedly, automatically.

The corridor echoed with noise, with voices, music, footsteps. Above all, the soft moan of poverty. People were everywhere, their shoulders against his, their feet under his, their faces—wet-mouthed, hollow-eyed, filthy skinned—close to his.

The floor, the walls, the ceiling were made from bare sheet metal that boomed. Doors punctured the way to the stairs, which had been dropped into deliberately-left voids and welded into place. There was a lift, which sometimes even worked, but he wasn't stupid. The stairs were safer because he was fitter than the addicts who'd try to roll him.

Fitness was relative, of course, but it was enough.

He clanked his way down to the ground floor, five stories away, ten landings, squeezing past the stair dwellers and avoiding spatters of noxious waste. At no point did he look up in case he caught someone's eye.

It wasn't safe, calling a post-Armageddon container home, but neither was living in a smart, surveillance-rich neighborhood with no visible means of support—something that was going to attract police attention, which wasn't what he wanted at all. As it stood, he was just another immigrant with a clean record renting an identikit two-by-four domik module in the middle of Clapham Common. He'd never given anyone an excuse to notice him, had no intention of ever doing so.

Street level. Cracked pavements dark with drying rain, humidity high, the heat already uncomfortable. An endless stream of traffic that ran like a ribbon throughout the city, always moving with a stop-start, never seeming to arrive. There was elbow-room here, and he could stride out to the pedestrian crossing. The lights changed as he approached, and the cars parted as if for Moses. The crowd of bowed-head, hunch-shouldered people shuffled drably across the tarmac to the other side and, in the middle, a shock of white-blond hair.

Wong's was on the corner. Wong himself was kicking some plastic furniture out onto the pavement to add an air of unwarranted sophistication to his shop. The windows were streaming condensation inside, and stale, steamy air blew out the door.

"Hey, Petrovitch. She your girlfriend? You keep her waiting like that, she leave you."

"She's a courier, you *perdoon stary*. Where is she?"

Wong looked at the opaque glass front, and pointed through it. "There," the shopkeeper said, "right there. Eyes of love never blind."

"I'll have a coffee, thanks." Petrovitch pushed a chair out of his path.

"I should charge you double. You use my shop as office!"

Petrovitch put his hands on Wong's shoulders and leaned down. "If I didn't come here, your life would be less interesting. And you wouldn't want that."

Wong wagged his finger but stood aside, and Petrovitch went in.

The woman was easy to spot. Woman: girl almost, all adolescent gawkiness and nerves, playing with her ponytail, twisting and untwisting it in red spirals around her index finger.

She saw him moving toward her, and stopped fiddling, sat up, tried to look professional. All she managed was younger.

"Petrovitch?"

"Yeah," he said, dropping into the seat opposite her. "Do you have ID?"

"Do you?"

They opened their bags simultaneously. She brought out a thumb scanner, he produced a cash card. They went through the ritual of confirming their identities, checking the price of the item, debiting the money from the card. Then she laid a padded package on the table, and waited for the security tag to unlock.

Somewhere during this, a cup of coffee appeared at Petrovitch's side. He took a sharp, scalding sip.

"So what is it?" the courier asked, nodding at the package.

"It's kind of your job to deliver it, my job to pay for it." He dragged the packet toward him. "I don't have to tell you what's in it."

"You're an arrogant little fuck, aren't you?" Her cheeks flushed.

Petrovitch took another sip of coffee, then centered his cup on his saucer. "It has been mentioned once or twice before." He looked up again, and pushed his glasses up to see her better. "I have trust issues, so I don't tend to do the people-stuff very well."

"It wouldn't hurt you to try." The security tag popped open, and she pushed her chair back with a scrape.

"Yeah, but it's not like I'm going to ever see you again, is it?" said Petrovitch.

"If you'd played your cards right, you might well have done. Sure, you're good-looking, but right now I wouldn't piss on you if you were on fire." She picked up her courier bag with studied determination and strode to the door.

Petrovitch watched her go: she bent over, lean and lithe in her one-piece skating gear, to extrude the wheels from her shoes. The other people in the shop fell silent as the door slammed shut, just to increase his discomfort.

Wong leaned over the counter. "You bad man, Petrovitch. One day you need friend, and where you be? Up shit creek with no paddle."

"I've always got you, Wong." He put his hand to his face and scrubbed at his chin. He could try and catch up to her, apologize for being... what? Himself? He was half out of his seat, then let himself fall back with a bang. He stopped being the center of attention, and he drank more coffee.

The package in its mesh pocket called to him. He reached over and tore it open. As the disabled security tag clattered to the tabletop, Wong took the courier's place opposite him.

"I don't need relationship advice, yeah?"

Wong rubbed at a sticky patch with a damp cloth. "This not about girl, that girl, any girl. You not like people, fine. But you smart, Petrovitch. You smartest guy I know. Maybe you smart enough to fake liking, yes? Else."

"Else what?" Petrovitch's gaze slipped from Wong to the device in his hand, a slim, brushed steel case, heavy with promise.

"Else one day, pow." Wong mimed a gun against his temple, and his finger jerked with imaginary recoil. "Fortune cookie says you do great things. If you live."

"Yeah, that's me. Destined for greatness." Petrovitch snorted and caressed the surface of the case, leaving misty fingerprints behind. "How long have you lived here, Wong?"

"Metrozone born and bred," said Wong. "I remember when Clapham Common was green, like park."

"Then why the *chyort* can't you speak better English?"

Wong leaned forward over the table, and beckoned Petrovitch to do the same. Their noses were almost touching.

"Because, old chap," whispered Wong faultlessly, "we hide behind our masks, all of us, every day. All the world's a stage, and all the men and women merely players. I play my part of eccentric Chinese shopkeeper; everyone knows what to expect from me, and they don't ask for any more. What about you,

Petrovitch? What part are you playing?" He leaned back, and Petrovitch shut his goldfish-gaping mouth.

A man and a woman came in and, on seeing every table full, started to back out again.

Wong sprung to his feet. "Hey, wait. Table here." He kicked Petrovitch's chair-leg hard enough to cause them both to wince. "Coffee? Coffee hot and strong today." He bustled behind the counter, leaving Petrovitch to wearily slide his device back into its delivery pouch and then into his shoulder bag.

His watch told him it was time to go. He stood, finished the last of his drink in three hot gulps, and made for the door.

"Hey," called Wong. "You no pay."

Petrovitch pulled out his cash card and held it up.

"You pay next time, Petrovitch." He shrugged and almost smiled. The lines around his eyes crinkled.

"Yeah, whatever." He put the card back in his bag. It had only a few euros on it now, anyway. "Thanks, Wong."

Back out onto the street and the roar of noise. The leaden sky squeezed out a drizzle and speckled the lenses in Petrovitch's glasses so that he started to see the world like a fly would.

He'd take the tube. It'd be hot, dirty, smelly, crowded: at least it would be dry. He turned his collar up and started down the road toward Clapham South.

The shock of the new had barely reached the Underground. The tiled walls were twentieth-century curdled cream and bottle green, the tunnels they lined unchanged since they'd been hollowed out two centuries earlier, the fans that ineffectually stirred the air on the platforms were ancient with age.

There was the security screen, though: the long arched passage of shiny white plastic, manned by armed paycops and monitored by gray-covered watchers.

Petrovitch's travelcard talked to the turnstile as he waited in line to pass. It flashed a green light, clicked and he pushed through. Then came the screen which saw everything, saw through everything, measured it and resolved it into three dimensions, running the images it gained against a database of offensive weapons and banned technology.

After the enforced single file, it was abruptly back to being shoulder to shoulder. Down the escalator, groaning and creaking, getting hotter and more airless as it descended. Closer to the center of the Earth.

He popped like a cork onto the northbound platform, and glanced up to the display barely visible over the heads of the other passengers. A full quarter of the elements were faulty, making the scrolling writing appear either coded or mystical. But he'd had practice. There was a train in three minutes.

Whether or not there was room for anyone to get on was a different matter, but that possibility was one of the few advantages in living out along the far reaches of the line. He knew of people he worked with who walked away from the center of the city in order to travel back.

It became impossible even to move. He waited more or less patiently, and kept a tight hold of his bag.

To his left, a tall man, air bottle strapped to his Savile Row suit and soft mask misting with each breath. To his right, a Japanese woman, patriotically displaying Hello Kitty and the Rising Sun, hollow-eyed with loss.

The train, rattling and howling, preceded by a blast of foulness almost tangible, hurtled out from the tunnel mouth. If there hadn't been barriers along the edge of the platform, the track would have been choked with mangled corpses. As it was, there was a collective strain, an audible tightening of muscle and sinew.

The carriages squealed to a stop, accompanied by the inevitable multi-language announcements: the train was heading for the central zones and out again to the distant, unassailable riches of High Barnet, and please—mind the gap.

The doors hissed open, and no one got out. Those on the platform eyed the empty seats and the hang-straps greedily. Then the electromagnetic locks on the gates loosened their grip. They banged back under the pressure of so many bodies, and people ran on, claiming their prizes as they could.

And when the carriages were full, the last few squeezed on, pulled aboard by sympathetic arms until they were crammed in like pressed meat.

The chimes sounded, the speakers rustled with static before running through a litany of "doors closing" phrases: English, French, Russian, Urdu, Japanese, Kikuyu, Mandarin, Spanish. The engine spun, the wheels turned, the train jerked and swayed.

Inside, Petrovitch, face pressed uncomfortably against a glass partition, ribs tight against someone's back, took shallow sips of breath and wondered again why he'd chosen the Metrozone above other, less crowded and more distant cities. He wondered why it still had to be like this, seven thirty-five in the morning, two decades after Armageddon.